I0604167

STONELANDS

Joseph Malik

Published by Oxblood Books, Gig Harbor, WA, USA

Edited by Monique Fischer and Sarah Lyon
Cover design by Lynn Stevenson

v1.01.20250718

Library of Congress Control Number: XXXXXXXX
ISBN: 978-0-9978875-9-4 paperback

Register at www.josephmalik.com for updates on new releases.

author@josephmalik.com

CONTENT AND TRIGGER WARNING

STONELANDS includes profanity, as well as graphic descriptions of sex and violence. Some of the language and sentiments you are about to encounter involve racism, sexism, ageism, ableism, body shaming, and homophobia.

Although the U.S. military, and particularly the U.S. Special Operations Command, was becoming markedly more progressive at the time of Project ARCHSTONE, this appears to have been a provisional shift, and an extremely fleeting one. The authentic language and sentiments are therefore presented here, unvarnished and as witnessed while working with elite units during the Global War on Terror.

The views expressed in this publication are those of the characters and should not be conflated with those of the author. The views expressed in this publication do not necessarily reflect the official policy or position of the Department of Defense or the United States government.

This is a work of fiction. All characters are products of the author's imagination. Any resemblance to actual persons, living or dead, is entirely coincidental.

Key aspects of U.S. military tradecraft and capabilities, as well as certain Department of Defense (DoD) agency names, policies, missions, operational compartments, and functions, have been altered, fictionalized, redacted, or omitted as necessary to comply with *DoD Instruction 5230.09 Clearance of DoD Information for Public Release, DoD Instruction 5230.29 Security and Policy Review of DoD Information for Public Release,* and findings by officials at the United States Special Operations Command, the Defense Intelligence Agency, and the Defense Office of Prepublication and Security Review (DOPSR).

CLEARED AS AMENDED
For Open Publication

Department of Defense

OFFICE OF PREPUBLICATION AND SECURITY REVIEW

*"Our technologies permit us to manipulate time and space.
"They leave distance annihilated."*

— Michael J.K. Kratsios, Former Acting U.S. Under Secretary of
Defense for Research and Engineering

14 April, 2025

ᛁᚾ ᚢᛒᛋᛏᛁ ᚾᛚᛏ ᛦᛁᚦ ᚾᛚᚠᛏᚱᛏᛁᚱ ᛁᚾ ᛁᚱᚾ ᛦᛁᚦᛁᛚ

One must howl with the wolves one is among.

— 9ᵗʰ-C. Norse proverb

CONTENTS

AUTHOR'S NOTE

Beginning in the early 1990s, shortly after the collapse of the Soviet Union, rumors swirled through the scientific and intelligence communities regarding the black-market availability of a substance colloquially known as red mercury. Red mercury is alleged to be critical in the manufacture of advanced and theoretical weapons, including, but not limited to, missile guidance systems, radar-absorbent coatings, and miniaturized multi-stage nuclear weapons.

To this last point, red mercury is a ballotechnic explosive which detonates with a pressure and temperature capable of compressing secondary nuclear material sufficiently to initiate a fusion reaction with no need for a fissile primary. American physicist and Manhattan Project veteran Samuel Cohen explained the development and workings of red mercury at length in his autobiography *Shame: Confessions of the Father of the Neutron Bomb*.

A proliferation of spurious claims and fabricated shams involving phony red mercury during the Global War on Terror prompted a broadly accepted theory among scientists and intelligence experts that red mercury is a fiction. Despite this, at the time of Project ARCHSTONE, the black-market rate for viable red mercury was in the neighborhood of one million dollars per gram, making it one of the most precious—and deadly—substances in the world.

The International Atomic Energy Agency, the U.S. Arms Control and Disarmament Agency, the Nuclear Regulatory Commission, and Lawrence Livermore National Laboratories all continue to publicly maintain that no such substance exists.

For Guff.

STONELANDS

I

EMERGENCE

"The consul Atilius Regulus, when encamped at the Bagradas river in Africa, fought a stubborn and fierce battle with a single serpent of extraordinary size, which had its lair in that region. When it was finally killed, its skin, a hundred and twenty feet long, was sent to Rome."

—Aelius Tubero (74-11 B.C.), *Histories*

Brothers Wilderness, Olympic National Forest, Washington

L iam's father was a Marine.

It was the only thought in Liam's head as he ran. A Marine. A Colonel. The toughest man anyone had ever met. Killed a guy in a cave in Afghanistan by sticking a knife in his eye.

Liam was not a Marine.

Limbs clawed and swatted him in the murk of forest twilight. Roots and vines snagged his feet. His back twinged as he stumbled, an old injury from Iraq.

Not Iraq. Kuwait. He jerked himself upright and ran on.

Branches broke behind him, rotten logs thundering under inhuman weight on clawed feet moving fast.

Kuwait is not a combat deployment.

The monsters were close.

Oh, Dad, help me. I was a bad son. I wasn't brave. I didn't fight. I'm not fighting now.

Brittany screamed somewhere ahead. Beautiful Brittany, from the rock-climbing gym, with her steady hands on belay and wide-eyed questions about his time in the Army.

Her .44 snubby shattered the night. Her bear gun.

A tomahawk hung from Liam's belt, not much more than a small trail axe for making camp. He was an idiot for coming out here without his own bear gun.

He was an idiot for coming out here, period.

It was time to stop running. He'd need his wind, and if he was going to die, he would die here and now, and he'd die fighting, dammit. He ducked behind a massive trunk, gnarled and six feet wide, flipped the leather guard off the 'hawk, and slipped the lanyard around his wrist. He choked up on it a few inches, back down a few, found the sweet spot.

Help me, Dad.

The tomahawk was the ideal weapon for this, he remembered from a week of training at Ft. Bragg, what seemed like an eternity ago. Edged weapons controlled space. Edged weapons controlled time.

Help me be brave.

Edged weapons got you out of shit like this.

As if there'd ever been shit like this.

Liam gripped the handle as the crashing became immediate and there it was, a massive shape in the darkness, bipedal, ogrish, a sense of tusks and clawed hands. He swung as it rocketed past, landing late and biting deep into glute and hamstring. It pivoted, roaring, and swiped at him with—it took a moment to register—*a sword.* He smashed the weapon arm with the tomahawk's shaft, felt the bone snap, and yanked.

Instructors had called it a "degloving action"; the sharpened juncture of blade and haft sheared a fillet from elbow to wrist and took the thumb as well. The sword fell into moss and tangles and the monster howled and flailed, and Liam was right back at Bragg, robotic, working by rote: shoulders, biceps, thighs, stepping away from swipes and lunges and treating anything it threw at him as a target.

Cut the strings and the puppet can't dance.

It collapsed, twitching and gurgling in the dark.

He contemplated looking for the sword, but time was short; there were more whatever-they-were behind it.

Brittany screamed again, deep in the woods. Screams beyond fright, cascading like shuddering heaves of vomit.

He raised the tomahawk and ran toward the sounds of death.

COPY 001 of 010

SPECIAL ANALYSIS GROUP

Washington, DC 20340

OPORD ███ PROJECT ARCHSTONE (~~TS//SAR-ASW//WAIVED~~)

(U) References:

(U//FOUO) FM 3-05.102 Army Special Operations Forces Intelligence, September 2001; ADP 2-0 Intelligence, August 2012 (U); FM 3-05.130 Army Special Operations Forces Unconventional Warfare, September 2008 (U//FOUO);

(U) Time Zone Used Throughout the Order: UNIFORM

(U) Task Organization. REF 3.(d)(2)(c) BELOW.

1. (~~TS//SAR-ASW//WAIVED~~) SITUATION. ███████ requires immediate technical and tactical support to a critical CONUS mission. Enemy forces UNK; REF Annex F 5.(a-e). Participation supports the intent of ███

(a) (~~TS//SAR-ASW//WAIVED~~) Area of Interest. OTHER. REF Annex F 4.(a)(3)(a) BELOW.

(b) (~~TS//SAR-ASW//WAIVED~~) Area of Operations. OTHER. REF Annex H 1.(c)(1) (b) BELOW.

2. (~~TS//SAR-ASW//WAIVED~~) MISSION. ███████ will support ███ Special Analysis Group at FOB WINTERSTONE REF Annex H. 1.(a-f) in accordance with ███ will perform Special Reconnaissance Operations in preparation for anticipated ███ necessary supporting actions in order to establish an enduring mechanism for future missions.

3. (~~TS//SAR-ASW//WAIVED~~) EXECUTION. Commander's Intent:

II

MY BROTHER'S KEEPER

Dépaysement: Fr.; the feeling of not being in one's home country; the sense of being a foreigner.

Cape Anguille, Newfoundland

Logan Shines-at-Night looked for all the world like a man kneeling in his own grave.

Bent beneath filtered sunlight, working with his hands in a depression in the earth, he was a lean man, deeply tanned, in a faded khaki T-shirt and an olive-green ballcap smeared gray with old mud dried hard, a dark braid dangling. Surf sighed a few hundred feet away.

Scraping with a trowel, he swore and stabbed the ground, freeing a fist-sized knot of dirt with blackened fingers and an oath.

"Dr. S.?" called an undergrad from the edge of the dig. Her name was Millie, and she was pale and freckled with a red ponytail beneath a once-pink knitted hat, as dirty as he was from shoulders to toes in mechanics coveralls. She was also, he forced himself to remember, wildly off-limits no matter how fiercely she flirted.

"There's a car."

His voice was a bright baritone, resonant and measured. "One sec," he said, rubbing with a thumb where he'd thought he'd seen a flash of—of all things—silver.

Ancient Norse silver.

Sand and loam crumbled with gentle pressure from numbed fingers, and he had it, the object of his attention, perhaps the very reason he'd come to this rain-swept rock pile.

A 1952 Roosevelt dime.

"Son of a bitch," he growled.

"Got something?"

"No. What are you doing right now?" His words had a distinct Blackfeet cadence and clarity, a holdover from a life on a Reservation that felt light-years from here.

"Bagging," she sang. Millie liked bagging.

He raised his voice above a squeaking drove of gulls as the wind kicked up again. "Okay, go see what they want. How's Kenny coming on the drone?"

"The transmitter's shot. We'll need to order another one."

Logan grunted. He hadn't foreseen *repair quadcopters attacked by birds of prey* as a line item, and this was the third incident in as many months. The eagles native to this area apparently viewed the drones as territorial threats and destroyed them in diving attacks at nearly a hundred miles per hour. "Go see about the car," he said. "I'll be up in a sec."

She pouted showily. "I was bagging."

He waved her toward the road. "Just go see what that is."

Logan saw a black SUV through a break in the trees as he climbed a rope ladder out of the pit. The SUV had been black when it had left wherever it had come from, anyway. Silver-white road grime spackled the sides, which made sense; the nearest airport was at St. John, a four-hour drive. They'd have arrived on the island in the dark.

The engine shut off, and a door opened with a warning bell from the ignition, followed by two more doors opening and closing. Feet hit the brushy rock with crunching noises.

Whoever they were, they were staying.

Voices approached. Sharp, martial projection, not academics.

Logan was a rangy man in his early forties, marathoner-thin and light brown, with hard dark eyes and Algonquian cheekbones above a scraggly beard. Six feet three inches in the air, the dirt-encrusted yellow flash of a Ranger tab was barely discernible against the jungle green of a baseball hat spattered in the same months-old mud as the rest of him.

Approaching him was a medium-sized, very white, office type guy—clean-shaven, soft hands, dressed for anything *but* Newfoundland in a tie and charcoal overcoat around a slight paunch. Tan wingtips jutted from beneath tailored trousers that broke in the way only suspenders can cause pants to break. Two even whiter guys, if that was possible, stood behind him: clipped hair, manicured beards, and expensive mountaineering jackets in muted colors. Despite the facial hair, every inch of them read military.

"Help you?" Logan asked.

"Steve Paulsen," said the suit.

Logan shook his hand as it was offered. "Logan Shines-At-Night," he said.

"Good to see you again, *Mon Adjutant*," said Paulsen. "I guess it's 'Doctor,' now?"

"'Professor,' thank you," said Logan.

"Apologies. Your assistant said 'Doctor.'"

"My assistant says a lot of things," said Logan. "Have we met?"

"OEF Trans-Sahara," Paulsen said. "We met at the French

Embassy in Addis. You were a *sergeant-chef* with the Legion at the time. I was a short colonel with Third Group."

Logan took in a long breath. A Special Forces commander. Former, by the look of him. "I apologize. It's been a long minute."

"It was a diplomatic function," Paulsen said. "I wouldn't expect you to remember. You had a great story about an Issa man who'd had his hand bitten off by a camel."

The memory stirred. Logan spoke to the others behind Paulsen as the details came back. "The guy had a camel he used to beat," he said. "Finally, he sold it. Ten years later, at a market, a camel sneaks up behind him and bites his hand off. Turned out to be the same camel. A lot of lessons there. What can I help you with?"

"Do you still drink rum?" Paulsen asked, and one of the bearded guys—a non-commissioned officer, judging from his beefy build and black square-toed shoes—offered Logan a varnished wooden box, roughly the size that would comfortably hold a bottle of liquor. Gothic letters burned into the wood spelled DIPLOMATICO above an inset reproduction of a gold doubloon. Venezuelan. Probably older than most of his students on this dig.

"I do," Logan answered. "You have my attention. What's this about?"

"Is there a place we can talk?" Paulsen asked.

Steve Paulsen and the Rum Bringers followed Logan up a set of grated metal stairs into a modular office nestled in the trees higher on the hill, muddy, but otherwise tidy. An eagle feather dangled from a dream catcher above a row of multicolored crystals in a window facing the sea. Lavender and incense wafted gently through the space, pushed along by a quiet heater set high in a wall.

"No generator?" Paulsen asked at the silence.

"There's a solar farm on the other side of the hill that they're dialing in out of Acadia." The batteries were five years ahead of any commercial technology, and it had taken months of begging to convince the university to put them all the way out here. Logan ran some water and scrubbed his hands before opening the box and bottle. "Clean tech," he added, by way of explanation.

He shook out four red plastic cups from a sleeve on a utility sink next to a refrigerator, opened the top freezer, and cracked some ice out of a tray. He dropped a few pieces in each cup and added a couple of fingers of rum, waiting for the spiel.

There was always a spiel with guys like Paulsen, blatantly D.C. with the gray suit and British-tan brogues, clad in his sense of duty like a ballistic vest.

The guys with him . . .

It was a look he knew well; an American soldier who doesn't want anyone to know he's a soldier, but has no actual idea how to hide it, beard or no beard. Powerful necks expanded from their designer alpine jackets, but they didn't have the long-limbed builds of mountain guys; they were heavy-chested, with thick, veined hands. Logan put them at either side of six feet and each outweighing him by a good margin. The edges of a tattoo sleeve peeked out where the larger one's jacket caught up on a black ceramic Rolex Submariner. SEALs.

"How long have you been out here?" asked one. The other picked up a stub of sweetgrass from an ashtray and sniffed it cautiously.

Logan handed them their drinks. "Forever," he answered. "It's this or the office. You can probably guess how I feel about desks."

"We can relate."

The rum was everything Logan remembered—and many things he'd been working to forget. Tobacco, figs, and oak carried him to a bar in Djibouti City; 13ᵉ *Demi-Brigade, la Légion Étrangère, Squadron Reconnaissance.* The elite of the elite. Heady days of khaki shirts and *kepis*, of bar fights and beautiful women and rum and cigarillos and holy shit, Algeria: sixteen Legionnaire *Commandos Desertiques* and a twelve-man American Special Forces team, backs to the wall in a Biblical-era fortress outside Tamanrasset against a battalion-strength horde of jihadis. Screaming for air support into four radios in three languages. The dropping of hearts into guts as ammo belts clinked up their last few links, bolts slamming home dry as anti-aircraft cannons mounted to the beds of Toyota Hiluxes started to light up the walls.

He raised his cup. "To absent friends."

"Indeed," Paulsen said.

The taller guy slammed his, then eyed the others awkwardly.

"So, you're from D.C.," Logan said, pouring him more.

"How did you know?" Paulsen asked.

It was a gift Logan had always possessed, honed scalpel-like by ten years in the Legion surrounded by men from around the world. Every tribe had its tell.

Logan shrugged. "And I'm guessing one of you is . . ." He eyed the taller, tattooed guy up and down. "A sergeant major? Senior NCO?"

"Master Chief," he said, and put his hand out. "Sean Stannard."

Logan took it and they locked eyes. "Navy?"

"SEALs," said Stannard.

"Buck Decker," said the slightly shorter one, extending his hand. "I'm a SEAL Team Commander." Logan shook it, noting he didn't say which team. "Stannard's my Chief," Decker added.

Stannard nodded to Logan's hat. "Rangers? I thought you were French."

"I was born in Montana," Logan said. "My mother's Blackfeet. I served in the Foreign Legion and earned French citizenship. I attended Ranger School as part of a training exchange."

"Why the Legion?" Decker asked.

"I was working on my doctorate at the Sorbonne when I felt the call."

"You could've joined the Navy, been a SEAL," Stannard suggested.

"I wanted a challenge."

Stannard ground his teeth silently. Decker let out a low whistle.

"So," said Logan, turning to Paulsen. "What do you need, Colonel?" It was now soldier talk, so he might as well address the senior officer in the room. "Is it still 'Colonel?'"

"Yes." Paulsen looked for a place to sit not covered in old mud, failed to find one, and shifted his feet before leaning against a countertop, wiping it first with the palm of his hand. He appeared to not know where to start.

Logan started for him.

"You have no jurisdiction here," Logan said. "We're funded through the school. If there's a DoD problem with us digging here— an undersea cable or something, you need to take it up with—"

"This is not about that."

Logan leaned against the sink and swirled the ice around in the rum. "Okay."

"We're with the Defense Policy Agency," Paulsen said, producing a card.

Logan took it. Dark, laser-etched metal. Very heavy. "'Special Analysis Group,'" he read aloud. "Never heard of you."

"You wouldn't have," said Paulsen. "We provide subject matter expertise on national intelligence problem sets."

"This has to do with me, how?" asked Logan. He opened the refrigerator door and tucked the card between two bottles of beer on a shelf.

"What the hell?" asked Stannard.

"If there's a bug in it, the electromagnetic field from the fridge would block it," Decker said. "He's had counterintelligence training. I'm guessing DGSE? French intelligence?"

"Something like that," Logan confirmed. "So, talk to me about this problem set.”

“We have a concern in Washington State,” said Paulsen.

“I don’t,” Logan noted, speaking around the rim of his cup.

“You might,” Paulsen suggested.

Logan grunted. The room was still except for the rumble of surf and the hum of the heater.

“An exercise in the mountains west of Seattle may have discovered something of considerable archaeological value,” Paulsen said.

“Skokomish land,” Logan noted, interested.

“Not quite,” said Paulsen. “That’s the problem. But yes, it’s on indigenous land.”

“And I’m the only Indian in the world, is that it?”

“Do you know how hard it is to find an archaeologist—”

“Ethnoarchaeologist,” Logan corrected.

“I thought you were an archaeologist?” Decker interrupted.

“Ethnoarchaeologist,” he repeated. “I interpret archaeological findings. My master’s was in anthropology.”

“Cool,” said Stannard. “My kids love dinosaurs.”

Logan sighed.

“—with a Top Secret clearance?” Paulsen finished.

Logan raised an eyebrow. “Why the hell would an archaeologist need a Top Secret clearance?”

“The project we’re working on in Washington is extremely sensitive. Your clearance was renewed just before you left the service, so you were still cleared Secret, just suspended. It was a small matter to reactivate it. From there, Top Secret is simply ‘need to know,’ so it was easy to—”

Logan finished his drink and refilled it. “You reactivated my clearance?”

“Well, yes. We had to, so we can talk to you about this. In fact, if you’d be so good as to put your phone in the fridge—”

“Wouldn’t anything you tell me have to be releasable to

France?"

"You're a dual American citizen," said Paulsen. "You sign two pieces of paper and you have a NOFORN clearance. You'll need to surrender your French passport. Temporarily, of course," he added at the look Logan gave him. "There's a little more involved to read you in, some of it will be Special Access, compartmented, that we'll have to—"

"Jesus," Logan breathed. "Come on. What is this?"

"I can't tell you, here," said Paulsen. "But we're prepared to pay you."

"You'd better be."

"We'd bring you on at a consulting rate. Two weeks of 24-hour ops, at two hundred dollars an hour."

"That's . . ." Logan did some quick math. "Okay, that's a lot of money."

"After taxes, almost exactly what you owe on your student loans," Paulsen said, and Logan winced inwardly. "You hand this site over to the undergrads. You come see our problem, you write us a white paper. You're back here in fifteen days. We ten-ninety-nine you and offer you the thanks of a grateful nation."

And I can eat more than canned soup on an adjunct professor's salary, Logan told no one, though the words rang in his skull like gunfire.

"If you've disturbed an ancient site, you're going to need a lawyer, not a digger."

"We've got one," said Paulsen. "The two of you can talk when you get there."

Logan took Paulsen's card out of the refrigerator and held it up between two fingers. "I trust this number works?"

"You won't need it. We have a jet waiting at St. John."

"Of course you do." Logan said. He twisted the stopper back in the bottle and shoved it into a leather shoulder bag on the counter. "Give me an hour, maybe two. I need to pack, and it'll take a while to square this all away."

"Take your time," Paulsen said.

The business jet was midsized, clean and white, with semi-swept wings and a sharp nose. New white seatbelts on eight chocolate leather seats inside gave the appearance of frosted cupcakes. Logan had to duck his head considerably, and he took the first forward-facing seat on the starboard side, halfway back, away from the sun. He tucked his legs in and snugged the seatbelt tight as Paulsen, Decker, and Stannard all chose seats in the front, facing backwards.

After the long car ride, Logan had determined these were men of few words.

Three possibilities existed: they'd been unable to discuss the mission ahead of them; they'd been intimidated clear to hell by being in a confined space with a professor, much as he himself had often been back in his military days; or, and he found this most likely, they'd simply had nothing to say to him.

The little jet whined to life, rumbled into the sky with a few bumps, and banked westward. Logan took a long swig from the bottle of rum and passed out in his seat.

He awoke to tires screeching as they touched down at Fort Lewis, a sprawling base outside Tacoma, Washington. A short, cold, very wet walk across the tarmac—someone carried his bag for him, which he thought was a nice touch—and into a battered Blackhawk, rattle-can black and already spun up. An Army Chief Warrant Officer handed him a low-profile, high-speed ballistic helmet, coyote brown, and they belted into front-and-back facing seats, extremely comfortable leather ones. In white letters, a red morale patch affixed to the back of the pilot's helmet read:

STOP SCREAMING
I'M SCARED TOO

Logan slipped on a set of Ray-Ban aviators, eliciting an appreciative nod from the Chief, and it was the military exactly as he'd left it: the gallows humor, the tang of grease and aviation fuel, the vertiginous lurch as the bird hopped off the pavement.

Within twenty minutes, they were skids-down in a hurricane-soaked forward operating base in the foothills of the Olympic Mountains. The skies were the color of pavement above sheets of rain driven sideways. He had to double-check his phone because he didn't believe his watch; it was, in fact, barely after three in the afternoon. It could have been six in the morning. Or six at night.

As he stepped out, pine-carpeted cliffsides gave way to tangled knives of mountaintops that screamed up into the sky, primeval and wild and disappearing into the storm. Logan wondered why the hell he didn't live out here.

A team of soldiers rushed out to greet them and take their bags. Logan turned up his collar and followed Stannard, Paulsen, and Decker up a flight of expanded-metal stairs into a large modular building well out of the mud.

He handed both his passports to an Army Sergeant First Class at the desk immediately beyond the door, a broad, powerful man in his mid-twenties with an eyebrow-length shock of red hair clipped exactly above his ears; technically Army regulation but irreverently close to the standard. Tabs for Special Forces, Rangers, and Airborne decorated his upper arm above his unit insignia. Logan noted the sergeant wore no nametapes. He'd seen operators downrange in fully sanitized uniforms, but never this. There weren't even Velcro tapes for name and branch identifiers.

"I thought you guys were SEALs," Logan said, turning to Decker.

"New paradigm," said Paulsen. "We're all one big happy family."

"Since when?" Logan asked.

"We'll talk inside," Paulsen promised.

The last Logan could remember, these spooky types of troops referred to themselves only as "Task Force," with code words for individual operations. Task Forces were the highest and shadowiest echelons of Special Ops. The go-getters. Not troops you'd relegate to menial duties.

Guarding this building was not a menial duty.

"Open your bag, please, sir," the sergeant said. It was not a question.

Logan's briefcase was a battered shoulder bag sewn from bullhide, dark with wear and now nearly black with rain. He unzipped it.

The soldier looked inside and grunted. "You'll need to leave your laptop, your phone, and anything that transmits wirelessly. Smart watch, anything like that."

Logan dug the items out. The soldier placed them in one of the small, square lockers behind the desk and handed Logan the key, then a numeric keypad connected to the computer on the desk. "Choose a six-digit PIN, sir. One you won't forget."

Logan punched six numbers into the pad—the date he'd joined the Legion, in European format. A moment later the sergeant handed him a key card designating him UNESCORTED ALL ACCESS with a small digital fob behind it on a split ring and a lanyard. "Keep this visible at all times. Swipe your card, enter your PIN, and the code from the fob. Every door except this one."

"Sure. Why not this door?"

As if in answer, the laminate far wall of the modular slid open— there had been no indication that it moved—and Paulsen placed his hand on a scanner on the brushed-steel wall behind it.

"How did you get the permits for all of this?" Logan asked.

"How do you mean?" asked Paulsen.

"Someone had to sign off on this," said Logan. "Your funding, the equipment—you built a town out of modulars in the middle of a national forest without anyone noticing?"

The scanner bleeped, and Paulsen took out a card and fob from around his neck, identical to Logan's. He consulted the fob and punched in a series of numbers. "You could land a UFO out here and no one would notice," he replied.

"Ah, so that's why I'm here," Logan joked. At least, he hoped it was a joke.

"You wish," Stannard grumbled. "It's weirder than that."

The steel door opened with a pneumatic hiss. Beyond was a hallway, twenty feet long, with faux-wood paneling and a round, glass, airlock-looking door at the far end.

The steel door shut behind them after a few steps, and Paulsen swiped his card at the airlock and punched in another run of numbers using the fob around his neck.

"Jesus," said Logan. "What is this place?"

"You'll see," Decker promised.

Beyond the airlock was the same kind of industrial-use building he'd seen in dozens of locations around the world, only much higher-tier: raised floor panels of faux granite, cherry-wood walls, expansive cubicles with sleek monitors and computers humming, air conditioning, the smell of coffee and new carpets. He guessed it hadn't been here long.

A few soldiers milled about. One clicked around on a laptop at a common-area desk. Logan didn't need to see shoulder tabs to know they were also Task Force personnel, as no one stood up at Paulsen's entrance, no one yelled *Attention*, no one so much as nodded in the Colonel's direction. Decker and Stannard wandered off wordlessly.

A large sergeant called Colonel Paulsen by his first name. "Hey, Steve," the sergeant said. "Is this the guy?"

Logan was definitely in the realm of a Special Forces Group, where ceremony fell apart and the rules became whatever they had to be to get the work done.

"Hey, Tommy," said Paulsen. "Come meet the Doc."

Like the sergeant at the front door, this sergeant also had no nametapes, not even an identifying U.S. ARMY on his uniform. Six opposing Master Sergeant chevrons were clear in the center of his chest, however, as was a combat medic's badge on his shoulder. Both arms sported the Task Force flash, with Airborne, a Ranger tab, and Special Forces stacked above it on the left.

"I'm Sergeant Duchamps," he said. "Call me Tommy. I'm the medic for Det Four."

Detachments, Logan thought. So, they were working in units smaller than platoons, but larger than standard four- or six-man teams. "Duchamps," he repeated. "*Et vous français?*"

"*Je comprendre meiux le français que je parle le français,*" Duchamps replied, so quickly and fluidly that it surprised Logan. *I understand French better than I speak it.*

"*Bon accent,*"Logan commended. "*Ça va.*"

"It's a lot less hassle to learn French than it is to understand a Frenchman trying to speak English."

"Can't argue with you, there," said Logan, extending his hand. "Logan."

Duchamps took it. "Call you Doc?"

Logan nodded to the combat medic badge. "I prefer 'Professor.' Anyway, we should be calling you 'Doc.' You're the medic."

"Pleasure to meet you. Glad you're here, Professor."

"I hope we won't need you, Doc," Logan said.

"This way, Professor," Paulsen said as he unlocked a door to an office. "The relics."

The lights flickered for a moment, then stayed on as if reluctant. It was a small conference room, with a dark, varnished oval table and five faux-leather chairs, a drop-down viewscreen, and a projector mounted in the ceiling at one end.

"This is it," Paulsen said.

Several impeccably preserved medieval weapons lay on the table: swords, daggers, an axe, a shield, and a gorgeous nasaled helmet sitting upright on a mail aventail that sprawled like a small blanket. Wire loops tethered yellow tags to each, the cards scrawled with arcane code in black marker.

"You found these out here?" Logan blurted. Nothing from the Viking era had been found on the West Coast. Ever.

"We'll get to that," Paulsen promised.

Logan traced a finger across the handle of an early Migration-era long saxe, its broken-back design a work of brutal perfection. Next to it lay a sword with a roughly Tenth-Century handle and grip in magnificent condition, and a plain wooden roundshield with a central boss beaten to hell. The daggers were odd, with fat leaf-shaped blades, long handles, and rings at the ends of the grips.

His heart slowed. They were clearly reproductions, far too new to have been recovered from a dig, although several were dinged and scarred from recent use.

The helmet sat at the end of the table, the most authentic piece in the room and breathtaking, reproduction or no. He picked it up.

The mail was threaded through a leather band riveted to points along the bottom edge of the rim. Most reproductions of Viking-era helms he'd seen attached their mail through hundreds of drilled holes, something no one would have been willing to do in Tenth-Century Scandinavia. The mail itself was every bit as authentic— mostly flat metal rings, every four linked with a thick circle of wire flattened at the ends, drilled, and pinned. Even as a reproduction, it belonged in a museum.

"Interesting, huh?" said a female voice.

She was made of mahogany and nearly as tall as he was, scraping the underside of six feet in flats with soft almond eyes, a delicate nose, and a mane of black curls atop a dark blue suit jacket and skirt. He guessed her heritage as Somali or possibly French Creole. It was good to see a familiar face, he thought. Or, at least, familiar facial features.

"Jamila Fournier," she said.

"I'll leave you two," said Paulsen, and disappeared.

"You're the lawyer," he assessed.

"The suit gave it away?" she asked, taking a seat at the head of the table.

"Head of the table sure does." He set the helmet down and took a seat at the far end, by the toys.

"Professor Logan Shines-At-Night," she began. "Montana State University."

"That's me."

"You're a bird of rare plumage," she commended. "French Foreign Legion. Impressive. Even around here."

"You know the Legion?"

"I've seen your dossier. You're quite the badass, for an anthropology professor."

He pulled the bottle of rum from his shoulder bag, uncorked it, and took a swig. "Well, I'll let you in on a secret," he said. "All anthropologists are badasses of one stripe or another."

"Really?" she deadpanned.

He motioned to her with the bottle, and when she shook her head, he put it away. "You'd better believe it. For instance, our dissertation defenses are actually fights to the death with ceremonial weapons on a rope bridge above a volcano."

She feigned interest. "Amazing. Where?"

He sipped at his rum. "Borneo," he said, matter-of-factly.

"Well, I'm glad I chose law."

He nodded. "You should be. You're not going to tell me what

this is about?"

"We're waiting for one more."

A pale, black-bearded, heavyset man in a charcoal sport jacket set a camel-hair overcoat on the back of a chair and dried his hands several times on his chinos. He picked up the saxe, said, "Whoa-a," put it down again, and stuck out a meaty hand to Logan. "Bob Valentine."

"Logan Shines-At-Night," Logan said, standing and taking it. Bob's grip was warm and powerful. He guessed Bob had been an athlete at one time, or perhaps was one of these strongman competitor types who wolfed down beer and cheeseburgers after a hard day of bench-pressing axle assemblies. "I trust you two've met," Logan said, motioning to the end of the room.

"We have not," said Bob. "Bob Valentine," he said again, and headed to her end of the table.

"Jamila Fournier," she said, shaking his hand. "Bob—short for Robert?"

Valentine grinned. "No, Bobby. Bobby Fett."

Jamila and Logan shared a glance. "You're joking," Logan challenged.

"Bobby Fett Maverick Valentine," he insisted, digging in the pocket of his folded jacket and producing business cards. He handed one to Jamila and returned to the artifacts in two strides to hand Logan a card with an affirming nod. **B.F. VALENTINE, M.S.M.S.E., PH.D.,** it read. **ANTIQUITIES RESEARCHER.**

"My parents were awesome," Bob added.

"Apparently," said Logan. "Antiquities? With a materials science degree? Can I ask what your doctorate was in?"

"Archaeometallurgy," said Bob, his tone cheery. "Medieval and pre-medieval weapons technology. I'm surprised we've never worked together. By the way, I bought your book."

"Oh, that was you," Logan grumbled. "I was wondering."

"Viking expansion as a market-driven economic strategy," Bob recited. "Brilliant. Loved it. Early-Medieval Globalism."

"It made sense at the time."

"That's all right, my thesis did, too," Bob assured him. "So, do you not believe yours anymore?"

"I'm not drunk enough to have this discussion right now," Logan told him, and changed the subject. "Ever seen a helmet like this? Look at the inside, the leather strip. Only minimally drilled."

"Hand-hammered," Bob noted, turning it over. "Iron, not steel. The slag inclusions are linear, see? We'd need to polish it to be sure. Wow, riveted links. *Hand*-riveted links. This must have been a pain in the ass to make."

"That's what I was thinking. It's a museum-quality replica."

"It's not a replica," Stannard said as he stepped into the room with two soldiers behind him—a tall Army captain with a tight blond brush cut and a can opener of a chin, and a medium-sized Sergeant First Class, male-type, about the same color as Logan, skin like wet sand at sunset. Latino, Logan figured, or Arabic. Or East Indian. Or Cheyenne. He quit guessing.

"Master Chief," Logan greeted Stannard.

Stannard was in uniform, sleeves rolled, and he was impressive. Massive pectorals and enormous traps shoved at the camouflage pattern every time he moved. Logan figured he was probably built like an old-time carnival strongman. Sleeve tattoos encased both his arms, including several prominent Norse symbols.

"Nice ink," said Logan.

"Thanks." Stannard crossed the room to Logan and turned his right wrist over. "Check this out." A lone rune in thick ink dominated a good bit of real estate before morphing into the other designs around its periphery. His body spray hit like insecticide.

"Huh," said Logan.

"It's a Viking rune."

"It is very much that," Logan agreed. He kept his tone flat. The rune was also very much more, but he didn't want to get into it at the moment.

"I'm sorry, what were you saying?" Bob asked Stannard, setting the helmet down exactly as he'd found it, upright on its skirt. "Not a replica?"

Stannard deferred, leaning against the wall. "Sergeant? Please."

"My name's Quinn," the sergeant said by way of introduction. "I'm an intel sergeant on the team that recovered these pieces."

"'Recovered?'" Logan repeated, perking. "Continue."

"They didn't 'recover' them," said Bob.

"I know," Logan assured him. He leaned forward interestedly, his hands on the table. "I want to see where this goes."

"Well, sir," said the sergeant, not flustered in the least. "The local nationals, we call them LN's, attacked our team using these weapons you see here. We took all this off the bodies."

"They attacked your team," Bob repeated, picking up the sword and eyeing down its length before setting it down again. "With these?"

"Yes, sir."

Bob nodded to Jamila. "Well, it's a good thing you've got a lawyer here, son. You just wiped out a whole pack of LARPers."

"LARPers?" asked Stannard.

"Live-Action Role Play," said Bob. "Dungeons and Dragons, but acted out."

"Respectfully, sir," said the sergeant, "this wasn't that. We were on the other side of the—"

"Sergeant," warned Stannard, "They don't have ARCHSTONE, yet."

"Apologies, Master Chief." Quinn addressed Logan and Bob again. "As you were, gentlemen. We were in an area where there couldn't be anyone doing that, sir. These are real weapons."

"They can't be real weapons," said Logan. He picked up the saxe. "Yes, these are real; they'll kill you, sure. But if this was authentic, it would be a thousand years old. This weapon is almost brand new."

"Yes, sir. They were using them."

"Well, okay," said Bob. "But look, nobody does this. May I?" he asked Logan, who handed him the saxe.

"This is a steel edge," Bob said, "hand-welded into a spine of iron bands that were twisted into a braid while red-hot. You can see the grinding marks, which means it wasn't finished on a modern belt. It was done with a stone. I don't know where these came from, but the only reason to make something like this" —he shook the saxe in his fist—"is to pull some kind of elaborate hoax." He set the saxe on the table again.

Logan agreed. "You've been had, Sergeant. Doctor Valentine"—he'd almost called him *Doctor Bobby Fett*— "is correct. You killed a bunch of nerds. Skilled nerds, nerds I would have loved to have had a beer with. Nerds who succeeded in pulling one over on you. But nerds nonetheless."

"So, you're saying those weapons are authentically made," said Stannard.

Logan looked to Bob, who picked up the sword, stood away to make some space, and spun the weapon around its long axis in his hand a few times. He stood it in his fist and struck the pommel, noting the harmonic center where the blade moved the least.

He tried a couple of slow cuts. Despite his bulk, the big man had a sensei's somatic focus; the sword, which Logan had always envisioned to be a blunderous, crowbar-like weapon, was graceful and snakelike in his hand. Bob tried a couple of faster cuts in the air, flipped it, caught it in a reverse grip, and flipped it back again, falling into a crouch with the sword out in a guard.

"It's a beauty," Bob admitted, standing. "As good as it gets. The design makes sense, too. May I see the shield, Professor?"

Logan handed it to him. Bob slipped his hand into the grip behind the center boss and settled into a stance with the ease of an otter sliding into a pond.

In his element, Logan thought.

"The way you use this thing," Bob said, raising the sword, "is, you keep a sword like this *behind* a roundshield. Hollywood gets this wrong all the time. These Norse-type swords don't have handguards because you don't"—he moved the shield aside and took a wide, slow swing with the sword—"you never do this. You use the edge of the shield as the handguard, which is why these shields don't strap to your arm. It's why the saxe, that little sword, also has no guard. This is all meant to be used together. This is as authentic a set of reproduction gear as I've seen. It's all exactly period. Except the daggers. The daggers are . . . well, they're weird."

He let the shield and sword down to his sides. "But they're reproductions. The professor is right. There is no way in hell these are originals, unless they've been oiled and dusted weekly and kept in a glass case for a thousand years. If, somehow, they were, they'd be priceless. Nobody would be out here in the woods playing with them. Not in the rain, that's for certain. Professor?" he asked Logan, welcoming input.

"I agree with Doctor Valentine. I don't know what happened here, but you don't need an archaeologist," said Logan.

The room was silent as eyes met. Logan could feel something wanting to be said, but damned if he knew what it was. He waited.

"These are the guys we want," the captain said to Stannard. "Give 'em the show, Master Chief."

"Jamila?" Stannard offered. She opened a manila folder Logan hadn't noticed and took out two stapled contracts, sliding them down the table with the practiced ease of a woman used to handing out contracts.

"These are your read-ons for ASCENDANT WARDEN and ARCHSTONE," Jamila said. "These are compartmented Top Secret programs. We need you gentlemen to fill in the first page and initial the boxes at the bottom of each page thereafter. You're agreeing that no information on these projects will be discussed in anything other than a secure classified area, nor with anyone who doesn't first use the codewords ASCENDANT WARDEN or ARCHSTONE for the appropriate project. Leaking the information you're about to be given is punishable by life in prison."

The captain spoke. "When you're done, there's a room across the hall. The door access code is the number from the fob behind your key card. Be sure to badge in individually. Ms. Fournier will stay behind to answer any questions you might have. Take your time. We'll wait for you."

Logan stepped off the bottom stair of the modular into the mud as the wind and rain lashed at them. It was like standing on the deck of a ship in a storm.

"You are shitting me!" Bob yelled. His golden trench coat was immediately drenched. Logan's gray Patagonia puff jacket was water-resistant, but in no way up to this task.

A six-man team waited for them in camouflage rain gear, body armor, and ballistic sunglasses despite the gloom. They wore low-profile helmets with lights and microphones, and their carbines had suppressors and quick-reaction holographic optics. One wore half a Ghillie suit, scarecrow-esque, strings of mud- and leaf-colored jute flapping in the storm and his face striped in jungle colors. He carried a camo-splotched bolt-action rifle with a skeletonized stock and almost a full meter of scopes and attachments. The magazine was blocky, squarish, 30-caliber, doubtless one of the obscure precision cartridges American Special Ops loved so much. Neat piece, whatever it was.

Dwarfing the sniper, an absolute Godzilla of a man cradled an enormous belt-fed light machine gun with a scope and bipod, attached to a polymer umbilical disappearing into a pack.

"Is that a Mark 48?" Logan asked with a considerable degree of awe. They'd been custom-built by Fabrique Nationale, the French arms maker, for American Special Operations at the outset of the war. He'd never actually seen one. In the right—or wrong—hands, a Mark 48 could bring down a 747.

The soldier nodded with a grin. "Her name's Sally."

Stannard and Paulsen, in the same gear as the others minus the body armor, joined them in a moment. They carried compact carbines with collapsible stocks, stubby scopes, and suppressors on short barrels. The suppressors wouldn't remotely silence a seven-inch barrel, Logan knew; operators employed suppressors to reduce muzzle signature and keep the noise below the level of shouted commands.

Stannard offered Logan a pistol from his leg holster. Black, full-frame, a Sig with a reflex sight that looked expensive.

Logan glared at him. "I don't want that."

"You might," Stannard assured him.

Logan accepted it, dropped the magazine, ran a functions check in a flurry of clicks and slaps, and smacked the mag home. He chambered a round and decocked it so smoothly it sounded like one motion.

"Damn. Shoot much, Doc?" said the Mark 48 gunner.

"Where are we going?" Logan asked, raising his voice above the wind. With the Sig in his hand, he really wanted a smoke right now; specifically, one of those little vanilla-dusted cigarillos he gave up a decade ago. Of course, without a hat, the rain would have put it out in moments.

"Through those trees," said Stannard, pointing through the storm as the team began a comms check. The trees, a hundred yards away, were shadows in the downpour.

These guys were packing a lot of heat for a hundred-yard hike. Logan didn't like it; it made his pulse elevate. You don't carry a goddamn Mark 48, much less comms and camo, for a twenty-minute

     Joseph Malik

nature walk. And the troops were amped, nearly antsy. They either really wanted to go through those trees, or they really, really, didn't.

Logan addressed the team. "Which of you has a compass?"

A soldier rooted through a bellows pocket and tossed him one, a Suunto with a mirror. Logan stuck the pistol in his jacket pocket, opened the compass, and beckoned Bob close as the soldiers dialed in their mics and earpieces. "Can you use one of these?" Logan asked Bob.

"Points north, that's all I know."

"Red needle is north, yes."

"Sure."

Logan raised the compass to his eye, opening the mirror. Rain hammered the lens as he moved a red box on the dial until it bracketed the red needle. He took it down from his eye and wiped the face with his thumb. "From here," he told Bob, "The opening in those trees is zero-two-niner. Damned near north." He spun the dial until the red needle sat in a black box opposite the red box, then turned himself around so the needle pointed into the red.

"The needle is your friend. His name is Fred. Red Fred. *Red Fred lives in the Red Shed.* Got it? Red Box. Red Shed."

"Okay."

"Say it back."

"Red Fred lives in the Red Shed."

Logan closed the compass and handed it to Bob. "Stay behind me, goddammit. If anything weird happens, get on your belly and crawl south. Keep Red Fred in the Shed and keep crawling until you hit this clearing. Don't ever look up. Watch the compass and crawl until you're out of the trees. Do you understand?"

"I do."

Logan took the gun out of his pocket. "Say it back to me."

"If anything goes wrong—"

"If anything weird happens," Logan corrected. "We don't know what 'wrong' looks like."

"—fair point. Drop and crawl. Watch the compass. Keep Red Fred in the Shed."

"Or you're dead."

"What is this?" Bob asked.

"I have no idea," said Logan, and they moved out, walking fast.

The team fanned out as they crossed the edge of the modular village, with Logan and Bob in the middle of a modified wedge. Logan heard someone say, "Sniper up," and the scarecrow with the scoped rifle sprinted ahead, gazelle-like, disappearing in the rain.

"Do I get a gun?" Bob asked.

"No," Logan, Stannard, and Paulsen chorused.

They followed a two-track road until it ended at a red and white sign nailed to a tree that read DANGER UNEXPLODED ORDNANCE. A yellow triangle sign nailed to another read DEATH HERE below a black skull-and-crossbones.

They stopped. The wind tore at the trees overhead in waves of white noise.

A single trail between the signs led into the dark.

"EOD?" Logan asked. *Explosive Ordnance Disposal.*

Stannard shook his head and touched a finger to his lips.

"Compass," Logan hissed to Bob, who handed it over. Logan pocketed it, pointed to the sign, and drew his finger across his neck. Bob crawling into live ordnance was probably not a great idea. "Change of plans," Logan whispered, leaning close. "Stay behind me, whatever happens. I've got you. Do not leave my six."

They moved out again, this time in single file, three meters apart, with Logan and Bob in the middle.

It was nearly silent beneath the understory except for splashes and trickles of water and the distant rushes of wind. They traversed a small ravine, navigating around blowdown and storm damage. The undergrowth was as thick and lush as any jungle Logan had seen anywhere in the world. Had it been fifty degrees warmer, it could have been Guatemala.

The sniper was nowhere to be seen. Posted up on overwatch, Logan guessed.

Moss and cold fog clung to everything. Rain spouted and hissed, and trees glistened with water. They slithered forward, nine coils of a snake, any sound they made masked by the sizzle of the wind far overhead and the dregs of the storm snaking through the canopy.

The team's ability to move this fast out here with virtually no sound was startling. Logan, raised in the woods, had never seen so many people in one place with fieldcraft as good as his own. The exception was Bob, of course, who huffed and stomped behind him like a buffalo. Logan leveled no blame; Bob had spent his life doing other things than creeping through the forest killing stuff, and there was no fault in that.

The ground was otherworldly, dense with thick carpets of green over crumbling wood. He was glad he'd worn waterproof hikers—he hadn't even thought about it when leaving Nova Scotia. Bob wore some kind of upscale dress boot, which Logan guessed was better than nothing but likely not by much.

The team started up a hill, this one much lighter in vegetation and opening into a mossy glen. The air was heady with the scent of mushrooms and the sweetness of decay, the smell of healthy earth. The purity of the air, here, Logan thought, more oxygen than a man could—

They stopped.

A fifteen-foot ring of woven living branches flanked with leaves and wisps of bright green moss, baldly artificial out here in a world of tangles and ancient gnarled trunks, hung in the air, perfectly vertical. Levitating.

Logan broke the silence. "*Qu'est-ce que* fuck?"

The intertwined branches formed a torus a foot thick. At the inner edges of the ring, the tips of the branches sprouted into lace, forming symbols Logan assessed as alien writing.

The team fanned out further. Paulsen approached the ring and beckoned Logan and Bob, who slipped and tripped the last few steps through shin-deep moss.

The ring was ancient and very obviously alive, at once artificial and organic, a place of such immense power—the Blackfeet called it *medicine*—that Logan's head buzzed.

And it's just hanging there. How . . . the hell . . .

Paulsen's voice was quiet. "Through there, three klicks, is where our teams ran into the guys carrying those weapons you examined."

Logan kept his voice as low. "You mean up the hill?" he asked, nodding past the ring.

"No."

Paulsen extracted a stick from under the moss with a little digging and a yank. He sent it spinning into the center of the circle, where it vanished in an explosion of light and a burst of green sparks.

Logan trained the pistol on the flash with both hands, surprised less by the flash than by the calm that flooded him, slowing his heart and deepening his breathing, just as it had in the good old days. The red dot on the Sig rested exactly in the center of the ring without so much as a wobble.

Old habits.

Still the badass, huh, Professor?

"You are kidding me," he said, lowering the weapon. Emerald traces coursed along the arboreal veins of the ring, then sputtered and faded.

"Where did it go?" Bob asked, his voice clinical and level.

Paulsen balled his hands on his hips. "It went to ARCHSTONE. We're sending a recon element, and I want you on it."

III

SOLDIER'S THINGS

"The old world is dying, and the new world struggles to be born: now is the time of monsters."

— Antonio Gramsci

Analytical Control Element

Forward Operating Base WINTERSTONE

Mt. Jupiter, Washington State

Back at the base, with everyone out of their combat gear and still damp, Paulsen, Stannard, Bob, and Logan watched over the shoulder of ARCHSTONE's senior analyst, Todd Medved.

Medved was a slender, bookish man in his late twenties with rimless glasses and tousled dark hair, in a blue Oxford button-down two sizes too big for him. Logan noted the Luminox dive watch on his right hand and the Ranger scroll adorning his coffee mug. He knew the type: a forty-pound-brain who'd had the balls for high-speed training, but whose commander likely considered too bright to risk throwing out of planes with a knife in his teeth more than a couple of times. Special Ops intel. An envious position. All the intrigue, half the arthritis. Medved's station consisted of three large, curved monitors with a screen resolution Logan had never imagined possible. Each screen was marked on its bezel with a yellow TOP SECRET sticker.

Logan realized what was wrong with the place, now: it was far too upscale for a military facility.

The desks were sleek black steel with cherry surfaces, not blanched pressboard. A few of the analysts had hipster-style standing desks. The workspaces were twice the real estate of standard government cubicles, specialty stations eight feet on a side with frosted glass panels comprising the tops of the walls. Full-spectrum bulbs glowed from overhead fixtures. The floors here, as in the team room, were granite-looking raised utility panels, not gray industrial carpet. Bookcases lined the cubicles, along with cherry wainscoting to match the desktops. Special Operations apparently had a budget that other militaries only dreamed of.

A prompt appeared on the center screen. Medved typed in a long password and digits from the fob around his neck.

What Logan saw next was a video feed, likely from a drone, much clearer than he remembered. A world generated in crisp infrared, laser-etched in shades of gray. "Give this about thirty seconds," Medved said as the video rolled. "This is a feed from ARCHSTONE. The other side. We took this two weeks ago."

Logan could tell by the shades of graphite and silver in the IR that it was hot, wherever it was. The ground fell away in ripples of canyons, sharp slabs of mountains angling against the sky in the far distance. A low-altitude pass.

"You have GPS signal in there?" Logan asked.

Medved paused the video. "Actually, no. We had to send a team with it, since we can't transmit through the Arch. We ended up outfitting the drone with an air pressure sensor to maintain altitude hold. As far as stabilization, we had to make altitude corrections manually. Otherwise, you just set the Course Lock and hope it stays within line of sight." He clicked the mouse and the video rolled again.

"Huh," said Logan. "Quite a bit different from here. Volcanic badlands. Fairly standard alluvial fan. Those rock formations are interesting. What's the base—holy shit." Something massive collided with the bird. The feed rocked diagonally and went to static.

Medved rolled back the feed to the moment of impact and clicked through the frames until he got what he wanted.

Logan's jaw dropped.

Bob's jaw dropped.

"That," said Paulsen, "is our problem."

Feathers surrounded a hooked and massive beak.

Behind it, the video froze on a Viking-era helmet identical to the one in the other room, above the mail-draped shoulder of a man apparently riding whatever had destroyed the drone.

Riding the thing with the beak.

"You're fucking with me," Logan growled.

"I wish we were," said Paulsen.

"That's a . . ."

"A dragon," said Stannard.

"A gryphon," Bob corrected, his voice awed. "A hippogriff, maybe."

"A what?" Stannard asked.

"A gryphon," Bob repeated. "Half eagle, half lion. A hippogriff is half eagle, half horse. They're mythological animals. This is . . . yeah, bullshit. Funny, not funny."

"This is a long way to go for a joke, you guys," Logan added.

Medved's face was insistent. "I assure you, gentlemen, this is no joke. These things—we've been calling them dragons—have been eating our drones over there. They're some kind of predator."

Logan shook his head. His team had been getting their drones wrecked by eagles. The similarity was jarring, but it also lay far past where reality ended.

"A gryphon with a human on its back," Logan scoffed. "In armor. Yeah, right. I did not come here to be fucked with. What's your real problem? What's actually going on, here?"

Paulsen's eyes were level, all Colonel, in charge of the situation. "You're not being fucked with," he assured them. "This is why you're here. We didn't know who else to call."

"Looks like a knight to me," Stannard said. "Fuckin' Round Table, right? Crazy."

Logan chewed his lip for a long minute before speaking. Things like this didn't happen. Not anymore. He thought back to hazy Blackfeet stories told by firelight: the story of Star Boy, who lived in the sky, and the messengers from Napi, the Creator, who would visit the medicine men and the storytellers thousands of years ago. Visiting from . . . well, from who the fuck knew.

"Well?" Stannard needled.

Why not now?

Because we haven't done anything lately to deserve it, he thought glumly.

"Okay," Logan said, finally. "You're paying the bills, here, so let's just get through this.

"He would—theoretically—look like one of our historical knights because armor serves pretty much the same function no matter where it was developed. There are only so many ways to kill a man using a hand weapon. Bob, back me up, here. Play along with them."

"Sure," said Bob. "Mail, interlocking rings, what you have back there on the helmet and what this guy is wearing, is extremely effective at stopping edged weapons, and even impact weapons, believe it or not. It would make sense to see someone—like this, whatever this is—wearing this."

"We used mail on Earth all the way back to the Chalcolithic," Logan added.

"The choco-lithic?" asked Decker.

"*Chalco*-lithic. The Copper Age. Before the Bronze Age."

"They used armor back then?" asked Stannard.

"Of course. Until the invention of gunpowder, mail and helmets stayed more or less the same for three thousand years," said Bob.

"I thought it was all, like, bearskins and shit until, like, Sparta," said Stannard.

Logan ignored him.

"What about castles?" asked Paulsen.

Logan looked up from between his hands. "What about castles?"

The footage blinked and zoomed, and in the right-hand corner of the screen—which quickly became the center of the screen, grainy and pixelated—a pair of square towers came into focus against one of the mesa walls.

"Castles like that," said Paulsen.

Logan stared at it for what felt like forever. The room seemed to be spinning gently counterclockwise. "Yeah," he finally said. "That's a castle, all right. Embedded in the mountain." He shook his head. "What are you getting at, here? Where are we going with this?"

"Is it possible our teams went back in time?" asked Stannard.

"No," said Bob. "Time travel is impossible."

"Yeah, but that's a wormhole," Medved insisted. "It's technically possible, given an Einstein-Rosen bridge and enough power—"

"And," Bob argued, "you need a Kardashev Level II civilization, and we're not even close."

"A what?" asked Stannard. "What?"

"A Kardashev Level II civilization," said Bob. "A Dyson sphere."

Stannard's brow furrowed. "The vacuum cleaner?"

"Christ in a Camaro," said Medved, rubbing his forehead.

"A Dyson sphere is an artificial structure around a sun that harnesses its energy," said Bob.

"We don't have one of those," Stannard noted.

The room held its breath.

"Right," said Bob, with immense and granitic patience. "So, who the hell does?"

Stannard pointed at Bob authoritatively. "The Chinese."

"I promise you, they don't."

"How do we know?" Stannard asked. "I can get SOCPAC on the horn, we can ask them."

Medved massaged his face with both hands, breathing deeply.

"It doesn't matter," said Bob, speaking quickly to derail the entire topic. "The energy isn't the only problem. You can't travel in time without also having the computational power to calculate your temporal location in *space.*"

"I'm not tracking," said Stannard.

Bob picked up a compressible stress ball from Medved's desk and moved it slowly through the air from left to right. "The sun is moving, right? The solar system is in an arm of the galaxy, also moving. On top of that, the universe is expanding."

He circled the ball with his finger, turning his body to continue the line of travel. "We're orbiting the sun. And spinning. If you tracked my finger, you'd see that we're traveling in a helix. All the planets are effectively chasing the sun."

"That was actually disproved," said Medved.

"In the original model, the angle was wrong," said Bob, "but it's still a helix. The sun is moving, and the planets are in a disk at a sixty-degree angle to the ecliptic. It still makes a helix."

"Okay," Medved grumbled. "You're not, technically, wrong. Where are you going with this?"

Bob continued. "Well, the Earth spins at, what, a thousand miles an hour, right? And we're orbiting the sun at, I think, seventy thousand miles an hour? The sun is moving at a hundred and twenty miles a *second*. Half a million miles an hour. We have no idea how fast the universe is expanding; it changes several times a second. So, if you go back in time for just a few minutes, but stay where you were, you'll be in outer space, several thousand miles behind us. So, to travel back in *time*, you need to figure out where you also have to be in *space* to hit that same point in time. To do that, you have to know the speed at which the universe is expanding, and has expanded, at every moment. That takes computing power that we don't have. Won't have."

"You have so fuckin' lost me," said Stannard.

"The *USS Eldridge,* in World War Two," said Bob. "Philadelphia Shipyard. The idea was to bump the *Eldridge* forward or backwards in time, just a smidge, to render it invisible to radar. Not much. A couple of seconds. We had the ability to do that much seventy years ago. The power is not the problem with time travel. The math is the problem."

"The math," said Stannard.

"Eyewitness accounts report that the *Eldridge* disappeared, right before everyone's eyes. But when it reappeared, sailors were embedded in the hull and the decks. If they moved the ship through time, but didn't bring it back to the correct point in space ..." He put his hands a foot apart and slammed one into the other.

"I call bullshit," said Decker.

Bob shrugged. "Look it up," he suggested. "So, unless this thing, The Arch, is calculating literally the position of every single thing in the universe all the time"—he waved at the screen— "and ... come on, it's a *tree,* guys ... then it's a hyperspace rift. We don't know what's powering it, but it's a hell of a lot of power."

"We can also be assured it's not a door through time," Logan added, figuring he might as well say something, since they'd brought him all this way and the conversation was way off the rails, "because what we're looking at over there—assuming it's real—is definitely not ancient Earth. The gryphon—"

"Dragon," Stannard incorrected.

"*Gryphon,*" Logan insisted, "—demonstrates it. This means that what you're showing me, if it's real, and I'm still not sold," he said, turning to Paulsen to drive home the point, "would be another world, populated by what appear to be bipedal aliens with much the same body mechanics as humans. And, for whatever reason, they're stuck in what looks like the Late Dark Ages."

"How the fuck do you know that?" asked Stannard. "You've had this for five minutes."

"How do you not? You've had this for weeks."

"Well, they have fuckin' dragons," said Stannard. "What do we do about that?"

"Gryphons," Logan corrected, for what felt like the hundredth time. "And I don't know."

"Okay, tell me this, Docs. You think they're stuck in the olden days? We're looking at a, whatever, Chocolate-a-rific society?"

"Yes and no," said Bob. "Maybe that's their level of tech, but it's always possible that they're stalled at that level of technology for any of a thousand reasons. In a case like that, I'd expect them to be more advanced than us in every other possible capacity."

"Yeah, but castles. And armor, and shit," said Stannard. "Days of old and all that. Right?"

Bob handed off to Logan, who folded his arms professorially and said, "Assuming, once again, that this is real, then, sure."

"Keep going," said Decker.

"A castle is just a fortress, a place where you can rest and rearm troops. The designs have been pretty much standard throughout human history. Given a certain level of technology, a castle is a castle." He gestured to the screen. "Pull up the castle again, and let's look at the front of this thing.

"See?" he said a moment later once the image populated. "This structure appears to go back into the mountain. It's not a castle, per se. These aren't even towers. These are organ pipes, volcanic structures. This would be a natural structure that the inhabitants have turned into a gatehouse. It's an opening to an underground facility."

"Huh," said Decker. "What else?"

"Well, these guys wouldn't have gunpowder. You can tell because the towers outside aren't rounded. Rounded towers were a defense against cannon fire. They wouldn't use big siege weapons, either, because they left the tops of the towers flat. No one's ever thrown big rocks at them.

"The main gate, here, is a pretty standard design that goes all the way back to the Roman era. These two towers make a kill-zone. There would be another door inside, leading into the mountain. If they decide they don't like you, they close both doors on you and fire arrows from the sides and probably above, and that's it. Roll credits."

"You really know this stuff," said Medved.

"I fought in Africa, where it's all basically castles, old forts, ancient power projection centers of one type or another. It doesn't matter if you take a cave and stack rocks around it with acacia branches instead of razor wire, fortifications are how armies function. Frankly, looking at this, it could just as easily be any number of desert fortifications here on Earth that are based around caves."

"You're an archaeologist?" asked one of the analysts.

"Ethnoarchaeologist. I interpret artifacts. I'm a Norse researcher. I don't know much about medieval archaeology outside of one specific period. I don't even know how to use a sword."

Eyes turned to Bob.

"What?" Bob asked.

Stannard put his hands on his hips. "If they're stuck in the olden days, we should be able to go in there and roll these chumps, right? Too easy."

Logan turned to face him, his ears ringing as his blood turned to steam. "What?"

"I said—"

"Oh, I heard you," Logan assured him. "I'd suggest you reconsider your choice of words."

"Meaning what?" Stannard huffed.

"Meaning I'm *pikun'i* Blackfeet. So, say that again and I'm gonna fold you in half several times and run you through that shredder." He pointed to his right.

"What the fuck?" Stannard started. "Who do you think you—"

"What is there to go in there and 'roll' these people for?" Logan demanded.

Stannard's face reddened, incensed. "They attacked us! First, they came over here and killed two hikers, then we sent a team in there and they—"

"What would you do in their place?" Logan asked.

"Whose side are you on?" Stannard growled.

Logan stared down at him for a long moment. "I gotta tell you, I don't know, right now."

"Frenchie, man," said Stannard, shaking his head in disapproval. "You're just a fuckin' Frenchie. You're not even American."

"My people were here long before yours, *nap'iquan*." The Blackfeet word for *white man* came out like profanity, which it often was, only one letter removed from their word for *sugar,* both things the Blackfeet had never had much use for.

Stannard puffed up his chest and squared himself off. "Yeah, and we took this land from you. You wanna try to win it back? Come on. Let's go, Tonto. Step into the church."

Paulsen stepped in front of Stannard. "Stand down!"

"You're lucky," the massive SEAL said over Paulsen's shoulder. "Goddamn hippie Frenchie faggot. You get in my face again, I'll waste you."

"Better men have tried," said Logan, but it was a reflexive answer from a decade prior; no one had so much as spoken harshly to him in years. Besides, Stannard had fifty pounds on him.

"Master Chief, get out," said Paulsen, pointing Stannard toward the door.

Colonel Paulsen and Commander Decker stared at each other over the rims of their coffee cups in Paulsen's office.

Commander's Office, Standard Issue, One Each. The chairs were comfortable and the walls were white, decorated with exactly one cardboard box's worth of militaria: a folded flag in a shadowbox, a couple of group photos in long-lost and very hot places, a rack of challenge coins and a Masai war club on the desk in front of an array of three monitors. A coffee machine simmered in the corner, completely against regulation, but nobody who gave a shit would ever know the compound existed, much less inspect anything in it.

The insignia on the two men's mugs—the crossed arrows of Special Forces for Paulsen, the SEAL trident for Decker—marked allegiances like house sigils.

Decker, like Master Chief Stannard, was thickly built and dangerous, a pit bull right down to the high and tight haircut, reminiscent of cropped ears.

"I don't like this professor of yours," Decker started. "Stannard doesn't like him, either, so I *really* don't like him."

"He's not for you to like," said Paulsen. "He's the man we need."

"He's a pothead anti-government commie. He's French, for fuck's sake."

"He's American. He's an archaeologist, and he's a commando."

"He fought for France," said Decker. "I call 'em like I see 'em. And what the hell does that even mean, 'commando'? He hasn't been through the same training as us. I don't know his capabilities. You don't. We have nobody we can call, nobody to vouch for him. Do you know anyone who served in the French Foreign Legion? 'Cause I don't. We can't even get a goddamned annual report on the guy. I wish he and Sean had gone at it, just so I'd know what we're dealing with."

"He'd have killed Sean," Paulsen said soberly.

"Bullshit," spat Decker.

"He made it through Ranger School."

"Everyone makes it through Ranger School."

"Honors graduate. Top marks."

"Whatever. For all we know, he still could've been the biggest shitbag in the entire French Army, and goddamn, that would be saying something, wouldn't it?"

Paulsen rocked back in his chair. "The Legion isn't the French Army. They're technically mercenaries."

"Oh, that makes it much better."

"He's done some pretty ballsy shit."

Decker leaned forward. "Well, he didn't do it for *America*. I know you're a hybrid-driving liberal fuckstick, so it may not mean much to you, but it means a hell of a lot to me. At his core, he's French. When he decided to join the fight, he stood in front of another flag and saluted. I say, fuck that guy."

"He's the right fit."

"That's exactly the problem. That line of thinking, right there, is why we have . . ."

"What?"

". . . *Her*," Decker seethed, nodding toward the door.

"Oh, come on," Paulsen began. "This again? Major Easton? Really?"

"She's terrible for morale and unit cohesion. She's disruptive."

"She outshoots you, and you hate her for it," said Paulsen. "Let it go."

"It's not that. A woman on the team is disruptive. You know that, Steve. And this guy, this Professor? He's native. Like, hardcore native."

"You have a racial problem, Buck? You?"

"I don't care about that. You know me. I don't care if this Logan guy is bright green on the outside. I do care that he identifies as Indian instead of American—"

"He's an *American Indian.*"

"Yes, he is. And he has a burr up his ass about the U.S. Government. He sides with native people against us, even here in America. That should tell you something. What's going to happen with the natives over there? Whose side do you think he's going to be on when we get there?"

"You think I chose him because he's Indian?"

"I don't know," said Decker. "But I look at the composition of your teams, and it's We Are The World in that locker room. Every team of yours, it's a Rainbow Coalition. Pretty sure Hodges is a goddamn queer."

"That's not against regs."

Decker tapped his finger on the desk. "No regulation against me transferring his ass, either, if I find out he is. I don't want any faggots showering with my guys."

"You need to temper that language, Buck."

"Fuck you. And anyway, this major, your 'sniper'"—he made air quotes with this fingers and sneered the word—"banging her spotter? When I catch them, I'm gonna court-martial them both. End her career."

"You have no proof," said Paulsen. "Personally, I think you can't live with the fact that a woman, trained by the Air Force—"

"Oh, here we go," Decker said, rolling his eyes.

"—stomped the dogshit out of your *personal* sniper team. Your own guys, from your own SEAL Team. What'd they come in at? Twenty-eighth out of thirty?"

"She's not a sniper," Decker insisted. "She had no business being there. It was the 'International Sniper Competition.' Females are not allowed the sniper designation."

"If she hadn't been there, your boys would have come in twenty-seventh. Get over it. Major Easton is the fourth best shooter in the world right now. We're lucky to have her."

"Someone's having her."

"You're way out of line."

Decker sipped at his coffee. "Stannard sees it."

"Stannard sees a lot that a man in his position shouldn't see."

"Meaning?"

"Meaning Stannard's a misogynist."

Decker set his mug down. "You guys really love that word, don't you?"

"It's a word you'd better get used to. Stannard's bad for this team."

"He's a hell of a Chief."

"Nobody likes him," said Paulsen. "Nobody, Buck. That tells me a lot. Stannard has no place in Special Operations."

"He's been operating sixteen years. He's top of the pyramid."

"I don't care. He's poison. I'd transfer him back to Quantico if it was up to me."

"Well, it's not up to you. Stannard's with me, so he stays."

"Lucky you," Paulsen said, his tone dismissive.

"I think this professor is you trying to prove a point. I think this Professor Sun Shines Out His Ass, this goddamned French, Indian, whateverthefuck, is the crowning achievement of your tenure here."

"He's going," said Paulsen, with finality. "And so is Major Easton, and so are the others, including her spotter, and including Hodges. The team works well together. The problem is, they fall apart when Stannard's around. That tells me the problem's with him."

"Yeah, bullshit."

"Fix your senior enlisted. That's an order. And do it fast if you ever want Stannard on a team again, because I'm moving him to Ops until I'm convinced. You have a briefing in ninety minutes."

Logan munched an egg salad sandwich from a vending machine and a packet of crisps he'd never heard of—a DoD-contracted knockoff that tasted like salted air.

He was alone in the chow hall. It wasn't dinner, yet, and the line cooks were between shifts. No phone, no laptop. The facility was secure. He drummed his fingers.

He'd popped out to check his phone to find a message from Millie, a picture sans text, a selfie from her private living unit on the dig site, brandishing what he'd guessed was the new transmitter. Her coveralls had been unzipped nearly to the waist, and while it wasn't a boudoir photo, it certainly wasn't unintentional. He was more confused now than ever.

It was probably a good thing he had to leave his phone in the front office.

His stomach roiled. The vending-machine coffee could have doubled as engine degreaser.

The desks here were nice. The chairs were nice. The food? Abysmal.

Paulsen, in suspenders and no jacket, his sleeves rolled halfway up his forearms, slid into a seat across from him. "This seat taken?"

"It is now."

"You have a problem with Stannard."

Logan let out a long sigh, as if deflating. "Guys like him are the reason I didn't join the U.S. military to begin with."

"He's not all bad."

"Yes," said Logan tiredly, "he is. Have you seen his tattoos?"

"A lot of guys have sleeves. That's how the military is, here."

"Not that. Did you see the Othala rune on his right arm?"

It appeared he had Paulsen's interest. "I don't know what that is."

"It was the first thing he showed me. It's a Norse rune, but it's also the divisional insignia of two famous Waffen SS units. It's a white supremacist code. They use it as a dog whistle."

"Just because he's into Norse heritage—"

"Out of all his ink—the raven flag, the Valknutt, the SEAL trident—he shows me that first. He was looking for a reaction. He knows I know what it means because I'm a Norse expert. He showed it to me because I'm brown. I see this all the time in my classes. Norse heritage has been co-opted by the Aryan movements."

Paulsen pursed his lips. "Are you sure it's a Nazi symbol?"

"One hundred percent."

"We've heard scuttlebutt about white-nationalist movements in Special Operations," said Paulsen.

"It's not scuttlebutt," Logan assured him. "Every military in the world, every intelligence agency in the world, knows you have a problem with *seig-heil*ing assholes in your elite units. It's all over the newspapers in Europe. And Stannard's one of 'em, so you've got a problem."

"I—I can't . . ."

"I understand he fulfills a necessary function in your organization. But he's a nationalist and a bigot, and that's the last thing you need in there. Your Sergeant Major—"

"Master Chief," Paulsen corrected. And there it was, Logan thought. The calming officer-speak, the poker face. Problems laid open the way a surgeon opens a wound, analysis wielded like scalpels. This was the conversation they were having. Logan fell back into soldier mode and barefaced his way through the next few minutes, gloves off, officer to officer regarding a problematic NCO.

"—whatever," Logan said, "Stannard's far too small-minded to be dealing with anything this vast in scope. You want a racist running this show when you're dealing with another species? Because that's what they're going to be over there. Another species. They might even look like us, but they're not us."

"Yes, but . . ."

"If you really want to do this, you need to send him packing and get some senior enlisted leadership who've conditioned themselves to *think*."

"I've moved him to Ops, but I can't fire him. He's our senior enlisted leader."

"Then you have a problem."

Paulsen ground his teeth, and Logan could see he'd hit a nerve.

"We need you in there," Paulsen said. "Through the Arch. The other side. That's why you're here. Valentine could have done the weapons assessment. We brought you because you're an operator who knows this stuff."

"I *was* an operator. A long time ago. That life is behind me."

"You've had some of the best training in the world: small-unit tactics, improvised weapons, desert survival. Plus, you did a HALO jump with our guys in Germany, so you've trusted the U.S. military with your life at thirty thousand feet."

"Twenty."

"Just do this, Professor. Please."

"I want nothing to do with this," Logan said, and it hurt with the world-wrecking force of all half-truths. He was a few hundred meters away from an anthropological discovery that would change history, and yet merely touching it constituted anathema. Their approach would be an abomination, he could feel it.

Moreover, the scenario had an intellectual itch to it that told him facts were missing somewhere. And now Paulsen was in front of him, asking for a decision that he'd have to make based purely on need-to-know information, a circumstance under which he'd been nearly killed more than once and fucked over more times than he could count.

The words came hard. His stomach cramped.

"Keep the money," he said, looking down at the table. "Fly me to Seattle and buy me a ticket back to my dig. I'm done here."

He didn't want to be done, and that was the bitch of it. He wanted to see the other side of the rift more than he'd wanted anything in a very long time.

He wondered if, somewhere in this gerbil maze of Top Secret gadgets, they had a mind-wipe ray they could hit him with before he left, because he'd spend the rest of his life mourning this path once it had vanished.

"I need a mission specialist," Paulsen countered. "A cultural expert. None of us know what we're going to run into over there. We need someone to keep us from getting into exactly the situation we had before; the situation Stannard thinks this will be. We need you. Not someone like you. You."

Logan grumbled wordlessly.

"What'll it take?" Paulsen asked.

"I told you what it'd take, and you're not firing him."

"I can't. It's complicated, but I can't. Anything else I can do? Name it, Professor. I'll open the safe."

Logan stared at his coffee. At the laminate grain on the table between them. He watched the moment go by.

Goddammit.

He was not going to watch the moment go by.

"You're right," he said. "Okay? You're right. I'm the guy. Everything I've done in my life, from digging arrowheads as a kid, to—well, the Legion, even meeting you all those years ago—has put me in the position to do this. I see what I'm meant to do, now. For the first time in my life. Maybe the last. What do I want?"

He leaned back in his seat.

"Senior analyst. That's what I want. Classified papers laying the groundwork for first contact with an alien race. Think of it! An entire found civilization, first discovery. I want to write it. I want a career doing this, right here. A house on one of these mountains, coming in to work on horseback in the winter. I want to die of old age doing this. But God in Heaven, the fuckin' military? Really?" He threw his head back in exasperation. "This is where my shot comes from? You assholes?"

"We could bring you on as a GG-15," Paulsen offered after a moment's thought. "A senior-level intelligence officer. That's an easy get. Immediate contingency hire. We need an S-9, anyway; a Civil-Military Officer. You'd be the DIROPS CMO, Director of Operations for Civil-Military Operations. You would *technically*—on paper—outrank Decker. I could write a justification and start the wheels turning by close of business today. It would put you right across from me on the org chart. You'd call the shots for our interactions with the people over there."

"You'd do that?"

"I could have you hired by the time your consulting contract is up."

"Huh."

Paulsen pointed at Logan. "But you have to go over there, first. See it for yourself so you know what we're dealing with."

"Fuck."

"Ride out these two weeks. Then, take this consulting money. Pay off your debts, find yourself a log home with a gorgeous view up in these mountains. You step into a government job the following Monday at a hundred-thirty grand a year and the administrative weight of a full-bird colonel. In five years, we can put you in for a career appointment to Senior Executive Service—effectively a one-star general. And you can stay as hippie as you like. Bring your crystals and your candles. Smoke pot and play the bongos in your office. Nobody will fuck with you."

Logan had to hand it to him; the man knew how to bargain. "Really?"

"No one even knows this place exists. Who's gonna drug-test you?"

Logan laughed in disbelief. "Yeah."

"Yes?" Paulsen confirmed.

"Yes," said Logan, chuckling. "My God, absolutely."

"You and I will call the shots," Paulsen promised. "That's the smart move, here, you're right. You handle the cultural side. I handle the military side. I can see now, more than ever, that you're the right guy for this."

"That—okay, yeah," Logan stammered. "This is exactly what I want. But I'd rather be shot in each testicle than do this Stannard's way. That's my problem. The way he views this goes against every fiber of my existence. I won't go in there considering the locals as hostiles. I won't be part of some jingoistic—I can't."

"You won't. This isn't a commando team. This is a task-organized team of Crisis Operators, drawn from across the Joint Special Operations spectrum. Special Forces, SEALs, Civil Affairs, Rangers, Marine Corps Raiders. Wherever we found someone who has what we need. Selected individually, based on their skill sets. The absolute best in the U.S. military at what they do. Not only direct-action guys, but linguists, medics, conflict mediators."

"Isn't that unorthodox?"

"Less and less unorthodox as we drift further from conventional warfighting. We have a Staff Sergeant out of Seventy-Fifth Rangers with a Master's in Structuralism who speaks six languages. We even found a guy in the Reserves, a prior service Marine with three degrees, who's spent the last fifteen years volunteering for missions in the ass end of the world mediating small wars before they become big ones. Son of a bitch snuck into Ranger School when he was in the Corps. He's crazy. You'd like him."

Logan, about to brave his coffee, stopped with his lips on the rim. "What do you mean, 'snuck in?'"

"He wasn't authorized. After Airborne, he just walked over and stood in line. By the time anyone figured out he wasn't supposed to be there, the cadre was so impressed with him that they lobbied his command for an exception to policy so he could stay."

Logan stared at him.

"These are the kinds of people I look for," Paulsen promised.

Logan swirled the coffee around in the cup thoughtfully for a bit. "You said you put Stannard in Ops?" he said, finally.

"It's already done. He's in the rear detachment. Tommy Duchamps, the Det Four medic, will be your Team Sergeant when you go over. You've met Tommy."

"I have. And Decker?"

Paulsen sighed. "Decker's your Team Leader. We had some injuries, I'm sorry."

"You can't have everything, I guess." Logan crumpled up the rest of the plastic around the sandwich and tucked it into his shoulder bag. "So, what's there, Colonel?"

"What?"

"On the other side," Logan said. "What's over there that you need so damned bad you're willing to risk lives for it?"

Paulsen turned up his hands. "Knowledge."

"You don't send guys like Stannard anywhere in the name of 'knowledge.' This mission is insane. It's gonna be as dangerous as it gets. Why that asshat?"

"Stannard is attached to my Ops Chief. There's nothing I can do about him. But knowledge? Like you said: there are *other beings* on the other side of this. This changes everything we know about everything. It's going to change the landscape of politics as we know it. Of science. Of culture. It's going to change history."

"You don't have to sell me on that part," Logan said "Plus money, power, recognition, awards, yeah, I get it. Look, I wouldn't miss this opportunity. As an academic? As a historian? As an anthropologist, even? Put me in, Coach. But I'm not going as a commando. The only way I'm going in there is as a cultural advisor

first and foremost, an anthropologist second, and a soldier only as a
last resort. That means that Commander Dick Wrecker—"

"Buck Decker."

"—him—he does what the fuck *I* tell him to."

"You'll outrank him. Technically."

"Make sure he knows that. I don't take orders from him. I don't
like him. I don't trust him. I think he and Stannard are two peas in
the same pod. Which wouldn't be so bad, but that pod is a white
pickup flying Confederate flags. I don't have time for their bullshit."

"I think that's a little—"

"I'm not looting an indigenous homeland. He'll have to put a
bullet in my skull before we bring back so much as an arrowhead. Is
that perfectly clear?"

Paulsen let out a long, measured breath. "Yes."

"That's my line in the sand. No looting."

"No looting," Paulsen agreed. "I'll start drawing up the
paperwork. You'll be a contractor for the next two weeks, but we'll
make it clear that you're filling this slot as a Fifteen. Decker will
scream, but I don't care. It would do him some good to have adult
supervision. Two weeks, and it'll be on paper. Go chew sand with
these guys for a couple of days. That's all I'm asking."

They stood, and shook on it.

"Pre-mission brief at fourteen-hundred," said Paulsen. "Be
fifteen early and meet the team."

"Of course."

"You'll need to stop calling me 'sir.' I no longer outrank you."

The briefing room was standard: one long table, maybe fifteen
sleek office chairs, with a viewscreen at one end and, like many of
the other rooms in this place, a ceiling-mounted projector at the

other. There was also a computer monitor and keyboard at the head of the table.

What set this room apart was the shrine on a small veneer computer desk against the far wall.

It was the kind of makeshift shrine you'd see anywhere you'd find human beings practicing religion. Electric tea lights in this case, battery powered, their LED flames shimmering on a framed picture of . . .

He had to look more closely.

. . . Chuck Norris.

An offering bowl stood before a gold-framed eight-by-ten of Chuck, shirtless in a black vest, cracking his knuckles. In the bowl: bullets, a can of chewing tobacco, a packet of jalapeno cheese from an MRE, a twenty-dollar bill. A spare rack of candles stood along the right side.

"Wow," he said under his breath.

"You're an archaeologist?" someone asked from behind him.

"More of an anthropologist," he said, turning to see a small, thin, very Black young man. Clean-shaven head, cocksure, projecting, but his eyes flashed with intellect, which always gave Logan hope with the tough ones. A Sergeant First Class, he saw, and realized dully he hadn't seen one junior enlisted soldier. Who did the actual work around here?

"What's the difference?" the kid asked. Soldiers began filing in behind him, taking seats.

"Archaeology is a field of anthropology," said Logan.

The soldier pursed his lips and nodded, clearly processing. He reached around Logan and took a candle from the rack, turning it on with a button set in its base before setting it before Chuck and saluting solemnly. "So, what's your favorite dinosaur?"

Logan sighed. "Dinosaurs are paleontology. I study people."

"Dead people?"

"I find they're usually the best kind."

"Often," the soldier agreed. He stuck out a hand; small, thin, calloused. "Braxton."

"That your first or last?"

"Does it matter?"

"Not really, no."

"You?"

"Logan."

The young sergeant grinned. "Well played. Coffee? Logan?"

"Love some. That bullshit in the cafeteria . . . Dear God."

"Yeah, the vending machine coffee is a war crime," said Braxton. "You got to know where the officers set themselves up. We're right outside Seattle, here, man. They do coffee right. This right here?" He poured a paper cup and set out another. "Paulsen gets this from a place down the mountain. They roast it daily. You take anything?"

"Nope."

He sipped at his coffee. "Like your women?"

"Nonfat, extra-hot, and all over my crotch when I'm driving."

Coffee spurted from Braxton's nose as he held the cup away and stomped his foot. "Goddammit, that burns! *Fuck you, man.*" He laughed. "Oh, shit, I'm gonna die."

Logan clapped him on the shoulder. "Come, brother. Sit with me."

"Yeah, but no more jokes. I can't take another one of those."

It was a twelve-man team—twelve-*person* team, he realized, as there was one woman—but likely a standard Special Forces setup with two redundant six-person teams, Alpha and Bravo. He'd worked with SF enough to remember that much.

They were motley, he'd give them that. Every bit as muddled and nonlinear as any group he'd seen in the Legion. Not only were they racially diverse, but wildly disparate in bearing and personality, which was evident even as they sat around the table.

He had time to take notes, as anthropologists do, as they waited for the briefing.

Braxton, next to him, was likely Ghanaian or some other West African in descent from his features, outgoing no doubt as a survival mechanism honed on whatever godforsaken streets he'd grown up. He knew the type. Being cool to people gives them hope, and Logan, probably like Braxton, had grown up in a town with hope in short supply.

There was a fireplug of a Korean soldier, five foot six with a bodybuilder's neck and shoulders, laughing with a corn-fed, jug-eared professional-wrestler type who was a full foot taller, taller than Logan's six-three by a handspan and probably weighing in at three hundred pounds. He was definitely the one he'd seen earlier with the Mark 48.

Two young men in rolled sleeves stood at the coffee machine looking like salt and pepper shakers, lean and whip-strong with neck and arm tattoos, standoffish. Some kind of team, he figured, maybe a sniper-spotter pair or the tactical intelligence guys.

The woman . . .

The woman.

Dark, expressive eyes and a skeptical set to her mouth gave the impression of buried high voltage lines. German, French, WASPy, a mousy brown pixie cut accentuating a hint of Alsace-Lorraine in her cheekbones and a petite nose. Her uniform top strained against powerful shoulders; slender fingers with no polish spun a pen above a Moleskine notebook with an orange CLASSIFIED SCI sticker on the front cover. She was a major, he saw from the gold oak leaf on her chest, and her chest, he noted, was not what he should be staring at. He pulled his eyes away.

Officers, man. You want no part of that.

Tommy Duchamps, the medic, was the last sergeant from the team to enter the room, apologizing. He was greeted by his first name, and several of the troops rose to greet him with handshakes and hugs. Tommy was clearly well-liked, even if he was from a different detachment and therefore a different family. Logan loved it all: the camaraderie, the gentle ribbing between units, the brotherhood.

Christ, he'd missed it.

Decker and Stannard entered next. Paulsen followed, with Bob Valentine in tow, carrying the swords and some other artifacts. Two soldiers followed them, younger, uniformed, probably analysts.

Medved, the former Ranger turned senior intelligence analyst, was the last one in, and he closed the door behind him. Bob set the weapons at the end of the table. Everyone stared at them.

Medved took the seat at the computer, at the head of the table. The room quieted as Commander Decker walked down the table and stood before the drop screen. "Good afternoon, team," he said, and was greeted with a chorus of *Good afternoon, Sir.*

"A few shakeups," Decker told the room. "I'm still covering down for Major Nesbitt until he heals up. Tommy Duchamps, the medic from Det Four, will be covering down for Master Chief Stannard. Tommy's our Team Sergeant until further notice. We'll have an extra medic. Let's hope we don't need him."

Tommy waved, and the team applauded. Decker waited for the applause to die down before continuing. "Chief Collier will be the Alpha SAW gunner, and his swim buddy, Chief Delacroix, the Alpha medic." He motioned to the two raily, tattooed guys. "They're off my old team, Det One."

"Well, no one's perfect," joked the big machine gunner from the back.

"He's shaking up the whole damn team," Braxton whispered to Logan in the murmurs and catcalls that followed. "Right before this? Really? Now? Fuckin' Squeals."

Logan said nothing. The Navy SEAL swim buddy concept was one of the many ideas he felt the U.S. military had connected solidly with and then run into the ground: taking two elite troops who'd been working together since their initial days in qualification and keeping them side by side for a career. It built a cohesive two-man structure who could finish each other's sentences and anticipate the other's movements, but it also created insular small teams that could be excessively problematic to integrate. It was brilliant and idiotic at the same time, U.S. military to its core.

"And we have an addition," said Decker. "On this mission, and likely a few to follow, we're adding a mission specialist. Doctor, would you care to introduce yourself?"

Logan took a deep breath. He'd been hoping Decker would make a case for him joining the team as an outsider, explaining why the commander thought he should be attached to what was almost certainly the most elite collection of special operators in the world.

No such luck.

The room hung suspended on a thread.

He stood, turned, then took a moment and met each face around the table. "I'm Logan Shines-at-Night," he said finally. "I'm a professor of ethnoarchaeology at Montana State.

"Ethnoarchaeology, for those of you who don't know, is the reverse-engineering of cultures through archaeological findings. I specialize in the period of Viking expansion, from 793 to 1066 AD. After seeing what your teams brought back, Colonel Paulsen approached me to consult for your operation. I will accompany you through the Arch on these initial missions as a cultural advisor."

Colonel Paulsen spoke up from the back of the room. "The professor is a former *Adjutant*—a Warrant Officer—in the French Foreign Legion."

There were murmurs around the table. "Well, fuck me," Braxton said, his voice round with appreciation.

Paulsen continued, skirting those seated, moving to Logan. "He served with the Airborne Desert Commando Regiment of the Foreign Legion's Thirteenth Demi-Brigade. He saw extensive combat in North Africa during combined ops with Task Force."

Standing beside Logan, he added, "He's HALO qualified, and a graduate of the Foreign Legion Desert Commando School in the Horn of Africa. He was also Distinguished Honor Graduate at Ranger School."

"Fifteen years ago," Logan added, holding up a finger for emphasis.

Paulsen coughed theatrically. "They didn't have to know that," he grumbled, clapping him on the shoulder. A few soldiers tittered.

Logan winced. "After an intro like that, they're due a little expectation management."

"My point is, he could have served in this unit," Paulsen continued. "Think about how you'd want to be treated if you were asked to come back in ten or twenty years for another mission. Afford the professor the same respect."

"Or he'll kick your ass," someone suggested.

"That is a distinct possibility," Paulsen agreed, his tone solemn. "He's going in as your advisor and mission specialist this time. However, the paperwork's in motion for him to join this operation permanently as my civilian counterpart. When he comes on staff in fourteen days, he'll be your S-9 DIROPS CMO, and a GG-15."

Logan could have kissed him. Paulsen had informed the room that the new guy outranked their detachment commander, at least on paper. Very officer; very political.

"I have *got* to finish my Master's," Braxton swore.

Logan addressed the room. "The Colonel's right. You won't have to carry me. I'm a little long in the tooth, but I can still ruck, I can still shoot. I'm a desert rat from way back, and from what I've seen, this looks like it's going to be desert."

"On that note," said Medved from the computer. "We should get started. Sergeant Holton?"

Logan took his seat as Paulsen retired to the back of the room behind Medved, and one of the uniformed intelligence analysts took the spot at the head of the room. He was in his early twenties, physically nondescript except for his clipped hair and being exceptionally fit. He could have been any of Logan's students on an athletic scholarship.

The projector clicked to life, displaying a PowerPoint slide, a stark black rectangle dominated by a winged skull with a SCUBA breather valve in its mouth and the Task Force logo emblazoned on its forehead. The ridiculous thing all but had the words "a Stannard and Decker design" underneath it.

A series of letters and slashes in orange adorned the top of the slide, a classification. He had never in his life seen one as long. It was every bit as arcane as the alien writing in the edges of The Arch.

Is the writing a warning?

"I'm Sergeant Holton, intelligence sergeant for the ACE," —the Analytical Control Element, Logan remembered after a moment, Medved's office—"and this is your mission brief. This brief is classified Top Secret, Special Access Required, Multiple Programs, Waived." He looked to Paulsen, then to Logan. "Is he . . . he's French, right, sir? Are we good, here?"

"He's been read-on," said Paulsen. "Continue."

"Yes, sir. As you were, team. If anyone does not have both ASCENDANT WARDEN and ARCHSTONE special accesses, you must leave now." He gave it a moment before continuing. No one rose.

He loosened up considerably, talking to the room as if they were his best friends. "All right. Here's what's up. Todd?"

Medved played a roll of video footage, freezing on what appeared to be a high-angle view of Alpine mountains in the dead of winter, only with a clearly alien rock structure, jet-black, stabbing into the sky from the center of the range like a cavalry saber.

"Wait," said Logan, out loud. "What? Snow?"

"It's a trick of the eye," Braxton assured him. "A black-thermal composite. That's not snow, it's sand."

"We'll get there, sir," Medved promised Logan, from behind his laptop.

Holton continued, "The Arch, as we call the structure down the road here at FOB WINTERSTONE, appears to connect to a near-identical Arch on the other side, made of stone, atop this ridgeline. This stone arch is, well, ARCHSTONE.

"It's hot, people. The ambient air temperature at ARCHSTONE averaged one hundred eight degrees at seventy percent humidity when we were in there. Your heat index will be over a hundred and fifty Fahrenheit, as hot as the hottest inhabited places on Earth. It may be hotter in the valley."

"Drink water," someone called. A few people laughed.

Logan didn't get it, and looked to Braxton, who explained, "Drill Sergeants yell that shit nonstop in Basic."

Logan nodded in agreement. The Legion had done much the same. Armies were armies.

Holton added, "This image is a reverse thermal scan, Black-Hot, and yes,"—here, he nodded to Logan— "the sand is showing up white, but we had to recalibrate the thermal just to see anything at all. The sand is hot. Some of the rocks, as you can see, are much hotter."

This brought groans and murmurs as Medved continued from his seat. "ARCHSTONE is on a hilltop eight klicks from a canyon that we're interested in."

Stannard spoke up. "The team will perform an airborne insertion once you're through the Arch."

"Excuse me, Master Chief, but if we're jumping in, how do we exfil?" asked the big machine gunner.

"You're gonna walk, smartass."

"Then why don't we walk down?" the Korean guy asked.

"Todd?" Sergeant Holton said, deferring.

"Funny you should ask," said Medved. "Time is at a premium. Beyond ARCHSTONE, time appears to flow differently. We're still working on the calculations. It's a function of the wormhole, as best we can figure."

"It's not a bug, it's a feature," someone needled.

Medved stood, walked to the front of the room, and continued. "We were over there for thirteen hours flying the drone and collecting footage, but here at base it was only ninety minutes. The previous team had been gone for ten hours and returned with only ninety-six minutes of footage. So, the difference isn't constant, it fluctuates wildly, and at the moment, we have no way to predict it. You need to get back here as fast as you can once you've reconned the area. Also, going through the Arch, you'll need to follow each other as closely as possible. It may take a few minutes, or perhaps even hours, for the entire team to assemble on the far side."

"Wait a minute," said Duchamps, looking up from calculations on his notepad. "So, if we're over there for, say, two weeks, and we get back here and it's been, say, a day? Are we getting paid for two weeks, or one day?"

"One day," said Decker, eliciting a chorus of groans.

"Yeah, bullshit," argued Duchamps. "How is that fair?"

"Do you want to explain this to Finance?" Decker asked. "You want to, what, get one of them read-in on the program? And then what? How do they justify it to someone who doesn't have ARCHSTONE access? Explain to me how this could work any other way, Tommy. No, go ahead. I'll wait."

"Yes, sir, but that's not—"

Stannard finished the sentence for him. "What? Fair? Grow up. You're in the Army. Deal with it or I'll transfer you right the fuck out of here. Next question."

"Master Chief, the sergeant has a legitimate question," Logan insisted. "What happens if he's injured over there? What if he's injured and ends up on the other side for a significant period of time? He comes back here, his wound's been infected for three weeks, and you have to chopper him to Fort Lewis, but maybe to them, he's only been at our FOB two days. How do you fix that without spilling compartmented information?"

The room fell silent.

"He's going to be on another planet," Logan continued. "Suppose he picks up a parasite that doesn't respond to any antibiotic on Earth. Maybe he catches a strain of flu we've never seen. It gets loose in Seattle and kills half a million people, and we all end up testifying before Congress. Are we going to forge documents? What's your plan?"

"I don't know," said Stannard.

"Kind of figured *you* didn't," Logan said.

"We'll talk offline," Paulsen said.

"My recommendation is none of you get injured," Stannard suggested. The room groaned. "And don't catch any fuckin' flu," he added.

The slide show flipped to a shaded relief map.

"All right," said Medved. "Here's the canyon."

"How high does that drone go?" Logan marveled.

"We put this together from several passes," said Medved. "We didn't get a fifty-thousand-foot shot, if that's what you mean.

"All right, team. Note the location of the second Arch, the arrival Arch. That's ARCHSTONE. You'll insert off this cliff, it's four hundred meters. You'll bury your chutes in the DZ and proceed through the phase lines until you reach the end of this canyon, twenty klicks in. You'll have a map—well, this map—but you will not have compasses. Compasses don't work there."

Duchamps spoke up. "Well, how the hell do we—"

"You'll deadhead off the map," Stannard interrupted.

Medved continued, "We can't get the drone down inside that canyon. We lose the signal. This is a Special Reconnaissance operation. You will document as much as you can."

"What do you mean, you lose the signal?" asked Logan. "Why do you lose the signal?"

"We don't know."

"So, it could be radioactive," Logan theorized. "Is that why the rocks are so hot?"

"Unlikely," said Decker. "Ionizing radiation doesn't affect signals."

"So there is ionizing radiation."

"We didn't say that."

"That drone has a MASINT suite, doesn't it?" Logan asked.

"How the hell do you know about MASINT?"

"The blatant evasive? That's your play, here?"

"You're pissing me off, Doc," said Stannard.

Logan ignored him and pointed a finger at Decker. "I'm asking you again, Commander: is it radioactive?"

"Not the area where we're going. To the best of our knowledge."

"Jesus Christ," Logan muttered.

"This will be a covert insertion," Medved insisted. "Once you reach the floor, you will proceed on foot.

"Fun time: Guess the Phase Lines. There will be a prize for the first correct answer. Leaving the DZ—" the drop zone, Logan deduced, though it took him a moment, "—you'll double back, and at zero degrees and one klick off the Start Point you'll cross Phase Line CLAPTON.

"The entrance to the valley—" He clicked to the next slide. "—is Phase Line FREHLEY. At FREHLEY this becomes a recon mission. You will proceed to the end of the valley, which is Phase Line HETFIELD—"

"Guitarists?" the Major guessed. "Rock guitarists?"

Sergeant Holton tossed her a Kit Kat bar.

"— and hook a right for two klicks to within visual range of this structure, which we've named The Citadel. Phase Line LEMMY is your Limit of Advance, the base of the mountain that forms the Citadel. You will hole up somewhere short of LEMMY and document the Citadel to the best of your ability. Collect any relevant intel on its defenses, its purpose, and if possible, the strength and disposition of troops within."

Logan shook his head, sighing slowly.

"Is there an issue, Professor?"

Strength and disposition of troops struck Logan like ice on a cracked tooth. He didn't want to start a fight about the purpose of the mission, though; not in front of the kids.

Fortunately, he had something else to dicker about: "Lemmy's a bass player," he said.

"Lemmy is God," Medved corrected.

Logan sipped at his coffee. "My mistake."

"You will avoid detection at all costs," Medved continued. "Local nationals are likely hostile. You will avoid intentional contact. If contact is inevitable, Professor Logan and Major Easton are your Cultural Support Team—"

So, her name was Easton, Logan noted. No one wore nametapes, but she was the only major at the table. He nodded to her, and she nodded back.

Wow, those eyes. They just . . . simmer.

"—let them handle interactions with local nationals. If combat is inevitable . . ." Medved motioned to Bob Valentine, who stood.

"My name's Dr. Valentine," said Bob. "I'm an experimental combat archaeologist."

"How could you not be?" someone from the back joked.

Bob smiled. "I have a doctorate in archaeometallurgy—the materials science of ancient weapons."

"Write down the big words," Braxton warned the room, clicking his pen. "We'll look 'em up later."

Bob put his hands in his pockets and slouched, talking easy, in his element. "On the other side, you will likely run into humans, or humanoids, likely using swords of varying sizes, made of mild steel. Their armor appears to be wrought iron. Your weapons will penetrate anything they have. Maintain a stand-off distance; your sniper team—"

"Marksmen," Decker corrected.

Paulsen let out an exasperated breath through his teeth.

"—what's the difference?" asked Bob. When no one answered, he went on. "Your snipers need to keep overwatch. Move by bounding, engage at range. The local people are likely very, very good with their weapons. If they get within thirty feet of you, you're dead."

A rumble of low curses followed.

"Thirty feet?" Stannard asked. "With hand weapons? What the hell can you do in thirty feet?"

Bob picked up a leaf-bladed dagger from the table and threw it down the long side of the room, where it sank in the wall a hand's breadth from the fire alarm handle. Concerned cries alighted from around the table.

"Someone call Maintenance," Braxton quipped.

The room's attention was galvanized on Bob. "If you sat down with an artificially intelligent CNC machine, you couldn't come up with a better throwing knife.

"Every weapon they have is likely this well-refined and task-specific. This is problematic for you, because right now we have very little idea of what their combat styles look like. Tactically, you'll be in a purely reactionary zone once you get within reach of their weaponry."

Logan made a point to apologize to him about . . . well . . . everything. *Never underestimate the guy with all the letters after his name.*

"—know about close-quarters fighting will apply," Bob was saying. "You'll need to improvise, against an enemy who's been doing this their entire lives, and who certainly has an entire combat system that optimizes weapons you've never seen. Hand to hand, you will likely lose."

"Holy shit," said the Korean kid. "Are you coming with us?"

"Oh, hell, no," said Bob.

"They need armor," Stannard stated. "They need to go in there with plates."

"Absolutely not," said Paulsen. "At a heat index of one-fifty? Full armor? Do *you* want to do it?"

"I'd go in a minute," Stannard offered.

"You won't be wearing body armor," Paulsen told the room. "You'll be carrying full combat loads, though."

"Well, that's good, because we still need to tell them about the goddamn dragons," Stannard grumped.

"Aw, what the *fuck?*" Braxton yowled.

"They're not technically dragons," Bob assured them. "They're some kind of winged aerial mount. It appears to have an eagle's head, and they ride them like horses."

"They've been beating the shit out of our drones," said Medved.

Logan raised his hand. "My team, back in Newfoundland, has been having a similar problem, interestingly. Birds of prey, killing our drones. Eagles, mostly. They're super-territorial. These things, if they're related to birds of prey somehow, might be . . . uh, well . . . you know what?" he said brightly, "I'll just shut up, now. Who's working on this? The xenobiology?"

"We're working on getting some biologists out here, but there's a hangup with clearances," said Paulsen. "We don't have enough read-ons for a full scientific team at the moment, but rest assured, we'll get there."

"'*We'll get there?*'" Logan asked, his voice round with disbelief.

"We're working on it," said Decker. "I'm sure it's fine. Anyway, what're we gonna do, send a bunch of nerds in there before our teams? They need to know what we're up against."

"Up against," Logan muttered.

"So, air assets," said Major Easton, returning to the topic at hand. "I imagine that gives them a recon capability that we'll need to keep in mind. Is there anything else we need to worry about?"

"Not that we're aware of," said Paulsen.

"Your most likely enemy course of action is that they'll spot and assess while staying distant," said Medved. "The most dangerous enemy course of action is an aerial attack by mounted cavalry on the gryphons."

Swearing and groans seethed from all sides of the table.

Stannard spoke. "Get pictures. Get readings. Don't get seen. I wish I was going with you."

The silence that followed wasn't lost on Logan.

"Are there any questions?" Paulsen asked.

Logan raised an index finger. "One more."

"Figures," Stannard huffed.

"The Unexploded Ordnance signs on the way to the Arch. Does EOD work in the area? And also, what are we looking out for in the approach to the Arch?"

A few people chuckled. Logan looked around the room. "Did I say something funny?"

"The signs are a cover," Decker said, pushing off the wall behind him. "Most of the soldiers on this base believe we're out here cleaning up UXO—unexploded ordnance—from World War Two on an Indian burial ground. It explains the fence, the secrecy"—here, he gestured at Logan and Bob—"the experts coming and going. You've noticed we don't wear nametapes."

"I did notice that," said Logan.

"If the support personnel ask, we tell 'em if this goes sideways, we don't want the Five O'Clock News to know who was out here fucking with a burial ground. In the meantime, none of them dare go past the signs."

Paulsen added, "Every soldier knows you do not screw with UXO. It's an easy way to wind up dead, with everybody shaking their heads at what a dumbass you were."

"So, the other soldiers out here? They don't even know about the Arch?"

"Of course not," said Paulsen. "They're not read-on. The read-ons for ASCENDANT WARDEN and ARCHSTONE are apportioned. There are only around a hundred for each. There are a few at the director level, but most of the read-ons have to go to the teams, the Ops shack, and key individuals in the ACE—the Analytical Control Element—in the intel shop. The Deputy Director at the Defense Policy Agency is the highest, I think."

"The SOCNORTH Commander," corrected Decker, referring to the Special Operations Command for North America. "No one on his staff, though."

"Really?" asked Paulsen.

"He doesn't attach teams to anything unless he's read-on," said Decker. "He's kind of a dick about that."

Logan spoke up. "Are you telling me the President doesn't even know about this place?"

"That's correct," said Paulsen. "Nor the Joint Chiefs, nor anyone on the National Security Council. In fact, outside of SOCNORTH and our Deputy Director, no other agencies are aware of its existence. We intend to keep it that way."

The ready room buzzed.

It was effectively a locker room, with benches set inside oversized yellow cages of two-inch steel mesh lined with racks to their eight-foot ceilings. Equipment snapped and clicked, men laughed, men swore. Music played from somewhere, a singer growling over looped beats and barre chords. The air stung with Pine-Sol and weapons lubricant, and it carried Logan back.

"How long since you've jumped?" Decker asked from outside Logan's cage.

Logan pulled at straps and buckles on the pack he'd been given, a towering expedition rucksack in heavy nylon, speckled in multicam, doubtless built custom for Special Operations. It had held a sleep system, a bivouac system of some type he'd never seen, a gas mask, his plate carrier with front and back plates and all its associated web gear, and his helmet and comms gear, all of it arrayed on the floor. He had a lot to sort out, but first things first: make sure the damned pack fits. Blisters festered fast and would take a man out in days, if not sooner.

"Do you remember?" Decker asked. "Your last jump?"

"A military jump? It's been a long minute," Logan admitted. He sat, reached for a black duffel bag, and took out a weapon-looking device, a steel blade with carbon fiber. "Though if I'm jumping with all this shit, I'm gonna need my other foot."

He pulled up his pant leg, exposing a shaft of gleaming chrome-moly steel, a high-tech ball and socket disappearing into his hiking boot.

"Oh, Jesus Christ!" Decker yelled. "No! Full fucking stop!"

The hum of locker-room talk and laughter dropped its pitch and became the murmurs of concern that hailed discovery as a crowd gathered outside his cage door.

"You think they pulled me aside at the airport because I'm brown?" Logan said. He opened a valve to release a vacuum lock and eased his prosthetic off its liner, a few shades lighter than his own skin and extending a few inches below his knee. The hiking boot stayed on the foot.

Decker's mouth dropped open as Logan removed an antibiotic towelette from a package and wiped the inside of the socket thoroughly.

"Cool," said Braxton, ducking under someone's arm and coming into the cage. "That's a nice one, too. IED?"

"My buddy and I were the first IED injuries of Coalition members in Algeria. I was a trend-setter." He proceeded to clean the inside of the blade prosthesis with a fresh towelette.

"You are full of surprises," Tommy Duchamps said from the

doorway. "Anything I need to know, as your medic?"

"No," Stannard said, pushing his way through the gathered mass. "Because he's not going. You're out, Doc. Pack your shit."

"Paulsen makes those calls," Logan said, not looking up. "You don't."

"I'm your Ops NCO."

Logan set the leg down on the bench. "And I'm a contractor. I don't work for you. I work with—not 'for'—his boss." He pointed at Decker.

"Well, we didn't know you were disabled," Decker said.

"That's because I'm not."

"You only have one foot!" Stannard cried.

"I have three feet," Logan corrected, gesturing. "One for my left leg and two for my right."

"Goddammit," said Decker. "You know what I mean."

"No, I don't," Logan said. "Explain it." He nodded to Stannard. "Use small words if it helps him."

"You watch your smart mouth. This is a liability. I won't have it," said Decker.

"A liability?" Logan challenged. "Can you switch your foot out for a better set of performance characteristics? Don't tell me you wouldn't if you could. I've run marathons on this thing. I've skydived with it."

"That's not the point," said Stannard.

"That's . . . no, that's exactly the point," Logan said, thinking about it visibly and looking between the two prostheses.

"What if something goes wrong? What if it breaks?" Decker asked.

Tommy Duchamps cut in, smooth and professional. "It's carbon fiber and spring-tempered steel. There's nothing that could break it that wouldn't already take off a leg, anyway."

"I guarantee you it will outlast all of us," Logan said. "And to your earlier question, Doc, the knee's intact, and I've got almost three inches below. There's some minor loss in proprioception. Unstable terrain is a little tricky at a sprint, but not much more than it would be for anyone. If we're out there for more than a few days, I'll need to clean the liner. I'll bring a spare and everything I need."

"Do you take anything?" asked Duchamps. "Opioids? Anticonvulsants? Beta-blockers for phantom limb pain?"

"God, you know your shit," Logan said appreciatively. "No. Not for years. The occasional ibuprofen. Shots of vitamin B."

"B6? B12?"

"Bourbon."

Duchamps laughed. "All right, Professor. You're good by me."

"And so, we meet these people," said Decker. "They see that. What happens then?"

"I'll put the other one back on, first. I've been wearing it the whole time, and you didn't know."

"You're disabled," said Decker.

"I identify as performance-enhanced."

"Smartass. Do you park in a disabled space?" Stannard asked.

"No. I'm not disabled."

A long moment passed.

"I don't like it," said Stannard.

"Funny, I didn't like it, either."

Major Abby Easton's cage was across the hall from Logan's, and both their doors were open. His peripheral vision picked up on her unbuttoning her fatigue blouse—boy, did it ever—and a flick of his eye took in a stomach carved like a river over stones below a gray sports bra. She hung the shirt on the cage wall and fought her way into a Frogskin, a skintight, flame-resistant top for wear under armor and load-bearing gear.

"Cultural Support," said Braxton, from the cage next to Logan.

He reminded Logan of the bad motherfuckers back on The Rez, the scrappy guys who used to fight for fun. He remembered the Knife-In-The-Back twins from high school, Clarence and George, who'd drive clear across Glacier Park to Kalispell to hang out at a truck stop and start fights with passers-through. He wondered where they were now.

They'd probably think I'd sold my soul to the devil to get where I am.

"What's that?" he asked. He hadn't been listening.

"Cultural Support teams, Doc. They used to be called 'Female Engagement Teams.' Special Ops, female-type. They engage with the female population in countries where we men aren't allowed to. She's our XO, and your team leader. She's also our sniper."

"Huh," said Logan, glancing back to watch her shrug into a plate carrier arrayed with pouches of double-stacked magazines.

"The major's hardcore," said Braxton. "The Army doesn't let women attend sniper school? So she went to an Air Force school and *killed that shit.* Top of her class, turned around and took fourth in the International Sniper Competition."

"You don't say."

"Whupped Decker's team something fierce, too. His clowns barely finished."

"Wow," Logan breathed. "I bet that's going real well."

"Yeah, he kinda hates her."

"I imagine so."

"You know, she used to play football? Not, like, Powder Puff; she was semi-pro. Tight end. Thousand-yard seasons back-to-back, still runs a four-five forty. Look her up on YouTube. She'd be in the NFL if this country made any damn sense."

"Well," said Logan. "I should probably go introduce myself."

"No need," she said, and he jumped; she was in his doorway. "Never seen a woman in a locker room before?"

"Actually, no," said Logan. He met her eyes, and she held them, challenging. *Interesting.* "Apologies, Major. I was of the mistaken impression women weren't allowed in combat operations."

"Only technically," she said. "Administratively, I belong to an intelligence unit in Virginia. Special Operations retains operational and tactical control. I've had three combat tours this way."

"Good," he said.

"Do you prefer Professor or *Adjutant?*"

He thought about it. "I'm a civilian. 'Professor' is fine."

"Here's the deal, Professor. I carry my own gear. I use the same latrine you do, so cope. I'm your XO, your Cultural Support Officer, and your long gunner. I rock an IWI DAN in three-thirty-eight Lapua—" He knew the rifle, an Israeli sniper's piece, but he knew the caliber only by reputation. A SEAL had schwacked a bad guy at well over a mile with a Lapua right when he'd left the Legion. "—and I can drop a running man at fifteen hundred meters. If you forget everything you think you know about women, we'll get along fine. Just don't help me, don't try to *save me*, and don't test me. I've already passed every test in the Army, that's why I'm here. Are we clear?"

"Yes, Major," Logan assured her. "Do you prefer 'Major?'"

"From you?" she asked, looking him up and down. "Yeah."

"Fair enough," he said, but she'd already turned away. She returned to her cage and stepped into a parachute harness, snugging it down with effortless, mechanical precision.

"And this is Special Ops, is it?" Logan asked Braxton.

"Best gig in the Army, Doc."

"A little unorthodox to dual-hat cultural support and sniper."

"Why? When you gonna need 'em both at the same time?"

Logan thought about this.

"Anyway," said Braxton, "unorthodox is how we roll. Task Force saved my life."

"How's that?" The Frogskin they'd given him was scratchy with sizing, and he pulled at it before throwing the plate carrier over his head. Nothing fit quite right.

"Well," said Braxton, pulling on his own chute and harness over his load-bearing gear, "I was in a leadership school to get my rocker, and the instructor's one of these guys with the skinny hands and a gut, you know? He's running down all ninety-two steps of the Military Decision-Making Process. This asshole spends three days teachin' us what to do in a crisis, so I knew he was full of shit. Who the fuck has three days to figure out what to do in a crisis?

"A few days later I'm outside his office, and he's up on the wall, Employee of the Month or whatever, his official photo, right? Instructor of Whatever. This motherfucker got *four* ribbons on his rack, the three you get for Basic Training and one you can get for mopping a floor real good. He got to Staff Sergeant with *four goddamn ribbons.* He's got no deployment badge, and he's got a Marksman badge, like, hit twenty-three out of forty. Punkass can't even shoot. Slick-sleeve motherfucker holds my career in his hands, and I wouldn't trust him to fold my shirts.

"As you can imagine," Braxton continued, tightening a strap around his thigh and adjusting his crotch, "it was detrimental to my morale. I barely graduated. Attached to Special Ops on a tour to the Sandbox six months later, as a Staff Sergeant," he added for emphasis, "and realized there was a whole other side to the Army, where we get the shit *done.* Found my people. Results-oriented, not process-oriented, you know? I went to Ranger School when I rotated back, tried out for SF after that, made it first pass. Commo pipeline, second rocker, Task Force, *bang,* here I am. That motherfucker's probably still at the Schoolhouse, quoting regulations, and me, I'm about to parachute into another dimension beside a goddamn *cyborg.* Love my job, hate the Army. You good?"

"Sure," Logan said.

Braxton's story wasn't much different from men he'd met in the Legion Commando Brigade. Outcasts, wanderers, adventurers of all stripes, all of whom possessed that certain cut above at whatever it was they did, and to a man they had no time for useless people. Commandos were commandos.

He went back to donning his parachute over his plate carrier and all its attached gear. It felt alien and awkward in its entirety. He knew he'd get used to it again, but right now it felt . . . off. Everything was uncomfortable, different. All the balance was wrong. There were straps on the parachute rig that he didn't remember, and it didn't make any sense. He tried not to take it as an omen.

He turned around to find Major Easton in his cage, well inside his personal space, close enough that he could smell baby powder and—he had to think about it before he placed the scent—fabric softener.

"Can I help you, Major?"

"No, but I can help you. Your chute's upside down."

The team met up at the base of the stairs outside the Ops modular, the same place Logan had met them on his first foray into the woods. They were dressed for the desert in the rain, wildly incongruous, necks and faces splotched and slashed in tan and brown, Logan's included. Even through the paint, he recognized everyone from the briefing, and he tried to remember names.

The occasional eye flicked to his blade prosthesis. They'd all heard the fight with Stannard and Decker. He wore it like a trophy, the leg of his trousers cinched around it. Decker said nothing.

Logan carried his pack underslung sideways beneath his reserve chute, hitting him in the knees with every step. They'd outfitted him with a coyote-brown, stubby, suppressed rifle with a shitload of optics that he originally thought was an M4 but was pleased to learn was in fact his old friend, the Heckler & Koch 416, an ultra-reliable version of the American carbine and as it happened, his issue rifle in the Legion. On closer inspection, he noted the team all carried HKs, top of the line; no cut-rate weapons, here.

They'd given him half a dozen thirty-round magazines, which he personally viewed as excessive. If he had nearly two hundred locals trying to kill him, he'd probably have it coming.

They'd also issued him a pistol, a compact Sig, blocky, ugly, and murdered-out in flat black carbon steel. He wore it strapped across his chest above the HK's magazines, with a mag seated and two more on his left hip. It was like being surrounded by compatriots.

In addition to Major Easton's regular load of chutes, web gear, and rucksack, she carried a black waterproof flight case at her side that looked like something a musician would use to protect a priceless instrument, stenciled with KARMA DELIVERY SERVICE in white two-inch letters.

She was probably the fast-mover with the skeletal rifle he'd seen on his first trip to the Arch. The scarecrow who'd run like a gazelle. *Runs a four-five forty. Back-to-back thousand-yard seasons.* In a Ghillie and face paint, there'd have been no way he could have known she was a woman.

Forget everything you know about women.

They moved out, trudging under their packs, chutes, and combat loads. This time, no one ran.

The team members had to give each other a hand up the hill to the Arch; their gear was so heavy, and the moss so slick, it took considerable effort and more than a few falls before they assembled at the suspended ring.

Logan was struggling.

"Been a while, huh, Professor?" asked Martin, the big guy with the machine gun.

"I haven't humped this much gear in years," said Logan. He was glad they'd left the armored plates out of the carriers. "So, the fun question: how do we get through? You have a rope swing or something?" The Arch hung suspended three feet off the ground. "Or is Martin here just going to throw us like footballs?"

"The minute you touch it, it'll suck you through," Braxton said. "So they say."

Logan drew the Sig, racked the slide, decocked it, and put it away again. "You first," he said.

Martin grinned his insane grin and dove headfirst into the Arch, cradling the Mark 48. He disappeared with a whoop, a green flash, and a kick of sparks.

"Go!" yelled Decker, and the next soldier dove through, and the next, and the next, until it was Logan's turn.

Heart hammering against his ribs, he took a deep breath and thrust both hands into the Arch.

The world flipped inside out.

There was no flash, no light inside the rift, only darkness and the sensation of violent motion. He was body-surfing, rag-dolling in the sea, tossed about by immense tidal forces, his pack gyrating at the ends of its tethers and cracking him like a whip. *This was an idiotic idea; what's to keep it from ripping us all limb from limb?* All he could do was curl into a fetal position and cover his face with his forearms.

He landed on his side in hard, baked dirt, dropped from a few feet like falling out of bed. He understood now why they'd insisted he wear elbow and knee pads.

"Well, whadja' think?" asked Braxton, as he and Major Easton's spotter—a Marine named Foster—heaved Logan to his knees, and then upright. Foster was a fine-boned, shrewd-looking young Gunnery Sergeant, clear-eyed and model handsome even through the camo facepaint.

Logan dusted off his gloves. A fine layer of powder puffed up and shimmered in the sun. "Not fun," he admitted, spitting sand off his tongue. "Wow, it's hot."

Hot was an understatement. It was easily over a hundred Fahrenheit and humid in the manner unique to desert depressions, reeking with the faint Play-Doh smell of sand and rot.

This place has everything, he thought.

Major Easton popped into existence in midair a few feet from him and fell with a grunt and a crash.

"Major," said Logan deferentially.

"Shut up."

Logan bit down on his water valve. The heat was nauseating.

It was gorgeous, though. Stunning vistas stretched in every direction, a tapestry of red and gold desolation under the deepest blue sky he'd ever seen. A ringed planet, pink splotched with purple, took up a tenth of the horizon as it peeked over the edge of the canyons, a lone slender white ring canted forty-five degrees. "That's a sight," he said aloud. "The moon!"

"I know, right?" said Braxton.

They stood atop a knob of rock, surrounded by vastness: rock-strewn sandy valleys stretched between volcanic ridgelines; the alien blade of a mountain, miles high and rising to a point that looked barely big enough to stand atop, was red, not black as it had looked in the thermal. The canyon they were about to recon stretched flat for miles until it doglegged off a spur into . . . well, he'd find out what it doglegged into.

Lemmy.

It doglegged into Lemmy.

From what he could see, looking out from over a kilometer up, it was the kind of terrain he knew well, fouled with jagged boulders and wind-sculpted obstacles on the hardpan below.

Major Easton rose to one knee with a long groan and adjusted a pair of wraparound Oakleys, spitting repeatedly. "Okay," she said, seeing the moon and sagging slightly. "Wow."

Another soldier appeared several feet past her and nearly ten feet above the ground, screaming obscenities as he fell and landed with a cloud of dust.

"Is that the last one?" asked Decker.

The team sergeants did a head count. Logan was on Easton's team, Team Two. He was the seventh body on a six-man outfit. Lucky Number Thirteen.

"I seem to have one extra," she joked. "Some straphanger."

"It's cool," chided Martin. "We'll probably shake him after this next part."

The Korean soldier dropped his ruck and walked to the edge of the mesa, peered over, and let out a low whistle. He motioned at Decker and beckoned him to the edge.

They conversed in low tones. Decker returned to the team. "Take a knee, everybody. Martin, assist Park. Leave your ruck."

Logan dropped to one knee and shook out the kink in his back as his pack rested on the ground. It was glorious not having to carry it, even for a few minutes.

Park and Martin began beating on the rocks with hammers of some type. Driving pitons, Logan saw. He watched as Park threaded nylon webbing through the eyes, tied it off, and gave a thumbs-up to Decker. Martin returned to his pack and attached it to his harness.

"Let's go," Decker said.

Logan waddled over near the edge with the team. The cliff fell away in an overhang a few meters down, the ledge cantilevering into space. It was a perfect spot for a static-line jump.

"Range finder says four-zero-six to the hardball," Park announced. "Twelve hundred feet. Anything feels hinky, the wise man grabs the handle." By which he meant to cut away the main chute at the first sign of trouble and pull the reserve. With only a few seconds of descent, there wouldn't be time to fix much.

Waves of heat radiated from the desert floor, obscuring

granular details of the ground below. Logan handed his carabiner and static line to Park, who hooked it to the webbing in sequence. He'd be jumping behind Martin and before Major Easton; fourth in the stick.

Decker went first, which Logan grudgingly admitted was very cool. The SEAL commander's yellow line unraveled from the bag and the canopy unfurled—a high-performance, gray, rectangular military ram-air chute. It looked like the RA-1, the rig Logan had trained on for his HALO certification.

"RA-1?" he asked Major Easton, as the next chute popped, exactly in Decker's wake.

"Modified," she said. "Controls are the same. It's a little faster, a little touchier. Reserve is automatic when you cut away. Yellow handle."

Martin ran off the edge.

"*L'appel du vide,*" Logan said to her with a shrug. The literal meaning was "the call of the void." It still amazed him that the French had a word for the attraction of jumping from high things.

"Get some," she returned.

Logan saluted her. It was instinctive, and the thing to do at the time, thumb tucked, fingers tight, palm outward in the Legion manner, giving them a glimpse at who he used to be. Older now, maybe; gravely injured once, certainly; but still fearless.

She returned it with an American salute; slow, courteous, professional.

A thumbs-up from Park, and Logan rumbled off the edge as fast as he could manage, really no better than a waddle with all his gear, but at the last step he planted the blade, bounced off it hard, and arced over the edge as if he'd had a small trampoline.

His ruck threw him forward with a sickening lurch, wildly off-balance. He'd done this a hundred times—a hundred and eight, to be precise—and there was always the irrational fear that he'd topple over headfirst under load, the chute would tangle around the ruck, and he'd burn in; or he'd tumble backwards as it opened and a line would foul around his neck, popping off his head like a doll.

But none of it happened, as it never did. He tucked his knees and leaned into the wind as the canopy opened with an easy, familiar ruffling followed by a stout impact. He didn't have to look up to know it had gone without fault, but checking the lines was tattooed across a part of his brain.

The lines were flawless.

The stabilizers, the fabric wings at the edges of the canopy, were pressurized. That was something new. It was a well-behaved system, and completely silent.

He reached up for the steering toggles, right where he'd left them over a decade ago. The rig braked smoothly, the canopy easing forward without a hint of side-slip, and he swung out into the valley and followed the others.

The big ringed planet hit him in the solar plexus. *Who would believe this?*

If we were smart, we'd ride these thermals as far as we could. What a view.

He cut loose his ruck to the end of its tether and set his feet on it, an old trick to stabilize his frame that had only taken years to get right, but the first time he'd done it with his blade. At that moment he either passed Martin's wake or lost a thermal because his chute burbled with turbulence and dropped several feet before finding itself again. "Easy, girl."

Below him, Martin and Decker had started to circle. The ride was almost over.

Logan wheeled, flared, braked, and touched down with the confident grace of a robin on a power line. His pack barely made a sound as it kissed the hardpan.

He stepped over his ruck as he landed, jettisoned his canopy, and walked away as it collapsed.

"Who the fuck are you?" asked Martin incredulously, on his ass with his chute behind him, rock-throwing distance away.

Major Easton came in hot, raising a cloud of dust as she stumbled and slid on her knees, dragging her gear and swearing epithets.

Logan headed her way. "We gotta talk landings sometime, Major." The string of vulgarities that followed assured him she was, without a doubt, old-school Army. He stretched his hand down to her. "Gimme your hand, ma'am."

"Eat a dick."

"You do you." He unclipped his harness as he strode back to his pack and canopy, took out his entrenching tool, and attacked the sand with broad, expert strokes. An inch of shiny sand gave way to baked silt. Tough digging. "How far down do you want this stuff, Commander?"

Decker was on his hands and knees twenty yards away, pulling at straps and untangling himself. "Like I give a fuck. Just bury it. Canopy, harness, everything."

Logan was sitting on his pack against a boulder, suckling at his bite valve and watching the moon, when the rest of the team finished burying their gear. He noted Major Easton had buried the rifle case and would probably need to do so on every trip, at what had to be a thousand dollars a pop.

The American Special Ops problem-solving process illustrated. Apply money.

Unbelievable.

Her sniper rifle rode in a padded bag on her ruck. She carried a suppressed HK 416 street sweeper like his on a sling attached to a carabiner at one shoulder, and wore a sand-shadowed jute Ghillie draped over her rucksack with the hood thrown back. She'd either painted her previous Ghillie desert colors, or she had one lying around for every environment. Neither would have surprised him.

There was no foliage here that they could see, but from the ranges where she could engage, it wouldn't matter much. She'd be another lump in the distance. Foster wore a Ghillie, as well, not much more than a hooded cape over his pack. Like her, he carried a street sweeper hanging off one shoulder. What Logan figured was a spotting scope the size of a fire extinguisher bulged from a padded bag on one side of his ruck.

"You're just like a pig in shit, ain't you?" Braxton asked Logan. "Goddamn desert rat over here. Man, we *hate* the desert. Why are you like this?"

"*Quand on a pas ce que l'on aime, il faut aimer ce que l'on a*," Logan said as he donned his ruck.

"What's that mean?"

"If you don't have what you love, love what you have," said Tommy, passing by, nearly doubled under his ruck.

Logan clipped the HK's sling through a carabiner on one shoulder, the same as Major Easton, and shrugged. "It's pretty around here."

Around them, the team loaded up.

Logan didn't let on how miserable the place made him; how the heat and the humidity triggered the urge to vomit from anxiety and loss, much as the scent of a specific perfume can extinguish a man's heart like a cigarette tossed in a gutter.

He didn't tell them he'd been avoiding the desert since the day he left *la Legion*. He hadn't gone into treasure hunting or searching for lost civilizations, even though it's what appealed to him most, because that bullshit invariably led you back into the desert and he was done with deserts.

Still, here he was, sand in his teeth, rifle at his shoulder, a ninety-pound ruck and the never-ending sweat drips of rift valley wasteland. Cozy as a roach in a baseboard.

Know thine enemy.

The worst part of it was, he was more in his element at this moment than he'd been anywhere on Earth in a long time.

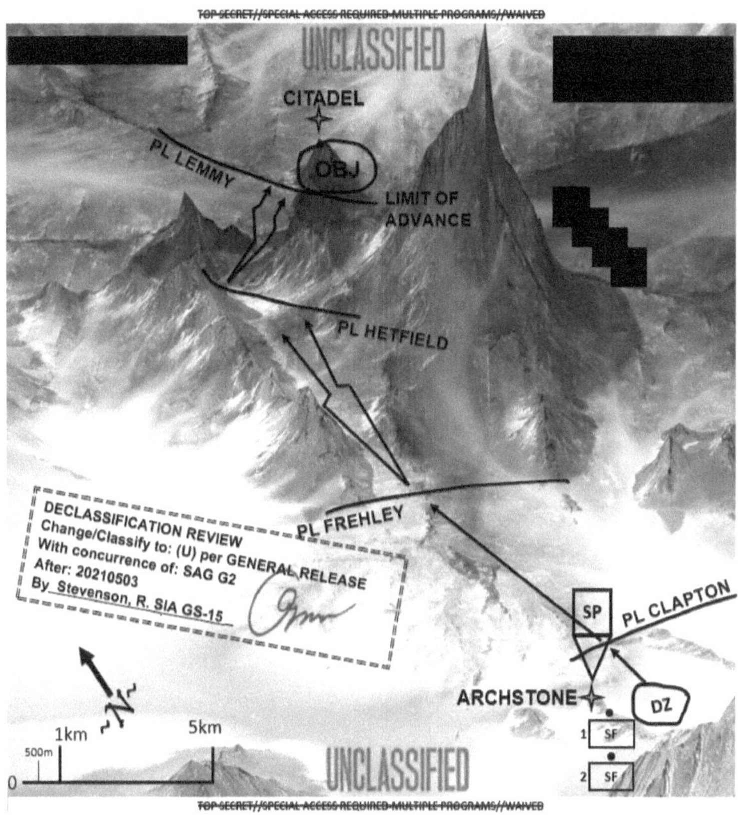

Multispectral and thermal (Black-Hot) composite of the ARCHSTONE canyon complex, with preliminary DET 2 reconnaissance mission phase lines.

IV

TERRA NULLIUS

"Earth was not found, nor ether-Heaven,
A yawning gap, but grass was none."

> — Snorri Sturlson, writing on the lands of
> the gods in the *Prose Edda*,
> Iceland, c. 1220 A.D.

Logan knew within an hour that this was the wrong team. American troops weren't used to fighting in the desert as much as they were acclimated to fighting on top of the desert, which was an important distinction. Americans fought their desert wars from islands of America carved into the sand and rock.

Even this ultra-elite team of Special Operators weren't desert fighters. They were fighters in the desert, sure, and good ones, he had no doubt, but they weren't scorpions who could bury themselves in the sand, becoming one with the heat and the grit while remaining lethal and invisible. They were chimps, scurrying from cave to cave. Avoiding the desert.

They were tough, he'd give them that. But the rate at which they burned through water, the heavy footsteps in the shallow sand, the wasted motion vaulting rocks best gone around . . .

Their packs were too heavy. They were provisioned as if they'd never be able to draw water from the sand, or find bugs or snakes to eat, or pull acacia branches into fortifications for protected rest. Maybe they wouldn't; maybe there wasn't anything like that on this planet. But you didn't carry your world into the desert with you. You carved your world out of the desert, which entailed a considerably different approach.

They weren't lean. They were Americans, heavy with muscle, buoyed by protein bars and weightlifting and CrossFit to make them the most lethal warriors who had ever lived, but needing a chopper to carry them into the arena, like knights of old hoisted into their saddles by crane before a joust.

He tried not to resent them, thinking back to Bob huffing through the jungle and how much slack he'd cut him.

This was that, only the team was in his element, now.

In his ears, a cliché, a stupid off-the-cuff remark he'd heard a thousand times in the States on an 80-degree day in Montana: "It's the humidity that gets you." But it was true. High desert, sandy desert, desert where the wind blew the humidity away? That was manageable desert. Easy desert. The human body was effectively a water pump. Water in, water out, keep feeding it. An uncomfortable proposition, but not a complicated one.

Sub-sea-level deserts could be outright damp. It was the great irony of their existence. Sweat took forever to evaporate below sea level, so people never cooled off. Eventually it caught up to them and they'd redline—literally turning bright red—and go down. Every time. The fundamental physics of death.

The key to thriving in the desert, any desert, was realizing your limits and planning around them. The world made the rules.

In low desert, you moved at the speed of evaporation.

And Americans were worse at nothing in the world so much as slowing down.

The Legion had been adapting their soldiers to desert combat for nearly 200 years. Their official march, *Le Boudin*, is sung at 88 beats per minute, a painfully slow cadence compared to the typical 120 beats per minute of every other service in the world.

Mars ou meurant, "march or die," is the unofficial motto of the Desert Commando Regiment, because at anything other than a march—a slow march, the Legion march, the *Le Boudin* march—you wouldn't reach your destination alive.

Again, the math was simple: an army would cover more terrain at two miles per hour for six consecutive hours than at four miles per hour for two hours before collapsing for four hours to recover.

In the desert, slow was fast.

The superhuman Special Operations pace of nearly five miles per hour, effectively a race-walk, could kill in the desert after thirty minutes. He'd seen American commandos, suicidally convinced of their physical prowess, crashing on the first day of desert operations in East Africa and needing to be choppered out because they were moving too damned much.

It was the SEALs, more than any others, they always had to scrape off of the sand; SEALs never slowed down. Throughout his career, he'd seen dozens of SEALs laugh at the "lazy Frenchmen" lounging in the heat and moving at half-speed everywhere, only to watch the same SEAL flopping in the sun like a landed trout a few hours later. He'd expected the Marines to be the problem children, from what he'd always heard of the American military, but Marines, by and large, were obedient and had a healthy respect for danger.

Similarly, the "Group Guys"—the Special Forces teams—had an innate sense for when they were out of their element. They took direction from the desert rats and adapted well. They were also, to a man, very, very smart.

Bravo Team, Major Easton's team, was mostly Group. Collier and Delacroix, the salt-and-pepper shaker duo with the neck tattoos, were SEALs in Alpha Team. Decker's team.

Decker was a SEAL.

Decker was pushing them hard.

He'd bring it up away from the team when he had the chance. He just hoped that Decker didn't kill them all, first.

They rested a bit later, among the rocks, drinking water and adding electrolyte packets to their bottles and bladders, adjusting boots and straps. The sun was a sledgehammer, but it was moving across the valley from left to right and had started to throw a shadow from the right-hand cliffs. "We should make for that shade," said Decker, pointing. "It'll be cooler over there."

Logan thought about pulling Decker aside right now—heat was the subject of the conversation—but something was off. The idea of heading for the other wall raised his hackles,
though he couldn't remember why. Some shred of training, though, knowledge long dormant and now atrophied, tapped meekly on the bars to its cage.

He scanned the canyon wall through his optic, and noted a series of dark spots along it. He flipped the magnifier behind the optic and spun the ring to maximum, and it all came back to him. "Absolutely not," he said after another moment.

"It's hot as balls out here, Doc," said Decker. "We need to get over there."

"Yes, it is cooler over there, which is why you've got those den and burrow entrances along that side. Take a look. Look ahead of us, where there's the overhang."

Rifles came up and dials clicked as the team scanned the wall. "What the hell are those?" Decker asked.

"I don't know," said Logan, "and I don't care to find out. Predators build dens like that. Specifically, nocturnal predators, who want as little sunlight in their homes as possible, which is why there aren't any on this side. I recommend we stay near this wall and make damn sure we return on this side. Whatever lives in there comes out at night. In the meantime, you sure as shit don't want to wake it up."

"Check out the professor," said Major Easton, visibly impressed for the first time since he'd met her.

Foster, looking like a sweaty, murderous Muppet in his Ghillie with his pack sticking out the back, pulled out a plastic-coated map and checked their location against the landmarks along the mesas. He beckoned Logan over. "Whatdya think, Doc? I think we're here." He put a finger down on the image.

They were dead reckoning off visible land features, though the view was largely blocked by a maze of smooth-swept, skull-like boulders and rock piles crumbled from the cliff edges not yet battered smooth by the sand and wind.

Logan had a solid memory of what the valley had looked like from the air. Down here on the canyon floor, it showed as nearly flat, with only a few features on the map—very little to work with, and the drone hadn't brought back any imagery of the ground at this level. A long ridge scraped the sky atop the canyon to their right, with the alien spire rising into the sunlight as a terrain fixture.

"We've gone four thousand paces," said Foster, tapping a string of beads on his chest. "Four klicks. None of these rock piles are on this map, but four klicks puts us right here. See that little spur?" He pointed off to the left. "That's that, I think." He tapped the map, and Logan nodded in agreement.

"Looks good. Nice work."

"Am I nuts, or are we not going north?" Foster asked him quietly.

"I've been thinking about that," said Logan, and he had. "I know the map we saw in the mission brief had this canyon laid out heading north from the Arch, but if compasses don't work here, then north is arbitrary. If this sun moves east-west like ours does, we're actually heading south."

"That's what feels wrong," Foster agreed. "I wish I'd brought a compass."

"Medved said there are some kind of deposits all through this valley that screw with bearings," Logan said. "They couldn't verify it, because there are no GPS satellites."

"Maybe we call the sun's movement east-west, mark this as south, and then at least we can stick-and-shadow it going forward if we get hung up," Foster suggested, reminding Logan for the dozenth time since they'd arrived how much he enjoyed working with Special Operations. Stick and shadow was easy; you put a stick—a knife, a rifle, anything—in the ground, marked the end of the shadow, waited a while, and marked the end of the shadow again. A line from the first mark to the second would give west to east. It was fail-safe; assuming, of course, this world rotated eastward.

"I like it," he said. "Call it south. Flip the map." He put his fist out, and Foster punched it.

Major Easton came over to see what they were talking about, and Logan relaxed on his pack while she and Foster worked it out.

She approached Logan once they were done.

"You figured all that out?"

"No," said Logan. "Foster figured it out on his own. I merely agreed with him. Everything he said makes sense."

"Mind if I ask . . . just how smart are you?"

"We're about to find out."

Decker got everyone up, and they broke into their respective teams. Logan motioned Decker to him, away from everyone else.

"What's up, Doc?" Decker asked with a cocky grin.

"You're moving too fast," Logan told him. "You need to slow these people down. Save your water, save your energy."

"You heard the briefing. Time is at a premium. We move, we move fast. We get this done and we get the hell home. If you can't keep up—"

"I can keep up," said Logan, "but if you drop one of them with heatstroke, you'll have a whole set of problems you're in no position to deal with right now."

"They'll drink water. They'll be fine."

"No, they won't," Logan insisted.

"Yes, they will."

"You're pushing the limits of human endurance!" Logan hissed.

"That's what we do!" snapped Decker. "Quit being a fuckin' pussy and fall in."

"You understand, you're the problem, here."

Decker pointed away from himself. "Fall the fuck in. Now."

"Sure."

Ninety minutes later, they were fourteen kilometers into the canyon, haggard, exhausted, and panting.

They'd blown right through Phase Line HETFIELD, doglegged at the end of the valley, and were still moving hard within two thousand meters of the Citadel, well within observation range if they'd either move out into the canyon a bit more or get some elevation. Some of the rocks were tall enough to offer what had to be spectacular views. There was no reason to move fast.

Hell, there was no reason to move further.

They hugged the left wall, a hundred meters away from the base of the cliffs, Decker's team ahead by two hundred meters and still moving far too fast. Bravo Team had fanned out into a lopsided chevron with the long arm away from the ridgeline, Martin and his belt-fed taking up the slack on the short side, with Logan in the center behind them all feeling like baggage. He watched the sky at regular intervals, thinking of that goddamn gryphon or hippogriff.

Dragon, he thought.

Stannard was an idiot.

He stepped over a suitcase-sized rock. The sand was baked into a crust here, scattered with broken stone pieces anywhere from feet to meters across, some of it wind-blasted, some of it sharp, all of it dusted with the red-gold metallic sand like talcum powder. The ground shimmered, opalescent, as they moved.

On the other hand, the battlespace owners here have air assets.

Which means we are idiots for not flying in while it's clear. They could easily have drifted the twenty klicks to what the team was calling The Citadel. This was the big idea: get close. Get readings. Get pictures. If possible, get a good look at The Citadel and get a feel for—what had Medved called it?—"size and disposition of troops." It felt part and parcel to Stannard's bullshit redneck idea that they were going to go in there and "roll these chumps." He seethed at the thought.

Decker was still moving too damned fast and his team would be out of range in moments. Logan's earpiece crackled. "Keep the fuck up, Bravo," said Decker.

The earpieces were an interesting solution; some genius in the S6, the communications shack, had rigged up the teams' helmet mics and earpieces to old-school, two-way radio transmitter-receivers with a thousand-foot range. No massive antennas, no cell networks.

However, it meant he still had to listen to Decker kvetch and grumble when having a few hundred yards between them was starting to feel like a blessing. He was about to turn the volume down on the receiver when he heard someone calling *Break break break.*

"We've got movers," said the voice. It sounded like Park, but Logan couldn't be sure. Bravo Team went to their bellies.

Logan scanned under the nearest rock to ensure nothing came out of it to investigate him—an old habit that he liked to keep around.

They listened.

"Six pax—" said Park, the Korean bodybuilder. Logan

recognized his voice but it took some thought to realize he meant six personnel; he thought "pax" an odd choice of abbreviation, "—foot patrol, half a klick at two o'clock. Unit unknown. Equipment follows: hand weapons. Body armor . . . ah, shit, I dunno, Roman-looking? Weird, man. Like, armor. Not . . . not ballistic armor. They do not, say again, do not, appear to have seen us. They are continuing their sweep, moving toward our three o'clock and increasing their distance. Over."

"This is Six," said Decker's voice. "Assessment on—well—are they human?"

"Negative, Six," said Park. "Definitely not human. They look . . . big. Stand by."

Foster unpacked the spotting scope, which took about as long as Logan thought it might. He set it up on a rock and peered into the eyepiece.

"Sniper team confirms," Foster reported. "Six individuals. I make them eight, maybe nine-er feet tall. Ah, I think it's Martin's family out for a picnic."

"Asshole," Martin muttered off-mic, loud enough for Logan to hear.

"Received," said Decker. "Stay low and move out."

"They'll have the sun at their backs," added Martin. "They're gonna be harder to see the later it gets."

Logan didn't respond. He was watching the sky.

Bravo Team picked their way through the boulders, slowing to a literal crawl in the name of cover and concealment, which contented Logan for many reasons, not the least of which because it infuriated Decker. Also, hugging the left rim of the canyon with the sun traversing to the right meant they could shelter in shade, and the ten or so degrees of difference felt glorious.

Great, it's only a hundred and forty right here.

Using the pistol grip of the rifle as a brace in one hand, Logan crawled from a refrigerator-sized rock to the shady side of a boulder twenty feet away. The pack and combat gear made staying low excruciating. He leaned on his pack against the rock and rested.

"Doc, you gotta move," said Major Easton, her voice coming through the headset. "Keep up."

"Get with the fuckin' program, Professor," Decker seethed. His annoyance was apparent even over the comms. "We will leave you out here. Over."

"You can kiss my fry-bread-eatin' ass," Logan told him, not keying his mic. He sipped at his water valve, scanned three-sixty and overhead, and moved for the next piece of cover, a pile of rocks the size of a two-story Colonial some fifty feet away. "Moving," he told the team.

"Tommy, this is Six," said Decker as Logan muscled across the hard pan on hands and knees. "Where the hell are you? Over."

A span of silence followed.

"That's not good," Logan whispered to himself, still moving.

"Sergeant Duchamps," said Decker, "report. Over."

Logan drank more water and took the moment to relax while they sorted it out. Broken comms was someone else's problem. They had commo sergeants.

"Alpha Team, hold," said Decker. "Anyone seen Tommy?"

More silence.

"He was right—" the voice cut off abruptly.

"Say again? Over." Decker said.

More silence.

"Fuck," Easton muttered, snapping down the bipod and the rear support on the sniper rifle and posting the weapon on a rock. She threw her hood over her head and shrugged herself up to the weapon, the movement intimate and vaguely sexual, even in the shapeless mass of her Ghillie. "Bravo, weapons hot," she said. "Watch your sectors. Move up on my go. Over."

Logan covered behind the nearest rock, smacked the bottom of the HK's mag out of habit, shaking any sand out of the stack, and chambered a round.

"Alpha team, we're coming to you," said Easton over the radio. "Bravo, go."

Hodges and Martin exploded from cover at a sprint, disappearing again thirty yards ahead.

"We're bounding," said Braxton, tapping Logan on the shoulder. He hadn't even heard him approach. "Two by two. You're with me."

"Set," came the call over the earpiece.

"Brax," said Easton. "Go."

"Moving." Braxton took off from behind the rock like someone was chasing him with a chainsaw.

Logan had been that good on his feet ten years earlier. He dropped on the left side of a boulder the size of an executive desk a good second after Braxton had posted up on the right side and braced his rifle on his left shoulder.

"Set," he wheezed into his mic.

"You okay, Doc?" Braxton said with a grin.

"No," said Logan. "Too old for this shit."

"Set," came the call, far too soon.

"Tower," said Braxton, pointing to a mushroom-shaped boulder probably twenty feet tall.

"Moving." Logan followed him, staying on his left.

As they ran, the supersonic crack of suppressed 5.56 shattered the sky, intimately familiar but wildly out of place in the still of the rocks. The echo rolled off the cliffs and seemed to go on forever.

"Fuck," said Logan, as they set up again.

"Contact, contact, contact," said a voice, icy and calm. It sounded like Park. "Contact left, three hostiles, forty meters.

Correction, make it six—repeat, six—hostiles. Eleven o'clock. Closing."

Another report ranged through the canyon.

"How the fuck does he know they're hostile?" Logan fumed to Braxton.

"'Treat all ARCHSTONE personnel as hostile,'" Braxton recited. "I don't like it, either, Doc. But here we are."

"We don't even know what they want!"

"Set!" came Martin's voice in the headset.

"Fuck!" Logan yelled, moving out.

As Logan sprinted, the air detonated around him, hammering his eardrums and lighting up his body with cold shock-sweat. He dove for cover behind a small boulder and rolled onto his pack to look around as the echoes faded, because his initial, scattered thought was an artillery strike.

It took him a second.

The sniper rifle.

Major Easton was twenty yards behind him, right where they'd left her, a shambling pile around the rifle. He saw her throw the bolt.

He'd never been in front of a sniper at this range; it was the kind of thing a shrewd commando worked to avoid.

She wasn't running suppressed like the rest of the team, and as he thought about it, another old memory shoving its way to the surface: snipers hate heat.

Suppressors trap heat, and in the desert, shimmers from a hot suppressor would distort the view of a target at long range. The .338 could hit at well past a mile.

The noise rattled his mind. He didn't remember the ballistics tables verbatim, but he knew at this range the .300 magnums delivered four thousand foot-pounds of energy, enough to shatter the volcanic rocks around them and turn hard cover into concealment.

"Go!" yelled Braxton.

They moved.

The world erupted again.

He vaulted a boulder, nearly landed on Martin, fell face-first, and the carbine drove the holstered pistol into his chest. He lurched upright, sucking in wind and sand, coughed, and fell over again, blind and gasping.

The world tunneled away as the big gunner pulled him ahead at a run, nearly all twenty pounds of the Mark 48—Sally, he remembered in a haze—and her feeder umbilical raised to his shoulder with one hand and dragging Logan by the handle on the nape of his load-bearing gear with the other, inhumanly strong, a machination grown in a lab.

Martin dropped him behind another rock. "You okay, Doc?"

"I'll be fine," Logan spat. "Fuck. We shouldn't be doing this."

"I have the professor," Martin said into the headset.

"Is he down?" asked Braxton.

Martin had the toneless, rapid-fire cadence of an air traffic controller, or an announcer reciting terms and conditions at the end of an advertisement. "Negative. Took-a-header-we're-three-zero-yards-ahead-of-last-position-bearing-zero-come-get-him-we'll-take-next-bound-over."

"Thanks," said Logan.

"You good?" Martin asked from behind the eyepiece of the machine gun, draping one hand over the buttstock near his cheek.

"Yeah. But—"

"You gotta keep up, Doc."

"Goddammit—"

Martin punched Logan's shoulder, and Logan took the cue and posted up beside him, unclipping his rifle to brace it against the side of the rock on his left shoulder. "I got you," Logan said, swearing under his breath.

"Moving," Martin told his mic. He skirted the boulder and blasted forward like a wingback coming off the line. Braxton appeared beside Logan an instant later. He was startled at how quick they were. He remembered stories, now, of American Special Forces Groups with their own personal training staff, nutritionists, sports physicians. Professional athletes on par with anyone alive.

"You good?"

"Fine. Wind knocked out of me." He was fairly certain he'd cracked a rib; it was getting worse, but he could work around it. "I'm fine," he insisted.

"That's two I'm fine's, Doc. So, bullshit. We'll get you checked out when this is over. Can you move?"

"Of course."

"All right. On me. We gotta get past those two."

"I can't even see them," Logan said. The multicam was incredible, and he wished he'd had it in Algeria back in the day. The mottles and mixtures of color formed an optical illusion that tricked the human eye and smeared itself into any surroundings. If the troops stayed still, they disappeared unless you knew right where to look. "What are we doing?"

"Contact right!" came a yell from ahead—not from the headset.

"Right?" asked Braxton. The prior contact had been to the left. "Ff—"

Any further communication was lost as Sally, Martin's machine gun, opened up like the voice of God among the rocks ahead, three identical three-round bursts followed by a ten-round suppressing burst—impeccable trigger technique.

Logan still couldn't see anything moving.

Braxton pointed his index and middle fingers to his eyes, then pointed them left, ordering Logan to watch the approach from the canyon wall, the left approach, where Park had first reported contact.

Martin and Sally kept blasting.

Braxton dropped his pack with two successive quick-releases Logan hadn't even realized existed. His water bladder was still on his back, attached to his web gear in its own camouflage sleeve. It was like a magic trick.

Another 5.56 added its vote to Sally, brighter, sharper, cracking out now and again. Braxton motioned that he was moving up and Logan was to stay put, tapped the top of his helmet, and jerked a thumb toward Major Easton. He ran toward the gunfire, scuttling in a crouch, and Logan realized Braxton meant the sniper was covering him.

Logan settled his eyes on the left flank and scanned the approaches to their position as the firefight raged on.

I want to see *the monsters.*

The shooting stopped as abruptly as it had begun, as shooting always did.

Logan waited for it to start again, as shooting always did.

"Doctor Logan, come in, over," Easton's voice crackled over Logan's earpiece.

Logan cursed, taking a hand off his handguard to key the radio. He was posted on the left side of the rock, shooting with his non-dominant hand, and everything was now backwards on his kit. It took him a moment. "Logan."

"Where the hell are you? Over."

"About forty meters ahead of your last position, on the left," he said. "Watching your left flank."

"Anything?"

"Negative," he said.

"Roger. Stay there. Over. Break," she said, indicating she was now talking to the team at large. "I've lost visual on all hostiles. Anyone have a visual?"

"Negative."

"Negative."

"Negative."

"They're nine feet tall," said Decker's voice, irritated. "They don't just disappear."

"Bravo, status report," Easton said.

"Foster, up."

"Martin-up." One word. Switched-on, the big guy was a robot.

"Hodges. Up."

"Braxton, up."

Logan fumbled with the button on his transmitter, swearing. "Logan, up. Uh . . ."

"Logan?" asked Major Easton.

"I'm good. I, uh, fell. Might have cracked a rib. I'm fine."

"Medic," said Easton. "Hodges, get with Logan."

"I'm fine."

"Not an option, Professor."

Logan saw the movement out of his right eye, a rock shimmering, standing, running. Someone in camo moving fast.

They were so fast!

The medic dove low and came in beside Logan, head-first, as if stealing second. Clouds of red-gold dust shimmered in the sun as he rolled upright.

The medic was very tall, with Ethiopian facial features greased white and tan in blotches. He had the whitest teeth Logan had ever seen, perfect Hollywood pearls. "Talk to me," he said, moving to one knee and shouldering his rifle but keeping his suppressor pointed at the ground, his head on a swivel. Decker was blathering into their earpieces. Logan turned the volume down and noted Hodges was doing the same.

"I fell," said Logan. "Buttstock hit me in the chest. Right on the pistol. It hurts a bit."

"Did you hear a crack?"

"No."

The medic—Hodges, Logan remembered, now—pushed on his sternum. Logan winced as it shot sparks into his spine. "Yeah, that hurts."

"Any coughing? Blood in your spit?"

"Nope."

"Trouble breathing?"

"A little tight."

"All right. Vitamin I. You got some?"

"Ah, somewhere." He had ibuprofen in his medical kit, which was somewhere on his vest, which he didn't have the hang of yet. Hodges had a small packet in his hand and was already ripping it open. He held up one huge pill.

"Eight hundred," he said, indicating eight hundred milligrams. He handed Logan the rest of the packet. "Take another in an hour if it doesn't get better."

"That's . . . a lot," said Logan.

"You can take twenty-four hundred in twenty-four hours. If sixteen hundred doesn't help, we'll move on to something stronger."

Logan nodded and took the pill with a slug of water from his bite valve.

He turned up the headset volume on the bodypack to find Decker was in deep shit.

"—drag marks? Anything?" Decker was asking.

"Negative, Six," said a voice.

"Jesus Christ," said Decker. "Who saw him last?"

"He was on my left. I was scanning right, over," someone else said.

"How long has he been gone?" asked Decker.

"Three—four mikes," the same voice said.

He's been gone four minutes?

"Gone?" Decker repeated. "They're both fuckin' gone?"

We're missing two, now? Uh-oh. "Who's gone?" Logan asked Hodges, who shrugged.

Decker was yammering into the radio.

"We've got our guys," Hodges told Logan. "Let Alpha sort it out unless they—"

"—Break break break—"

The Mark 48 opened up again.

Longer, this time.

"What do you see, Martin?" asked Decker as the echoes faded.

"Movement-three-o'clock-they're-behind-cover-now," Martin answered. "I-got-stoppages-feels-like-bad-ammo."

Logan keyed his mic. "Everybody hold your fire."

"Belay that order," said Decker, "Doc, stay off this line unless addressed. You're not in charge."

"They've got us on two sides," Logan replied. "We're pinned. They have freedom of movement. Let the major and me go out and talk to them."

"Doc, shut your hole. That's an order."

"Oh, fuck you," said Logan, not keying his mic.

A flash of motion out of his right eye, among the rocks, where he'd figured Alpha Team was hiding. It was hard to tell with the camouflage, but someone was . . . he had to pull his eye off his optic to be sure.

Standing up.

"Oh, what the f—" Logan groaned.

"COME GET US, YOU FUCKERS!!" the soldier yelled. He was a good fifty yards ahead and the waves of heat off the floor and the opalescent dust obscured fine details. A belt-fed weapon came up, leveled at the hip, and the furious chatter of 5.56 in short bursts thundered through the valley. "GET SOME!" the soldier yelled, and moved up, out in the open.

"FIGHT ME, BITCH!"

Shouts over the earpiece, and another soldier stood up, running to him, weapon raised and whooping.

The SEALs.

Logan quietly prayed Major Easton would shoot them both.

The guy with the belt-fed pitched forwards, his buddy straining to catch him, and the monsters appeared. Towering, behemoth, ungodly, they rose out of nothing with leviathan hand weapons—Swords? Clubs?—and engaged, so close that nobody dared fire. In a flurry of atrocity both men were down, and the creatures vanished again as quickly as they'd appeared.

"Holy fuck," said someone over the headset.

Logan felt for his quick-releases, dropped his pack, and sprinted for the fallen SEALs.

The monsters were nowhere in sight, against all physics and logic. Maybe they had some kind of camouflage. Maybe they were made of the sand.

Maybe they *were* the sand.

He ran on.

He made twenty yards, ducked behind a slab of volcanic slag the size of a bus, and caught his breath.

It was hot. His chest screamed at him.

He eked his right eye around the right edge of the rock, looking for the bodies, working out a plan.

There were no bodies.

He checked behind him, triangulating. He was where he was supposed to be. There was a three-story skull-shaped rock on his right with a small arch on its top; the SEALs had gone down about ten yards this side of it.

But they weren't there.

He rested against the stone, raising his rifle to his shoulder to use the optic, framing their last position, scanning for drag marks.

The optic was dead, the reticle gray against the red-gold of the sand.

"Oh, come on." He flipped it on and off.

Nothing.

His headset was quiet. He turned the volume dial and keyed the

SEND button. "Break, break. Logan."

No bleep. No static. No voices.

"Oh, fuck me . . ."

He scanned the rocks behind him again. Nothing. No motion, no shooting.

The team had peeled, God knows in what direction, and he hadn't heard the order. Because for whatever reason, all his electronics were out. The team would now be scurrying rock to rock, staying low, invisible in their camo. He wouldn't see them any more than the monsters would see them.

Any more than he could see the monsters.

We can't get the drone down in the canyon. We lose the signal.

He sank against the boulder.

Not only had the team fallen back, but people this far forward were vanishing at an alarming pace. They'd lost two, and God knows how, even before the SEALs got killed, and now the SEAL bodies had vanished as well.

When he didn't show up at the rally point, they'd surely figure he was one of the vanished.

One of the dead.

They weren't coming back for him.

He was alone on an alien planet.

The team, down to eight from its original thirteen, gathered in a horseshoe five hundred yards back, along the sunny side of the canyon.

"We're aborting," said Decker. "We're aborting and getting the fuck out of here."

"We leave no one behind," Major Easton said.

"Bullshit," said Decker. "There's no bodies, Abby. We saw

Collier and Delacroix go down. Where'd the bodies go? What about Park and Tommy? They're gone, too."

"Exactly," she said. "We don't know if Park and Tommy were killed or captured. They could be in enemy hands. Hell, they could be back there alive, with scrambled comms, wondering where we are. And what the fuck happened to the Professor?"

"Who cares?" Decker asked. "He's not even one of us."

"Oh, fuck this," said Abby, dropping her pack. "Gunny, let's go. We're traveling light."

"Moving, ma'am," Foster offered, wriggling out of his gear.

"As you were," said Decker. "I won't allow it."

"It's not for you to allow," she said. "This is my team. We can get the professor, and any survivors, and get back here. We might even catch you. Team Two, fall in under Commander Decker."

Decker's mouth formed a tight line as he breathed out through his nose. "Fine, but take Fields."

"Absolutely not."

"You two are not going anywhere unsupervised," Decker insisted, pointing at them and then at the ground emphatically.

"Oh, Jesus Christ, Buck!" Abby bellowed. "What is your problem with me?" She strodeover until she was directly in front of him, half a head shorter, but broad-chested and challenging. "Say it! Go on!"

Decker put his hands on his hips and scanned the faces of the team. "You're fuckin' your spotter!" he blurted. "There, I said it! You're fuckin' him"—he pointed to Foster—"and I'm gonna end your career! Bitch!"

Abby's eyebrows went up. She blinked several times. Her mouth moved, but no words came out.

Foster broke the silence. "I'm gay."

"What?" Decker snapped.

"I said, I'm gay." He spat in Decker's direction in punctuation. "You sheep-diddling hick."

The desert was very quiet.

"Okay, I did not see that comin'," Braxton admitted.

Someone snorted, and the team burst out in hoots of laughter. Martin moved in front of Foster and turned to face Decker. He didn't have to say anything.

The others joined him, forming a literal wall between Foster and Decker.

Abby turned back to Decker. "You are so screwed."

"Yeah, well, you're off this fuckin' team," said Decker. "Both of you."

She looked back at the team eclipsing Foster. It was the tension-breaker they'd needed.

"We'll discuss who's off what when we get back," she said.

"I'll have your rank," Decker promised.

"Oh, you will," Abby assured him as he walked away alone. She called after him, "You'll be wearing it!"

She shucked her Ghillie and unstrapped the shorty HK along with a breakaway ruck, half the size of her big pack, which she slung and cinched tight. "Martin," she called. "Hodges, you too."

The big soldier jogged over to her and Hodges followed. Hodges was nearly as tall as Martin, but reedy and smooth in all his motions in a way that reminded Major Easton of a ballet dancer. "Ma'am?" Martin asked.

"Make sure Luke gets back," she said, referring to Foster by his first name. "Go to Paulsen, give sworn statements on everything that happened back there, all the way till now. Stay with Luke. Don't let any of Decker's boys, those goddamned SEALs, near him. Twenty-four seven, Luke has company until I get back with the professor. That's an order. When I get back, we'll straighten this out."

"Wouldn't he be safer with you, ma'am?" Martin asked.

"No. If I take him with me, Decker will leave us both over here."

"He wouldn't dare," said Hodges.

"Oh, he would," she said. "Take my gear back. Foster takes the rifle. You have extra water?"

"A couple liters," said Martin.

"I got some," said Hodges. "A big thing of Gatorade, too."

"Gimme all you can spare. Put 'em in my bag. Hodges, I need your 5.56 mags, and your break-and-shake ice packs. Hurry."

"It'll be dark soon," Hodges warned.

"Yes," she agreed. "So, take that hill. Get home."

She vanished before Foster even realized she was gone. It was the sniper's gift; she just melted away.

Luke scrambled up a rock and scanned left and right. There was no sign of her.

"Come here, asshole," said Martin, gesturing to Foster with both arms. "Bring it in." The horseshoe collapsed on Foster, throwing their arms around him.

Martin held Foster's helmet in both his hands like a proud uncle. "Nobody's gonna fuck with you, don't worry," he promised. "They gotta get through me. You're my boy."

V

DESCENT

Before Sir Richard Owen coined the term Dinosauria, dinosaur skeletons were thought to be the remains of dragons.

— Owen's Report on British Fossil Reptiles, *1842*

Phase Line HETFIELD plus 500m

L ogan picked up his pack from behind the rock. He made a quick sweep of the area with his rifle in one hand, still pissed at the dead electronics. He set the weapon down while he donned the towering ruck.

"Fuck fuck fuck fuck fuck," he told no one.

The moon was still up; it had barely moved, which he thought was interesting. The sun, however, would definitely set in the next few hours. His watch had stopped, which was also interesting. It was an automatic Suunto, no battery. There was no reason he could figure for it to have stopped.

He checked his headset again. Still nothing. For giggles, he clicked the flashlight on the underside of his rifle.

Dead.

"Fuck."

He leaned against the rock. It was a desert commando's natural position; you exerted as little energy as you could manage and exposed as little of yourself to the sun as necessary. He was at his best in the shade, drinking water and relaxing.

Only those who didn't hope to get out of a desert alive wouldn't keep a running inventory, and he knew his. He had a day's worth of water, seven liters; maybe a day and a half if he stretched it and didn't do anything stupid, like . . . fight.

He had food for what Americans considered three days: nine of the American MREs—"Meals, Ready to Eat," which soldiers joked constituted three lies for the price of one—plus a handful of energy bars. It was easily a week's worth; far more than he would be able to consume before he died of thirst.

But he had a plan for that.

The arch atop the high skull-shaped rock, thirty feet tall and jutting from the desert floor like the stripped bones of a horned giant, offered the best shelter. The top had a couple of wind-sculpted shallow caves, and the arch appeared to have an overhang offering top cover. It was smooth and rounded and getting up it would be a bitch, but he'd deal with it in due time. It was about a hundred yards off to what he was now calling west.

Scampering from rock to rock, he thought of the old cartoons in which Wile E. Coyote sneaks across a scene, disappearing behind a tiny tree against all physics, his tail jutting from one side while his nose appears behind another some distance away. It was what he tried to emulate.

Scan. Run. Freeze. Scan.

Repeat.

At the area where the SEALs had gone down, he knelt, swept the area with his rifle, and inspected the sand, reading its stories.

He could clearly see the footprints of the first SEAL, the fine dust kicked up, the harder dirt cratered under the edges of boots running under load. Brass glinted under polarized lenses, a breadcrumb trail back to the rock the kid had run out from.

The footprints led directly into impressions of a struggle. Blood had congealed in the dirt, black and thick, a lot of it, an arterial hit. Impressions of gear in the shiny dust where a body fell hard. No twitches, no thrashing. No struggle.

Nothing further.

And no drag marks. He put his eye next to the ground, looking for impressions.

Vanished.

His buddy's footsteps ended, too, not much further back. Blood, impact, no scuffle. Also no drag marks. He was simply gone, as if he'd been taken up by angels. Or a UFO.

The creatures left no tracks.

Jesus.

At the base of the skull-rock, he broke out his entrenching tool and attacked the hardpan. This time, it gave way to soft sand six inches down.

He cut an index-card-sized hole in the thick rubber wrapper of an MRE, wiggling the food packets out. He put it all into his bellows pockets except for a packet of Skittles, which he nibbled one at a time as he worked.

It had been an unusual request, but their S-4, the supply and logistics component, had come through: a four-foot square piece of clear polyethylene, not much more than heavy-duty plastic wrap. He unfolded it and placed it across the top of the hole with rocks pinning each side and a fist-sized rock in the center, an inverted cone. As the air cooled overnight, the humidity would condense on the underside of the plastic, trickle down the liner to collect at the lowest point, and drip into the MRE bag.

As an afterthought, he raised one corner, knelt, and urinated into the hole. He'd need to recover as much fluid as he could manage. It would taste awful, but he'd drunk worse during *Aguerrissement Zone Desertique,* Desert Hardening, in Commando School. Forty sweating, filthy Legionnaires choking down hot piss-flavored water in front of the instructors in their impeccably pressed uniforms, to get a checkmark in the Go column and move on to the fun stuff: finding and defusing mines.

He wouldn't have to worry about mines this time.

Probably.

The skull-rock was an easy climb, on the shady side at least. The side facing the dropping sun was too hot to touch for long, even through his gloves. The side casting shadows was manageable; the carbon-fiber blade at his foot dug hard into the textured stone and he was up it in short order, even with his pack and rifle.

From the top, beneath the small arch, he had a gorgeous view. The canyon, the moon, and the Citadel, with mountains far in the distance.

He tossed a rock through the small arch. Just to make sure.

Nothing happened.

He shucked his pack beneath the overhang, which was nearly tall enough to stand under, dug out a liter-and-a-half bottle of water, an electrolyte packet from the MRE, and a small, plastic-coated foil bag of chocolate-filled pretzel pieces made in—he held the fine print out at arm's length—Grand Prairie, Texas.

America, goddammit.

He leaned against his pack in the shade. He still had a shitload of ammo. What a country.

There was still the question of what lived in the dens and warrens on the west side of the canyon, and what their range for foraging was. Did they fly? Could they climb?

He had a hundred and eighty rounds.

But no flashlight.

And there were still two squads of invisible nine-foot monsters out there somewhere, leaving no tracks.

Abby moved as fast as she could, sprinting from cover to cover, slamming water from a bottle whenever she found shade. The sun was going down behind the canyon, and it would be dark in—well, she didn't know; there was no way to know how long the days were here—but night was coming, and she didn't want to be out here if she could avoid it. She kept Logan's warning about nocturnal creatures dwelling on the right side of the canyon in the back of her head and pulled it out to move faster when she started to flag.

She keyed her radio again. "Logan, come in, over."

Silence.

If Logan was alive and moving back for the mesa and the Arch, she might have gone right past him. She keyed the radio again.

Assuming, of course, his radio worked. If it didn't, it would explain why he missed the fallback order.

Hadn't there been something about the drones losing telemetry down in the rocks?

They'd had radio contact, and then, at a certain point, radios had cut out. Right about the point where Park had vanished, which wasn't far from the last point anyone had seen Logan.

Maybe there was something in the rocks that scrambled comms, or drained batteries, or killed electronics.

Compasses don't work down here.

She reached into her belt pouch and broke hers out, flipped the cap open, and watched the dial.

North.

Logan and Luke had argued over north versus south. She was heading arguably south, now—what they'd called south, anyway, the sun would be setting on the right shortly—although the needle showed north. She turned the compass around, and the needle spun back toward the area where they'd had the encounter.

Definitely a magnetic anomaly in that direction.

Enough to break a radio?

She aimed herself in the direction of the needle, took another slug of water, and charged for the next cover.

A three-story haystack outcropping jutted from the canyon floor fifty meters ahead on her right. It would afford the best view of the valley.

She moved for it, skirted the base, slung the HK, and grabbed a protrusion on the side where it leaned slightly away. With a heave and a scramble, she was five feet up.

The next part was tricky, a mild overhang but plenty to grab. For one sketchy moment her feet swung out over the desert, but she pulled hard and muscled up, caught a toe on a bump, and from there it was pretty much a ladder with easy handholds.

Getting down would be a bitch in the dark, but she'd be able to surveil the area right now and if she had to spend the night, there wasn't a better place. Maybe from here, she could even find out where the bodies of the SEALs went, or even see the professor out there somewhere. She stood on the top of the rock and scanned the canyon floor.

"Major," Logan said, emerging from the overhang. She started so hard she nearly fell off.

"Thank God," she breathed, and hugged him as he approached, which surprised her as much as it seemed to surprise him. "You okay?"

"I'm fine," he assured her and clapped her on the back. Her muscles were like slabs of stone. "Is anyone else coming?" he asked. "Is Foster down there?"

She let go and stepped back, straightening her gear, realizing she'd overstepped decorum. There was something ridiculously attractive about him, but she couldn't identify it. Certainly, his easy competence, but competent men were a dime a dozen in Special Operations. "What? No," she said. "Just me. What happened to you?"

"My radio died. Actually, everything did. My optic, my flashlight. Everything. Something down there wiped my batteries."

"Did it wipe the spares in your buttstock?"

He glanced over at his gear. "There are spares in the buttstock?"

She covered her face with her hands and growled profanities. Competence had its limits. "You didn't try to get back to the Arch?" she asked after a pause.

"It will be dark soon. I wasn't going to get lost down there. Figured I'd wait till morning."

"Okay," she admitted. "This"—she gestured around them—"is the smart play."

"Thanks. Please tell me you didn't step on my still."

She looked at him quizzically. "Your still?" She had an image of him making whisky, cobbling together some Gilligan's Island contraption to pull alcohol out of the sand. It was absurd.

"Solar still," he said. "Rocks, plastic. Makes water. You didn't disturb it, did you?"

"I didn't see it," she said. "I hope not."

"You'd know it if you saw it. I was hoping I could get some water out of this sand and head out early before it gets too hot to move. In the meantime, I figured, maybe you'd come back for me. If you did, this is where you'd go to get a look over the terrain." He gestured around them. "Right?"

"Smart," she admitted. And that was it. He wasn't just smart; he was *smart*. Smarter than she was. He was operating on a whole other level, a standard deviation above the end of the bell curve where she and her teammates lived.

"Let me show you something," he said. "You have the same scope on that thing that I do, yes?"

"Probably."

"Check this out." He led her across the top of the small outcropping.

He'd set up a camp under a shelf: a thin bivy sack, his pack to lean against, a couple of opened packets from an MRE refolded neatly, and a leather-bound copy of—she had to look twice—*The*

Cosmology of Epicurus, with a bookmark. His rifle leaned against the side of the overhang with a black boot sock pulled over the barrel, the dust covers tight on the scope. Beside it, a pair of binoculars stood in a wind-blasted depression in the rock.

"Quite the bachelor pad," she said, impressed.

"Best spot I could find," he admitted. "The view's pretty nice. In fact,"—he handed her the binoculars—"check that second peak, about a hundred meters up. Eleven o'clock."

She did a slow arc through the sector. "What am I looking for?"

"You'll know it when you see it."

Rocks, more rocks, even more rocks. Long shadows, getting longer. "I don't . . . Oh, my God," she breathed, and spun the magnification ring. "The Citadel. It's right there."

"About fifteen hundred meters, I figure."

"Wow," she said. "We were so close."

"We are so close," he corrected. "How much water do you have?"

"I don't know. Three liters, plus some Gatorade."

"You're not going to make it back to the Arch on three liters. What were you going to do if you didn't find me?"

"That wasn't an option."

"You sure you're in the right Army?" he commended. "Anyway, I've got six liters. I might get a half a liter tomorrow morning from the still. That's almost ten for the two of us."

"That'll get us back."

"If nothing goes wrong. But hear me out."

"Oh, God," she groaned. "No. We're not heading for the Citadel."

"How'd you know what I was—"

"Because of course it's what you're gonna do! Because you're insane. Absolutely not. Limit Of Advance. *Limit*," she repeated. "*Of. Advance.* Besides, nobody fucks with Lemmy."

"True. But it's a lot closer than the Arch."

She sighed.

"We head for The Citadel in the morning," he insisted. "Look, we show up on their front door. We make first contact. Hats in hands."

"After we fired on them," she offered.

"We don't know that the patrols we fought were even theirs. The video feed I saw back at the base showed a human-sized being, in Norse armor, on the back of a horse-sized creature, with The Citadel in the background. Those creatures we attacked were much larger. How do we know they're not, I don't know, at war with the owners of The Citadel? Maybe we did them a favor."

"My mission is to get you back."

"You called an audible on that one. How is this different?"

"Are you kidding me right now?"

"Look at it this way. If they're at war with those other . . . beings, maybe they know where they would have taken Park and Tommy. And if they're on the same side, maybe Park and Tommy are there. They'll see us, they'll know we've come for our people."

"Oh, I hate this."

"We're so close. Look at it! We're right here! They could be in there. And they have to have water."

Profanities spread under her breath like torrents of scales from a gifted cellist. "We don't speak their language. We don't even know if they're human. What are we going to say? How are we going to say it?"

"We're not going to learn their language until long after someone goes up to them and shakes hands. Do you think that person should be Decker? Stannard?"

She groaned and leaned her rifle next to his, flipped her scope covers and ejection port cover closed, and shrugged out of her pack. "We should be going up there with a battalion stationed in this valley. The two of us? Just walking in there? This is your plan?"

"The two of us are far less threatening," Logan admitted. "We could definitely make the argument that we come in peace if we don't have an army behind us. Besides, you're the Cultural Support Officer. I'm the incoming S-9. Who's it going to be, if not us?"

She stared out into the desert. "Let me think about it overnight."

"We're staying?" he asked.

"It's getting dark and we're better off up here. You have an E-tool in your ruck?"

"A what?"

"Entrenching tool," she clarified. "Shovel."

"I do." He unzipped a pouch on the side of his pack and pulled it out, still folded. "What's up?"

She took it from him. "That far side is downwind. It's now the latrine."

The sunset was spectacular. The ringed moon fringed a froth of clouds to the west with heliotrope and violet, rendering it unbelievably detailed, exploding in orange and rust from beneath as the sun slipped under the mountains in the distance. The temperature in the canyon dropped twenty degrees in a matter of minutes. Logan actually shivered.

It was amazing how fast you acclimated.

"Why do you think the sun's going down, but the moon isn't?" Abby asked. She'd shucked her Ghillie and her load-bearing gear and sat against the overhang in her sweat-soaked Frogskin top and a set of clear ballistic eyeglasses, watching the ring growing against the darkening sky and digging at an MRE pouch of enchiladas with a brown plastic fork.

"I have no idea," Logan said. "The moon's definitely moving, but slowly. You can see the rings are tilting more. Valentine would probably know. He's the smart one."

"Yeah," she said. "Who is that guy? 'Knife Guy.'"

"Ancient weapons guy. Bob Valentine. Bobby Fett Maverick Valentine."

"'Bobby Fett?' You're kidding me."

Logan shook his head. "I wish I was."

"'Knife Guy,'" she said again, announcing it like a superhero's name and miming throwing a knife at the horizon. She slumped. "He'd love this. It's a shame, though. He wouldn't last ten minutes out here."

"People can surprise you. You never know what someone's capable of. I would have bet my car he couldn't throw a knife like that."

"Well, I wouldn't have expected some egghead professor to be a former Foreign Legion badass, either. Sneaking up on me, no less."

"Like I said," Logan said, shaking a few more pretzel pieces into his mouth, "people can surprise you."

"You're hanging in with the big kids pretty well, old man," she teased. "Paulsen says you've worked with SF before."

"This is not my first rodeo," he agreed. "Actually, I've found that Legionnaire commandos and American Special Forces get on very well."

"Why's that, you think?"

He ripped the package open along its length to get the last one out, a recalcitrant little bastard tucked in the deepest corner. "Peer review."

"Say that again?"

"In our commando schools," he said, popping it into his mouth, triumphant, "we're subject to a series of peer reviews. The instructors would flunk Legionnaires out if others in the platoon didn't like them. All the assholes, the me-firsters, the idiots who did stupid crap that might get everyone killed, they didn't make it."

"SF does that, too."

"Yes. That's why Legion Commandos and Green Berets get on so well. You become a Commando only if everyone you worked with on the course wants you to be one. You can ace every test, every exercise, but if you're not the kind of soldier other soldiers think they can count on, you can get all the way to graduation, forty days in the desert, and be standing in formation and not get your brevet. They'll walk right by you. And they do; a lot of Legionnaires are miserable assholes."

"A lot of American soldiers are miserable assholes," she added. "Which is why SFAS—Special Forces Assessment and Selection— does the same thing. It's possible to pass Assessment with top marks and still not get selected. To make it into Special Forces, you have to be someone people want to work with."

"Right," said Logan. "As opposed to goddamn SEALs. All you have to do to become a SEAL is be tough. That's it."

"That's plenty," she said.

"It's not enough. SEAL candidates' peer reviews are for 'personal and professional growth,'" he insisted, making air quotes with his fingers. "Unless you're a complete dirtbag, your evals can't wash you out."

"The instructors use it as ammo against you," she argued. "Those evals make it harder. They find out where your weak points are, and they pile it on."

"That's not remotely the same thing. In the end, to become a SEAL, you don't have to be mature, and you don't even have to be likable."

"I get your point, I think. As long as you're still standing, you win."

"Exactly. This is why, with SEALs, everything comes down to a dick-measuring contest. 'I've been through the toughest training in the world.' Well, hey, great," he said, taking a swig from his water bottle, "you're tough. Good for you. Lots of people are tough. My grandma's tough. Most SEALs consider themselves exceptional men for reasons that are largely unremarkable.

"What makes an operator is maturity and mindfulness. I've met mature, likable SEALs, but that's not what got them onto the Teams. If you're a SEAL, then as far as I'm concerned, you've never been measured on maturity. Those two asshandles wanted to show everyone on the team how tough they were. That's why they're dead, and that's why we're stuck on this goddamn rock instead of enjoying a beer and a bacon cheeseburger at some roadside joint down the hill from FOB WINTERSTONE right now."

"Wow, that sounds good."

"Doesn't it, though?"

They watched the moon for a bit before he spoke again. "I keep a cold, dark place in my heart for zealots. That includes evangelicals, training officers, and fuckin' SEALs. Once you start believing you shit sandalwood, you're useless to anyone who matters."

"Well, this isn't going to make you happy," she said, pulling herself cross-legged. "Decker has it in for me, big time. And for Foster, too."

"Oh, Christ," Logan griped. "What's his problem with Foster?"

"Foster's gay."

"Seems like a good kid. Hope he finds a nice fella."

She stared at him.

"Ooh, wow," he said a moment later, on reflection. "I bet Decker hates that. Does he know?"

"He does, now. I've known for some time, but Foster just came out to the whole team. Like, right before I headed out. A few hours ago."

Logan nodded, watching the horizon. "How'd they take it?"

"Really well," she admitted. "They're a good team. The kid's had a tough run. His last sniper, in the Marines? They were in a relationship. He was killed about a year ago, hit by a drunk driver in London on R&R. So stupid."

"Dear God."

"It really tore him up. They sent Foster home from Afghanistan. I was just coming out of the sniper course and needed a spotter. Paulsen found him at Quantico, drifting, working on ballistics and powder loads, and took him in. He needed a place, you know?"

"I do," Logan admitted. "I do know."

"Well, Decker's apparently had it in his head this whole time that Foster and I were . . . well, yeah."

Logan cleared his throat. "Gettin' some stank on the old hangdown?"

She choked, spat into the crook of her elbow, and coughed several times. "Don't make me waste water. Asshole."

"Apologies."

"Jerk."

"That fuckin' guy," Logan said, referring to Decker. "Ol' Dick Swackhammer."

"That's a better name," she agreed. "I like 'Swackhammer.' Anyway, he called us out in front of the whole team. Accused me of sleeping with Foster."

"In front of the team?" Logan clarified.

"Yeah."

"Like, just now?"

"Right before I left."

"Jesus, what an asshole."

"Believe it. And then Foster came out."

"In front of the team," he repeated.

"He saved my career. Probably ended his, though."

Logan whistled quietly. "Solid brass on that kid."

"I'm scared for him. For his safety. He's gay, and he made Decker look stupid."

"That second part's not hard. But you're right, the SEALs are gonna have a field day with him. The team's watching him?"

She stood and went over to her bivouac site. "You bet. Martin's got his back."

"No one better, I'd guess," Logan assessed. "You know, you've probably got a pretty good case against Swackhammer at this point, I'd think."

"We're calling him Swackhammer from now on," she decided from under the archway, where she was digging through her load-bearing gear. "And yes, I do have a case against him. The team will be giving sworn statements to Paulsen when they get back."

"Great. Whatever they need from me, they've got it."

She ducked around the rocks to meet up with him again. "I *need* you to have a word with Swackhammer."

"Two words," Logan promised.

She handed him a couple of small, cold, round objects and closed his hand around them, the motion dominating, the touch surprisingly intimate, her gaze lingering. His first thought, feeling them in his fist, was coins. "What's this?" he asked.

"Batteries for your optics and your tac light," she said. "Be careful with me."

"What?"

She closed her eyes and blew out a laugh that turned into a long sigh. "Wow, I'm tired. Be careful with *these*," she reiterated.

"Get some sleep, Major."

Logan was exhausted, but the fresh battery for his scope made the view interesting. Night vision technology had come a long way, and this little jobbie was crystal clear. There was a lot to keep his attention.

It was fairly light out; he'd been right about the moon and the ring. There was enough illumination to read by once his eyes adjusted. The scope worked by light amplification and yielded outstanding resolution when coupled with the magnifier.

The night smelled of damp sand and ancient desert, a faint metallic tinge.

Major Easton snored softly.

He doodled in a blank notebook, plotting out a possible course to the Citadel, copying down the landmarks as best he could. A wide path, possibly a road, led to the Citadel in a straight shot up the canyon, easily discernible. There was one glitch in the plan: high walls bracketed the path on each side, likely the sides of a long-collapsed lava tube. It was the mother of all fatal funnels.

He swung the rifle over to the canyon wall to the west, sighting in along the cave entrances, and his heart jumped at wriggles of motion. Many wriggles of motion.

Snakelike and massive, the creatures slithered down the canyon wall by the thousands. Ten feet long, twenty feet long, perhaps longer. He thought of bats leaving a cave, but they weren't flying, nor were they dropping to the hardpan below. They were climbing down the rock face.

Climbing down meant they could climb up.

He woke her with a toe to the sole of her boot. Not a kick; a nudge. She leaped awake, coming to a three-point stance like a superhero landing from a building.

"Whatever lives in those caves over there?" he said. "They're coming. Fast."

She picked up her rifle and flipped the scope covers open. "How many?"

"I don't know. Thousands, it looks like. They're maybe a mile away."

She scanned the wall, the openings, and the floor at the base of the cliff. He put his rifle up and did the same.

They were still cascading out of the dens. The valley floor at the cliff base rippled with them.

"What are those?" she wondered.

"No idea," he said. "They didn't fall off the wall, though. They're climbing. They can climb."

"Shit," she said, lowering the rifle. "Shit shit shit shit shit."

"The positive part of this is that I didn't see anything else moving out there. It's not like there are, I don't know, herds of elk passing through or anything for them to feed on. At least, I haven't seen anything. Maybe they're not carnivorous. There wouldn't be enough for them to eat if they were; not enough to sustain that many of them."

"Maybe something else comes out later that we haven't seen. Maybe they eat those."

"Wow, that sucks," he said.

"I'm here to hand out the hard truths."

"And I appreciate it. How much ammo do you have?"

"I don't know. Ten, maybe twelve mags. You?"

"Six mags. Forty-five rounds for the pistol."

"So, we've got about six hundred rounds. That will make some holes."

"There's way more than six hundred of them."

"They're not all coming this way, are they?"

"Well," he said, raising the weapon to his eye again, "not all of them." Most had turned south, hugging the canyon wall, either on it or along its base.

She braced her carbine on the overhang and maxed out the magnification. "Weird. They're sticking to the rocks. Like, sticking on them. They hit the rocks and latch on, quit moving. Am I seeing this right?"

A few moments passed as they watched.

"It's possible these rocks aren't wind-blown," he admitted. "Maybe there's some, I dunno, mineral or something that they scrape off? This weird shiny dust? Who the hell knows. Although if they can scrape off rock, I sure as hell don't want one latching onto me."

"Okay, I'm never sleeping again," she announced.

"That's a terrible idea. We have no idea how long the night is.

Get some rest. If anything else happens, I'll wake you."

"You'd better."

She was out cold again in moments; it was a soldier's talent.

The creatures each seemed to find a rock, settle in, and stay still. They didn't appear to pose a threat, but there was no way to know what one would do when faced with a human being, or anything that would get in the way of what appeared to be its meal. It was enough to keep him intensely awake, even in the heat and the sweat.

He wished they'd move more. He found it infuriating being bored by something that had the potential to kill him.

His mechanical watch had come back to life after leaving the Dead Zone that had wiped all his batteries. After three hours, he felt his eyes prickling over, and he woke Major Easton.

He was out and snoring before she'd even set herself up.

VI

TRIGGER POINT

"My little friend I lull to rest
But outside, a face looms at the window."

—Icelandic lullaby (traditional)

Forward Operating Base WINTERSTONE
Mt. Jupiter, Washington State

Coffee steamed untouched in Commander Decker's SEAL-trident mug on Paulsen's desk. It was late in the afternoon, and Paulsen adjusted his frameless reading glasses. The rain smashed at the roof of his office.

"No bodies, nothing," said Decker. "The major went back for that idiot professor and went radio silent about an hour into it. We waited as long as we dared after that. That hike up the back side of the mesa was a real bitch. It's steeper than it looks. We had to side-hill it and switch back a dozen times."

Paulsen put his head in his hands, elbows on his desk. The debriefing report was, frankly, unbelievable. Invisible monsters. Scrambled comms. Bad ammo. Disappearing personnel.

Every Team Chief's nightmare consisted of going into a

situation blind and learning he was completely and disastrously unprepared, and Buck had stepped in it. And good.

"You should've seen these things, Steve. They were something out of a movie. Fuckin' aliens. They were invisible until they were right on top of us."

"Well, hell," said Paulsen. "I wonder if we can see them on thermal."

"Fuck yeah, let's go find out," said Decker.

"Your team's not going anywhere," Paulsen agreed. "We're standing down Team Two. You all take thirty days, decompress, get counseling—"

"Counseling." Decker snorted. "Christ, you're such a pussy. Fuckin' counseling."

"This is not a suggestion, Buck. Every surviving member will check in at Behavioral Health by close of business tomorrow. That's my standard, and you know it. Death on the team? Stand down thirty days. You've had six deaths. You should be standing down for a year."

"My boys are above your standards."

"Your boys didn't come back," said Paulsen. "Mine did. And they're going to counseling, all of them. La-dee-dah-dee everybody."

Decker swore under his breath. "I'm not getting weepy over this, Steve. Sure as hell not over her. Much less am I gonna shed a tear for that sorry-ass French faggot you sent into harm's way. Neither one of them had any business going in there, and I fuckin' told you that. Your hotshot commando turned out to be a little bitch, by the way. He was whining the entire time: 'We're moving too fast.' 'It's too hot.' Couldn't keep up. This is on you."

"Collier and Delacroix were your troops."

"They were ambushed," said Decker. "War happens. When we go back in there, we're rolling heavy. I want a company-sized element. I want arty set up in the end of the valley. I want drones with Hellfires. We are gonna fuckin' own that place, no matter what it takes."

"Well, we'll see when we get there. We're standing down for a while. And you're sure, there was no sign of any . . ." Paulsen gestured for continuation, eliciting a response around an unspoken issue.

"We didn't get that far," he said. "We were about two klicks from the Citadel. If they have an operation to produce the stuff, it's got to be inside. There are some caves along the east side of the canyon, we don't know what's in there. The Professor thought there might be some kind of critters living in there, but I dunno. It sure looks like a mining operation to me. I think he—" He shut his mouth tightly. "—no."

"Go on."

"I . . . fuck. Okay, off the record?"

"Sure."

"I think it was just him being Native. I think he knew there was something in there, and he didn't want us looking. I think he was bullshitting us."

"You think it's in there?"

"We were getting some weird compass readings. Does red mercury—"

Paulsen cut him off with a glare.

"Does *it* screw with compass readings?"

Paulsen shrugged. "No one has ever officially gotten their hands on it in the wild. It's not like the NRC is going to hand us a vial of it to play with. It's radioactive, it's explosive, and it's a million dollars a gram. That's all I know. No idea if it's magnetic, but mercury's a metal. So . . ." He shrugged. "Maybe?"

"Can we get any, like, papers on this stuff?" Decker asked. "I hate not knowing what we're dealing with."

"All I've got is what you've seen. These are classified Special Nuclear Materials. All they've told us is that you can't put more than five kilos of the stuff together or it'll wipe out Seattle. We'll find it, we'll bring it back a few drops at a time, and we'll let them deal with it."

"And we get promoted."

"Goddamn right."

"Take the night off, Buck. Grab a beer at Cooper's. Raise a glass to your boys. I'm going home."

Decker stood and pushed his chair in. "Thanks, Steve."

Paulsen's email refreshed, and refreshed again. "No worries."

It refreshed again.

And yet again.

Decker closed the door behind him as Paulsen scrolled an incoming raft of emailed sworn statements from Team Two surviving members and realized there was no way in hell he was going home.

Martin, Foster, Braxton, and Hodges sat at a booth in a corner of Cooper's Tavern, a waterside joint in Brinnon down the mountain from FOB WINTERSTONE. They'd cleaned up and changed into comfortable civvies, and now the team sprawled, listless, stunned into quiet. Braxton toyed with a plate of fried food. Luke slowly turned his beer around on a coaster.

They could have been any bunch of college students after a tough exam, or perhaps any group of Ultimate Frisbee players who'd lost the afternoon's match.

Fields, the intel sergeant for the team, wasn't with them. A hardcore introvert, he was doing his own thing, and that was fine.

"That was some bullshit," Martin said for the fortieth time.

"The fuck were we supposed to do," said Luke.

"This is so wrong," Hodges admitted. "I was just getting to like that professor dude, too."

"Man, that guy was up Stannard's ass," Braxton chuckled, shaking his head. "No goddamn fear."

"Good instincts," Martin muttered.

"He woulda been great to work for," said Braxton. "I was looking forward to that."

"Foreign Legion Warrant," said Martin. "Bad motherfucker."

"Couldn't run for shit, though."

"He had one leg, asshole. And he was two hundred years old."

"Raise a glass, yeah?" said Martin, hoisting his bottle of beer.

"To the professor," agreed Braxton, raising a rocks glass with something clear and three ice cubes in it. "Wish we'd known you better, sir."

"*Au revoir.*"

Glasses clinked.

"The fuck am I gonna do about Abby," said Luke. "Two shooters, now. I've lost two shooters. God," he told his drink, "I loved her."

Hodges cleared his throat. "I thought you were—"

"Not like that," Luke snapped. "I dunno. She was decent. She was hard, but God damn, she was a good person. Just, good, you know? All she wanted was to be the best at whatever she did. That was it. That was her life. Who does that? I'm so pissed, you guys. I could kill that asshole."

"Get in line," said Braxton.

"She might make it," said Martin. "She's gonna walk through that door any minute and order a shot."

The door swung open as if on cue, and in strode a line of Navy SEALs, ARCHSTONE Detachment One, nine of them with Stannard at the head—tattoos, beards, muscles, and cargo pants interchangeable to a man.

"Aw, fuck me," said Martin.

"Doesn't he have war crimes to commit somewhere?" Braxton grouched.

"Hey, girls!" shouted one of the SEALs. Stannard led several over to the table while a few stayed at the bar to order drinks.

Stannard grabbed a chair from a nearby table, swung it around backwards, and sat on it. "You motherfuckers wanna tell me what happened?"

"It's in my report," said Martin, sipping his beer. "You can read it."

"I'd like to hear it from you," said Stannard.

"We're not in a secure environment, Master Chief. You know that," said Hodges.

"You both shut the fuck up," said Stannard, waving a finger at Braxton and Hodges, clearly inebriated. He'd obviously pre-funked in the car.

"Are you drunk, Master Chief?" asked Braxton.

"I said shut the fuck up," said Stannard. "This environment's as secure as I make it. If I say it's secure, it's secure. Now, what the fuck happened?"

"Nope," said Martin. "No chance."

"See, that's a thing about you Army faggots I can't stand. Motherfucker, I outrank you. Call me fuckin' sir."

"No chance, fuckin' sir," said Martin.

"Ha ha ha," said Stannard. There were now six SEALs behind him.

"We're sorry for your loss," Luke offered. "They were our teammates, too."

"Shut it, you crayon-eating jarhead fuck," snarled one. "You ain't one of us. You don't fuckin' know. What the fuck do you know? You don't know fuck."

"See, it's that kind of witty repartee that makes me wish I'd joined the Navy," said Braxton.

"He's just sad because his girlfriend got whacked," said another, shaking Luke's shoulder and making a pouting face. "You gonna cry about your girlfriend?"

"This is not something you want to be doing right now," said Luke quietly, his lips barely moving. The color had drained from his face, and Martin put a hand on his arm.

"Hey, we're being nice," said the SEAL. "We're sad, too. Face it, bro, she was the most prime cut of meat in the whole operation. We were hoping you'd at least share at some point."

Luke leaped up out of the booth, the table upending. Martin and the rest of the team held him back.

Stannard laughed as Luke seethed wordlessly, his eyes crazed. "You boys want to take this outside?"

"We'll deal with it later," Braxton assured him, adding, "Fuckin' sir," as they left.

As the SEALS walked away, Stannard's phone went off.

"What's this about?" Decker asked as he opened the door to Paulsen's office, Stannard behind him. It had been a long day, and Decker was running out of time for bullshit.

"I'm glad you're both here. Sit down." Paulsen opened a manila folder atop a small stack on one corner of his desk as Decker and Stannard sat. "I've got sworn statements here from five members of Team Two—"

"Aw, shit," Decker swore, rolling his eyes.

"—yeah," said Paulsen. "You wanna talk about this?"

"About what?"

"They all attest that Delacroix and Collier broke cover and charged, disobeying protocols, showing wanton disregard for rules of engagement, and endangering the team."

"Bullshit," said Stannard. "They would never—"

"You weren't there, Master Chief, so please."

"Those are my SEALs," Stannard insisted, "I trained those

boys."

"Which is why you're here."

"This is crap," said Decker. "We were attacked."

"If that's your statement, that's your statement. I'm going to need it in writing, though. At this point, there's going to be an inquiry."

Decker snorted. "Fine."

"Well, you say that. All five statements corroborate that the team wanted to wait for Major Easton to return, and you overrode your acting non-commissioned officer in charge, Sergeant First Class Martin. Your exact words, according to these statements—"

"—Aw, Christ—"

"—were, and I quote, 'Fuck that bitch'—"

"—come on—"

"She was a bitch," Stannard concurred.

"—they're alleging that you left two members of your team in hostile—"

Decker pounded his fists on the table. "You're goddamned right I did! *You* go in there, Steve! Take a goddamned team and go see for yourself! You'll be out of there with your tail between your legs in five minutes."

Paulsen put the papers down and took off his glasses. "I swear to God, Buck. If I find out that you left another officer in enemy hands as a retributory act . . ."

Buck stood. "You weren't there. Anyway, what are you gonna do? Whole goddamn thing is compartmented. You're gonna convene a court-martial? How?"

"I don't know yet," said Paulsen. "I honestly don't. But there will be an investigation."

"Oh, bullshit."

"With this many sworn statements, there's no way for me to not start one."

Decker cracked his knuckles and stood. "Fine," he told Paulsen,

"This isn't over. Not by damned sight."

"No," said Paulsen. "It's not. I need a statement from you before close of business tomorrow."

"Oh, you'll get one," Decker said on the way out the door.

Several hours later, Luke Foster was headed to the gym to meet Martin when the SEALs caught him in a long hallway.

Luke had no doubt that by now Decker had informed the SEALs in Det One of everything that had happened; at least, how it had happened from his point of view. It was not going to go well.

Three SEALs stood at the end of the hall, in patriotic-themed workout gear, tattooed, bearded, and massively muscled.

There was no place for Luke to run.

"Well, well, well," said one of the SEALs.

"It smells like bitch in here!"

"Smells like a goddamn faggot."

"That's weird. I didn't think there were no faggots in the Marines."

"You were wrong."

"Wrong about a lot of things. Figured he was banging Wonder Woman all this time. Who are you fuckin', faggot? Who are the other fags, here?"

The door opened behind Luke, and where he'd expected to see Martin stepping in to save the day stood Bob Valentine, hulking and sloppy in rain-sodden running pants and a maroon MIT hoodie.

"Heh," said one of the SEALs. "There you go."

"Oh, hello, gentlemen," Bob said cheerily. "Am I interrupting something?"

"Get out of here," one of the SEALs warned. "You didn't see nothin', fatass."

Bob winced and let out a long, pained sigh. "I'm afraid I did, son. How about you boys let this young man go about his business. There's no need for this to get . . ." He searched for a word. " . . . complicated."

"You might want to leave, sir," said Luke.

"Oh," Bob assured him, "I wouldn't miss this."

Quiet laughter rang down the hall as the SEALs looked at each other in disbelief. "This is too good," one admitted.

Bob's tone was distant and academic as he turned and fiddled with the crash bar mechanism on the door. "You know what your mistake was, gentlemen?" He pulled on the bar a couple of times before facing them again. The scholarly eccentricities drained from him as he lowered his head, bison-like, and growled, "You didn't lock the door."

Two rushed Bob, and one tackled Foster, who sprawled, slithered, and went to the deck with his hands full. The SEAL was superhuman, every inch of him cast from lead, and Foster failed in throwing him and wound up on his back, failed in unseating him as he passed the guard, and finally covered his face and tried to work out how he was going to get out of this as the SEAL beat on him with hands like bricks.

The pounding on his arms and ears stopped and the weight disappeared. He peered out from between his arms to see Bob heave the SEAL over his head by the midsection, flipping in midair like a breaching whale and driving him through the floor as they landed.

Lights flickered overhead as Bob stood, a gridwork panel hanging tenuously below a struggling fluorescent tube. Groans, weeping, and the hiss of water filled the destroyed hallway. A steel water-bottle filling station lay in the middle of the corridor; a pipe sprayed sideways over two bodies lying face down. A third hung by his shoulders and one leg through a smashed floor panel, dangling above the nest of cabling some feet below, rag-dolled.

Bob looked over the wreckage, pushing at his neck in either

direction. "Are you all right?"

"Holy shit," Foster wheezed, looking up at Bob from his elbows and tailbone.

"Ring rust," Bob quipped, massaging one his hands. By way of explanation, he added, "I wrestled at Stanford. Don't they teach you boys five-point throws? Or is it all this"—he gestured around him—"'submission hold' bullshit?"

Someone moaned, regaining consciousness and clearly not enjoying it. Blood swirled in the water around a SEAL's head as one of his legs kicked at a puddle in slow motion. White gypsum peeked through a spiderwebbed concavity in the wall directly above him.

There was nothing for Luke to say as Bob reached down a hand. His strength made Luke think of a horse on a friend's farm, an animal that hadn't crossed his mind in years. "Are you hurt?" Bob asked.

"I'm in so much trouble," Luke said, collapsing into himself.

"They're in far more trouble than you are," Bob promised. They stepped through the spray of water and Luke felt baptized, saved. Washed clean.

"We need to help them," Luke said.

Bob steered him toward the door. "Fuck those guys." He jimmied the bar, wiggling something jammed in the mechanism, and pushed it open. "After you, Marine."

Martin was charging down the hallway in an Army T-shirt and black rain pants, dripping and pissed off. "You okay?" he called.

"Don't go in there right now," Luke suggested, looking behind him.

"Luke, what's back there?" Martin asked through gritted teeth.

"About six hundred pounds of SEAL paté," said Bob, clapping Luke on the shoulder.

"Oh, fuck," said Martin.

"And a, uh, minor plumbing issue," Luke added.

Martin headed for the door.

Luke called, "Hey, Martin, you don't want to—"

"Fuckballs!" Martin roared from the doorway. "Holy shit, Foster! What did you—what are you, The Hulk?" He pulled out his phone, punched numbers, and told whoever was on the other end, "Yes, this is Sergeant Martin, Det Two NCOIC. I'm at the gym in Building Two-One. We need medics. Three casualties. Get Ops over here, too, with a water shutoff tool. We've got water in the electrical, and, holy shit, there's a"—he snorted and started to laugh—"there's a guy stuck in the floor. You're gonna need a chainsaw . . ." The door closed, and his voice trailed off behind it, murmurs punctuated by the sporadic cry of alarm.

"I imagine Colonel Paulsen's going to want to talk to us," said Bob.

"I imagine so."

VII

DAWN

Yet they were made of earth and fire as we,
the selfsame forces set us in our mold.
To life we woke, from all that makes the past.
                    — Thøger Larsen (1875-1928) [tr. from Danish]

Phase Line HETFIELD plus 500m

Morning hadn't quite come, but it was on its way. After five combined shifts, Logan and Abby had made the night out to be fifteen hours long. The exact timing of sunrise would be impossible to figure this far in the canyon. The shadows would stay for some time.

Logan poured the water from the MRE-wrapper catch basin into an empty bottle. The solar still had produced more than he'd hoped, nearly a liter. Should he have to do it again, he wouldn't piss in the hole. As it was, they'd had enough water between them to use the collected condensation for hygiene, sparing him the horror of drinking it.

He was smoothing over the sand when Abby came down.

"Good morning, Major." His voice was quiet, the bass removed, a directionless murmur commonly heard diffusing through library stacks.

"You can call me Abby," she said in an equally quiet voice. "I mean, if you think about it, we've slept together."

"Like Swackhammer's gonna let that slide," he grumbled.

"We're still calling him that, huh?"

"Oh, yeah. It's a thing now."

"Wait till we go back and tell him we've made first contact. How are you feeling? Your chest, I mean."

"There's a pistol-shaped bruise right on my sternum. It's okay as long as I don't think about it."

"Tough it out. Hey, you swapped out the blade," she said, motioning to his foot.

"I don't want to surprise them quite yet."

"There'll be plenty of time for that, I'm sure. Ready?"

He took a deep breath. "*L'appel du vide,*" he swore.

"You said that before," she noted. "Foreign Legion motto?"

"Not quite. *L'appel du vide* means 'the call of the void'."

"The call of the void," she repeated.

He ran a functions check on his rifle as he spoke. "*L'appel du vide* is the feeling you get when you're looking down from a great height, and you have a vision of what it would be like to jump. You're not suicidal, you just want to know what it would be like. That ache. That longing to jump. The call of the void."

"I get that all the time. I didn't know it had a name."

"In English, it doesn't. Metaphorically, the French use it to mean something you shouldn't do, would never do, but have the urge to experience. Every now and again, though, people like you and me?"

"Yeah?"

He slapped the magazine into place and chambered a round in punctuation. "We get paid to jump."

"Let's do this."

She scurried around the rock. He followed, and they bounded from position to position, pausing, waiting, relaxing, scanning between each movement. The pink-purple moonglow and the crimson breaking light made for long shadows and easy travel. They crossed the first few hundred yards without incident and backed up to a towering stone pile, drinking water and catching their breath.

"Not bad for an old man," she chided.

"I hate running," he said, sucking at his water valve, "but once I got my new foot, I couldn't find a good reason to quit doing it."

"When I get out of the Army, I'm never running again," she vowed. "I'll do something else. I'll bike, I'll swim, I'll hike the goddamn Appalachian Trail. But no more running. I'm done after this. I used to love it. The Army takes everything that's supposed to be fun in this job, and they suck all the fun out of it."

"That's what armies do," said Logan. "The Legion excels at it. Everything we do? Totally humorless. Rappelling, jumping out of airplanes, shooting guns, beating the crap out of each other, blowing stuff up. It's supposed to be fun, and it never is. When I was a team sergeant, I used to tell my men that it was our duty to steal the fun back. That was the key, I found. Have fun, but look miserable."

"You look like you're having fun," she observed.

He grinned. "I'm not in the Legion anymore."

The sun broke above the canyon. They were still in the shadows, but the skies instantly morphed from purple to an intense lapis blue smeared with wisps of heliotrope condensation, rendering the edges of every shape in the valley intensely sharp and surreally vivid.

"Oh-h, wow," she said.

"That's amazing." There had to be greater words than *amazing* somewhere, but the vertiginous reminder of being on another planet had reduced his brain to a quivering blob of ballistic gelatin. "Just . . . wow."

"Ready to move?"

"No, but yes," he said.

Scan . . . scan . . . up . . . run . . . cover.

Scan . . . scan . . . up . . . run . . . cover.

He was exhausted after their second break. It felt pointless. It felt arbitrary. She was a machine, a Terminator robot. She'd never get tired. As he remembered from the hug last night—and what was up with that?—she was made from the same material as the blade on his leg. They were still in the shadows, and it was probably only ninety degrees, but much harder to put out the effort with the damned humidity.

He kept up, but he was having a word with her when the sun came fully out.

Far behind them, the mighty stone needle jutted into the sky, three-sided and inhumanly high, but an easy marker for the way back. Several structures like it, though only dozens of feet tall, now blocked the end of the valley, creating a chokepoint that funneled any foot traffic approaching the Citadel.

He saw immediately why Medved had called Limit of Advance. The last approach to the Citadel, right at LEMMY, was a lava half-pipe with veritable razors for walls, leading up the hillside to the towers. It was the kind of place an army would get hewed down with artillery or murdered with gas and left to rot in the heat.

A hundred meters from the half-pipe, she rested against a boulder. "They're gonna see us coming the minute we pop around these rocks."

"Yup."

"I don't like that," she said.

"Yup."

"Ideas?"

"You can probably hit from here. You could post up on that little—"

"No," she said. "You're not going in there alone. Besides, once you're inside, I'd be useless. What do you think's in there, anyway?"

"I've been in places like that. Small castle. A few big rooms, probably an armory, barracks. There will be routes out the back. There'll be a well, if we're lucky."

"You're sure?"

"No, but there's a fortress like it in the A'aggar highlands in the Sahara. The towers are hollowed-out organ pipes at the end of a canyon, same thing, and the structure is a series of caves under the mountain. It's just like this. Basalt columns, lava fields, fissures, a deep well. It's half a mile in the air, though. It's not this damned hot. It snows."

"In the Sahara."

"Yeah."

"That's the weirdest thing I've ever heard."

"Well, the day is young."

"Oh my God," she moaned quietly, a hand on her forehead. "This is insane."

"It's about to get insaner," he muttered. "No more running, no more hiding." He rummaged in a bellows pocket and produced the bottle of water from the still. "We need to wash off this paint. No headgear, no sunglasses, we sling rifles. We approach empty handed."

"I hate it, but yes," she said. She wet her shemagh and scrubbed her face. "This water smells terrible."

He rubbed at his face with his own shemagh. She was right; the water smelled like it had been used to mop the floor of a kennel. "Would you rather use it for this or drink it?"

She quit what she was doing and stared at him until she had his full attention. "It's a shame you're right all the time."

"Tell me about it."

"You're kinda hot. But it's a deal-breaker for me."

His heart punched him in his fractured rib, but he poker-faced it. "I'd rather be right than cute."

"See what I mean?"

"Let's do this."

"Wait," she said and reached to her belt. She unscrewed her suppressor and affixed a fighting knife with a six-inch blade to the end of her barrel. "They'll want to see our weapons, I'm sure. I'd suggest we remove mags. If they ask, these are close-quarters weapons."

"Well, that's intellectually disingenuous. It's not a bad idea, though."

He followed suit. The HK had an empty attachment point beneath its stubby barrel, but he hadn't recognized it as a mounting point for the knife on his leg.

"What about pistols?" he wondered, slipping the Kydex sheath over the blade with a click.

"Brass knuckles," she suggested. "They're big, fuckin', brass knuckles."

He dropped the mag from the Sig, cycled the action, and thumbed the round back into the magazine before shoving it in a pocket. If they confiscated it, he didn't want to give them a loaded weapon. "I really don't like going in there with no weapons," he said.

She forced a pained, cynical smile. "And yet, here we are."

"Come on. Where else should we be?"

"You said something last night about a roadside bar and a bacon cheeseburger." She clipped her rifle sling through the carabiner on her shoulder.

Logan sighed. "Yes. Yes, I did."

"Get us through this in one piece, and it's my treat."

"Wow, a date."

"Call it what you want."

The slog up the collapsed lava tube to the main doors was nothing shy of hellish. The ground was smooth volcanic glass coated in dust, and it might as well have been made of ice. Logan had to wonder if it was why they used gryphons for their recon; getting up and down from the valley was a real motherfucker. Assaulting this place on foot was out of the question.

He wondered if whoever lived in the Citadel had been watching and laughing for the past three hours as he and Abby had helped each other up a hundred times.

Bruised, sweat-soaked, frustrated, and coated in glitter, they stood before the gatehouse towers. Hundred-foot columns, volcanically formed, melded into the canyon wall, impenetrable. The rock face between them was flush with the cliff face and peppered with arrowslits.

A cave entrance led between the towers, massively high and worrisomely dark.

"That's a bad idea," Logan observed.

"Agreed."

"They had to see us coming. I vote we wait."

They didn't have to wait long; the shadows inside the tunnel shimmered, morphed, and began to move forward.

Contact.

It was the hardest thing he'd done in years to not raise his rifle as the darkness extended from the mountain in human-shaped forms, shadows coming alive. But after a few seconds it became clear that they were humanoid, bipedal, with dark complexions like oiled hardwood, and onyx hair. They were clad in black and silver, formal and severe. A delegation.

Three at the forefront wore flowing robes, several behind were in various types of dark clothing, and a dozen more followed in Norse-looking mail and helmets.

The three at the front approached Abby and Logan while the others hung back.

They appeared to drift, their footsteps light on the ground, and Logan wondered if they even left prints in the shining dust, thinking of the missing footprints at the combat site.

At five feet eight, Abby towered over them, the tallest coming to her nose and the rest considerably shorter, slight of build and androgynous.

Their faces were lean and dark with tones of walnut and gold, white facial tattoos in fine curving lines and dots over elfin features, and straight black hair pulled back from delicate pointed ears pierced by gemstone hoops of varying gauges and diameters.

Svartálfar, thought Logan. *Black elves.*

His brain raced.

In Nordic legend, the Svartálfar inhabited an underground heaven, separate from the shining elf-lands of Aelfheim above.

Had Norse chroniclers traveled here? Had these beings traveled to Earth long ago? That was sure as hell Norse armor and weapons on the door-kickers standing in the back.

He had so many questions.

There were also the *Dökkálfar,* the demon-elves, the tricksters. The Evil Ones. Were these Svartálfar or Dökkálfar? Good? Evil?

Did they even know, themselves?

He put both his hands up, his palms open; a gesture of peace, of hailing. Abby did the same, and the three Svartálfar—he hoped they were Svartálfar, anyway—closed within arm's length.

One put its hand on Logan's, its touch surprisingly cool, folding its fingers over his. His brain convulsed.

It was the psychic equivalent of a mirror splintering on the far side of a room and revealing a window.

The breadth and energy of each of the beings was a thing alive, sprawling, a communal oneness. He saw himself from fifteen angles—their angles—his head down, his hands up; he watched them react to the shock of the touch and saw how out of place he looked. How out of place he was.

What followed wasn't so much a distinct thought as it was an idea, an image planted in his head that they wanted him to understand: a nation under the desert. Innumerable, and yet, oddly, one. With it came an alarming realization, a near-death glimpse of his own individuality and the horror inherent in his consequent frailty.

This was their desert, their canyon. And . . . more, a shadow of thought beneath it, something darker, sinister. A flash, and it was gone.

Something else lived here, resided here, but he couldn't get back to it.

Their world was under the desert, and yet they owned—shared—the surface, as well. And he now knew, the being drilled it into him, that they were one people because you couldn't survive here alone. The single, overwhelming fact of their existence: no one survives here alone. And with it, a question.

Do you travel alone?

"As you, we are of many, but we travel alone," said Logan, out loud.

They seemed to get it.

"Where am I?" Logan asked. "Who are you?"

An indeterminable shadow of meaning, a thread grasped and tugged with utmost care and concentration until it came loose and expanded. An image. A concept. The name of this place: rocks glimmering under the sun. He could almost hear it, almost repeat it.

He flashed back to the idea, hovered over it, the archaeologist's gift, trying to uncover without disturbing; brush on bone; the gentle breath atomizing the ageless shroud.

The being touching his hand poured it into his mind again, slower. This time, near-words. A world of rock and stone.

"The Stone Lands," Logan said aloud, and the being nodded, its almond-shaped, nearly human, dark eyes boring deeply into his.

It released his hand, and he was back to the heat and the sun and the rock everywhere, leaving such a vast and fitful debt that his overwhelming urge was to slip the leash of his lone mind and rejoin them. He reached for its hand again but stopped himself, though a bubble of longing tightened in his chest under the ache from his fall-bruise.

Holy fuck, it was hot.

"Sown. Lanz," repeated the being, and gestured around them. A slight lisp to the words, and a hint of catlike fangs as it spoke.

"Who are you?" Logan asked, but they were already melting back into the tunnel. The being, and the two with it, motioned for them to follow. Logan looked to Abby, only to find her looking back at him. Simultaneously, they nodded toward the tunnel.

Logan went first, feeling relieved, if only slightly, with Abby watching his six. The soldiers brought up the rear, their armor creaking and jingling in step.

The tunnel entrance was dizzyingly high, intricately carved with symbols and images on crossbeams and arches within, all of them gilded with the opalescent sand, powerful and vibrant against the dark stone.

He'd been right about it being a kill-zone; murder holes flanked the anteroom and perforated the ceiling. A recessed pocket door of stone, a foot thick, was open but would have cut the room down to probably twenty feet long when closed. Nowhere to run.

Zero survivability.

Beyond the pocket door, filtered daylight illuminated the hallway through what Logan originally figured were vents to the surface, but passing beneath he saw they were crystals several feet in diameter, either glowing of their own accord, or perhaps some sort of fiberoptic pathway to the desert above.

How would they have fiberoptics, but still be fighting with swords and mail? So many questions. Did they have a way to harness the energy? Was killing not that important to them?

Imagine the technology you'd have if you didn't spend all your time building weapons.

On that, they had neither taken the rifles nor even asked about them. Logan figured wherever they were going, these people were comfortable enough that they saw literally nothing as a threat.

The corridor wasn't long and led to a set of broad, grand steps carved into the rock leading down into an arena of carved stairwells that flowed to tunnels and corridors, all of it illuminated from above in near-daylight, all of it marked in their lettering, glimmering in the light.

He'd been in castles before. He'd helped excavate Viking fortresses and burial mounds. He'd been in towers and keeps all over Northern Europe.

This was no castle.

It was a realm, an underground world, the vast arena before them merely a waystation with hundreds of tunnels doubtless to far-flung corners of their dominion.

The room with the stairs was immensely larger than any keep still standing in Europe; an inverted tower hewn into the rock. Where northern European castles had inner great towers forty, fifty feet across, this space was wide enough to stage a stock car rally.

Down the stairs, landing after landing, weaving left, right, down more stairs, to one of a hundred, maybe a thousand doorways sunken into the rock. Who knew how far it went?

He tried to grasp the writing above the door, but it was gibberish. Symbols, a scrawl. Vaguely reminiscent of the vine tips forming lace around The Arch.

The beings led them into a smooth-walled chamber hewn from red and black stone, thirty feet on a side, well-lit with a high ceiling and a doorway on the far end. The Svartálfar proceeded through the far exit, at which point a wall slammed down from above with a thunderclap of stone on stone, blocking Logan and Abby in.

Logan sprinted for the doorway they'd come in, his skin flushed and prickling with shock and self-hatred for being so stupid. Abby ran ahead of him, much faster. Neither of them reached the far door in time. It also crashed shut, the soldiers outside.

The echoes faded through the hallway outside. Inside the room—now clearly a prison—it was very, very quiet.

They sighed in unison.

"Well, fuck," said Logan.

"He didn't say anything to you?" Abby asked. She was sitting on her pack, leaning against the wall. It was dry, and cool, and three of the quartz-looking fixtures fifteen feet overhead fed light into the room. Pillars of light danced from above, still alive with dust motes riled by the doors.

"Nothing," he said. "There was . . . an image. Something dark. Something big. Something they're afraid of. I couldn't see it for more than an instant. Then he showed me who they were. What this place is. They call it The Stonelands, I think. That's all I said to him: 'Stonelands.' He said it back. Now, we're here."

"They can read minds, or something," Abby said. "Telepathy. Shit, I wonder what they saw in my head. It's weird in there."

"What were you thinking about?"

"The big thing was how hot it was," she said. "I was tired. I was hot. That was the biggest thing in my mind, I swear to God."

"Well, it's cool in here." He dug through his pack and tossed her a bottle of water.

"We're gonna need that to get back," she said.

"How adorable. You think we're going back."

"You think we're not?"

"This sure looks like an oubliette to me."

"Oubliette?"

"A French word, from *se faire oublier,* 'to be forgotten.' An oubliette is a hole you throw someone in so you don't have to think about them ever again."

"So, what do we do?"

"Settle in." He put a brave face on it, but the background music in his head was the final credits, and this was indeed it—a tragedy. The entire cast dead on the floor. Bring up the house lights. Thank you, everyone, drive carefully.

She stripped the knife from her carbine's barrel and pulled the suppressor from her thigh bellows pocket. "Fuck that," she said, screwing it on. "They have to come back in here. We'll shoot our way out."

"They don't necessarily have to come back in here," he said. "But sure. If they do, I'm all for it."

"You're gonna want your suppressor—"

She cut off as they both heard the sound. A trickle, growing to a spatter, then splashes.

A blade of water a few feet across spouted from the rock at waist-height, folding crystalline before breaking on the floor and draining away a few yards later through a series of cracks.

"Fuck, are they drowning us?" Abby asked.

The water was certainly draining away; the room was not filling.

"Guess not," said Logan.

"Bottles," they said in unison, and scrambled for their empties and dashed to the spout, filling them.

When the bottles were full, they filled bladders from their packs, then drained the bottles in long gulps and refilled them. The water was cold as snowmelt and tasted miraculous, and Logan fought the urge to stick his entire head under the spout. They refilled the bottles and drained them again.

The water showed no signs of stopping, but no signs of flooding.

"Of course, we both have brain amoebas, now," he joked. "You know that, right?"

Abby shed her web gear. "No fucks to give. Since that's still running, I'm gonna sponge off."

"I was thinking the same thing."

"You have a washcloth?"

He dug out a packable towel, a strange thing a few millimeters thick that felt like a chamois. Allegedly it would mushroom into a full-sized towel by absorbing water. He'd never seen one, nor used it. "I have this."

"Use your knife and cut off a corner," she suggested, stripped down to black hi-rise training shorts. She was striking, sheathed in cables of broad muscle from the ankles up with nudges of veins in her shoulders and arms. Jockish. Tough. Shameless. She tossed her sports bra aside.

She caught him staring as she stepped into the water. "Yes?"

"I'm sorry," he said. "You're,"—he didn't want to say *beautiful*, though she absolutely was, "—impressive."

"Thank you," she said, scrubbing her armpit. There was a matter-of-factness to it, a barefaced lack of modesty; she could have been any guy in any locker room at any gym. "Fuckin' Army says I'm overweight." She tossed him a small bar of soap, clearly pinched from a hotel room. "That's all we've got, so make it last."

He stripped to his skivvies as well, folding his clothes. "You're shitting me. Overweight? You?"

"The Army still has its head up its ass with BMI," she said. "I have to get measured with a tape because I'm over my allowed bodyweight. I mean come on, most of us are. Park is a bodybuilder, like, legit. He has a wall full of trophies. And Martin? Ha!"

"Well, yeah, no shit." He himself would have had no such problems. He hadn't stepped on a scale in years, but at just under six feet three he was mostly legs—well, leg—a hobbyist half-marathoner with a desert fighter's build. He wet the soap, scraped it with the piece of towel, and scrubbed.

"But Decker?" she continued. "Writes me up for it. Just me. Puts me 'on notice,' even though the only one on the team who makes weight is Braxton. Decker even put a de-rog in my annual report. And Stannard—*ugh!*" she growled, swiping at the air. "Oh, fuckin' Stannard. For the next week after I weighed in for this team? Cows. Pictures of cows all over my cage, on my gear, slipped into my briefing materials. He thought it was funny as hell. That guy hates women. Hates them."

"Me think he doth protest too much."

"You think?"

"I think. Stannard needs to do some serious self-evaluation."

"Meaning what?"

"Meaning he needs to put a dick in his mouth and see if the taste agrees with him."

"That'd be a moment, wouldn't it? Wow, your chest," she said, changing the subject.

He looked down at the bruise from the pistol, where he'd fallen. "It's fine." Leaning against the wall next to the fountain, he released the vacuum lock on his prosthesis.

"You want a hand?"

He pulled it off along with the liner and held both under the water. "I got it."

"That must've been awful," she admitted, looking at the stump. Three inches of skin protruded from beneath the knee, crossed with slashes and tucks of scars. He scrubbed at it.

"Zigged when I should've zagged," he quipped. "If you could throw me my towel in a second. Getting over there to grab it will be a pain in the ass."

"Place needs a towel rack."

"And an ADA bar," he added.

They scrubbed, dried, and dressed, in the most unsexual-while-baldly-intimate series of moments he'd ever shared with a woman.

Sitting on their packs again, the water still running, he said the unsayable.

"They're not gonna kill us," he said, and hoped he hadn't jinxed it. He screwed the suppressor onto his barrel as he spoke, though.

"You don't think?"

"Nope. What did you tell them? In your head? You said you were thinking about how you were hot, and tired. Probably thirsty, yes?"

"Well . . . yes."

"And here we are." He gestured around them. "It's cool in here, we can rest, looks like they turned on the water."

"You think?"

"I was probably wrong. They may simply be letting us cool off."

"You're just getting my hopes up, right?"

"No. Imagine you lived out here and you found a dog wandering in the desert—roll with me on this for a second," he insisted at the face she made. "What would you do? You'd bring it inside, you'd put it in a corner, probably block off the rest of the house so it wouldn't chew on anything or shit on the floor, give it some water, let it rest and cool off for a while. Right? Then you'd see what it's about."

"See if it's something you want to keep."

"Or put down," he admitted.

They were quiet for a while.

"I hope Luke's okay," she said.

"If Martin's got his back, I'm sure he's fine."

"We need to keep him on the team. I like having a gay spotter. I feel safe around him," she said. "I can sleep. No offense."

"None taken," he assured her. "It's gotta be tough."

"It is. You know how men are terrified of prison? That's what it feels like, being a woman in the military. Every minute. Always on guard, never being caught alone. You choose your friends carefully, you vet your companions, you choose your teams as best you can. And even then, you don't know. You never know. Out there with Luke, I can go to sleep without wondering if I'll wake up being held down."

"Jesus," Logan said. "Why do you do this?"

She sighed. "Because I'm better at this than most people will ever be at anything. For me to do anything else is a waste."

"Usefulness, competence, and belonging," he muttered.

"What's that?"

"In every aspect of your life—friends, relationships, family, work—you're at peace only when you have usefulness, competence, and belonging. I was lucky. I found mine in the

Legion—well, the Commandos—and I found it again at the head of a classroom, and I found it yet again out in the dirt with a trowel in my hand. And it all came together, right here—well, out there. I'm where I'm supposed to be. If this is it, if we die in here, this is what was supposed to happen all along. I'm okay with that."

She cradled the moment until it passed.

"Do you have family?" she asked, quieter.

"No."

"That's a short answer," she observed. "Parents? Brothers and sisters?"

"My parents are long dead. My kid brother's doing a hard twenty in Great Plains."

She raised an eyebrow. "Wow. Girlfriend?"

"I was engaged a couple of years back."

She settled herself on her ruck, getting comfortable. "Tell me about her."

"She was a stripper."

"How military of you," she deadpanned.

"Gotta hand it to her, she beat that student loan problem. She was working her way through a doctorate in marine archaeology."

"Doctor Stripper. Nice pull."

"I can pick 'em," Logan admitted. "She got poached by a treasure-hunting outfit owned by some Eurotrash billionaire while she was working on her thesis. She's somewhere in the Tropics, last I heard, wreck-diving from a hundred-foot yacht."

She raised an appreciative eyebrow. "Not bad."

"Oh, I agree. It was one of those once-in-a-lifetime opportunities. But, what do I know? She never writes. You?"

"Not really seeing anyone, now," she sighed.

"'Not really?'"

"There was a thing with a guy back in D.C., but it was more of a . . ." Her voice trailed off. "—Thing," she finished, crumpling slightly.

"It was just one of those things," Logan sang, gruffing up his voice into a respectable Louis Armstrong. She tossed a rock at him. "I understand," he said. "I've had my share of, um, things."

"Undergrads?" she guessed.

"The preferred industry term is 'trip hazard.'"

"Oh, that's outstanding," she said, and rolled her eyes.

"You have kids?"

She snorted derisively. "That ship has sailed."

Logan turned completely around on his pack to face her. "You're a young woman, still."

"Cancer. I had all the plumbing taken out."

"Oh, Abby, I'm so sorr—"

"Don't," she said, cutting him off with a raised hand. "I wish I'd done it when I was twelve. I was miserable. I had cancer for years and didn't think anything was out of the ordinary."

"I do not envy the female of the species," he admitted. "That really sucks."

"It did," she agreed. "I'll adopt someday. Just gotta find a guy who's okay with it. Shit," she said, and crumpled fully against the wall, looking up at the ceiling. "No one's okay with it. You know that? Nobody's okay with it. It's like every man in the world needs to plant a flag in a goddamn uterus."

They were silent for a long time.

"No one on the team wears a wedding ring," Logan said. "Not even Paulsen."

"Nope," she said. "It's the Island of Misfit Toys. We're loners, all of us. Permanently single, divorced. If we do have kids, it's always a situation where we never see them. I think it's a selection criteria for this project. There's a lot less explaining when someone goes missing on another planet."

"There is that," he admitted. "Speaking of which, I wonder if Tommy and Sergeant Park are in a neighboring room."

"Do you think?"

"No, but hopefully, our hosts will be along shortly, and we can ask."

They were quiet again for a while. Logan didn't think anything of it; stillness was a skill she'd have learned as a sniper, or possessed to get her there. The ability to be alone in your head for—he didn't even know—days? Weeks? Jesus.

"Could you make anything out of the writing in this place?" she asked at last.

"No. I only saw it for a moment. There's no way. Good sign, though, that they have a written language. That will make it much easier to learn to speak it. Maybe."

"Do you see these kinds of inscriptions a lot? Is this, like, a common thing?"

"Yes, but unfortunately, most inscriptions are graffiti."

"Seriously?"

"About ninety percent. The Vikings were huge on graffiti. Like half of what they carved, all the way across Europe, was basically 'Sven was here.'"

"We haven't changed, have we?"

"Not really, no. The Romans drew dicks on everything. And I mean *everything*," he enunciated. "We find dicks carved into trees from two thousand years ago. Not long ago, someone found a metal sling bullet from ancient Greece with the words 'I Hope This Hits You In The Balls' cast into it. Soldiers are soldiers."

"Some things never change."

"Soldiers don't."

Logan was lying on the stone floor against his pack, tapping his foot to the music in his head, when the door opened.

Abby reached for her rifle, and Logan put a hand up. "It's all right," he told her as he stood.

This was not the being who had communicated with him outside the gatehouse; the white dots and lines on his face—her face?—were different, and she, definitely a she, was taller and—he had to look carefully—older. She was in a lighter-weight robe than anyone had worn outside, more silver and less black, and he could see the outlines of breasts swaying under the fabric.

Logan approached, his hands up.

The woman, clearly the leader, gestured to the room. Logan wasn't sure how to communicate his thanks, so he put one fist in the other hand and bowed his head, as he would in a dojo. It seemed a universal sign of respect and thankfulness, and it appeared to get the point across. He gestured to the water, which was still running, and did it again.

She nodded.

This is good, Logan thought. *They nod agreement. Another linguistic breakthrough.*

"Abby, let me do the talking at first, okay?" he said.

"Fine by me, I fucked it way up last time."

"No, you saved our lives," he insisted. "Let's just stick to one narrative right now."

He put his hand up again and pointed to the being's hand, folding the fingers of his left hand over his right. *I want to speak again.*

The reaction was immediate. She stepped forward and gently took his hand, and a hundred things exploded across Logan's mind, a violent riptide of concepts and images, a psychic kaleidoscope. He tried to grasp them all, but many were absolutely alien and dispossessed of any frame of reference. They faded the instant he looked at them.

The maelstrom quieted to a single thought, focused, clear.

Explain yourself.

Boy, he thought, that's a good one.

He took a moment to figure out what he would say, and finally pictured himself as clearly as he could, in a flash of memories as vivid as he could make them: a soldier in the Legion, a desert fighter. Digging up Viking artifacts. Examining the hand weapons at the FOB.

The Arch.

The being put a single concept, a vision, into his head.

Warrior.

Teacher, Logan responded, visualizing himself at the head of a classroom.

And then something new: puzzlement and a degree of respect.

Your people sent a teacher?

Logan didn't have to reply; his acceptance of the idea seemed apparent enough to make her speak to the rest of the room audibly. It was a musical language, guttural but lilting, sung in inflections and tonalities far beyond English, a slight lisp and there they were again, the fangs. Four human-looking front upper teeth and then a pair of vampiric canines, catlike and slender; a feral and not unalarming shade to a visage otherwise startling in its beauty and refinement.

They hadn't broken contact, and he could almost see the words as she spoke, flashes of meaning tearing by.

Speaking appeared to purify the thoughts they transferred by touch, distilling the concepts until the ideas shone, clean and honed. She was explaining to the others in the room that Logan was a teacher. Logan grasped the word for teacher as it flew by—*khos,* not an instructor per se, but a term of immense weight and reverence, referring to a master passing on knowledge.

"Khos," Logan said, and tapped his chest. Her grip on his hand loosened for a fraction of a thought.

"Khos," she said, touching her chest.

Hey, look at that, thought Logan. We're talking.

She spoke again, now, her thoughts crystalline, fully formed but fragile as cobwebs in the sun as the words spun on around them. *Have you come to teach us?*

"I have come to learn," he told her. "I will teach my people upon my return. We seek knowledge," he said, thinking back to Paulsen's rationale for the trip. "What is your name?"

Valla Kamè.

Valla, it seemed, was a title; not quite princess, not quite regent. Revered leader. *Precious one.*

My people call me Logan, who shines at night.

An already profound understanding and respect deepened behind the dark eyes. *Logan, Shining One.* "Logan *Kai,*" she said.

"Logan Kai," Logan repeated, tapping his chest. He gestured to Abby. "Abby."

Mate? Valla Kamè asked.

"Comrade," said Logan. "A great warrior of our people."

"Abè," Valla Kamè repeated for the room, who muttered *Abè* several times among themselves. "Shad-hai" was their word for *great warrior.*

Abby was watching the entire thing, rapt. "How are you . . .?" she asked.

"She's putting the words in my head," said Logan. Valla Kamè let him speak to Abby, pausing the influx of thoughts, quite graciously. "This is very hard. I think that's why the others are being quiet."

"I'll be quiet," she said.

"Thank you. Get the book out of the top of my pack. Please hurry."

She went to his pack and dug for it. It was heavy, battered, the pages still edged in gold. "I can't believe you brought a book," she said as she handed it to him.

"This is why," he said, not breaking contact. "Valla, this is a book of great teachings of my people. These are teachings of one of us who lived thousands of years ago, and those who followed. We still teach it today. My teacher gave it to me. I give it to you. A gift, from my people to yours."

She accepted it from Abby with her free hand. *We appreciate the gift of your teachings.*

"By the way," Logan told Abby, "your name is now Abè Shad-hai."

"Shad-hai?"

"It means 'renowned warrior.'"

"I can roll with that," she said with a nod. "Who are you?"

"They call me 'Logan Kai.' It means, 'Logan, the Shining One.'"

"'Kay. I mean, Kai."

"Right."

Logan turned his attention back to Valla Kamè.

"Yesterday," Logan said. "There was a misunderstanding. We thought we were being attacked."

Attacked. Yes. Shapeless, formless things appeared in the edges of Logan's mind, the dark corners creeping forward of their own volition. The creatures.

"A misunderstanding," said Logan.

No.

Interesting. "Our people went missing."

Missing. Yes.

"Do you know where they are?"

No.

"Are they alive?"

No.

"What took them? Killed them?"

"Sheth," said Valla Kamè. The word *sheth* seemed to mean *shadow,* and brought with it an immediate, shuddering fear; a distrust of the dark. Hints of looming things in blackness.

"We couldn't see them."

Yes. The explanation that followed was muddled, but as he understood it, the sheth could remain unseen until they struck.

"Who are your people?" Logan asked.

Our people descended from Vé. The word took Logan by surprise, sounding very close to the old English word for faeries: Fae.

"Do you have a name?" he asked. "Your people?"

One word, clear and powerful. *Sentinels.* Literally, "they who watch."

"You shouldn't have had to watch too hard," he said, attempting humor, "I shine at night."

A laugh, slow and heavy. Valla Kamè spoke to the others, and the room erupted in peals of silvery laughter. And *there* were the fangs, and holy shit, he thought.

Humor, Valla Kamè noted. *You would fit well with us, Shining One, Giver of Teachings, but you cannot stay.*

"She says we can't stay," Logan told Abby.

"Good," said Abby. "Let's get the hell out of here."

"Amen to that," he told her. "We have no intention of staying," Logan told Valla Kamè, and saw another flash, the Sheth, a mine? A dark place. Dark creatures in dark places carrying . . . *caring* . . . for something dangerous. Catastrophic. Destructive.

Whatever the dangerous thing was, the sheth tended it lovingly, and yet feared and respected it. The only thing he could compare it to was an image of farmers growing live hand grenades.

There was something terribly wrong in the valley, and the sheth were at the heart of it, and he couldn't make heads of tails of it. He followed Valla Kamè's thoughts down tunnels and warrens, each blacker and scarier than the last, and above it all, an immediate feeling of pressing time, a clock running down. Overwhelming, stifling danger.

They had built this underground world on a powderkeg.

"Why can't we stay?" he asked, and before Valla Kamè could answer, he heard the same question from Abby. At a glance, he saw she had joined hands with another Sentinel, who was likely telling her the same thing. Logan and Valla Kamè listened to her translation.

"Logan, this place is dangerous," said Abby.

"I'm getting that."

"They're giving their lives to be here," she said. "We need to go. Right now. Now, Professor."

"Hard agree," he agreed. *"Thank you,"* he said, slowly and clearly to Valla Kamè. "Thank you for the water, and the rest, and the teaching. I will implore my people not to venture beyond The Arch." He tried to think of the Arch, to give a clearer impression, and what he kept coming back to was the vision of Abby appearing in thin air and faceplanting in the dust. Valla Kamè smiled softly at the image. "We have come here to learn," said Logan. "We will remain on the mesa at the Arch, and we will watch. Is that acceptable?"

Do not return, Giver of Teachings. For your safety.

Logan tried to hide his disappointment, failed miserably, then realized that masking his emotions wasn't going to get him anywhere with a being that could read his mind. "I understand the danger," Logan said. "My life has been about finding this place. I want to know more."

We will show you more, but afterwards, you must go.

Again, the sense of a clock ticking down, a fuse burning, haunting every thought and image, hanging over them like an anvil on a thread. They were running out of time; for what, he had no idea.

Logan broke contact, stepped back, and saluted slowly and formally in the Foreign Legion fashion, palm outward, ramrod straight.

Valla Kamè returned it, and the others did the same. Abby saluted in the American method, but turned her palm at the last moment, getting with the program.

The Sentinels and their guards gave them time to gather their gear, and walked them out the second door, deeper into the underground world.

A tunnel opened into daylight a hundred feet further, and the entire subterranean realm sprawled before them.

They stood on a balcony of sorts, a dead-end a hundred feet above a jungle canopy that extended for miles. It defied imagination, vanishing into mist. The air up here was heavy with oxygen, comfortably cool, the world lit by massive fiberoptic crystals set in a ceiling hundreds of feet above. Motion flashed between the trees below them; zip-lines, possibly. Lights flickered deep in the understory.

"The Call of the Void," Abby quipped, looking down.

"Indeed."

What initially appeared to be a bird coming out of the trees became clearer as it neared—a gryphon with a rider on its back, circling higher and higher, headed for the light. Possibly headed for the surface. It made sense that they'd have a launch facility.

"Thank you," said Valla Kamè, in English, well-pronounced, adding, "Khos." *Revered Teacher.*

Valla Kamè motioned to the hallway, then to the light above the trees. It was time to go.

Logan nodded.

As they entered the tunnel, Abby laughed. "Decker's gonna have an aneurysm when he finds out you taught them the Foreign Legion salute."

Exhausted, filthy, sweaty, low on water, sand in their teeth and the sun setting at their backs, Logan and Abby stood before the levitating stone ring at the top of the mesa, as large as the leafy portal in the forest back home but this one carved into braids of rock, or hell, maybe even knitted from rock, who knew? Similar writing on the edges, as far as he could tell.

They turned for another long look at the ringed moon, the three-mile spike, and the canyons fading into the red-purple evening. Two gryphons and their riders, who'd flown overwatch for the past several hours—whether protectively, or to ensure they got out of town and stayed out, or some combination of both— winged their way across the canyon for the Citadel.

"You gave them a cookbook?" she asked.

"What?"

"Epicureanism. They're not going to figure that one out, someday?"

"Our word *epicureanism* comes from Epicurus, a Greek philosopher. He advocated happiness as the highest good, and pleasures in moderation."

"Happiness as the highest good as the teachings of our people? Isn't that, um, 'intellectually disingenuous?'"

"Touché," he said, smiling at her. "However, it's an old text comparing Epicurus with other great philosophers. If they ever translate it, they'll have a lot to talk about. Pretty much all the great thinkers in our history are represented in there at some level."

"You thought this through."

"Not really. Valla Kamè is effectively their queen. I didn't want to sit there empty-handed. You make do with what you have. What's really cool, is that in the gold edging on the pages, if you bend it just right, it makes a picture of ancient Greece."

She didn't hide her amazement. "I am impressed."

"I get that a lot."

"I bet."

They stared out at the moon, unable and unwilling to take their eyes off it.

"I'm never coming back here," she said. "And I'm okay with that."

"None of us are coming back," said Logan.

"I've always seen myself as sort of an astronaut. I mean, I'm out here in Task Force, where no woman has gone before, pushing the envelope."

"I'll say."

"It's funny, though. Because now, here I am on an alien planet, literally doing astronaut shit, and I want nothing so much as to go home and never, ever, come back here."

"We're not welcome." And what a shame, he thought. He'd give anything to return, to walk this world. Explore the underground jungles of the Stonelands. Ramble a while with strange new gods.

"Like that's ever stopped us before," she said. "We're the United States Army."

"All the more reason to shut this down," he said. "As your S-9, I'll be recommending no further contact with these people. My report will reflect a hostile, austere environment. Maximum risk to personnel and equipment. 'Local nationals possess military superiority and a vast intelligence network.'"

"You think they do?"

"They have air assets, and they can read minds. And there are invisible monsters down there. We're sorely outmatched."

"I concur."

They watched the sky for a while longer.

"Cheeseburgers," Logan said at last. "There was mention this morning of cheeseburgers. With bacon."

"And beer," she said. "Let's go."

VIII

RETURN

"When we talk about war, we're really talking about peace."
— George W. Bush

Forward Operating Base WINTERSTONE
Mt. Jupiter, Washington State

L ogan and Abby splashed and crashed through the last few yards of rain and ankle-deep mud to the Ops building. Floodlights blazed blue-white far overhead, illuminating what felt like a waterfall blowing sideways, absolutely bone-chilling after two days in the desert. Logan shivered as they ascended the stairs.

The yard was deserted. It could have been four in the morning; it could have been nine in the evening. Abby pulled the door open to the TOC—Tactical Operations Center—and a sleepy young Staff Sergeant at the desk looked them up and down.

"Major," he said, looking quite surprised. He stood, snapping awake, and reached for the phone. "Holy shit."

"Let me in," said Abby. "We're exhausted, we need to dump our gear and debrief."

"Yes, ma'am," he said, and unlocked the door behind him with a button on his desk, still holding the phone up. "You want me to call Commander Decker?"

"Fuck, no."

"Roger that, ma'am."

"Call Paulsen," Logan said. "Get him here as soon as you can."

"Don't tell Swackhammer or Stannard we're here," Abby added.

"Who?"

"Decker," she corrected herself. "Is that clear? Paulsen. Only. That's an order."

"Yes, ma'am. But—"

"No buts. Do you have a debriefer on shift in the Two Shop?" Abby asked, referring to the Intelligence office.

"I'll find out."

"We're not waiting to debrief," Logan interjected. "If you don't have a debriefer, wake Medved. He can be in his jammies, I don't care."

"Sir, it's twenty-two hundred."

"Do you see anyone else in this room who gives a shit?" Logan asked.

"No, sir."

"Atta boy."

Abby's voice echoed over the spray of the showers, fading in and out as Logan put his head under the nozzle, delirious with relief on the other side of the room as hot water beat his brains in. "Do you have a plan to deal with Decker?" she asked.

"I have a couple of ideas," Logan said, shutting the water off and reaching for his towel, coyote-brown and rough. "This debrief should be fascinating."

He heard her nozzle shut off behind him, and as much as he wanted to turn around to talk to her—okay, he told himself, not to talk to her, but Dear God in Heaven, to see that body again, and not solely out of the animalistic lust that rises from the joy of being alive after mission, but out of simple athletic admiration—he managed not to.

"Man, that guy hates intellectuals," Logan told no one.

"He hates you because you fought for France."

"I never fought for France."

"You were in the Legion, what do you call that?"

"I'm not a nationalist, for God's sake. I didn't fight for Sarkozy, I didn't fight for Hollande, and I sure as hell didn't fight for France. I fought for the same reason any sane man joins any war: there was fighting to be done, and better me than someone else."

She was wearing an identical towel around her waist, her breasts bare. "You stayed in for ten years."

He shrugged. "I was good at it."

He patted down his prosthesis and re-inserted his stump, sans liner, to get him back to the locker room.

"How long can you keep that on?" she asked, walking out behind him.

"I've worn it for seventy-two hours before. It's like boots. You technically don't ever have to take it off, but, gross."

In their respective cages, they dressed in civvies and cleaned their weapons until Paulsen arrived, his face drawn, no jacket, no tie, the top button of his shirt undone.

"Well, now I have to amend a whole shitload of reports," Paulsen deadpanned.

"Jesus, Steve," said Logan. "You look terrible. You okay?"

Paulsen reflected for a moment while Logan reassembled the last of his rifle, then seemed to decide to leave it at, "I've had an interesting day."

Logan checked that his weapon was clear. "I bet," he said,

punctuating it by releasing the bolt with a *clack.*

"Arms room's closed," Paulsen advised. "Lock it up in your cage. Turn it in tomorrow."

"Thanks. We screwed this one up, brother," said Logan.

"That's not the least of it. We're running out of SEALs at an alarming pace."

"We only lost two," said Abby, now loose and casual in jeans and a gray hoodie over a red T-shirt. "What else happened?"

"There was an incident with Sergeant Foster—"

"No!" said Abby. "Shit! Is he okay?"

"He's fine. He and Dr. Valentine got into a scrape with some SEALs. Three air-evacs, one critical, several thousand dollars in structural damage."

"We're gonna need a new archeometallurgist," Logan guessed. "Those guys don't come cheap, I'm sure."

Paulson winced. "Actually, Valentine's fine. He did most of the damage. Ever seen a rhino go after a car?"

"I have, actually."

"Dr. Valentine was a fifth-ranked NCAA heavyweight wrestling champion. Who knew? He went Incredible Hulk, destroyed a modular. Threw one of the SEALs straight through the floor. Smashed walls, ripped the plumbing out and beat one of them into a coma with a pipe."

"O . . . kay . . ." Logan dragged the word out, ready to believe anything at this point.

"It's been a strange day," said Paulsen. "Your team really went to bat for you. Both of you."

"The mission was a disaster," Logan said.

"I understand mistakes were made."

"Not mistakes," said Logan. "Malfeasance. Dereliction. Malice."

"Motherfuckery," Abby added.

"I need to file a report," said Logan. "I'll be recommending Decker's removal."

"Seconding, you mean," said Paulsen. "I need to know everything you two saw, to corroborate the reporting we received from—"

Abby waved her hands. "Steve," she said. "We were there. The Citadel. We made first contact."

"First contact?"

"We spoke to them," Logan said.

"Spoke."

"Spoke, yes," said Logan. "And they had a lot to say."

The debriefer had gone, the camera was off, the briefing room was empty save for the three of them. The door hung open, and beyond it the United States military awaited as it always did, pervasive, inescapable, and self-righteous in its ubiquity: the wood-paneled hall, the raised utility flooring, the smells of day-old coffee and the off-gassing of recently arrived furniture.

An enterprising Warrant Officer had made a last-minute run down the hill to Cooper's for a pair of bacon double-cheeseburgers, getting the order in right as the kitchen closed.

The fries were cold, but neither Abby nor Logan cared. Logan poured rum into Abby's bottle of Coke. Half the lights in the briefing room were turned out, but electric candles still flickered against Chuck Norris.

"So, question for the S-9," said Paulsen.

"Yeah, shoot," said Logan, biting into a room-temperature, sticky burger that was still amazing considering he'd been very nearly killed several times in the past forty-eight hours. Food was better, sex was better, sleep was better—everything was better after a hairy mission. It was the unwritten and inviolable law of being an Operator with a capital O.

Also, who the hell thought to put onion rings on a cheeseburger and where has this been all my life?

"These two factions, they're not at war?" Paulsen asked.

Logan spoke around his food. "That wasn't exactly how I understood it. I think there's a mutual respect, there, but that's as far as I got with it. Abby?"

"That was my takeaway, too. I assess with moderate confidence the Sheth are hostile to the Sentinels, but they appear to be hostile to everything. My assessment is that the Sheth keep people out of the valley, and the Sentinels appreciate the help."

"Well, maybe that's something we can exploit when we go back," said Paulsen.

"Go back, my ass," Logan snapped.

"We have to go back," said Paulsen.

Logan set his burger down and wiped both hands on a napkin. "What's worth getting everyone killed? We took thirty percent casualties on a recon mission. That's unacceptable by any standards. I vote we set up an OP,"—an observation post—"on the hill next to ARCHSTONE and take notes for the next fifty years. There's no reason to go—"

Paulsen slid an envelope across the table. Stapled to the outside was an orange coversheet marking it TOP SECRET/SENSITIVE NUCLEAR MATERIALS.

"Son of a bitch," Logan said. He opened it and handed half the papers within to Abby. "Really?"

"Red mercury," said Paulsen. "The place is loaded with it."

"Fu-u-u-u-uck," Logan groaned.

"What the hell is red mercury?" Abby asked, skimming the files. Several of the papers had the name HAYWARD NUCLEAR LABORATORIES in the headers.

"A nanophase material used in the manufacture of miniaturized nukes," said Paulsen. "It's also a key component in radar-absorbing paint, which could explain the weird readings we get in the valley."

"Jesus Christ," said Logan. His blood pressure was rising; his ears started to ring.

"You're not kidding right now," said Abby. "This stuff is there?"

"The valley is loaded with it. And we're out of it," said Paulsen. "Like, *out.* The processes we used to develop red mercury in the Fifties and Sixties have all been shut down. The last reserves in the world were stolen during the collapse of the Soviet Union, and the U.S. has been combing the black market for it ever since. The going rate right now is a million dollars a gram."

"Holy shit," said Logan.

Abby nodded in agreement.

"Super-dangerous stuff," Paulsen continued. "One reason it's so expensive is that you can't get more than a few kilos of it together or it goes supercritical, all on its own. And then you've got a huge problem. Something about the radiation feeding on itself. I don't understand it all, but we have to bring it back a kilo at a time, no more. They say five kilos is the tipping point. Plus, it's radioactive, so you don't want to handle a lot of it at one time, anyway. We'll need to bring it back with an eyedropper."

Logan didn't mention Abby's revelation about the Sentinels accepting shorter lifespans in return for their work "protecting," as they called it. Nor the overwhelming sensation of the place as a powder keg with a sizzling fuse. He got an uneasy feeling in his gut and shifted in his seat.

"You okay?" Paulsen asked.

A thousand thoughts were going through Logan's head and he didn't want to share any of them right now. The time would come, he was sure. "Yeah. Burger's not sitting right," he lied. "Ate too fast."

"Decker said something about tunnels along the east side of the valley," said Paulsen. "Are you tracking on that?"

"West side," said Logan. "The compass was screwed up. The sun moves left to right across the valley the way we were facing. We're calling sunset west. That puts the Citadel at the south end of the valley."

"The tunnels," Paulsen repeated. "Tell me about the tunnels."

"There are tunnels. I wouldn't go in there. There are things living in there that you don't want to fuck with."

"You don't think that could be a mining operation? Mining the red mercury?"

"Can red mercury be mined?"

"Hell if I know," said Paulsen. "It's not naturally occurring here. We had to create it. Who knows what's up with it over there."

"I don't think they're mining it. And I highly doubt they have nukes."

"What are the tunnels for, do you think?"

Abby spoke. "We saw creatures coming out of there, big snakes or maybe lampreys. They appeared to eat by scraping the surfaces of the rocks. Those rocks in the valley might not be wind-blown. They might have been scoured by whatever those are."

"I'd be curious to know what else is in there," said Paulsen.

"Well, I'm not about to go in there and find out," said Logan. "And I'm sure as hell not about to open that world up to the superior military of a country with a five-hundred-year tradition of ratfucking indigenous peoples."

Paulsen sighed and tapped his foot. "You don't have to frame it that way."

"I don't see any other way to frame it."

"Your country needs you," said Paulsen.

"My country needs to stay the hell away from there."

"We don't even know where the red mercury is. We need to find it, first," Paulsen said, ignoring Logan's last remark. "Any ideas how to reduce risk on an op like that? Going into the tunnels?"

Logan wasn't listening.

Paulsen was interested in the tunnels.

Decker had been interested in the tunnels.

There's red mercury in that valley, and they think it's in the tunnels.

Time to see who the smartest guy in the room really is.

"Logan?" Paulsen prodded.

"I'm thinking." It wasn't entirely a lie; he was thinking, but not about outfitting a team to explore the tunnels.

The Sheth were mining red mercury in the area around the Citadel, maybe not in the tunnels—probably not in the tunnels, given the number of snake-lamprey monsters that came out of there at night—but definitely nearby. The Sentinels were overseeing the process. They may not be *mining* it by any definition Logan would attribute to whatever they were doing, but rather, they were likely curating it to keep it from exploding, or whatever the hell it did when it went supercritical, which sounded like something really bad.

And, he guessed, the radiation in the valley was slowly killing the Sentinels, which is what they'd been trying to tell Abby. Giving their lives to ensure the Sheth got the work done. Saving the rest of their race, who likely lived far enough away for it not to be an issue . . . unless it exploded, probably. Which could explain why the Sentinels lived so damned far underground.

We who watch.

Watching over the most dangerous substance in the world.

He spoke carefully. Quietly.

"We shouldn't go back," Logan insisted. "We said no looting."

"This isn't looting," Paulsen said. "We make them a deal. An offer. Go back in there and find out what they'll take in trade."

"How about blankets?" Logan needled. "We could trade 'em blankets. That shit worked great last time."

"Come on," said Paulsen. "This is not that. This is national security. Our theoretical weapons program is at a standstill without red mercury."

"That's how you did it, isn't it?" Logan asked. "You didn't need authorization to set this place up. This is paid for by a skunkworks. By these guys—Hayward—right?"

"I don't know what you're talking about."

"Oh, come on. The desks. The high-speed computers. These modulars. Hipster tiny houses as the freakin' officers' quarters. Does DoD even know about this? Are we even authorized?"

"It's a complex arrangement, but Mission Delegation Authority rests with me," said Paulsen.

"Oh, shit," Abby breathed.

Logan raised an eyebrow. "You're telling me an Oh-Six greenlit a mission to another goddamn universe without so much as a bless-off from higher?"

"Who's gonna bless off?" Paulsen asked. "Nobody knows about this. The President of the United States doesn't know about this place."

"That's what I'm getting at. You can do whatever the hell you want out here, because nobody knows. You have zero oversight, as long as you deliver."

Paulsen nodded. "More or less."

Logan sat back and sighed. "Guys like Stannard run around screaming about conspiracies, the Illuminati, Bigfoot, and he's standing right in the middle of a conspiracy the whole time and doesn't even see it. Are you kidding me with this shit right now? Does he know about this?"

"The red mercury? No. Decker knows. Stannard doesn't. But let me tell you something." Paulsen motioned at Logan's rum bottle with his coffee cup, and Logan topped it off.

"I've been doing this for thirty years," Paulsen said. "I've had a top secret clearance since Basic Training. I came into SF from intelligence," he said, motioning to Abby. "And I was the intel sergeant on an SF team working Latin America before I commissioned. I have *seen—some—shit*," he emphasized. "I've greenlit strikes on terrorist leaders. I've run spy networks inside foreign governments. I've seen the guy I trained in interrogation techniques shaking hands with our President and being held up as a beacon of hope and democracy.

"There are no conspiracies," Paulsen continued. "That's the terrifying part. It's comforting on some level to think that there actually is a mastermind in control of everything, some puppeteer making it all happen.

"Some people are comforted by the idea that the world is flat, that the President of the United States is a lizard-headed alien, that high fructose corn syrup is ubiquitous because our masters are farming us for food. It makes some sense out of the world. It's comforting to think someone's hiding something from you—that one thing that would make it all make sense. Because, and this is far scarier, *none of it will ever make sense.* There are no conspiracies. The world is rudderless, reactionary.

"It doesn't make any sense up here at our level, either. And it never will. Everything I've seen in thirty years of doing this, thirty years surfing a top-secret internet that holds all the world's secrets, shows me that everything that happens is the *opposite* of a conspiracy."

"What are you talking about?" Abby asked. "There are conspiracies."

"There are secrets, yes. Nefarious goings-on, sure. But we're all making this up as we go along. Every world leader, every terrorist mastermind, every foreign spymaster"—he gestured around the office—"every commander of every Black Ops team. We all wake up, every day, have our first cup of coffee, check our phones, and start figuring out how we're going to unfuck whatever happened while we were sleeping. As I said, it's all reactionary."

"You're telling me—" Logan started.

"We're all idiots," said Paulsen, picking up his mug and nodding. He made it sound so simple.

"The war in Afghanistan," he continued. "The Pentagon called it a Sergeant's War because those unit-level decisions, which meant strategically dick in, say, Vietnam, became the defining actions of the conflict. A twenty-year-old sergeant decides to deploy a machine gun on the east side of a FOB instead of the west this morning, and when the badguys attack, that machine gunner inadvertently takes out the shadow governor of FuckMyLifeistan, who decided that morning he was going to run point because he couldn't get it up the night before and now he's gotta save face in front of his wives when he gets home. Suddenly,"—he gesticulated wildly, nearly spilling his doctored coffee—"*a world leader was assassinated by Special Forces'* and everyone's up in arms, and it was just some Infantry private with a mouthful of sunflower seeds who did a great job watching his lane. This kid changed the entire world and didn't even know it. How can you have a global conspiracy when it's this tenuous? How can anyone even claim control? Abby, you've been there. Tell me I'm wrong."

"It happens twice on a slow day," she admitted. "I never really put it together, though. I mean, there are people in power, right? People run things. Don't they—"

"Sure, every now and again you'll get a rich idiot who holds a lot of power, but they screw up far more than you'd imagine. They just have other people to clean it up. Powerful people are just people with the ability to hire people like us to recover the fumbles."

"That's why we're here?" Logan asked.

"You, especially," Paulsen said, addressing Logan. "Somebody screwed up. We ran out of red mercury, for whatever reason. It's not for us to know. Six months ago, a rift opens up to a world loaded with it, right when we need it. What are the odds of that?

"Six weeks ago, I was coming off a three-year gig breaking up a feeder operation for mafia assassins coming out of a former Eastern Bloc Special Forces school. I get orders to take charge of this operation. I didn't know what red mercury even was.

"I come back from leave, they fly me to this mountaintop, and Medved shows me those swords back there. I get on the internet looking for experts in Viking weapons and culture and find a dissertation on Norse expansionism written by one of the baddest motherfuckers I've ever met." He gestured to Logan. "There was no conspiracy to bring you here. You couldn't have engineered this set of circumstances if you wanted to.

"Abby, you're probably the one person in the Army who could find Logan over there and save him. It just so happened you were here. The odds of everything coming together to put the three of us in this place, right now—together, at this desk, discussing how to get red mercury back here . . . the mind reels."

"Recovered fumbles," Logan repeated.

"The framework that keeps the world running is made of stained glass, my friends. And right below it, seven billion people are involved in a rock fight. That's the true conspiracy. Our job is to patch the holes before they notice."

A moment went by. The words *before they notice* rolled around in Logan's head a few times.

"Okay," Logan said. "Hear me out."

Paulsen nodded. "I'm listening."

"From a civil-military perspective, we want to minimize interference in their world, in their culture. That's a moral imperative, here. Interactions between our cultures will be extremely damaging, on both sides."

"You think?"

"I know. This never goes well. It never has. Not once, in the history of mankind, has this ever worked. So, I've got to wonder if we can do this another way. Zero footprint. Low impact. No contact. So, let's look at a way to do that. How much of this stuff do we need? Really. How much?"

"As much as we can get, but we have to bring it back in small doses. They paint red mercury inside miniaturized nukes. That layer of paint detonates with enough force to fuse plutonium."

"Sweet Jesus," said Logan.

"The real trick is, like I said, it feeds off itself. Five kilos in one place runs the risk of going supercritical. When it does, it gets so hot that it'll melt a hole right through the ground. It sinks, and keeps going until it strikes groundwater, and then you get a steam explosion and you've got Chernobyl all over again."

"Holy shit," said Logan.

"My thoughts exactly," said Paulsen.

"If it's that dangerous, why do we need so much?"

"Because that's what we're instructed to get."

"This is the opposite of the discussion we had," said Logan. "You know that, right?"

"We can do this easy," said Paulsen. "We can make them a deal."

"This is exploitation," said Logan. He two-pointed his burger wrapper into a corner wastebasket in punctuation. "This is colonialism. It's worse than that, actually. This is theft."

"It has to be done," said Paulsen. "Look, if you help us with this, there's a much better chance this will go better for them. For the indigs."

"The indigs," said Logan, baring his teeth. "I could drown you in that fuckin' water fountain, I swear to God."

"Would you rather Decker be in charge of this?" Paulsen asked. "Stannard? This is going to go best if you're beside me on this. Be the voice of reason. You can moderate this thing. You walk away from it, and I don't know what the next guy's gonna do."

"Holy . . ." Logan grumbled. He swore in French, English, and Blackfeet. "Okay, what if we—I don't know—moderate this somehow? If we only need, what, a gram at time? How much of this stuff is a gram?"

"Two or three drops," said Paulsen.

"Then we minimize contact with the indigenous peoples. Not even minimize. Zero contact. If this is the mission, if we need to get this shit to keep this thing open, then we sneak in there, small teams, small footprint, and we steal it a drop at a time, like you were saying.

They never see us, we were never there. Special Reconnaissance. Operating behind enemy lines. Meanwhile, we write."

"I agree," said Abby. "This makes the most sense."

"That's going to take years," said Paulsen.

"You have any place you need to be?" Logan asked.

"That's going to be a tough sell, professor."

"That's your goat to fuck. I'm just here to hold the horns."

Paulsen rubbed his eyes. "Okay. The both of you, take some time off. Let me run it up the flagpole and see who salutes. I've stood your team down until they get counseling for the losses. Go get some sleep, both of you."

IX

SPARE PARTS

"My logisticians are a humorless lot. They know if my campaign fails, they are the first ones I will slay."
— Attributed to Alexander the Great

When Logan would reflect on it later, it was the only possible decision.

He swiped a new uniform and towel from the rack, unlocked his cage with his card and key fob, and filled his water bladder and bottles from the filling station in the hall.

The trick was going to be getting a new chute, and getting out of here fast enough carrying it, with no one watching. There was no way there weren't cameras all over this place, though he didn't know where. He didn't see any.

The heater kicked on at the end of the hall, and the noise startled him.

It took a lot to startle him, it always had, and he surprised himself at how not-okay he was with this. He tried not to think about how bad of an idea it was.

He kept rolling over the thought of telling Abby, to get her to come with him. She wouldn't, of course, and her sense of duty would send her right to Paulsen, and the whole thing would come down around him. It'd be over, he'd be fired, and there'd be no way to help anybody.

He couldn't tell Abby. That was it. The urge was palpable, though. Wow.

Really falling for her, aren't you?

Officers, man, he repeated to himself. You want no part of that.

Back to the problem at hand.

Chutes.

There had to be spare chutes.

No rigger, in any army, would pack exactly the requisite number of chutes and no more. Soldiers got superstitious; jumpmasters suffered from I-know-better-itis; some pain in the ass flag officer would invite himself along for the party at the last minute.

In the cage at the end of the hall, he found them. And miracle of miracles, his card unlocked the door. And why wouldn't it? On paper, he outranked Decker.

He fished out a canopy pack, rearranged the rest in an orderly manner so they wouldn't appear disturbed, and locked the cage behind him.

The supply cages to its immediate left yielded a bonanza: MREs, spare batteries, medical kits, night-vision goggles, and best of all, in a rigid plastic case, a small, fat, thermal scope with a rail mount, built to clip on at the end of his optic. It might light up the Sheth.

It might light up far more than he wanted to see.

This time, he managed to don the chute right side up on the first try.

It was three-seventeen in the morning and raining with the force of gods throwing axes when Logan stood before the Arch, aglow in the red wash of his headlamp, praying to his ancestors for protection and saying a quiet goodbye to everything he'd ever loved or wanted in this world.

Abby awoke at zero-five-thirty in a small modular home a hundred yards from the TOC, one of dozens of pre-fabs comprising the officers' quarters. Rain thundered at the walls and ceiling.

Like the rest of the base, it was considerably scaled-up from the Army standard of repurposed shipping containers; it had a covered porch, windows, a small kitchen, and a separate sleeping area; much more a stylish tiny house than a barracks.

It wasn't, she thought to herself, a bad gig.

A camouflage rain jacket lay across a brown corduroy loveseat. On a breakfast nook, half a glass of white wine stood resolutely next to a corked bottle of pinot grigio and a patrol cap. There was no stove in the kitchen, but some enterprising officer or contractor before her had installed an 18-bottle wine cooler next to the mini-fridge, and she sure as hell wasn't going to let it go unused.

Abby moved far slower than usual this morning. She could have slept through the day, but there were reports to file, asses to chew, Marines to find and slap on the back.

SEALs to fuck over.

The team would be standing down until they'd completed mandatory counseling, which would surely take weeks if not longer, so today was likely a DONSA—Day of No Significant Activity. She hadn't thought to check with Paulsen. Of course, Decker would know the plan for the day, but she had no interest in speaking to Decker right now.

She checked her phone. Sixty-one group texts on their secured team network, mostly about Decker. A few concerning the fight; Martin had sent pictures of what were apparently two SEALs lying face down in the wrecked hallway. A third, unbelievably, had been stuffed straight through the floor as if by a superhero.

Bobby Fett Valentine. Knife Guy.

She had to wonder where Stannard was in all this.

It was going to be an officer's day.

The issue, at the moment, was wardrobe. She pulled on a clean, folded uniform and cold weather boots, threw a Gore-Tex jacket over the top, and though she was authorized a maroon beret as a paratrooper on Airborne status, she decided that today she'd wear a cap, given the way the rain was raging at the outside of her quarters.

A tankless system brought water out of the tap near-scalding on command. She filled a mug and shook out an instant coffee packet from a box on the counter.

The rain in this place. She'd weathered tropical storms on the Eastern Seaboard less wet and violent, and significantly warmer. Apparently, here, it did this for months on end, threatening to sink the world. It boggled the imagination.

She could change into civvies later if they truly had the day off. Besides, the Gore-Tex was damned near drownproof; it was a long hike to the dining facility and—

Three heavy knocks at her door accompanied the announcement "Gunnery Sergeant Foster to see the Major!"

Smiling at his permanent formality and thankful as ever for Marines, Abby nearly knocked him off the nonskid deck as the wind caught the door. He was in civvies, a waxed canvas barn coat and a black watchcap, grinning, sheets of rain behind him in the distant floodlights. A devastatingly beautiful man looking as if the world had been lifted from him.

Dr. Valentine—Knife Guy—stood beside him, drenched in his camel-hair coat and a no-shit Indiana Jones hat.

"Major," said Bob.

"Doctor," she returned. "Gunny, how'd you know I'd be up?"

"How would you not be?" Luke joked. "Surprised you didn't wake me an hour ago for a six-miler in this lovely weather."

"Yeah, fuck you."

"Good to see you again, ma'am," said Luke.

"You, too. It's good to be back. Come in, please. Both of you."

Luke stepped inside and doffed his hat, ever the Marine. Bob did the same after a moment.

"Coffee, Doctor?" she asked, handing her mug to Bob.

"Thank you. Are you all right?"

"I'm fine. I heard you two had some adventures."

"It's been eventful," Bob admitted.

"I heard part of it." She dumped a pouch of instant coffee into a new mug, stirred it with a pen and handed it to Luke, then started the process yet again.

"Professor Logan came to see me last night," Bob started. "He, ah, told me about the . . . material. Over there. That we need to get."

"Did he," said Abby levelly.

"I think he may have done something rash," Bob said.

Abby closed her eyes and swore silently. "Such as?"

Luke spoke cautiously. "Did—" he began, wincing, "—did he . . . bring his gear back?"

"Of course."

"All of it?" Luke asked.

"As far as I know."

"Well, this is weird, ma'am, but we were just in the cages, and the Professor's gear is gone."

She was quiet for a moment; the coffee hadn't taken hold yet. "Maybe he was up before us, already did a turn-in. He's probably still on East Coast time."

"The arms room isn't open," said Luke. "The S-4"—the Logistics team—"won't even be in until zero-nine. There's nobody to turn his gear in to."

"Where . . . where the hell would he go?" she asked.

The coffee kicked in.

"Oh, shit," she said, grabbing her hat and throwing Luke his.

"Come on."

It was night atop the ARCHSTONE mesa. The heliotrope of the moon cast slate-blue shadows and was bright enough to read by, had Logan needed to. It was cool; well, desert cool, probably in the eighties. A beautiful night.

He tongued grit from his teeth as he clipped his static line's carabiner around the webbing, left in place by Park and Martin. He spun the locking ring. *You are out of your mind.*

He tucked Decker's static line and carabiner into his pack, leaving thirteen on the webbing. With any luck, they'd count the static lines, figure he walked, and start down the back side of the hill on foot, buying him hours. There should be enough prints from the team slogging up the back side of the mesa to confuse anyone trying to track him.

He zipped the top of the pack shut, triple-checked the carabiner, and took a run off the cliff.

Jumping in the dark was always tricky. Sky and ground blurred; you had to orient by feel in the critical first moments.

The chute unfurled and slammed him nearly through the harness, harder than last time, and he wasn't sure why. He checked his risers and lines, and from what he could see it was fine. Some odd result from the way this particular chute had been packed, maybe. He flared slightly, braked, steered away from the wall, and headed out over the valley.

The ringed moon gave him more than enough to read the terrain, and he oriented off the miles-high spike once he faced south—what the team was still calling north. This time, instead of spilling his front edge and spiraling for the floor, commando-raid-style, he popped his leading edge up and milked the ride for distance, hunting for thermals.

There wouldn't be as many thermals at night, but the sand was still warm below, because he didn't seem to be losing much altitude, if any. He was a few hundred feet above the edges of the canyon and moving beautifully.

The chute had a significant glide ratio and he'd probably pulled at a thousand feet, so if he could hit a couple of thermals, he might be able to squeeze out five or six kilometers, landing well past Phase Line FREHLEY, which would give him a two- or three-hour head start even if they came through the Arch right now and had their own chutes. Which they probably wouldn't, because nobody was crazy enough to do a night jump from four hundred meters.

L'appel du vide.

And there was the first thermal; he went to deep brakes the moment the air heated up, swung around, would have stalled had it been anything other than this chute, and with a little juking and massaging, he was lifting. At least, he figured, he should be lifting. He wouldn't know in the dark until there was a visible change in altitude . . . or he slammed into the desert floor and broke his remaining leg.

It sure as hell felt like lifting, though; his ears were popping, and in a few minutes, he could sense a definite shift in aspect to the spike. He'd probably gained a thousand feet, and he wasn't sure because he didn't have an altimeter on his wrist, so he needed to get the hell off this elevator, which was starting to feel like the sort of monster mountain waves he'd ridden in Death Valley . . . and Djibouti . . . the kind of superthermal that could suck you up to hypoxic levels in a matter of minutes. Hell, he didn't even know what the air was made of here. Nor did he have any sense of the gravity, though it was close.

Okay, everybody off the ride.

If he'd gained a thousand feet—and it felt like a thousand feet— he'd have gained four klicks of glide. He'd get six or seven kilometers total from here, and he might luck out and hit another thermal further down the canyon, hopefully one less aggressive, and make it nearly to HETFIELD. He braked, nosed down, and dove until he felt the air shift and cool. He leveled out and watched the moon on the mesas because damn.

A lurch; a yank; a rush of wind.

The canopy collapsed.

Instinct told him to cut away even before he fully realized what was happening; he yanked the handle and he was falling, leaning into the wind, waiting for the reserve to do its thing, but there was something else in the dark with him, tangled in the canopy, massive and shrieking as it rocketed past in gravity's claws, terrifyingly fast.

The reserve unspooled and popped, and he arced away. He was fifteen hundred feet up, judging from the moment the screaming ended.

It had all happened so fast.

It was several seconds before he realized a gryphon had attacked his canopy in the dark.

He dropped his front risers and raced for the floor as fast as he dared, lest they move in twos.

The tiny reserve, effectively a BASE jumping rig, had very little glide. He banked in tight circles for the floor, hit hard this time, and felt like he left a dent in the hardpan as his legs collapsed under him. The bruise from the pistol lit up like a flare.

He was glad Abby wasn't around to see the landing.

He lay in the shallow sand until his breathing slowed.

He tapped his headlamp to life.

He checked his prosthesis, still functional—Tommy had been right; the thing could take a hell of a blow—and started loading up his gear.

He didn't know where the gryphon had fallen. He didn't care. Anyone riding it wouldn't have survived the impact, sure as hell not in armor. If they hadn't survived, they weren't his problem.

He had larger problems, nine-foot-tall problems, and for all he knew, they were already here and closing on him.

From a cold start, an ARCHSTONE team could be ready to deploy in ninety minutes.

It took a series of logistical feats just this side of smuggling to not only obtain the equipment needed to explore an alien planet, but to deploy it up a logging road in a national forest while attracting zero attention with Fort Lewis practically within line of sight on a clear day. Abby thought of this often, and for all she knew about the military from her now-five years as an officer, she had no idea how it was actually done.

It did, however, remind her of a friend she hadn't seen in a long time—a young supply officer at her first duty station, freshly commissioned, who'd signed for their brigade's fleet of vehicles only to learn a month later it was short an entire goddamned armored bulldozer.

An enterprising Staff Sergeant had pulled the distraught lieutenant aside and assured her it was fixable, and sure as shit the two of them spent a year and a half quietly ordering "spare" parts, using the motor pool's technically unlimited repair budget.

Under the guise of Live Environment Training, the Staff Sergeant directed his young crew to, hand to God, assemble a sixty-two-ton, two-million-dollar bulldozer from the tracks up, using the back forty of the yard where no one would notice. Once they'd fired it up, the LT simply struck a line through the old numbers, noting the engine had been swapped—there was, after all, a receipt for a new one—and when she moved on to a broadening assignment, she handed the newly fabricated dozer over to the incoming supply officer in a battered ledger along with two hundred sixty-nine other vehicles. The Army never did figure it out.

There were ways, was what Abby was getting at.

Sergeants like the one who'd bailed out her friend were the kind who found the doors held open for support billets at SOCOM, the United States Special Operations Command. If you wore the SOCOM crest on your left shoulder, an arrowhead on a black oval the Army called the "Spear Cookie," it meant you were the absolute best in your service at whatever you did, be it commando or cook.

More to the point, the Spear Cookie meant word had gotten out about you, and you'd been tapped-in by a quiet cadre of professionals who looked for troops who solved problems rather than created them.

And if you got pulled from SOCOM to support the secretive world of Task Force—the U.S. military equivalent of being drafted by the Yankees—you were the master artisan of your craft, revered in hushed tones by those you left behind as you vanished into the shadowy world of compartmented operations.

A Task Force supply sergeant could get anything. And they had. Which was why this place worked at all.

In the cages, she now saw what Luke had seen, and she saw why he'd come to her at Oh-Fuck-Hundred hours.

Against all logic and reason, Logan's cage was empty. Or nearly empty. Looking through the two-inch squares of coated yellow wire, Abby could see his pack and rifle missing. His boots were also gone, along with his helmet and his load-bearing gear.

There was no way he couldn't have returned to ARCHSTONE.

The question was why.

She could think of literally nothing. Except, perhaps, the red mercury. "Oh, fuck," she muttered.

"He couldn't have gotten far," said Bob. "Right?"

"Well, you say that," said Luke. "Guy's as good as any of us. Or was. Those skills don't go away."

"We need to wake Paulsen," said Abby.

"If we do that, he'll send the SEALs," said Bob. "He'll send Stannard."

"Be a great way to get rid of Stannard," Luke offered.

"That would only complicate things," said Bob.

"Anyone have a better idea?" Abby asked.

Luke pulled his badge to the end of its tether and clicked open his own cage. "Yes."

"You can't be serious," said Abby.

"Never seriouser," he said, standing in the doorway with one hand on the cage wall. "We go get him; we're back here before anyone knows we're gone. We've got a few days' stand-down. That could be weeks over there. We do this fast enough, maybe they'll think we all went into town."

She opened the door to her cage. "We are breaking so many laws right now. We're going to get court-martialed if we get caught. You know that."

"I'll risk it," said Bob. "They can't court-martial me."

"You can't . . ." Abby's voice trailed off. "You can't," she finished. "I'm sorry, Doctor."

"This is gonna be hard, dude," said Luke. "Like, marathon-running through a desert hard."

"I might surprise you," said Bob. "If memory serves, I already have."

Abby began, "There's no way you—"

"If you two go in there alone, he's going to assess that you're the enemy. I guarantee neither of you wants a Foreign Legion Commando with that guy's IQ thinking you're out to get him. Take me with you. When we catch up to him, send me to talk to him. Just cover me and let me do the talking."

"He's right, ma'am," said Luke, unlocking one of the equipment cages while Abby swiped her card at another. She hoped to God there was a uniform big enough to fit Bob. They'd have spares for Martin, which would likely work.

She handed Bob a size 2XL uniform, neatly folded. "What are you going to do for boots?" His shoes were stylish, cap-toe dress boots with heavy hiking-style rubber outsoles and waxed cotton laces. "Even if we had something your size, you won't get them broken in."

"These will work fine," Bob insisted.

"Respectfully, Doctor—" Luke began.

"Son, have you ever worn a four-hundred-dollar shoe?"

"Your shoes cost four hundred dollars?" Abby asked in disbelief.

"Each," said Bob.

"Holy shit," Luke breathed.

"These are handmade, custom-fitted. They're far better leather than yours, better quality stitching. Much tougher. The soles are rated for a thousand miles. When we get back, I'll throw a fresh coat of wax on them, and they'll be fashionably distressed. All I really need are some good socks."

"We can get you socks," said Luke. "Do you know anything about rifles? Like, at all? Pistols? Anything?"

"Almost nothing," said Bob. "I haven't shot a gun in years. However, I'm far better with a sword than any of you. And a spear," he added. "And an atlatl, and, well, you get the idea. Let me handle the local weapons. Just keep me alive until we get that far."

Luke looked to Abby, who shrugged. "Why the hell not? Get dressed, Doctor."

Bob left, leaving Luke shucking out of his civvies and into a clean uniform.

"Pack an extra set of OCPs," Abby suggested, referring to their uniforms; *Operational Camouflage Pattern,* the newest and greatest camo.

"You think we're gonna be there that long?"

She opened her cage. "Don't get your heart set on coming back soon."

"How's that, ma'am?"

Abby let out a long breath. "The Professor might be right."

X

TRACES

Le bateau coule normalement
Fr.; tr. "The boat is sinking normally."
— French Foreign Legion idiom

Phase Line CLAPTON

"**Y**ou weren't kidding," Bob said. "It's really hot."

"Yes," said Luke, behind him. "It'll get worse once we're on the floor."

They were traversing the back side of the mesa, teetering on the ridgeline, which was maybe five feet wide on its spine. Luke was in the rear. Three pine boughs, secured to his pack with a length of 550 cord, dragged in the sand behind him, masking their tracks. It wasn't perfect—there would be drag marks until blowing sand smoothed them over—but maybe it would be enough to stump the SEALs.

The key to the trick, Luke had explained to Abby, was that SEALs weren't infantry. They couldn't be; they were Navy, and the Navy had no other combat arms ratings. As a result, all SEALs were originally machinists, electricians, radio operators, shore patrol cops . . . anything but infantry.

Conversely, Marine Corps Force Recon and Army Special Forces came almost exclusively from combat arms, which gave them a base of knowledge steeped in muscle memory, and therefore a set of instincts SEALs generally overcame through sheer grit. Even Abby had come into the Cultural Support Program from a slot as an intelligence officer in an infantry unit, where she'd spent three years training her ass off in basic infantry tactics right beside—and usually ahead of—the rest of the team.

No infantryman, even a boot Marine who'd been through the School of Infantry, would fall for the pine boughs trick. The SEALs likely might, Luke figured, because they weren't wired for it. They were wired for violence, not fieldcraft. That was fine; there were times and places for violent action. However, tracking a sniper team across a hostile alien planet was not one of them.

"We need to speed up," Luke told Abby, and Bob grunted. His feet kicked up clouds of opalescent dust. They'd rigged him with the smallest possible pack, carrying only his water, food, and minimal bivouac gear. It was still a slog for the big man, a rhino navigating the Sahara.

"Logan will be moving slow," Abby corrected. "These Legion guys, they crawl. Two miles an hour, maybe less. We can slow up a little, do twenty-minute miles, catch him in a few hours, and still not kill Bob."

"Thanks," Bob grunted.

"You need to keep wiping your sweat off," Abby told him. "Use your shemagh. In this humidity, sweat doesn't evaporate, so your only way to cool off is to get more water in you. To do that, you have to get it out. If you stop sweating, you're dead in twenty minutes."

"Well, that's good, because I don't think I'll ever stop sweating."

Paulsen's coffee maker was burbling exquisitely as he re-read an email to the Inspector General about Decker. It was nearly 1500 and he hadn't heard from Logan, Valentine, or Abby. Or, for that matter, Decker. Or Stannard. Anyone, really.

The day gets away from you.

He saved the email—he'd read it four times already, but he couldn't bring himself to pull the trigger on it—and put his mind back to where it had wanted to be all day: Logan's idea to steal the red mercury. It was beyond genius.

Best of all, it would keep the teams here occupied for the better part of the year; hell, five years. There would be scouting reports, maps to compile, debriefs, doubtless more Troops In Contact reports because that was just the way things went.

So many missions.

Missions would put him on the map. Exploration of an alien world, to say nothing of the recovery of, what, a billion dollars' worth of critical nuclear material? There goes General Paulsen. He ran a Task Force on another planet.

Things got crazy when he thought of the jobs to follow. He had three years left until he hit his thirty-year mark. He could make General by his early fifties and write his own ticket in the world of defense contracting.

Or, he reasoned, sign on with Hayward Labs when this stint was up and pencil himself a civilian gig running this show next to Logan. This was the last job he was ever going to have.

Logan was . . . he had the file here somewhere . . . forty-three? Ten years in the Legion; nine, really, as they'd promoted him in the hospital and kept him on exactly long enough to hit Adjutant.

He rifled through manila folders in his desk drawer until he hit it.

It wasn't much. Logan's academic evaluation from Ranger

School. A handful of classified debriefings from the incident at Tamanrasset, Logan not referred to by name but only as *Allied Team Sergeant,* a Legionnaire Commando in possession of such massive, chrome-plated balls he stood atop a goddamned castle with a grenade launcher while people shot at him with anti-aircraft weaponry, buying an AC-130 gunship an extra ninety seconds to set up a pylon turn and index targets below.

Drawing fire for a minute and a half, facing down an entire battalion, was a realm beyond suicidal; it was doing the hard thing for your men and taking whatever God decided to dole out.

And bless him, he kept the bad guys from looking up until things started exploding around them, and then, of course, it was too late. An AC-130 was like a tsunami; once you knew it was there, there was nothing you could do. This had been the new "Ghostrider" platform, too, upgraded with a 30mm chain gun and precision-guided groundburst munitions in addition to the ferocious 105mm artillery piece, a Sherman tank round thumping out every six seconds like God's own sniper rifle. It had shredded three hundred-plus optimistic jihadis in under a minute.

Logan had no idea how lucky he was to have had the damned thing on station pulling a low and slow inside Algerian airspace—wildly, war-startlingly illegal, and Paulsen's request after a barrage of intel reports indicating an imminent attack on the fort. Brass at Djibouti had scrambled a flight of Warthogs out of Bamako, but they'd still been over an hour away when Ghostrider showed up. It had been a big win for the Air Force, but an even bigger win for Paulsen.

And then the IED on the way back to Tandouuf. What had that been like? To survive the fight with no more than a couple of stitches, and then . . .

Not a word in here about it, either. Only a release from service, translated into English, along with a two-page records brief.

He skimmed it for the fiftieth time. Master's degree in

l'archaeologie at the Sorbonne, doctoral candidate. Class leader in Basic Training with *La Legion.* Full fluency in French. Rapid promotion, almost always on the day available; this, in an army where it wasn't uncommon to stay a junior soldier for a career.

Commando training in Africa, and other training to follow: combat tracking, jungle warfare in French Guiana, Ranger School, HALO, with a follow-on assignment to French Intelligence, No Further Information, which was almost unheard-of in the Legion, and he had to wonder how it had come about. On the other hand, he'd been an outstanding soldier with a formal education from one of the finest schools in the world, so who the hell knew what kind of exceptions to policy had been tossed his way. To a Legion officer, Logan would have been like finding a goddamned unicorn in the ranks.

Then, the part he'd really lost sleep over: The Legion had made Logan a Warrant Officer—for them, a career rank—three weeks before discharging him. It reeked of disciplinary issues. Looking at it now, through the lens of injury, it started to make sense. In compensation for his right foot, they were allowing him to wear a platoon commander's bar on his tie for the rest of his life. A mighty gift in an organization renowned for not handing out gifts.

Logan was forty-three years old. A lifetime ahead of him.

I need this guy to lead this operation.

I need this guy to be this operation.

He picked up the desk phone, but set it down as his secure personal phone buzzed. It was Stannard.

"Hey, Master Chief."

"Afternoon, sir. I understand she made it back last night, with the Professor? Did I get that right?"

"You did. She did a great job."

"Well, make sure they both come see me by C-O-B," meaning close of business. Paulsen thought it was a strange request, but he shrugged it off.

"If I see her, I'll tell her."

"Wait, she's not with you?"

"Why would she be?"

"Come on," said Stannard. "Don't fuck with me."

"I'm not fucking with you, Master Chief. She's not here. I haven't seen her all day."

There was a long pause.

"Huh," said Stannard, finally. "Her spotter needs to check in, too."

"They probably all went into town for lunch or something."

"Makes sense. Have them come by Ops if you see them?"

"Will do."

"Appreciated, sir."

Before he hung up, Paulsen said, "Hey, do me a favor, will you, Master Chief? Grab Decker when you see him and swing by my office. I've got the notes from the debrief last night, and they're . . . well, you should see this."

"We're on our way."

"A swallowfart," Stannard laughed. It was the third time he'd repeated it since hearing the word *Svartálfar.* "They swallow farts."

Decker chuckled. "We're definitely callin' 'em The Farts, man. That is too good."

"The Farts, and what are the other ones? The Sheth? Call 'em the Shits," said Stannard. "I can remember that. Farts are good, shits are bad."

"Do you understand how important this is?" Paulsen asked once Stannard had calmed down.

Medved and Holton had put together a gorgeous briefing, with detailed maps of the valley and inset ground-level pictures. Best of all, it showed the locations of the tunnels on the west—they now knew it was west—side of the valley.

"Oh, hey, shit," said Decker. "I do understand. Goddamn, right? Alien contact. E.T. phone home."

"And we know where the shit is, too," said Stannard, having been finally read-in on the red mercury. "We'll go get it. Too easy."

"They said something about snakes in there," said Paulsen.

"We ain't scared of no fuckin' snakes," said Decker.

"So, you think he was sandbagging us?" Stannard asked Decker. "'Cuz it feels like sandbagging, the way you tell it. I think he doesn't want us going in those tunnels."

"I think he was bullshitting, yes," said Decker. "I think this goes back to his whole Native thing about—what did he call it?—exploitation, right? If we need this stuff, and it's there, then I don't see what the big deal is. Maybe he does, but he's wrong."

"Well, here's the linchpin," said Paulsen, "the Professor's advocating that we don't go back in there, and I think he's right. I think we sneak back in there and steal it. Never let the Svartálfar know we're there. Dodge the Sheth. In and out, sneaky as thieves. Minimal disruption."

"No farts, no shits," joked Stannard. "Easy."

"Let me take the team," Decker insisted. "Gimme Det One. Det Four is half SEALs, gimme two of 'em, make 'em gunners."

"That's barely going to leave enough bodies for a rescue mission," said Paulsen.

"Rescue? Hell," Decker snorted. "I've seen those caves. I know the way. We have thermal goggles in the Team Shop. We'll see the fuckers coming. This is a cakewalk."

Paulsen folded his hands on his desk. "I want a risk assessment in my inbox before anyone moves."

"You'll have it in six hours," said Decker. "Give my boys the brief at"—he checked his watch—"zero-thirty, and we'll roll."

Paulsen shook his head. "No reason to rush this. You should still be on stand-down. You lost four—"

"We got this," insisted Stannard.

"I don't know that you do," said Paulsen. "Assemble your team, get me the reassignment orders for your backfill personnel in writing, and then produce a mission profile and a risk assessment, and then—only then—we'll see."

Stannard's phone rang at 1900 hours, and it wasn't good. It was Master Sergeant Broussard, the armorer, and he was livid. Three weapons missing, checked out to Ops.

"Sergeant," Stannard said, raising his voice above the noise of the bar area in Cooper's. It was a Friday night, the beer was flowing, Candlebox raged through the speakers, and who the fuck played Candlebox anymore except this was goddamn Seattle and they invented this shit, but the drinks were stiff and the place was packed with overly made-up jailbait and barely-legals sick of the same potbellied loggers, speed-freak ex-jocks, and starry eyed retail workers they'd known since grade school, glomming instead onto Navy SEALs, muscular, dangerous, and loud.

"Out here for training," he said to a girl for the fifth time in fifteen minutes. This time, she stayed, wedging herself between Stannard and the guy on the stool next to him, some half-toothed sad sack in a hunting hat with earflaps. She was an ex-highschool-cheerleader type in her last good years, hiding it with heavy makeup and dark lipstick, D-cups prominent in a spaghetti-strap black blouse. Like every other girl in here, looking for something different. Something new.

Something that would get her the hell out of this place.

Stannard motioned to the bartender to get her whatever she wanted.

"What's going on, Sergeant?" he said into his phone.

"Those fuckers never turned their weapons in," said Broussard.

"There were losses," said Stannard.

"No, we got those. You had three more check in last night. I need their weapons turned in at, not talkin' later than, *at,* fuckin' *at,* you get me? Zero-seven tomorrow."

"I don't know where they are," Stannard said. "I haven't seen them since they got back. Look, I'm sure it's fine, everything's locked up—"

The screaming on the other end of the phone was indecipherable. Stannard cupped his other ear against the bar noise.

"Nothing in their cages?" he asked, hoping he'd heard wrong. "What do you mean nothing in—"

"I'm Misty," the girl said, as he uncovered one ear. "I work at the Busy Beaver. I'm a server," she giggled, "not a dancer."

Stannard held up a finger. "Hang on, sweetheart."

"That's a good start, baby. Add another finger, and we got us a party."

The bartender slid Misty a shot of tequila, and gave one to Stannard.

Stannard pounded his back and tried to make out anything from Broussard's shouting. "Sergeant, I can't hear—I'll be back in a few hours, and I'll take a look. I'm sure it's nothing." He punched the hangup icon, and Misty threw the tequila into her mouth and opened it at him before swallowing.

"This isn't the only thing I swallow," she promised. "You got someplace we can go?"

Whatever Broussard was losing his shit over, it could definitely wait.

"I'm staying on a base up in the mountains. Is there a motel near here?"

"Two miles down the road. On the right. Meet you there?" He looked her up and down and there was no way in hell she was just a server at the local strip joint. Hell, he hadn't even known there was a local strip joint, but he knew a stripper when he saw one.

"I'll drive ya," he offered.

"Craig," she called to the bartender, "I'm leavin' my car tonight."

"No problem, Misty. Have a good night."

The guy in the earflaps had been replaced with a local boy Misty's age. Bigger than Stannard, softer, a longer beard, in a Carhartt jacket and an American flag hat. "This guy givin' you trouble?" he asked Misty, reaching around her and pulling her in.

"Fuck off, Brad," she said, pushing away from him. He held on to her. She pushed again; he held her tighter.

"Hey," said Stannard to whoever the fuck this guy was.

"Hey, yourself, grandpa. There's a bingo parlor down the way. Go find someone your age."

Stannard knocked his hat off, a move so fast the kid didn't have a chance to blink. No one watching would have noticed; the hat flew over the bar.

The kid pushed Misty aside. "Oh, you done it now, old man."

A flurry of motion followed, along with several loud cries even over the blaring of the jukebox, after which the much larger, much younger man was on the floor at the base of the stools, curled up and weeping. Stannard stomped on him several times.

He felt like stomping something.

The SEALs pulled Stannard away. As they helped him out the door, the bartenders screaming at them, Misty grabbed up her jacket and purse and followed.

At 0600 Stannard lumbered into the locker room, yawning and still moderately drunk, dragging a fog of perfume and sex-sweat with him into the aura of Pine Sol and weapons oil that hung in the ready rooms. It was a good smell.

Christ, he loved pussy. He'd never understand queers like that goddamn Marine spotter. Made no sense.

Everything looked in order. Team lockers squared away, one after the other.

"Armorer's an idiot," he muttered to no one.

He rounded the corner of the hallway between the cages, and remembered, now, this was where Logan's cage was. He flashed back to the whole thing with the artificial leg. Christ, what an asshole.

Assholes, everywhere.

Logan's cage was empty. Cleaned out.

"Oh, what the fuck," he muttered.

Did the dumb shit take his gear back to his hooch? The goddamn French probably slept with their rifles or some gay-ass shit.

Major Easton's cage was across the hall. She also hadn't turned her gear in, according to the armorer.

Empty.

"Oh, what the—what?" He shook his head several times, waking himself from the tequila. His head hurt. His back hurt. His dick ached; he could use one more go-round to wake up fully.

Her spotter, the queer little Gunny, had a cage next to Easton's.

The Gunny's cage was also empty. No rifle, no pack, no gear. It was as if he'd moved out.

As if they'd all moved out.

He pulled out his phone and speed-dialed Decker.

"Hey, Buck . . . yeah, I know what time it is. Look, we got a major goddamn problem."

"You want me to green-light two separate missions into

ARCHSTONE?" Paulsen said. He was in his office before 0700 on a Sunday and he hated every minute of it. "I want to make sure I'm understanding you correctly."

"Those fuckers are gone," said Stannard. "All their gear is gone. That goddamn fat boy professor? He's gone, too. They went over there, on their own. We need to know what they're up to."

"This would, literally, take every operator we have," said Paulsen.

"Bullshit. Send me with a half-team," said Stannard. "Give me the remaining four SEALs from Det Four and give me Senior Chief Johannsen out of Det Three with his Mark 48. IR scopes, and we'll take a heavy weapons loadout. Four belt-feds—a 48, three 46s—and a rocket launcher. Nothing will happen to us. We'll catch those guys, we'll find out what the fuck's up. And if anyone over there screws with us, we'll just hose 'em down and keep moving."

"I don't like it," said Paulsen.

"There's nothing here for you to like," said Decker. "I think it's a great idea."

Paulsen squinted and pinched off the bridge of his nose with his finger and thumb. "Sure, you do. It involves a rocket launcher."

Decker ignored him. "Keep Det Four back here. But, I want to plus-up with their Civil-Military Ops guy, Guffman. That will still leave you nearly a Det and half. A six-man team like Stannard's talking about can move like hell. If we hurry, they'll catch those guys, no problem. We have to know what they're thinking, Steve. We need that piece of intel, or this whole thing goes to shit. My team can't do it; we're already fitting out to explore the caves and bring you back the stuff. My team can't waste time chasing those assholes."

Stannard leaned forward in his chair. "Chase, hell. We already know where they're headed."

"They have a considerable head start."

"It's twenty klicks. We can make that in two and a half hours. We'll catch 'em."

Paulsen flipped through the mission brief once more. "You'd better."

XI

FIRST AMONG EQUALS

"Convictions are more dangerous foes of truth than lies."
— Friedrich Nietzsche

L ogan heard the bullet fighting air, a hummingbird thrumming a yard or two past his shoulder. He knew the sound well enough that he dove, the weight of his pack driving him into the dust and sand, and he was behind hard cover when the thunderous report of the .338 blew through the valley. Given the lag between the round and the report, he estimated Abby was a thousand meters behind him, which meant she was at an elevation. Likely shadowing him atop a ridgeline though damned if he knew how she got up there.

Hell of a second date. You sure are something with the ladies, aren't you?

There are two ways to evade a sniper: move fast, or move slow.

Moving fast had its advantages because of the flight time involved. If Abby was a thousand meters off, there was nearly a second of bullet travel between them. Technically, if he moved fast and changed direction every second, he should—again, technically—be able to evade any given round. The trick was to ensure he didn't repeat himself too soon; crossing into his own path from mere seconds ago would get him killed.

Moving slow relied on optics, distance, shadow, and dumb luck.

Multicam, the standard U.S. military uniform Logan was wearing, consisted of several dozen shades and colors, creating a blur to the human eye in virtually any surroundings. As long as he didn't make any sudden moves, he could—again, technically—ooze across an open space in multicam a fraction of an inch at a time without drawing a sniper's eye. This was also assuming she didn't possess a thermal scope, that she didn't have Gunny Foster with her on the big spotting rig, and a dozen other things he could pray about but probably wouldn't get.

Additionally, there was nearly twenty feet of bullet drop involved at this range, so it was equally likely she could guess where he was and sink a shot over one of the big haystack rock piles even if he thought he had line-of-sight cover.

He needed to run to immediate hard cover, and the next decent rock was thirty meters away, so it might as well have been on the big ringed moon.

He also didn't know the vector she was shooting from, so he wouldn't have known which side of the rock to take cover on even if he could reach it. A solitary rifle shot was directionless; the echoes rolled down the valley from wall to wall, obscuring the point of origin.

There was no follow-up shot, which likely meant she didn't have an angle on him.

It could also mean she was moving.

Screwed. I'm so screwed.

She'd dropped a running man at fifteen hundred meters with that goddamn rifle.

He checked his watch. Twelve seconds. Thirteen.

Fourteen.

A lifetime.

They sent the best they had to stop your dumb ass. Didn't see that one coming, did we?

Twenty.

His life ticking away.

A noise behind him; a huff, a heavy footstep on sand and hard earth.

And this is all I need, now. Invisible nine-foot monsters.

There were only so many ways to die, after all, and it was a privileged life that got to choose its end. He chambered a round and rose from behind the rock, shouldered his rifle and scanned with the optic in the direction of the footfall, waiting for the sledgehammer of a round through his chest.

Nothing.

Then, a shimmer; a mirage; the sand coming to life. The thing that stepped out of it was beyond huge, tusks and claws and teeth and walrus-like skin. An ogre with a sword like a guillotine blade.

A Sheth.

Every inch of Logan's body wanted to run in a different direction as he snicked off the safety and put a round center mass and two more into the pelvis—he had no clue what its physiology was, but with its hips shattered it sure as hell wasn't coming after him. The beast fell forward, bellowing. Logan retreated, and two more appeared behind it with a flash of something—an instant of opalescence—right before they showed themselves, and he wondered if it had something to do with the metallic sheen of the sand, the stuff the lampreys vacuumed off the rocks.

That was as far as his thought process got because they were upon him.

Another two rounds and the lead Sheth fell back. The one behind it came at him, brandishing another huge goddamned sword. He backpedaled, met the blade with the barrel of the rifle, fired—

And nothing.

He made distance, banging on the magazine, ejecting a round, and caught the blade with the receiver this time, sidestepping a thrust. He backpedaled and let the rifle swing from its sling on his shoulder, slamming against his knee, and he cleared the Sig as the Sheth froze with the sword over its head, ready to cut him in half.

Confusion crossed its face—genuine, almost human disbelief—before it groaned, crumpled, and fell to its knees.

Behind it was Bob Valentine, gone full Operator in ballistic shades and a boonie hat, the long, single-edged saxe from the relics table in his hand and his fist and uniform jacket bloody to the elbow.

With a swing and a *kiai*, Bob took its head off. Blood jetted skyward as it pitched forward, the head kicking up dust and rolling toward Logan.

The mouth still worked up and down, tusks and fangs clotted with sand. It blinked at him.

"Hey," said Logan.

The Sheth he'd shot in the hips groaned and gurgled, and Logan put three rounds into its head. The valley thundered for long seconds as the reports walked away.

"Professor," Bob panted. "We need to talk."

Logan fired two rounds into the last Sheth and snugged the pistol back into the chest rig. "I'd say we do."

"Sorry about all that," Bob said as he wiped down the saxe. Logan wondered where he'd obtained the sheath he slid it back into. "She wasn't really trying to hit you, you know."

"Uh-huh."

"I think she really likes you."

"Uh-huh," he repeated. "How'd you find me?"

Bob dug in his pocket and held up a compass. "Red Fred lives in the Shed."

"You're smarter than me, aren't you?"

"Yes."

Bob picked up the Sheth's cartoonishly large sword, resting it on his shoulder like a painting of a Swiss pikeman. He took a long look around the valley. "So, what's your thinking, here, Professor? What's the next move?"

Logan looked down toward the Citadel. "Warn 'em."

"Warn 'em," Bob repeated. He rested a foot on the rock where Logan had been covering. "Has it occurred to you they might very well kill you the minute you show up at the door?"

"The thought has crossed my mind," said Logan.

"And you're still going through with it?"

"Burning my bridges at both ends."

"I can see that."

"So, she's what, a thousand yards off to the right, I'm guessing?" Logan said, nodding to the ridgeline.

"About that, I'd think."

"Tell her she can shoot me if she has to. I'm doing this."

Bob turned to scan the ridge. "Like hell I'm going back up there. If she wants to talk to me, she can abseil down."

"So, hey, I told you my plan. What's yours? Fair's fair."

"Not much past this," Bob admitted. "Determine your motives, head back. File a report."

"And if I don't tell you?"

"We go back and Paulsen assumes the worst. No one wants that."

Logan let out a long sigh. "My motives are to let them know we're coming."

Bob adjusted his belt below his gut, which wasn't nearly as large as Logan would have guessed. The big man's wrists were nearly three inches across, the arms of a blacksmith, his hands immense.

Logan had seen offensive tackles at MSU with the same build, packed with explosive power. He'd have his hands full if Bob came at him.

"That's it?" Bob asked.

"That's it. The people here need to know what they're up against."

"The people."

"Yeah."

"You're on their side, now?" It was half a question, half a statement.

"I don't know whose side I'm on," said Logan. "But I'm sure as hell gonna give them a fair shot."

"Okay," said Bob.

"We done, here?"

"Well, if it helps any, we're not gonna kill you."

"Uh-huh."

"But you do understand, we have to warn Paulsen."

Logan let a moment go by, watching the skies. He sighed. "Then we've got ourselves a ballgame, don't we?"

"You don't want a war here, Professor."

"That's not true at all, Doctor. What I don't want is a long war."

"They'll send Stannard. He'll kill you."

Logan toed at the ogre head. "Well," he sighed, "I hope he tries."

"They're going to come at you with everything they've got. And then some."

"Then we'd better hurry," said Logan.

"Don't say 'we.'"

"I didn't mean you. No offense."

"None taken."

"They've got, what, a hundred read-ons for ASCENDANT WARDEN? About that many for ARCHSTONE? Steve can only send two dozen guys, tops, unless someone, somewhere, expands the program. I've been read-in to compartmented programs before. It's a real bitch to get more slots. For them to get as much as another platoon in here would take six months of kissing ass, and someone in D.C. or Bragg would want to know what the fuck was going on. Paulsen can't have the brass asking questions."

"Why are you telling me this?"

"Because there's nothing you can do about any of it. You kill me, there's a war. You don't kill me, there's a war. You've already said you're not gonna kill me."

"You've thought this through."

"Yes. Six months back home is still a considerable amount of time, here. It has to be. Plenty of time to train these guys up and get them ready for whatever Paulsen, or whoever follows him, throws at the Sentinels."

"Sentinels," Bob repeated.

"It's what they call themselves. Our word, not theirs. Theirs is really hard to pronounce."

"Your notes referred to them as Svart—Svartle—"

"Svartálfar," said Logan. "It means 'black elves.' You saw my notes?"

"No, I talked with the Major. So, *svart,* black, like 'schwarz?' *Alf*—elf—Black elves?"

"Black elves," repeated Logan.

"So, they're aliens who look like dark-skinned elves, right? They're not Drow, for God's sake." Bob paused after he said it and winced. "Are they . . . are they Drow?"

"What's a Drow?"

"A black elf. They live underground."

"Well, these are black elves, and they live underground. I wish I'd known about Drow, I'd have called 'em that. Hell of a lot easier to say. They're descended from a race called the Vé. I almost went with that."

"Vé. Fae. Faerie."

"We should be working together."

"I'm trying, here," said Bob. "Drow are generally considered to be evil, you know. The name comes from the Gaelic word for *troll*. The Irish and Scots thought trolls were, well, black elves."

"Interesting. The Norse got the Svartálfar and trolls mixed up a lot, too."

Bob gestured to the Sheth's head. "You can't tell me this is not a troll."

"It's pretty much a troll," Logan agreed.

Bob traded feet on the rock.

"Nice boots."

"Thanks," said Bob. "Let's assume, for the moment, this isn't the only portal from here to Earth. Or at least, not the first time a portal has been used."

It was interesting to Logan how fast they both could settle into intellectual conversation, even surrounded by dead monsters on an alien planet. "Do, let's," said Logan.

"Suppose our northern European ancestors traveled here. They meet these things, and they also meet the Sentinels. Maybe they used one word for both."

"So it seems," Logan agreed. "There are only a few mentions of either of them anywhere that we've found, so there's no way to tell, really."

"Are the Svartálfar considered evil?"

"By the Norse? Sometimes. If you're asking if the Sentinels are malicious, I don't believe so, but then, I don't even think the Sheth are. I think they're just doing their thing. They protect this place. We'd do no different. As for the Sentinels, if anything, they're benevolent, or they think they are. There's a sense of duty there that rivals our own."

"What do they look like? Seriously, do they look like elves?"

"Imagine the most beautiful human you've ever seen, but spun from obsidian. Five feet tall, pointy ears, delicate features, jewels."

"I'd love to meet them."

"You're more than welcome to join me."

"You know I can't."

"You definitely can." Logan dropped the magazine from his rifle, ejected a round, and performed a functions check. It was working fine, now. "Tell Decker you followed me. You wouldn't exactly be lying. We're what, two klicks from the Citadel? You came this far. Follow me for another half hour, come say hello."

"You're forgetting the whole thing about how they might kill us."

"Eh, I haven't forgotten," said Logan, picking up the round from the sand. He blew it off and reinserted it in the magazine. "It's worth the risk."

"To you."

Logan smacked the magazine home and chambered a round. It fed flawlessly. It was possible the impact with the Sheth's sword had knocked the round wonky in the chamber. "Yes."

"That's the problem," Bob said. "We can't be part of this. It's treason, at least for those two. They'll be facing court-martial when they get back just for coming this far. Their careers are over. They only came here to ensure you're doing the right thing."

"Am I?" asked Logan, hanging the rifle off the carabiner at his shoulder.

Bob adjusted his sunglasses and sighed. "We'll see."

As Bob walked away, Logan called, "If you roll the brim of your hat up like a bull rider and use the chinstrap to hold it there, it'll keep you a lot cooler."

Bob waved over his shoulder and kept walking. Within moments, he was gone.

Logan stood before the great gate to the Citadel and waited. He hoped they understood right and wrong the way he did. There was a definite angle to their morality that he in no way had a handle on, and he was diving into the deep end of meta-ethical moral relativism with this stunt. They'd had no Hammurabi, no Sermon on the Mount, no Emmanuel Kant.

Did they construe justice as an extension of equality? Did they recognize benevolence? Charity? Or were they beholden to deontological ethics and didn't give a damn about extenuating circumstances?

He was about to have his answer.

A lone female Sentinel, slight, very dark, very small, chest-high on him, came forward. Seven Sentinel troops stayed behind her, out of melee range, but he had no doubt they carried the kind of throwing knives Bob had demonstrated, and God knew what else. He kept his hands raised. He didn't dare touch his rifle.

She seemed to shimmer as she approached, otherworldly and powerful, a hologram of smoke and light in high-collared, form-fitting black robes lined with gold and open to her navel. She was, absolutely and without question, the most beautiful person he'd ever seen.

He caught a flash of silver tattoos tracing the curve of her breasts, inscribing a varnished undertone to her skin that carried down into a waist he could nearly fit both hands around. Her hair, blue-black in a series of braids cuffed with jeweled rings, was pulled back tight from chiseled elfin features dotted and lined with curlicues of silver. A colony of silver earrings gleamed in her right ear.

This was someone new, and she gave Logan his first assessment of how the Sentinels aged. She appeared much younger and more vibrant than Valla Kamè, achingly beautiful, and brimming with sexuality where Valla Kamè had been regal, measured, elegant. Understanding eyes the same pink-purple of the brightest spots on the moon regarded him with amusement; she appeared to be suppressing a smile. He was aware of her femininity on a fundamental, feral level.

She floated up to him in the weird Sentinel way of moving—he could see her feet, lithe and perfect with black nails on elegant toes; she definitely left footsteps, but she was so *smooth*—and she took his fingertips. He could smell her, a dusty-sweet scent he remembered from childhood when, while stalking a deer, a sparrow had alighted on the tip of his bow and he went on to hold it in his hand. The power of the memory was stunning.

They stared into each other, intensely close and intimate, and his immediate, overwhelming thought was what those eyes would look like in the throes of orgasm.

"Logan Kai," she said aloud. That was a wonderful start. She knew his name.

"And you are?" he asked.

A hesitation, as if the question itself was odd.

Yes, she answered with a touch of confusion. *I am.*

Ah, thought Logan, interesting. Semantics. Literalism. A pragmatic fuckup even on the unconscious level. He hadn't had any miscommunication of ideas with Valla Kamè, and it rattled him momentarily.

Let's start again. "What do I call you?"

"*Čer Aya.*" *Čer* was another honorific, like *Valla*, a rank or title below Valla, at least from the image he was getting. An advisor to a Valla. *Counsel,* he thought, pushing the concept hard—he noticed he squeezed her hand gently to drive a particular image or word home. She nodded.

She's a counselor—the counselor?—to the Valla. We're getting somewhere.

Her words in his head: *Valla Kamè instructed you to not return.*

"I've come to warn you," he said. "My people will follow me. They seek war. I must speak with Valla Kamè."

A flurry of thoughts: *You will not speak with Valla Kamė. Valla Kamė will speak to you. Valla Kamė instructed you to not return. Why do you disobey the Valla? You must never disobey the Valla.*

"The benefits of warning your people outweighed any risks to me for disobeying the Valla," he said.

Čer Aya's eyes widened and for a moment she radiated a sexuality that dwarfed the heat of the desert itself. The guarded smile nearly broke through. *You surprise us,* she said, and he got a flash of . . . arousal? Humor? Almost as if, to them, they were the same emotion.

"I often surprise myself," he admitted. And *there* was the smile.

Still holding his fingers, she turned, leading him by the hand into the Citadel. The soldiers fell in around them, this time in a ring. When they reached the stairwell room, they proceeded down the nearest stairs.

And down.

And down.

Čer Aya was silent as they strode, though she held his hand. He marveled at her control of her mind; it was, as far as he could tell, fully blank, yet she maintained contact, remaining available. In return, he asked her nothing, received nothing. He worked to stay in the moment, taking notes, enjoying the ride.

They descended hundreds of stairs, into a long, well-lit corridor that had no business being well-lit, far beneath the other chambers, the entirety of the hall engraved with their writing.

You have disobeyed the Valla, she said as they reached the end of the hall and stopped before an entranceway. *You will face punishment.*

Kinda figured, he thought.

"As long as I get the chance to tell her what's happening," he said.

You do not fear punishment?

"I accept punishment. I accepted the risk."

Valla Kamè admires courage. As do I.

"You should. What you do here is very brave." He envisioned the dark thing Valla Kamè had shown him, the dangerous thing they cultivated and managed—the thing he knew now was the red mercury—and sent the image to her; he felt Čer Aya's hand tighten on his, as if in shock.

You know of this? she asked.

"My people know of it. That's why I returned. I've learned they will send an army to take it from you."

You serve as a soldier in this army? An emissary? Negotiator?

"Yes. No," he corrected. "Not any longer. I was . . . ah, shit," he said, and the soldiers pushed them forward into what absolutely had to be a throne room, with Valla Kamè on a dais on the far end with what looked like several advisors, likely Čers, he assessed, on each side, in ornamental seats carved from red and gold polished stone.

The room was festooned with massive crystal and gemstone sculptures in dozens of colors. Black stone gargoyles, crouched and massive, flanked each side of the door, their details so lifelike they could have sprung into action at any moment. They'd be three stories tall if they stood.

He counted fourteen soldiers along the walls. Adding the seven around him, he was well and truly boned. "Uh oh."

Your return will anger the Valla, Čer Aya warned, her fingers locked with his. *I hope you live.*

"Well, now, that's nice of you."

Valla Kamè stood, the room stilled, and she spoke, the alien sibilance and musical tones echoing off the walls. Čer Aya translated.

You have disobeyed the decree of Valla Kamè. The Valla told you not to return, yet you returned. For this, you will face punishment.

"Yeah, fine, but—"

She spoke his words back to Valla Kamè, who spoke again.

You will face punishment.

"I will accept your punishment, but understand why I did this," he insisted, speaking directly to Valla Kamè.

Čer Aya translated as Valla Kamè spoke.

Your reasons do not matter. No one disobeys the Valla.

"Yeah, bullshit."

Given the length of the discussion that followed, Logan grasped that there was no direct translation.

He decided to go for broke as they continued to natter and hiss among themselves.

"We know of the red mercury," he said, again addressing Valla Kamè, while still holding Čer Aya's hand. Čer Aya translated as he spoke. Their term for *red mercury* was about nine syllables long.

"My people have known of it," he continued. "They did not tell me until I returned. My leader prepares an army to come here, to make war against you, to take the red mercury from you. It is valuable to us. So, please. Punish me if you must, but know that I returned only to tell you this. To warn you. To implore you to prepare for war."

Valla spoke.

Soldier, translated Čer Aya.

"Yes."

You came here as 'Teacher.' "Khos."

"Soldier," he agreed, "and teacher."

Soldier-teacher? You have shown us Teacher. Show us Soldier.

"What's that, now?" he asked, but she had broken contact and moved away as one of the soldiers in armor strode toward him. The Sentinel slid a sword from its scabbard, slender and short, and flipped a knife into his other hand with unnerving expertise.

The Čers stood, and the assembly with them. The other soldiers made space.

Valla Kamè barked an order. Logan didn't know what it was, but it wasn't hard to guess.

Kill him.

"Oh, fuck me," Logan grumbled. He pulled the hard plastic sheath off the knife attached to the HK's barrel and unclipped the carbine's strap from his shoulder.

He backpedaled as the Sentinel came in on a straight and simple vector, feet shuffling, and struck with the sword, overhand. Logan darted back and made more space with a slash of the bayonet. The Sentinel quick-stepped out of range. They circled.

He had his doubts.

Fighting close-quarters with the rifle had originally been Abby's idea, and he figured worst case, if things got too hairy, there was a round in the chamber and that would be that.

The Sentinel squared his body, raised his dagger hand in a hanging guard to protect his high left side, and engaged the knife with his sword. He toyed with the bayonet for a moment, fencing, testing Logan's strength and reflexes. He tried to push the rifle aside.

Logan was nearly a foot taller, far heavier, and his two-handed grip on the rifle gave him much more leverage. He looped the sword away in a textbook bayonet maneuver, stepped close, smashed the soldier in the helmet with the butt of the rifle while slipping a foot behind, and stabbed for the throat as he reeled, wounding him even through the mail—he could only guess their steel was wildly inferior to the hardened, spring-tempered steel of the blade—before waltz-stepping away. The soldier fell back and threw the knife, but Logan saw it coming long before it loosed, and he slipped it by merely twisting his feet—Foreign Legion Close Quarters Combat Day One: *use your feet to move your head.* The knife went wide by inches and clattered off the stone behind him.

Logan closed the gap, advancing again. The Sentinel kept one hand on his neck and fended with the other, holding his sword left-handed now, and all assembled understood the fight was over, or easily could be.

The soldier's sword rang against the floor as he dropped it. Logan stepped back and nodded in respect.

Other soldiers moved in and tended to their comrade. The wound didn't appear deep, but the fighting knife on the end of the rifle had punctured the mail, and the gathered soldiers regarded the broken links with interest and vocal concern.

Čer Aya returned to him. A soldier handed him the Kydex sheath for the knife, then stepped back with a fist over his heart and an offering gesture, as if giving his heart to Logan. Logan returned it with the Foreign Legion salute and slid the sheath back into place.

Čer Aya put her hand on Logan's shoulder. Valla Kamè spoke again.

Do all your soldiers fight this well?

Logan didn't think he'd call it "well," by any stretch. He'd been lucky that the Sentinel hadn't known how to fight against a bayonet; plus, he was bigger than the Sentinel, and, frankly, meaner, and both went a long way.

"Yes," Logan said. "Most of our soldiers are younger than me. Stronger. Different weapons. Better weapons. Those soldiers will come for the red mercury."

Valla Kamè spoke.

Did your people remove your leg as punishment?

"My leg . . ." he looked down and realized he had completely forgotten to swap out his blade for his other prosthesis. "No. I lost my leg in battle long ago."

What the hell kind of 'punishment' was I originally in for?

"My people are coming to steal from you. To make war upon you," Logan repeated. This brought murmurs and discussion, and Čer Aya's hand left his shoulder as discourse raged among the Čers for what felt like several minutes.

"Shad-hai Khos Logan Kai," said Valla Kamè, when they'd

quieted, which was all he got from it before it returned to gibberish—*great warrior-teacher Logan, the Shining One.* Čer Aya put her hand on his arm and translated. *Why would you betray your people's confidence? Why return?*

"My people betrayed me," Logan returned. "I have seen my people eradicate people like yours. They did it to my ancestors, long ago. They have done this to many, many nations."

Explain why your people would do this.

"I can't."

Yet you served them as soldier.

"I was a soldier for another nation. A different nation, a nation that no longer fights wars of conquest."

Yet you come here as a soldier for the nation you say wants to steal from us.

Valla Kamè was much quicker on the uptake than Paulsen.

"I came here as a teacher," Logan insisted. "Not as a soldier. I came here to learn about your people, so I could return and teach our people. This is what my leaders promised me. They lied to me."

You returned. You disobeyed.

"I disobeyed your people, and mine. There comes a moment in every man's life when he must decide who and what he's willing to die for." He looked into Čer Aya's eyes, then to Valla Kamè.

"I needed you to know what you now know," he continued. "I needed you to be ready when they come. I returned in the hopes that your people will fare better than my ancestors fared. This is why I have come. If I must leave now and never return, I understand. If you must punish me, I also understand."

Valla Kamè was silent for a long time. When she spoke, it was with deliberation and projection that even Logan could make out. It was a decree, to all present.

The warrior-teacher Logan Kai must not return to his people. He must speak to them no more of what he has seen here. This, we cannot allow. As punishment, Logan Kai will remain with us as our

Conditional Ally.

The title "Conditional Ally" had an odd ring to it; it was definitely a title, and yet a euphemism of sorts, and what he grasped from the translation was that it was a moniker they gave to non-Sentinels of . . . the concept was murky; *worth*, he decided, was the best word for it.

Useful outsider.

Who is now our bitch.

On a positive note, it sounded like nobody here would try to kill him again. So, that was something.

Čer Aya was now speaking—thinking—directly to him as Valla Kamè continued to speak. *However, as you live,* she told him, and it was Čer Aya communicating with him, now, *you must obey the Valla. If you disobey the Valla ever again, the Valla will decree punishment.*

"Yeah, let's not go through this again," he agreed.

Valla decreed once you shall never return.

Valla decrees now you shall never leave.

XII

RED SKY GREEN

"They now commingle with the coward angels, the company of those who were not rebels nor faithful to their God, but stood apart."
— Dante, *Inferno,* on those damned for lack of conviction

To call it a treehouse was to do it a tremendous disservice. It was a house in a tree—more to the point, the tree was central to the entire house concept—but that's where the idea ended.

It was an open design, one spacious room, a high ceiling with crystals set in the walls for light, and a pile of them on a central table. They weren't fiberoptic but glowed of their own accord. He hoped they weren't radioactive, but then, he thought, you can't have everything.

The most striking thing about the home was the construction: floors, walls, and even some of the furniture made from branches interwoven over hundreds of years into tight rattan-like surfaces. It all looked very much like the interlocking vines and branches of the Arch back on Earth, only varnished or hand-rubbed, all of it looking hundreds of years old.

There was no way the Sentinels couldn't have been responsible for the design and construction of the Arch.

Čer Aya gave him the tour.

It was twice the size of his own apartment back in Missoula. Against one corner rested a palatial canopy bed with posts of twisted and gnarled branches a foot across, rubbed dark with loving care like everything else, with gauzy, spiderweb-like curtains, likely insect netting, tied to each. The foot of the bed was stacked with heavy linens that looked to be rough silk in shades of blue and brown.

A carved hardwood trunk with gold hardware stood at the foot of the bed. Some things, he realized with a start, were remarkably similar between the worlds. Beds were beds. You put your shit in a footlocker by the bed so it was there when you woke up. That's what sentient beings did.

There was a massive table of living-edge wood, with five heavy, four-legged chairs to match, near a firepit set on a stone slab with a smokehole above.

There was no fire. The room could use one.

Shelves on the walls were bare, knitted from branches and small limbs. The floor was covered with knitted heavy rugs in ornate patterns. A massive bough forked through one corner of the house from floor to ceiling, broad leaves a verdant explosion against the wall, water trickling down. A large window faced out into the forest on each side.

The Sentinels' homes sprawled up the enormous trees—the trunk of this one must have been thirty feet across—and cantilevered out over the understory a hundred feet off the jungle floor, some higher, some larger; all of them connected with stairs and walkways. This one was directly in the middle of the . . . he didn't know what to call it. Village? Tree-town? Nearly a city. Beyond the windows, homes flickered like jewels in the half-light of the canopy, disappearing into the mist. He shivered. It was chilly.

"What do you call this place?"

She put her hand on his arm, and he repeated the question.

Red Sky Green, she answered, and it was as good a name as anything. The sky was, in fact, red, and around them all things were, well, green.

"It's beautiful," he said, and Čer Aya didn't need to touch him to translate. She smiled.

She opened a door he hadn't even seen at the back of the home. Within was an ornate, carved seat, and the sound of a waterfall from the wall behind. The toilet. He'd been wondering.

Crossing the room, she took a beautiful wooden goblet from the table and held it against the water trickling down the wide, forked bough.

He understood. The center of the tree supporting the houses was a sewer; the good water came from the main line, in the bough running through the center of the room.

She beckoned him to the far corner, where the floor was not wood, but tightly fitted stone. She stepped on one of the flagstones, and after a moment a blade of water, the same as he'd seen in the oubliette, cascaded from the wall. The bath. Shower. Whatever.

She motioned for him to try it, and he waved his hands. "I'll do it later," he said.

She motioned again, insistent, and pulled at his load-bearing gear.

"Yeah, okay," he said.

He took off his rifle and gear, hung the whole thing off the back of a chair—she picked it up and hung it on a peg on the wall; apparently there were standards, here. She put her hands on the top of his uniform, and pulled at it so the Velcro came undone, which surprised her.

He unzipped the jacket, which she apparently thought was amazing. She worked the zipper up and down, then held the teeth up close to her eye. He pulled the jacket off and handed it to her to play with. "Cold," he said, and rubbed himself. She worked the zipper a few more times and set the jacket on the table.

She untied the belt from her robe, dropped it from her shoulders, and stepped out of the garment. His breath caught in his chest and something primal rushed through him that he hadn't felt in a long time.

Čer Aya was hewn from varnished chestnut in long, supple curves, pencil-lines of silver gleaming against her skin in tattooed curlicues on both breasts and down to her navel. She was entirely hairless, and wasp-waisted, but her breasts were spectacular, and he had to wonder as to her age.

"Whoa," he said, and she touched his hand, clenched it hard, and the images that she put in his head—writhing explosions of gushing endorphins—startled him with their vehemence and shamelessness.

She let his hand drop and went to the shower/bath spout/whatever it was, he'd think of a name for it later, and washed herself. He stripped and joined her, and as he crossed the room, she stared at his blade prosthesis with the same intensity and fascination with which she'd regarded the zipper.

He was used to people staring.

He stepped next to her in the water, which was lukewarm and not entirely unpleasant but could have easily been twenty degrees hotter given the chill in the room. He put a hand on her shoulder, saying, "I'm cold," and she stepped back, deliberately putting a foot on one of the stones. The water temperature shifted after a second or two, becoming warmer. He moved over to where she was, putting a hand under the blade of water, and pressed the same stone. The water grew warmer still. He nodded, as did she, and when he moved back under the waterfall, still cooler than he liked but better than it had been, she knelt before him.

Questions raged. *Is this foreplay, or do I just stink and they're, I dunno, cool enough with their bodies that showering together is a regular thing? Is she merely showing me how everything works in*

*my new apartment? Is she examining me for a dissertation later?
Because whatever she was thinking a moment ago sure didn't feel
clinical.*

Her head bent low to examine the prosthesis, her braids
hanging heavy, drenched. She put her hands on the blade, tracing it,
examining it from all angles.

She put her hand on his knee above it and said, *Sword foot.
Jewel foot.*

"That's one way to think of it," he admitted, still wondering
exactly what was happening right now. Christ, she was stunning. He
vowed to roll with it.

A line of what he thought were rocks on a stone ledge turned
out to be hard-milled soap, agate-hued and semi opaque, which he
never would have sussed out except the one she'd used had a thin
layer of foam on it now. It smelled of raw earth with a touch of mint.
Soap was soap, and no matter how violently alien the world was,
some things were the same. The bed was the same. The trunk was
the same. Soap was the same.

He started to scrub his scalp, and she took him in her mouth,
the heat like a furnace in contrast to the water. His fingers tangled in
her wet locks as he swelled and collapsed against the wall and all
bets were off.

She'd made a fire.

Smoke drifted through the room, clearing slowly through the
hole in the roof now that it had warmed.

He'd removed his blade, and she snuggled next to him, tracing
the muscles of his chest and stomach with one finger. Her body was
warm, almost uncomfortably so. The Sentinels apparently ran hotter
than humans.

She smelled like old books, which was the craziest thing. Not the salt and earth of human exertion and lust, but the scent of dusty libraries and the tart sting of sheets aired for the first time after being tucked away in a chest for a season.

Running a close second for craziest thing was that he'd never been to bed with someone who could read his mind, who'd literally connected with him from the first touch with a clarity and intensity that took humans years, even a lifetime, to develop. He'd think of some part of her he'd want to explore, some way he liked to be touched, and she'd switch to it enthusiastically, brazenly. The reverse was true, as well; he'd known everything she'd wanted him to do, the moment she wanted him to do it. More, less, slower, faster. Wordless, instantaneous, saving her bell-clear voice for crying out to the rafters, her skin like hot silk.

Despite this, there was more that she wanted from a mate, he could feel it. She had a greater need, but he couldn't understand exactly what it was. Even her thoughts about it were a nebulous, confusing mishmash, as if she herself didn't have a clear idea. If she did, she seemed to have no way to articulate it in a manner he'd understand.

What he gathered, now that they lay together in the afterglow and she put calmer, less graphic and insistent thoughts into his head, was that the Sentinels sought a different sort of rush out of sex than humans. For Sentinels, sex was a portal to an intellectual and psychic fulfillment of which he could only grasp the barest notions. However, rolling around naked by a fire making each other feel good was her people's ideal way to spend an afternoon, and casual physical gratification didn't stop even when they were pair-bonded. The Sentinels were, as best he could gather, both pansexual and polyamorous.

Would he like a different mate? Another to join them? Two more? Five more? A male? She was happy to oblige. This was their prevailing pastime, and it was going on all around them right now, she'd assured him. It's why their beds were so nice.

For Logan, the subject of endless flirtation and teasing from students who could wreck his career, he felt like he'd discovered the great buffalo herds.

A man could make a go of it here.

She'd also made it clear that human men were massively endowed compared to Sentinel men. At his size, which he'd always considered adequately nominal, she'd compared it to scaling the highest tree in the forest. Even now, flaccid, she kept putting her hands around him and giggling quietly.

All this, however, was contingent upon him cleaning himself assiduously, and this was a point she'd driven home. Humans, she'd made it clear, were gross. The Sentinels were nearly hairless, nearly sweatless, their bodies both flawless and exquisitely jeweled. It was infuriatingly erotic. More than that, they were immaculately clean to the point where he'd felt he was begriming her somehow. He had to admit, it made it even sexier, given her enthusiasm for it. And that was fine; he'd been with weirder.

Still, she'd shoved him out of bed into the shower twice since the first one.

Humans, he thought, dozing. For all my meditation and yoga and sweetgrass, for all my family's medicine going back a thousand years, for my twenty years of schooling, I'm just another gross, sweaty, dumb human.

Another dumb human.

He started from half-sleep, and she laid a hand on his shoulder. He put his hand on hers, and she made a small, questioning noise, opening her mind to him.

He treaded carefully, putting the words into her head, afraid of the answer. His heart slammed against his chest as he voiced it.

"Čer Aya," he said. "Are there other humans in this world?"

XIII

CHARYBDIS

"More serpents lie under Yggdrasil
Than every unwise ape can think"
— Prose Edda

1600 meters SSW of Phase Line FREHLEY

The tunnel entrances loomed, twenty-five meters above Decker's position on the canyon floor. A pair of SEALs drove pitons into cracks in the mouth of the nearest entrance with hammers.

"Easiest thing ever," said Jeff Rollins, a Navy Lieutenant and Decker's number two man on the team. He was an earnest, red-haired, bucktoothed former running back from Boise State who'd joined up after graduation, cruised through BUD/S, and found his true purpose: shooting people and blowing shit up. Decker liked him a lot. The Teams needed more guys like Rollins.

Det One wasn't a full sixteen-man SEAL platoon, but a twelve-man detachment, what Paulsen called "a platoon minus." Decker had removed four of the enlisted billets from a SEAL platoon to effectively mirror a Special Forces A-team, but with four machine gunners instead of two, and every man an engineer/demolition expert. It was still a damned effective outfit.

Det One didn't have a Cultural Support Officer assigned; they were the only team that didn't. Det Two had Major Easton. Det Three, equal parts Army Special Forces and Navy SEALs, had a Special Forces Captain named Tanner with a master's in international conflict mediation from Georgetown.

Det Four had Guff.

Master Sergeant Jake Guffman was a large, tough, graying prior-service Marine still serving at the Methuselah-esque age of forty-one and having a hell of a good time. Guff had famously attended Ranger School as a Marine by simply walking across the tarmac at Ft. Benning fifteen minutes after graduating Airborne School, sliding into an empty slot at the back of a formation and hoping nobody noticed. In Decker's eyes, this level of audacity qualified Guff for Task Force more than anyone else in this entire operation.

After leaving the Corps, SSgt Guffman joined the Army Reserve and served several tours in the quiet, understated Civil Affairs Command, a Reserve Special Operations component responsible for humanitarian operations in the hairiest places in the world. Civil Affairs represents a fractional percentage of deployed U.S. Army troops, but accounts for nearly a quarter of the Army's combat casualties. It is hideously dangerous work, and Guff was great at it.

This wasn't Guff's kind of operation, but Decker had added him in a thirteenth billet for this one just in case, because Guff was the kind of guy you wanted around just in case.

This was a simple sweep and clear. They'd assault the tunnel with thermal optics, paint the walls with those big ugly bastards, and get out with the goodies. This was an easy one, and exactly what SEALs did best.

They threw down the lines. Powerful hands gripped the ropes and the platoon-minus walked up the walls. It took seconds.

The cave entrance loomed.

They'd outfitted short carbines with thermal-imaging

monoculars, rail-mounted seamlessly to their scopes. Decker raised his weapon to his shoulder, flicked the system on, and . . .

Nothing.

The cave, as far as he could see, was still and cold, blue-black. Nothing lived.

"Clear," Decker whispered, and the team passed it back.

He tapped the side-mounted light three times, and it flashed from white to red to green, illuminating the ground ahead. Green was harder on the eyes and burned through your intrinsic night vision, but green light was a hunter's friend, especially when traversing to a hide at night, because most animals can't see it.

He was betting the monsters couldn't, either.

Green light also had greater throw and revealed more detail than red light. The cave was wide enough to drive a Humvee down, and it vaguely reminded Decker of karez systems in northern Iraq, the tunnel-rat war of his generation, hand-fighting in irrigation systems dug in Biblical times, some of them fifty feet underground.

However, unlike a karez, the floor and the walls here were polished, devoid even of sand once he'd passed the immediate entrance. The green reflected crazily off curves of wall and floor until it dissipated far ahead. The tunnel was straight and uniform, immaculate, doubtless intentionally constructed.

And cold in the thermal sweep. Nothing lived. Nothing moved.

"Gotta be a fuckin' mine," he whispered into his helmet mic.

"This shit is man-made," someone replied. Reyes, the newest member of the team, from the sound of it.

"Not man," Decker said. It had been either the—what had Stannard called them? The Farts or the Shits—who had carved this. "These are asymmetric threats."

"Right," Reyes said.

The tunnel opened into a yawning hole after a few more steps, straight down, the green vanishing to black. Still nothing on thermal. "This is it," Decker said quietly into his headset. "Definitely a mine shaft. We got it, gentlemen. This is what we're looking for."

"How do we find the stuff?" asked Clark, one of the engineers, who was packing a Mark 46, the smaller, 5.56mm version of the Mark 48 machine gun. The team carried four of them, with a total of twelve thousand belted rounds in boxes strapped to the four gunners' packs. It was a ridiculous amount of heat.

Clark cradled the gun in one arm and waited as the team caught up to them, silent as tigers in the black.

"We'll know it when we see it," said Decker. "It'll show up warm. It's slightly radioactive. Not enough to hurt you unless you, you know, bathe in the shit."

"The problem, boss, is there's nothing to anchor lines to," said Rollins. "We're about six-zero meters in and we've got one hundred meters of line. If that bottoms out past forty meters, we're screwed."

"So we face-fuck the bitch," Reyes offered. "Australian rappel. I'll go. If I don't see the bottom by the end of the rope, I'll flip over and climb back up. Shit ain't hard, sir."

"I like it," said Decker, and the team brought the lines down from the cave mouth and dropped them down the slope, which was abrupt and glass-smooth.

"You two be goddamned careful down there," said Rollins, slapping Reyes on the helmet as he hooked himself up. Dewey, a linebacker-sized SEAL out of Alabama, Black as the air around them, did the same beside Reyes. Carbine in one hand and the other on a line, the two SEALs dropped into the dark. In moments, the green lights from their helmets were invisible.

"Whatdya got?" asked Decker. "Talk to me."

"About thirty meters of drop," said Reyes. "Hard floor, there's a tunnel here. Too easy, boss."

The tunnel shook with a massive impact. Decker's first thought was artillery.

"The fuck?" asked Rollins.

"Stand by, Six," said Reyes.

Another impact. Decker could feel it through his boots. "Talk to me," he told Reyes.

Another. Faster.

"I've got something on thermal," Dewey drawled. "It's down the tunnel, and it's . . . big. Oh, fuck. Fuck!"

Decker could hear clicks and clinks as the SEALs unhooked themselves, more rumbling, like distant explosions, increasing their cadence—were they *footsteps?*—and rounds being chambered. Full-auto fire from their carbines drove his eardrums into his teeth, the entire world being torn apart.

Caves were loud.

"Port line! Go! Get down there!" Decker shouted, and four more team members grabbed the left-hand rope. Their helmet lights lit up white—no more sense in hiding, after all—and they dropped toward the sound of the firefight. "Starboard line exfil!" Decker shouted into his mic. "Say again, starboard line is exfil!" Four more SEALs dropped down the port line, leaving Decker and Rollins, who grabbed the rope as the lights disappeared. Lightning lit up the tunnel as the belt-feds opened up.

It roared. The darkness seemed to tear in half at the sound. Whatever was down there, it was massive, thundering, furious.

Helmet lights scurried in different directions beneath Decker's feet as he dropped, and the world shook with muzzle flashes and roars.

Screams.

Someone was injured; someone was dead; a body flew by in the flash of his helmet light, a leg ripped out of its socket flashed past in the other direction.

Decker hit the floor hard, spun in a crouch, and leveled his weapon at the mass coming at him in pink-white thermal from a tunnel ahead amid the chaos and explosions, a chasm of fangs the size of an Airstream camper yawning on a serpentine neck. A flash of scales, horns, and claws. Beyond that he couldn't process it, he wasn't ready for it, but someone yelled *frag out* and that, he understood. He threw himself flat.

A grenade went off in the tunnel and the world shook, and shook, and kept shaking, and as he got to a prone firing position, he saw the dragon—and it was an absolute, no-shit *dragon Jesus Christ it was a dragon*—was backing away and disappearing down a slope. He got a sense of a snakelike tail far back in the tunnel, and then more grenades followed, and after five, six, seven blasts the thing went completely away, the thundering footsteps fading into the mountain.

The tunnel went quiet.

"Who's hurt?" called Rollins. "Count off!"

Of the twelve SEALs, three didn't answer, including Reyes, whom Rollins found sitting along a side of the tunnel, his headlamp off, staring straight ahead into the black, unresponsive.

"Get him out of here," said Decker. "Send a corpsman with him. Go. Go! Then get back here pronto." His pulse was digging into his chest like a mattock. For the first time in his life, it crossed his mind that he might be too old for this. "Rollins, Guff, get the bodies back up, then pull rear security at the top of the ropes. The rest of you, with me. We're gonna find that thing and finish it off. Let's move."

Rollins and Guff leaned against the tunnel wall at the edge of the shadow, looking out over the canyon. What was left of the two SEALs, what they'd been able to collect, anyway, was splayed out behind them. The corpsman, Conway, sat against one wall, keeping an eye on Reyes, who still hadn't spoken.

"This is moronic," said Guff, renowned for calling such things as he saw them. It wasn't a gripe; it was an observation. It was, in point of fact, moronic. "We don't even have litters. What's he thinking? Drag them all the way home?"

"I advocate we bury them here," said Rollins. "We rig up crosses and take their tags back. It's another planet. If they were astronauts or something . . ."

"Hard agree," said Guff. "It sucks, but" —he gestured around them— "I wouldn't mind being buried here."

"Let's try to avoid that," said Rollins.

"You know, we just fought a damned dragon," said Guff. "You know how awesome that was? That was a *dragon,* dude. Sir. Dude-sir," he corrected.

"Grenades didn't do shit, either," Rollins assessed. "Just pissed it off."

"Really did, didn't they?" Guff admitted. "There's a pissed-off dragon in there, Ell-Tee. Against seven guys." He knelt by the pile of SEAL gear they'd stacked on the glass floor away from the sand, opened his rucksack, and began taking pieces out of it. He tossed them in the pile with the broken equipment and filled his pack with water bottles and food.

"What the hell are you doing?" asked Rollins.

"You think those guys are gonna kill that thing?"

"No."

"I'd say there's a high chance it has another exit, and if it does, it's gonna come back through here, looking to hit those guys from behind." He set a machine gun and ammo bag next to him, resting the gun on its bipod.

"So, you have a plan?"

"Yup." Guff examined a piece of gear and jammed it in an external pouch on the ammo bag, which he attached to the back of his ruck. He lashed the machine gun to his ruck with a length of paracord from one of the late SEALs' packs.

"You're gonna carry that stuff all the way back?"

"Nope." Guff set the ruck on the edge of the cliff and scanned the side of the wall, looking up.

"I don't understand."

"I know, sir," said Guff, still examining the wall, now looking up with interest. "That's why you're not coming with me."

"Where are you going?"

Guff had clipped a long loop of paracord to his belt and the other end to the pack. "See? That's what I mean. I'm going up top, Ell-Tee. I'm gonna set up an overwatch up there with the forty-six and give you guys cover. When I see you moving out, I'll be on your left flank. I'll be two hours behind you. Pour me a Jack, double, neat. Don't wait up."

Rollins was still sputtering an answer as Guff spidered out onto the wall and started to climb.

A few minutes later, Lieutenant Rollins saw the pack swing out into space on its tether and rise out of view.

Rollins leaned against the wall and watched the shadows lengthen across the canyon. Night was falling.

Decker edged his foot forward and watched the darkness. That was the damnedest part of it, he thought, the darkness. It was absolutely, dead-ass pitch black in the tunnel. Nothing lit up on infrared when he flipped down his night-vision goggles; nothing showed in the thermal; nothing moved other than his team. The illumination from the green tac light vanished almost completely. The cavern was much wider here, and it began to slope downwards with his next step. This was the area where the dragon—and this was now a real dragon, goddammit all to hell already, the professor had been right—had vanished.

"Wary of the dark, sir, there are monsters about," Mike Balmore, one of his machine gunners, quipped.

"Shut the fuck up," Decker hissed. "Nicky, Garrett, hook left and see how far this goes."

"Six, this is Garrett," came the reply through his earpiece a moment later. "Drops off, right here. Another shaft, straight down."

"Stay the fuck away from it," Decker ordered.

"Aye-aye, sir."

"Buck." The whisper was so close behind Decker that he started.

"Jesus, Mike. Don't do th—"

They both heard it.

"What the fuck is that?" Mike asked.

"I don't know."

"Listen."

After twenty-two years in the Teams, Buck's ears earned him twenty percent from the VA—his tinnitus was deafening in these tunnels and the recent firefight hadn't helped. He looked around in the darkness, shining his light in all directions, and when he turned his head in one particular direction off to his left, his right ear picked up the scattered patter of distant—

"Rain," he said. "What the fuck? Sounds like rain."

"Running water?" Mike whispered.

"No. That's rain." It was, without a doubt, droplets impacting on stone, hundreds upon hundreds, distant, directionless. He flashed his underslung light from green to red to white, a thousand lumens tearing into the black, and . . .

Nothing. In any direction.

"Nicky, Garrett. Report."

"We're here, Six."

"You hear that?"

"Yeah, it's weird. Is it raining, boss?"

"Get back here. Now."

It was getting louder, the skies opening up.

Only there were no skies here.

"Oh, what the fuck," he grumbled. It was definitely the sound of something wet impacting on the marble-slick floor. Thousands of somethings. Getting closer.

Growing louder.

"What the fuck," echoed Mike, behind him, his white light on.

Garrett and Nicky's green lights were visible now. They were running, judging by the motion.

"Fall back!" Decker urged, and turned back up the tunnel at a run, away from the noise. They still had one line thrown down, and he grabbed it and slung his rifle and powered up the wall, hand over hand, walking straight up.

The rain turned to a torrent behind him, a downpour of white noise hammering at his ears and flooding the tunnel. Mike was behind him on the rope, and then he wasn't, and Buck was alone in the dark with the sensation of swift movement all around, thousands of nameless horrors in the black.

The screaming started.

Buck Decker climbed, and climbed, because somewhere at the top was daylight, and with daylight there might be a chance.

Guff looked out from the top of the canyon wall. It was three hundred feet to the valley floor, an easy slope once he'd gotten past the first thirty feet or so above the cave mouth, and from here he had a glorious view.

They should have thought to post a machine gun team up here initially.

Rocky interior desert highlands sloped away in the other direction, and a dry breeze puffed at him from the depths of gray, broken ground littered with piles of cumulate gray rock.

It was considerably less hot on the ridgeline; under a hundred degrees, and much less humid.

Brutal, but survivable.

He unslung his pack and unlashed the Mark 46, set it on its bipod on a flat rock, and took out a pair of binoculars. He found a good rock for sitting and scanned the horizon, wondering exactly what a dragon looked like on the wing.

Well, he'd know it when he saw it.

Too far away for radio comms with the team, and sure as hell out of range for radio comms with them in the tunnel, there were only three possibilities: the dragon would show itself and he'd put as many of his available three thousand rounds up its ass as he could manage; the dragon would kill everybody in the tunnel, in which case he'd wait until nightfall and head back for the Arch, because, while he killed good, Decker was at his core an aggressively stupid man living well past borrowed time; or he'd see the team moving out across the canyon floor, successful against whatever odds, in which case, he'd shadow them giving top cover until they reached the Arch, then scramble down and hike it out an hour or two behind them.

Leaving Rollins had been rude, he knew. The Navy didn't do things that way, and that was fine. He'd probably get in trouble when the team got back, and that was fine, too.

His goal was to stay alive long enough to get in trouble for staying alive.

As long as he was alive, he had options.

The going along this ridgeline looked tough, with lots of slopes and treacherous footing. He'd have a bitch of a time keeping up with the team, provided they got out, which was still a huge question mark. It had been eerily quiet.

Behind him, the sun had traversed a flatter bit of desert to what he decided to call west, setting past lower peaks and ridgelines, a series of smooth gray-red hills extending out into infinity below him, the ringed moon to the south.

Sun moves faster than the moon. What the hell is going on with this planet? He picked up a few rocks and toyed with them, trying to work out the orbits. It was, after all, something to do.

After a few minutes, he figured he had to be orbiting the moon, not the other way around.

That meant other, possibly habitable planets in the moon system around the ringed planet, which opened up possibilities.

If we built a rocket base out here, we could land on them all.

He watched the sun go down and the stars come out, and on the horizon to the west, so faint it almost looked like a star on its own, the lights of a village or maybe a small settlement atop a hill became progressively more distinct.

There was no way to judge the distance, but it couldn't be more than ten miles to the west. On Earth, the curvature of the planet gave a maximum view of three miles, assuming everything was level. The lights appeared to be above him to some degree, and of course he had no idea how large or small this world was in comparison to Earth, so he called it five miles plus, maybe ten, and scraped an arrow into the dirt pointing directly to the town, lest he lose it in the daytime, because it sure as hell wasn't visible during daylight.

He settled back, watching the valley ahead of him.

Four hours later by his watch, the moon cast blue shadows and lit up the surfaces of the rocks in pink-purple. It was as night as it was going to get and cooling off quickly. The stars were spectacular, much larger and brighter than on Earth.

At one point he thought he'd heard rain down in the valley, but the skies were clear.

Four hours.

He inched toward the cliff's edge on his belly and flipped his NVGs down.

The valley was crawling with snakes.

Huge ones, twenty, thirty feet long, climbed the rocks by the thousands along this side of the valley as far as he could see. The ground and the rock towers undulated with them.

It was simple math: if the snakes could climb the rocks to get down there, they could sure as hell climb the rocks to get up here.

He broke the Mark 46 down and tied it to the top of the pack, loaded all ninety pounds of gear on his back, and put distance between himself and whatever the hell those snakes were. He had no intention of finding out. And if the snakes had come out of the tunnels, they'd have gone through the SEALs, and that, Guff figured, was that.

To his credit, Master Sergeant Jake Guffman's first hundred steps were toward the Arch, and the Earth, and the Army, but a cool wind kicked up as he turned to admire the lights of the town on the horizon, flickering in the green of his night vision. He flipped the NVGs up to take in a long breath of the world under the lavender-pink of the ringed moon—because what a sight—and he had an idea. A once-in-a-lifetime idea.

Because goddamn.

What if.

After staring at the pinpricks of life to the west for five minutes and running every conceivable scenario, he could find no downside.

Guff turned on the thermal scope of his HK, swept the desert in front of him twice, and struck out for the town, eager to make first contact.

XIV

THE CIRCLE CLOSES

"I speak Spanish to God, Italian to women, French to men, and German to my horse."

— Attributed to King Charles V (1500-1558)

1600 meters SSW of Phase Line FREHLEY

The artificial sun overhead had gone to sleep, and Logan attributed it to fiberoptics and the sun outside having finally set. The cold was palpable, pinching. Čer Aya had given him a robe, such that it was.

The trunk at the end of the bed was full of the Sentinels' dressing gowns in various weights, though at Logan's height they fit him like kimonos, barely reaching his knee. He'd shoved the sleeves up his arms, but they barely fit around his chest, and he was wiry by human standards. There was a blown-glass decanter of wine, and small strips of meat charred over the fire but rare enough to still leak blood onto an irregularly shaped, rough-edged gray stone plate beside it.

Best of all, there was a map.

His evening was booked.

The fire crackled, and Čer Aya moved a lightstone—one of the

  Joseph Malik

yellow-glowing stones, roughly the size of a bar of soap on Earth—over the map. Four more anchored the corners. The map was larger than the table, spectacularly detailed. The canyon hiding the Citadel amounted to not much more than a couple of squiggly lines and a dot.

This world was huge.

"Countries," he said. She put a hand on his arm, he repeated the word, and she agreed. "Vallala," she said. The realms ruled by Vallas.

"Valhalla," he repeated. She nodded.

"You're putting me on," he told no one. "Valhalla."

"Vallala," she said with a smile, gesturing across the map.

Logan's world reeled.

Beyond Paulsen's spiel about the stained-glass floor to heaven and the rock fight below, beyond conspiracies, beyond the craziest thing he could imagine this ever being, it was worse than that.

This wasn't a rift in space-time.

It was a rupture in the firmament, and he was in deep shit.

"This," started Logan, speaking carefully to choose not only his words, but the images in his head as he spoke, "is important to me. Some of my people, our ancestors, spoke of a land called Valhalla, where they believed their spirits passed on to when they died. A land of sex and war, full of fae—Vé," he corrected, gesturing to her, "—and battles, and courage. A land where people never die again."

"Vallala," she said again, gesturing to the map once more. She draped herself against him, radiating like the fire, and in the touch came ideas. Thoughts. Sentences. *We call this land Elalion. It means, 'what I have seen.' Elalion varies in meaning depending on the speaker. When I say Elalion, I mean 'the world I know of.'*

Their communication was much clearer now, and he wondered if she was getting better at filtering the thoughts she was putting into his mind, or if he was getting better at sorting them.

"But the door," he said. "The Arch."

You speak of an old door. Yes, the old door. We never use it.

"Never?"

The Valla forbids it.

"Well, that's great, but no one ever disobeys the Valla?"

We never disobey the Valla.

"What if the Valla makes an unjust decree?"

The Valla never makes an unjust decree. If the Valla decrees it, we adhere.

"That seems . . . overly simple. You don't have—criminals?"

Those who violate the decrees face punishment. Until you, I had never seen one face punishment yet evade the wrath of the Valla. In my life, no one had done it. You impressed many of us, perhaps Valla Kamė most of all. You out-thought the Valla. Because of this, she considers you dangerous. She keeps you here so she can watch you, and to keep you under her decrees. She intends to study you.

"Well, that's fine," said Logan. "I like it here."

I like you here.

His hand tightened on her arm, and she pressed against him harder.

"It's interesting that you never use the door," he said. "Something—we don't know what—came through the door a few moons ago and killed several of my people. This is why my people have come. They were afraid; they sent soldiers. The Sheth killed some of the soldiers. Some of our soldiers who survived told our leaders of the red mercury. The leaders sought me because I teach the ways of the Old Ones. The ones who believed in Valhalla. My leaders thought I would understand you. And now, here I am. In Valhalla."

You have a word that we do not. I find it hard to understand much of what you say. Explain 'am.'

"What?"

'Am.' We have no such word.

"'Am?' It's what things, uh, are," he stammered. "Am is . . . is."

Boy, that was great. Ph.D., huh?

He rallied his thoughts and tried again. "It refers to generalization. It's a word we use to describe the state of a thing at this particular moment."

I thought as much. A capture of the world in its stasis, a momentary examination. Flaws exist in this thinking, for all things fluctuate. You often say something 'is,' as if to capture it with a net or pin it under crystal for study.

Nothing 'is,' Logan Kai. Things only appear a certain way. In time, they will appear differently. Things never 'are,' and you must learn that things never 'were.' You, certainly, have no 'am.'

"Well, yes, but . . ."

To learn our language, you must think as we do. You must begin by removing from your mind the idea that anything 'is.' Observe the world in its motion. Revel in the knowledge that all things change before you, always have, and always shall.

"Son of a bitch," Logan grumbled. "I'm going to need more wine."

Am, again.

"I need more wine," he corrected.

She refilled his glass with the decanter and said, "E khole nik-hu."

She repeated it, pointing between him and the wine. It took him a few tries, and she corrected him on his pitch and delivery. There were several ways to say the phrase. The rise in pitch determined the strength of his need and could also determine the amount or even the strength of the wine. Pitch could also be used to downplay the "I," to politely ask on behalf of another who might not be in a position to ask; or to emphasize the "I," if, say, he wanted wine and no one else around him did.

"Your language is—your language reminds me of music," he corrected.

Your people have music?

"We have music. I would love to hear your music."

I will show you our music. But our music will mean nothing to you until you understand our language. Our language defines our music. First, I will teach you language. Then, music.

She led him over to the bed and laid him down on it, fluffed a pillow behind his neck, and put her hand on his forehead. With his next exhalation he was flying, soaring, lifting above the room and into the city, and he could hear their voices, hundreds of them—thousands of them—and the music of their words formed undertones of English in the back of his mind. He relaxed and let it wash over him, listening with Čer Aya's hand on his head, until he passed out.

"Shining One, arise," said Čer Aya. "You have much to do, today."

He opened his eyes to find her standing over him, nude, spectacular, smiling. Bejeweled and gilded and warmer than the sun.

He rolled over, reached beside the bed for his foot, and had a moment of panic when he couldn't find it.

"My leg," he said. "I need my foot. And the sleeve."

She handed him both, her smile broadening. "I cleaned them for you."

"Thank you. How long did I sleep?"

"Long enough, it seems. You have done well."

Logan swung himself upright and pulled on the sleeve. "I did well? Did well at what?"

"You speak our language already. This impresses me. You speak other languages from your world, yes? Did you learn them as easily?"

"I speak three languages fluently, and bits and pieces of several more. This increases my confusion. I don't understand how I can learn a language in one night. It took me years to learn other languages." And he truly didn't understand, because he was sure as shit speak-singing it, with the clicks and pops and musical inflections. He was slower at it than she was, but he didn't have to think about it. It rolled out as reflexively as if he'd spoken it for years. What was interesting was that he spoke Sentinel as deliberately as he spoke English, with the same northern Blackfeet weight to the syllables.

He didn't do that in French; he spoke rapid-fire French, polished French, and while his accent was still slightly American with a touch of Dutch from a close Belgian friend in the Legion, he spoke it so fast that French natives often mistook him for Spanish. He had to wonder what ghosts were loose in the darkened halls of his inner being to make him approach the Sentinels' language in his Blackfeet accent instead of his French one.

He hadn't been conscious for the lessons, which made it even more interesting, and he turned the concept around in his head.

It was fascinating, exploring what you were capable of in the absence of purpose.

"Your people would call it magic." Her word for magic here carried a dubious connotation; a miracle, an unexplained phenomenon. How he'd grasped the meaning in context was a head-scratcher—they were past syntax and semantics and clear into pragmatics, in one night!—but he knew a different Sentinel word for magic, too, a word English didn't have, a more literal term for the power itself, and he poked his brain for a bit until he dug it up: *Čyeen.*

A simple, common noun. There was nothing mystical or occult about the word, nothing fantastical or whimsical. Čyeen was a current the Sentinels tapped into, and some could do it more than others, apparently. Čyeen was the energy of the world. Medicine.

"Do you have Čyeen?" he asked her.

"All have Čyeen. Others have more control than I, but I have some."

"Can I learn Čyeen?"

"We will teach you. You must learn it, to live with us. Life here, without mastery of Čyeen, would present near-insurmountable difficulty. I do not teach Čyeen well. We will assign you a khosa Čyeen." A revered teacher of magic. Which, he had to admit, sounded cool as hell.

He wondered what his Blackfeet ancestors would think of him. Things come around.

"My people revered my mother's father's fathers as powerful sorcerers," he said. "Perhaps I can make them proud."

"I promise you, you already do," she said, and with a gentle hand, she helped him off the bed. "Valla Kamè sends for you."

"For me? What did I do, now?"

She handed him a formal silver robe with black knotwork along the edges, then a black overcloak with silver designs. Both were extremely soft and heavy, likely silk, and looked expensive. The black overcloak draped atop the silver so that both sets of designs were visible, and he had no doubt they told everyone who he was in all of this. Court wear. Much like what both Valla Kamè and Čer Aya had worn on their first meeting. Official raiment, though too small for him.

He needed to learn how to read their language, which was probably written into the hem. Learning to read would take far longer than learning to speak, he could feel it.

"You have done nothing wrong," she assured him, helping him with his belt, which seemed needlessly complex; he'd need to learn to tie a tie all over again. "Your warrior-mate has returned. With more soldiers."

Logan perked. "Abby?"

"Yes. Abè Shad-Hai returned, with two warriors. Valla Kamè will speak with them when you arrive. She needs you to translate."

"Will they face punishment?"

"They will explain themselves. Then the Valla will decide."

"I don't want responsibility for their punishment."

"You have no options. Valla Kamè will punish you, as well, should you disobey. The Valla brought you here, kept you here, for exactly this."

"Do you know—" who the two warriors are, nope, can't say are. Think in Sentinel, "—the identities of the two warriors accompanying Abè Shad-hai?" It hurt his brain.

"I do not. Valla Kamè did not make this information available to me. Do you require it?"

"I'll know them when I get there," he grumbled.

It was, as best he could figure, two miles to the edge of the forest where the great tunnels led into the rock, and it was probably a thousand stairs up to Valla Kamè's chamber. He understood why Čer Aya had such magnificent legs. She made this walk every day.

Čer Aya took her place along with the other Čers, high in the dais. Logan was also afforded a place on the dais, though much lower and nowhere near the Valla.

Logan figured he was what they'd been waiting for, because his heart leaped as a moment later Abby, Luke, and—holy shit—Bob Valentine were all shoved into the room by a contingent of guards. They looked a little rough. Bob, especially.

Logan had to wonder how long they'd been out there. Judging by the time that had elapsed, he estimated they'd returned nearly to the Arch before changing their minds. Afterwards, they'd have had to proceed slowly, low on water, expending minimal effort. It could have taken all night, easily.

"Logan!" Abby shouted. She tried to push past the guards to get to him, but they held her back at weapons-point: swords, daggers, spears.

"Abby?" Logan called across the room. "Why are you here?"

"We're on your side on this," Bob replied. "We came to help you. To help them."

"That's right," she said. "Bob told us what you're up to. We want in."

"This was my screwup," said Logan. "I'll fix it. I told them that soldiers were coming to get the red mercury. They probably thought you were them. I'll straighten it out."

The Sentinels separated them, with several guards on each. One took Bob's saxe, which Logan found interesting, because they ignored the rifles and pistols.

"Tell us why you have our weapon," asked a Čer, which surprised Logan. He'd only ever heard Valla Kamè speak. "This weapon belonged to a great warrior of our people who disappeared the last pass of the moon."

Logan stared at her for a long time before he realized they intended him to translate; he could understand them, but Abby, Luke, and Bob couldn't.

"They want to know how you got the sword," Logan said. "It belonged to a great warrior of theirs, who disappeared." He noted that each of them had a Sentinel in personal contact. This was a test; the Sentinels wanted to see how truthfully he'd translate. He pretended not to notice.

"You speak their language?" asked Abby.

"Long story," said Logan.

"How long has it been?"

"A few days. They have, um, ways. Abby, please."

"Your soldiers attacked us," said Abby, addressing the Valla. She was trained to work with translators, and knew to speak to the speaker, not the translator. The deference would make it easier. "We defended ourselves. We brought their weapons back for study."

"What did you learn?" asked Valla Kamè. No anger, no

resentment, no punishment. She was much more interested in what her opponents knew. Logan found this fascinating.

"Logan can answer that question better than I can," said Abby.

"Logan cannot answer the question," Logan translated, which was weird, referring to himself in third person. "You must answer."

"Bob?" asked Abby, deferring. "What did we learn?"

Valentine spoke. "Your metallurgy sucks. We make stairs out of better steel than your weapons."

Logan translated. Murmurs broke out among the Čers.

Bob motioned toward a sword at a Sentinel's belt and mimed drawing it. The Sentinel looked to the Valla, received a nod, and drew the weapon.

Bob drew a fighting knife, the same type he would have attached to a rifle had he one, and held it in the flat of his hand, unthreatening. He put his sunglasses on, and through miming, instructed the Sentinel to hold the sword upright and demonstrated that he was going to strike the sword with the edge of the knife.

He struck the sword with the edge of the knife.

Logan would probably never cease to be amazed at the big man's body mechanics. The blow was beautiful, feet planted, hips twisting, three hundred pounds of mass and incalculable torque channeling into the end of one meaty arm. He could have been a heavyweight boxer showing off for a camera crew before a fight, knocking a heavy bag horizontal.

The blow staggered the Sentinel, who was probably half Bob's mass, even in armor. The soldier recovered, and when he looked at his sword, he gasped audibly.

Daylight was visible through the blade, even from the dais. The weapon was ruined, bent at the point of impact where the knife had cut a half-inch gash through the mild steel.

Bob pushed his glasses up on his forehead and showed the Sentinel the knife, which had a single, hair-thin chip in the edge of the blade. He offered it to the soldier. "Professor Logan, please let him know I'm giving him this weapon in exchange for his. I give it to him as a blessing and ask his forgiveness."

The soldier accepted it.

"Let them know their armor is useless against our weapons," Bob said. "And there's an army coming with much greater weapons than this little knife."

"I think they got that part," said Logan, but told the Valla anyway.

"Do you have these greater weapons with you?" asked the Valla, which surprised Logan again.

The three looked back and forth. "Absolutely," said Abby.

It had taken hours, and the sun was straight overhead and feeling heavy.

Logan had changed back into camouflage and his ballistic helmet. He was going down into the valley, and seriously, he thought, fuck this place. It's hot, it's full of monsters, women shoot at you. He'd set up a Sentinel helmet on a rock on one of the large wedges of stone roughly a hundred meters from the front gates of the Citadel, and a second Sentinel helmet on a rock another two hundred meters or so past that.

Logan peered back through the binoculars at a cluster of Sentinels around Abby, two hundred meters back, who had set up the Lapua on its bipod at the edge of the cliff. Two Sentinel soldiers waited with him.

A hundred yards, he knew, was bullshit; he could hit it with iron sights. Even six hundred, for Abby, would be nothing. This would impress the hell out of the Sentinels, but it wouldn't give away the extent of their capabilities. It was a good test.

He got the thumbs-up and told the Sentinels with him to take cover behind the rock.

The explosion of the .338 slammed through the valley, then once again. A full two seconds later, he heard the helmet hit the ground. He gave it another moment before coming out.

The helmet lay in the sand a good ten meters from its resting place, dented and torn; the iron had ripped apart like cardboard.

He tossed it to one of the Sentinels, who showed it to his comrades, and they went to look for the hundred-meter target as the Sentinels passed it back and forth.

They couldn't find the helmet at the hundred-meter mark. There was a depression in the rock where Logan had set it, nothing more. The bullet had carried four thousand pound-feet of force. The helmet had likely come apart like a grenade.

"It no longer exists," said Logan, by way of explanation. "The weapon destroyed the helmet. Entirely."

"Had I worn the helmet, I would no longer exist," said the Sentinel. "It would destroy me. Entirely."

"It would," agreed Logan.

Nothing else was said as they slogged up the lava tube.

XV

AND TWO FOR FLINCHING

Qui court deux lievres a la fois, n'en prend aucun:
tr. "Who runs after two hares at the same time, catches none."
— French proverb

Stannard mopped his brow with his shemagh. The sun hit like a freight train.

A half-team of Det Four SEALs, five operators, trudged behind him, every bit as miserable as he was, every bit as badass, gutting it out one step at a time. Doing the SEAL thing, as SEALs do.

This shit wasn't hard to figure. Logan, Easton, Foster, and Valentine had to have gone to the Citadel. There was nothing else around here, no place else to go. The Citadel had civilization, therefore it had water.

Aid and comfort from the enemy.

He had a plan for those fuckers.

One of his weapons men, Rodriguez, carried a Carl Gustaf, a man-portable 84-millimeter rocket launcher, atop his pack. If the Farts so much as raised an eyebrow, the team had eight high explosive rounds between them, each one a small bomb weighing over six pounds, enough to knock the whole fucking castle down, which would be the end of Logan, Easton, that goddamn queer Marine and the other idiot professor with them.

What the hell kind of gay-ass college-boy circus was that dipshit running, anyway? Where did he think he was gonna go? There was only one place to go. All Stannard had to do was get there and fuck shit up, which is what he did best.

The Shits, the giant invisible monsters, were less of a concern; the team had four flechette rounds for the Carl Gustaf, each of which would turn everything in a hundred-foot radius into spaghetti, and he didn't care if the Shits were invisible or not, Ol' Carl had a thermal sight. You can't hide heat.

Each round was more weight on top of their already considerable loads, and in this heat, it mattered more than it had probably ever mattered. This was the first thing he'd been through in sixteen years that had been as taxing as his initial SEAL training. The whole point of BUD/S was an experience so violently, soul-crushingly awful that anything you experienced in the real world of warfare would pale in comparison.

This was miserable. But then, he was good at being miserable. Being miserable pissed him off, and being pissed off energized him. That energy propelled him into more misery, around and around until it snowballed. Eventually, a few miles from here, he'd get to kill some motherfuckers, and that would make him feel better.

It was possible, too, that they'd catch them all before they got to the Citadel, and that would be far beyond enjoyable. Logan, Easton, and Foster were traveling with the fat guy, so it wasn't like they were doing sniper shit or even moving fast. They were probably deadheading to the Farts, and nobody could move faster than a SEAL team. The squad they were chasing were a lot of things— shooter, officer, French commando, Marine—but they weren't SEALs. They wouldn't—couldn't—tough it out down here. Not like SEALs could.

The greatest thing about this op was that he was in new territory, and the Laws of War applied even less here than they had in his past few wars. He laughed at the idea; it wasn't like the Farts were signatories to any goddamn treaty in the first place. Anything was fair play, and that included treatment of traitors, and oh, man, he'd let the team spend a few quality hours with them all before they buried them out here. His boys had done far more, for far less egregious transgressions, and Decker hadn't cared, then, either—

A thunderclap blew through the canyon. A heavy rifle shot, clearly .30 caliber. Several klicks away, but unmistakable.

Another, separated by the space of a bolt-throw.

Easton, engaging targets.

Speak of the devil.

"I got 'em, Master Chief," a voice said in his ear. "Bearing, I make it zero-one-zero. Given the distance of those shots, I'm betting they're hunkered down near the objective."

They waited.

There was no third report.

As good as she was, and he had to admit she was good, he was surprised there'd been a second.

So, they are doing sniper shit. Well, okay, then.

"Come on, motherfuckers," Stannard barked. "You know what to do."

Logan's team stood atop the mesa outside the Citadel, slowly melting in the heat, while Valla Kamè examined the destroyed helmet.

"Your weapon did this?" she asked.

"Yes," said Logan. He cycled the action on his HK, ejecting a round, catching it in midair. He snapped out a multitool and, with a few seconds of work, pulled the bullet out of the cartridge. He showed it to her, then handed her the bullet. Soldiers gathered to see.

This small tube"—he held up the rest of the round—"contains explosives." He dumped the powder into his gloved hand. "An explosion drives that small piece, called a *bullet,* through the weapon. The longest tube on the weapon directs the bullet. Our army trains us to direct the bullet over great distances."

"Over how great a distance can *bullet* kill?" asked Valla Kamè.

Logan decided to make it simple. "As far as I can see."

"You did not show us this. When you first showed us 'soldier,' at the breaking of your decree before me, when you fought our soldier. You did not show us this."

"I didn't see the necessity. It would kill your soldier to demonstrate it, and I had no intention of doing so. I came in peace."

"As it appears," said Valla Kamè, which might have been the nicest thing she'd said to him. "Will you train us to use the bullet?"

"It can take years."

"We have years."

"Each bullet will only survive one use. We would need to use what few bullets we have, in order to train your soldiers. Then, they would have no bullets to fight with. Without bullets, our weapons become mere clubs."

"Hey, Professor?" Luke interrupted. He had his spotting scope out, still, and was peering down into the eyepiece.

"Yes?"

"We got company. Three klicks."

Abby posted up behind the rifle and scanned the valley at twenty-four times magnification. Luke's rig had three times the zoom. "I don't see—"

"Dead ahead, coming down the middle of the valley. You'll see it."

"Oh, Christ," she groaned. "Really?"

"Yeah," said Luke. "They popped smoke."

"Oh my God. They are idiots."

He chuckled. "They probably heard those shots and thought you were shooting at them."

"Like I'd shoot twice."

"Well, they're SEALs. Counter sniper playbook, step one: smoke."

"Logan," Abby called.

Logan excused himself and hurried over.

"SEALs? You're sure?" he asked.

"They didn't come to talk," Abby said. "They wouldn't have popped smoke unless they viewed us as hostile."

"Pretty sure it's a heavy-weapons team," Luke said. "That'll be SEALs. For a moment I could see the back of one of 'em. The guy had a tube on his back, that's gonna be a Carl Gustaf."

"Not familiar with that one," Logan admitted.

"Eighty-four-millimeter reusable recoilless rifle," said Abby. "That thing could bring this whole place down on top of us."

"If they laser-sight us, they can hit from two grand," said Luke. "They'll be in range in fifteen minutes. That is, if they nut up and move again."

"I can take that weapon out from a thousand meters," said Abby, "but I can't hit it at two. I can get a round out there at two, though. I might even hit one of 'em at twenty-five if they'll hold still, but I can't promise I'll hit the tube and wreck it outside of a grand."

"Can you keep them pinned down?" Logan asked.

"I've got a hundred and seventy-six rounds left. I can spare a few."

"Luke?"

"What, shoot all the way out there? I've got the same piece you do, sir. These HK's are rated to six hundred, I might be able to hit at seven-fifty. Sure, I can get a round out to a grand. Shit, technically, I can lob one out to two grand, but it's not going to hit anything. At a thousand yards, a five-five-six drops nearly forty feet, and with these short barrels, it'll start to tumble way before that. When it gets there, it'll have the kinetic energy of a ping-pong ball."

"What's your drop at two grand?"

"Two klicks with a five-five-six?" He blew out a laugh. "I've never—I've never asked. A hundred feet, probably. But we don't know the air density, here, the gravity's different. At two klicks you have to factor in the curvature of the Earth, plus the Coriolis effect— what freaking hemisphere are we in? How fast does this planet spin? How big is it?"

Logan grunted. "What are the odds those guys know this?"

"Stannard can't even spell Coriolis," said Abby.

"Abby, we know you're at least within a minute of angle at two hundred meters, that's where the helmet was, right? It's what, a foot across? Two inches in any direction at two hundred meters?"

"More than that," said Luke, "she barely hit at two hundred meters. It was low, like, way low. For her."

"It's hitting at more than double this rifle's MOA on Earth, maybe even triple, but we can work with that," said Abby.

"Okay. So, we need to get you within, what, six hundred meters of them, before they get within two thousand meters of us," said Logan. "That's how this has to work."

"We can get there, but we need our Ghillies and we need to move, right now," Abby judged. "We'll be ahead of them by a couple of minutes."

"Okay," said Logan. "Make it happen. We'll draw 'em out if we can. Bob, you're with me."

Stannard rested on one knee in the shade of a pile of rocks. "Gotta wonder what the fuck she's doing," he grumbled. "Does she have us bracketed? Were they engaging enemies a minute ago? Why two shots? Why no more?"

"Maybe she shot both their dumb asses and she and the faggot are on their way back," suggested Smith, another of his weapons men. This team was almost entirely weapons men, with one medic.

"You know, I could actually see that," Stannard admitted.

"Master Chief, you don't think they were engaging Det One, do you?"

"We'd hear return fire," Stannard said, peering out around the rocks. "Let's sit here for a minute and see what they do next."

"We need to find an approach," said Smith, such a fundamental observation that Stannard rolled his eyes. "Right? We popped smoke, we got cover, now we locate and rush."

"Correct," Stannard said.

"Well, let's locate her."

"How the hell we gonna do that?"

"Wait till she shoots again," said Smith.

"And how the hell we gonna do that?" he repeated. "Go on. Tell me the next piece of your plan, Smith."

"I . . . I dunno, sir."

"When you do, let me know. Until then, we're gonna fuckin' wait. I'm not sending any of you assholes out there with a sniper sitting on top of us."

"She ain't a sniper. She's a goddamn 'target interdiction specialist.' How good can she be? She's Air Force."

"Better than you guys," Stannard grumbled, hating the words as they left his mouth.

"The only way to find out where she is, is to send somebody out there and get her to take another shot," said Smith. "I'll go."

"No, you won't," said Stannard. "Let's see what she does."

"You want me to throw more smoke?" asked Smith.

"Not till she shoots."

"She won't shoot till we stand up, though," said Smith, visibly confused.

"Right. We're gonna sit here for a while. Jesus Christ, warrior. Know when to take a fuckin' break when it's offered to you. I thought I trained you better than that." He keyed his mic. "Everybody chill. Hydrate."

Logan led the team down the hillside as quickly as he could manage. A small pack on his back held bottles of water and the bladder from his large ruck. Behind him, Bob carried only water in his pack, his hat finally done up like a bull rider the way Logan had recommended.

The Sentinels had outfitted the big man with a Sheth helmet that hung off his pack, ridiculously massive and padded to fit him, and a Sentinel roundshield. The Sentinel soldiers, in shirts of mail and leather outer layers, jingled and banged although they were far lighter on their feet than Bob. Logan was sure they'd bring the entire SEAL team's firepower to bear on all of them and that would be that.

They slipped, slid, and skidded down the hill. The Sentinels, even in armor, were sure-footed and nimble in a way that Bob sure as hell wasn't.

Logan, on his blade, HK on his shoulder by the carabiner on the packstrap, wasn't doing much better. He didn't have the moves anymore; not like he'd had fifteen years ago.

Bob chugged Gatorade, cold packs tied to the back of his neck with a shemagh.

"You gonna be okay, big guy?"

"I got this," Bob gasped.

"Don't you die on me out here," Logan warned.

The final approach was going to be heinous, and he motioned everyone down behind an enormous tower of rocks. They were a hundred meters out, still a long run in armor in this heat. He was stunned the SEALs hadn't heard them.

Come on, Abby. Come on.

As if on cue, the Lapua roared through the valley, terrifyingly close. The shockwave was tangible; the Sentinels flinched. The only thing Logan could liken it to was a fire engine rumbling past. It jangled the nerves and broke him out in prickles of terrified sweat.

Logan counted the seconds, five, six, and like clockwork, yellow smoke wove and puffed into the air behind a haystack-sized rock, joined moments later by red smoke, the colors mingling and clotting among a group of rocks exactly big enough to hide a small unit.

The smoke thickened and settled. The SEALs were moving.

Logan sprinted, crossing the gap as fast as he could, and leaped atop a coffin-sized boulder as he broke through the smoke and there they were, four, five, six bearded assholes, Stannard among them barking orders in the haze. There was a moment of shock on the big SEAL's face as he looked Logan's way, shoved his men aside, and brought his carbine up but far, far too slow.

Logan smiled as he held the red dot of the holographic sight on Stannard's chest, center mass, and squeezed the trigger.

Stannard hit the ground, the horsekick of the round knocking him limp as the world erupted in automatic weapons fire. Someone grabbed the drag handle on his plate carrier and pulled him to cover. Mark 46s rained brass and fire in every direction.

Smith tore at Stannard's gear. "And here I was pissed at you for making us wear plates in this shit, boss," he said as the firing died down. "You okay?"

"Return fire, goddammit. Kill that fucker. And throw more

smoke!" he shouted as Smith stood up and racked the bolt on his weapon back. "*She's* still up there!"

The team had fanned out three-sixty, and Stannard had gone to one knee watching their three o'clock from behind a good-sized boulder. Haze loomed in all directions, red, purple, yellow, rainbowed like one of Paulsen's goddamn prize teams.

Smoke worked both ways. Easton and her spotter sure as hell couldn't see them, but he had no idea where Logan was. He could be strawberry jam on the other side of a rock twenty meters away, or he could be running for elevation to get a bracketing solution without a scratch on him.

They peered through the haze, eyes above the stones or peeking around corners. Stannard flipped his thermal imager in front of his optic and put the rifle on top of the boulder he was sheltering behind, but it was so hot down here that everything shone pretty much the same color. Logan would be a shadow, if he could see him at all. Under the stresses of combat, his body temperature was going to be right about the ambient air temperature.

He flicked it off again. As it blinked out, he saw a shadow in the white blur of the thermal.

He turned it on. Nothing.

He turned it off, and the shadow reappeared as the images faded.

There was something straight ahead, behind the smoke.

He clicked the scope on and off, and got another momentary image of it in the flash of orange. A shroud of pink heat, registering last as the image died. Bipedal, round, big.

"Valentine?" Stannard shouted into the murk. His voice was pained, his chest on fire from the impact of Logan's round. "I see you, fat boy! Don't you move!"

A 5.56 rang out off to his right, a crisp, loud tenor compared to the expected .338 that had to be coming again at some point. A yell, a crash of equipment, a grunt of pain.

"Man down! Fuck!" someone shouted.

He fired three rounds in the general direction of what had to be Dr. Valentine, and tried his thermal again: on, off. Nothing this time.

Whatever it was, it was gone.

"Corpsman!" came the shout again. "Fuck! He's hit in the face! Hurry up!"

Sullivan, their corpsman, raced from cover, and fragments of meat and gore sprayed from his chest as if fed through a wood chipper. The .338 boomed across the world.

Ted Sullivan skidded in the dust, carried on only by momentum, and stopped on his side, leaking, his eyes still open.

Stannard hunkered down behind the rock. The smoke was thinning.

He keyed his mic.

"Gustaf," he said.

Logan grinned as he heard the shouts for a Corpsman, a Navy medic. They were SEALs, all right, definitely Stannard's boys, and they were hurting. And that was good. He'd plunked Stannard, although he swore he heard the redneck asshole berating Valentine—did they bring armor?

Armor wouldn't have mattered for the guy with the belt-fed rig who'd been dumb enough to rest it atop hard cover instead of firing around the side, though. A rookie mistake; the kind of thing a kid playing paintball should have known not to do.

These guys were a lot of things—brave, tough, heavily armed—but they weren't infantry.

They were calling for a medic, which Logan thought was ridiculous. He was pretty sure he'd hit the guy right through the eye, or slightly under it. Anything his body was doing at this point would be nothing more than electrical impulses searching for purchase.

Abby's rifle rang out like an earthquake, and he could tell by the sounds that followed—sheer panic, the collapse of someone in heavy gear, shouts—that she had a firing solution; some confluence of the smoke density and angle, likely an opening of a half-second or less judging by the rainbow billows settling into brownish fog. It wasn't much, but it was enough for her, apparently.

She was scary good.

Okay. Let's twist the knife.

"Stannard!" Logan shouted. "You wanna talk this out, buddy?"

A moment passed, and he knew they were looking for him.

"Professor, give up, now!" came the reply. "We can work this out!"

"Yeah, right," Logan called back. "The way I got this figured, you're down, what, two guys, now? And I'm pretty sure that was your medic. How's your chest, bud?"

No answer.

"I'm asking because that looked like it really hurt," Logan added.

"Fuck you, man!"

Logan's tone turned serious—a Warrant Officer addressing a senior NCO and letting him know exactly how things were, like it or not. "We have you from an elevation. You're gonna run out of smoke, brother, and she'll see you eventually. In the meantime, if you bust that hide, I'm gonna put a round right up your ass."

Silence.

"You can't move," Logan called. "Checkmate. Lay 'em down and come out with your hands on your head."

"Hey, Tonto?" Stannard said.

"Yeah?" Logan shouted around the pile of rocks.

"Fuck you."

Logan heard the rocket lighting up before it went off and threw himself flat. The backblast sent up a fresh cloud of smoke behind the rocks, and Logan looked up from his belly, hands interlaced on his head, and felt his heart fall into the center of the world as the rocket screamed toward the Citadel.

They waited for the impact. It would be enough to knock the damned thing down, and they all knew it.

The problem was, Rodriguez couldn't get a laser through the smoke. He had been aiming, literally, by compass.

They kept waiting.

They couldn't know it, because they couldn't see it, but the round went wide, missing the tower by fifty yards to the left.

The rocket kept its heading for another mile and a half, in a parabolic trajectory high over the waste desert of the Eastern Freehold, where it finally ran out of steam and fell out of the sky. When it landed, it pulverized a rock quarry, blowing open a new seam of prized black and gold marble and eventually making a down-on-his-luck quarryman who'd bought the rights to the place for little more than a handshake ridiculously wealthy.

For literally everybody else on the planet, however, it was a non-event.

"You wanna try that again?" Logan needled. "Pretty sure you missed."

"God, I fuckin' hate that guy," Stannard seethed. "Reload, goddammit."

"Sir," said Rodriguez, the weapons man with the Gustav, "there's no way we can—"

"I don't give a fuck. Use the flechettes this time and aim low. The goddamn Farts are up there right now fuckin' cheering him on, so clear the goddamn decks."

"Sir, the Law of Armed Conflict says we—"

"Do I look like I give a fuck about the Law of Armed Conflict?"

"Sir, we—"

"We're gonna destroy those assholes. And when he sees it, he's gonna fuckin' cry and wring his soft little hands and ask us to be nice to everyone, and he's gonna quit when he sees we'll do it again, because he's a goddamn liberal Frenchie pussy faggot hippie college boy. And then, when we have his team, we're gonna roast his balls over an open fire and watch that goddamn sniper eat 'em. And after that, we'll start getting creative."

"Sir, I—"

"You think we're fuckin' around, Rodriguez? If you don't want to be part of this, give me that weapon and go over there and put your gun in your mouth. I don't have time for your weepy Law of War shit. I got a war to fight, and *it ain't got no fuckin' laws.* Do your job, or go kill yourself."

Rodriguez was about to rebut when he fell back with a spear through his face.

The Sentinels, led by Bob Valentine, charged through the smoke, ululating and shrieking. The SEALs racked bolts and brought weapons to bear. 46's chattered and armored bodies fell, but only on one side of what was clearly a chevron; Stannard had a glimpse of swords and shields and the split-second thought that these guys were apeshit crazy, they were attacking a goddamn SEAL team with hand weapons. As he brought his rifle up, a monster in a fanged, painted helmet plowed into him like an enraged buffalo, and the last thing he saw was the rim of a shield driving his weapon to the side and blotting out the world.

Stannard snapped awake to a horrific smell. His first thought was gas, and he spasmed, wondering where his pack was. His mask was in it.

"Hi," Logan said. He tossed an ammonia packet into the dust.

Stannard rose to one elbow. He shook his head, rubbed at his nose. His hand came away with crusted blood. He had memories of being dragged, being carried, being beaten.

They were somewhere high, looking down on the valley. He needed water. "My team," he said.

Logan stood and stepped back. "Not so much."

Stannard looked around, saw the Citadel, the knights, the crazy little dark-skinned Farts in their weird-ass wizard robes. Of course, they were Black. How could they be anything else? It all made sense to him on some cosmic level, this guy standing up for his little brown brothers. "What happens now?"

"I don't know," said Logan. "Abby's coming. She'll probably want a word. Is Decker behind you somewhere? Are we doing this all over again? Because this is gonna get old real fast."

"Decker—" Stannard cut himself off with a laugh. "You dumb bastard. You think I'm the only one here? We know where the red mercury is. Decker's getting it right now. Kill me, bitch. You still lose."

Logan sighed, breathing profanities. "Tell me he's not in the tunnels," he pleaded.

"Die mad, pussy."

The Farts, and there were a lot of them, wanted to know what was happening. They spoke to each other in singsong tones, a language Stannard didn't know. It sounded like music.

Logan sang back to them.

Where the fuck had he learned their language? How long had he been over here?

Outclassed.

"They say you can't go in there," Logan told Stannard. "No one goes in there."

"Fuckin' Frenchie, man. There's a reason you assholes have lost every war you've ever fought. You got no balls."

"I need you to understand something, Sean," said Logan. Stannard recoiled at use of his first name. "Master Chief Petty Officer," Logan corrected himself, "excuse me. Whatever these people decide to do to you, it's out of my hands. You tried to destroy their home. They're pretty upset with you. Also, you had a flechette round in the recoilless. What was your thinking? Just indiscriminately kill anyone standing around up here? Civilians? Really?"

"I don't give a fuck."

"You might wish you had," Logan suggested. "Because I explained to them what it is, what it does. What you were trying to do. What happens next, here, is not me. My hands are clean. My ledger's balanced."

"Fuck," Stannard enunciated, "you."

"No," said Abby, stepping into view past the line of Sentinels with Luke behind her. "Fuck you, Sean."

She handed her rifle to Logan. Stannard was amazed at how naturally the skeletonized weapon melded into Logan's hands. From the easy way he held it, he looked like he'd built the damned thing. There was a lot about the Professor that he hadn't been told. Likely a lot Paulsen didn't even know.

For the first time in a long time, Stannard was worried. He'd figured he'd walk away from this, but now he knew the Professor was playing this game at an entire other level, and had been, the whole time.

"I was going to give you a message to send back to Decker," she said, "but they're telling me you won't get the opportunity. I'm sorry it has to end this way."

"What the fuck," Stannard growled. "You're gonna kill me? You, Major?"

"Not me," said Abby. "I had my chance."

"Yeah, and I shot you once already," added Logan. "Figure I'll let someone else have the privilege. And for the record, it was Doctor Valentine who put your lights out, and who ventilated your heavy weapons man."

"You're an asshole," said Stannard.

"I figured you wanted to keep score," said Logan. "I know I do."

Several of the aliens, the Farts, he couldn't even remember their actual name now, came through the line of soldiers. These were small women, mostly, with a couple of taller, effeminate men, also in dresses, all of them Black. Not even Black. He didn't know what the hell they were.

These who approached were more important than the others. More soldiers accompanied them, and they walked with ponderous weight, the weight of leadership. Everyone waited for them.

The most important, clearly, was an older, taller woman, flanked by younger women in revealing dresses with stunning silver- and gold-tattooed tits. He got an inkling of what Logan saw in them. He wondered how many of them Logan was fucking.

There seemed to be an argument between Logan and the important woman. Another, a woman so stunning he gasped at first sight of her, appeared to know Logan. Angelic, jet-black, alien, she was the most gorgeous thing he'd ever seen—fragile and innocent, powerful and terrifying. She kept putting her hands on Logan, hanging on him. She pleaded with him.

Oh, yeah. Logan was definitely banging her.

One of the soldiers handed Logan a sword.

Logan took it and spoke with the older woman again at length. She grew increasingly stern, and finally raised her voice and gave Logan a direct order. The young female alien stepped away from him.

Logan turned to Stannard.

"Sucks to be you," he said.

"Here's the deal," Logan said, looking down at the sword in his hand.

Stannard squirmed, which Logan found interesting; he hadn't taken him for the kind of man who'd squirm at this particular moment.

"They need me to prove my loyalty," Logan said. "They're still unsure about me. About us. They think this whole thing might be some kind of elaborate ruse. Frankly, I don't think they trust anyone who has the kind of weaponry we have. And, really, I can't blame them. So, I need to kill you. Sorry."

"Really?"

"Yeah. Get up. Die on your feet."

Stannard stood with some effort. "Sure."

Logan stayed well out of reach, the sword not quite at the ready, but ready enough. Stannard gave him space.

Logan motioned to Stannard with the blade. "If you weren't such a racist asshole, you'd have gone further than tattooing those runes on your arm. You'd have learned the history of those people. And you'd be losing your shit right now."

"What? Why?"

"There's a reason I called these people the *Svartálfar* in my report. *Svartálfar* is the ancient Norse word for the Dark Elves of the next world. You could have known that."

"So?"

"This woman behind me, the one who wants you dead, is their queen. She's called the *Valla.*"

"Like. I. Give. A. *Fuck.*"

"You will," Logan promised. "Stick with me. You're gonna love how this ends. The nations here are ruled by *Vallas.* Kings, queens. Regents. You know what they call this world? Three guesses."

"Fuck. You."

"Vallala," said Logan. Abby gasped behind him, and Logan saw Bob shrug to Luke.

"*W-what?*" Stannard stuttered. "What?"

"'Land of the Vallas.'"

He let it sink in.

"You incredible dipshit," Logan said, shaking his head as Stannard sputtered. "You made it to Valhalla and didn't even know it. All you could think to do was destroy it when you got here. And now, you're going to die here. So, any last words, brother?"

Stannard blew out a spiteful laugh. "I'm not your brother."

"That's it?" Logan asked, his tone surprised. "After all that, all this"—he gestured around them—"you're ending on the racist thing?"

"You're not gonna kill me," Stannard said simply. "You're bluffing."

"Am I."

"You're weak," Stannard badgered. "This is where you grant me mercy, so you look like the good guy to them. Go ahead, you French faggot. Cut me loose. Be the good guy. Win hearts and minds. Let 'em suck all your dicks tonight. Enjoy it while it lasts, 'cuz I'm gonna come back here with artillery and a full platoon of SEALs. I will burn this place to the fuckin' ground and there's nothing you can do about it."

There was nothing for Logan to say.

"You're fucked, now, aren't you?" Stannard guessed. "That was your only move. What're you gonna do? You're gonna be the bad guy all of a sudden? Kill me in front of everybody and ruin your rep with your new friends? Fuckin' Valhalla? Really? Bull-*shit.* Fuck you, man. I don't know what the fuck these things are, but Valhalla is run by men. By *white men.*"

Logan didn't know much about swords. He stepped in and aimed for Stannard's neck, hoping to take the head off in one blow the way Bob had done with the Sheth. He swung it hard.

Stannard got one hand up to block it, purely reflexively, and the sword took most of it off.

"YOU GODDAMN MOTHERFUCKER MY FUCKIN' HAND!!"

Logan recovered, wincing and swearing under his breath, and threw it again, harder, and Stannard ducked but not far enough. The top of his skull came off above the temples. Purple blood and pink-gray gunk vomited out as he collapsed backwards, convulsing.

Abby, Luke, and Bob fell in behind Logan. Several soldiers dragged Stannard's corpse away while it was still leaking into the dust.

"Yuck," Logan observed.

Valla Kamè, the Čers, and the palace guard faded back into the Citadel.

"Feel better?" Abby asked Logan.

Logan asked himself the same thing.

"I sure thought I would," he admitted.

Abby and Logan sipped wine on either side of a firepit at Logan's home. Logan had changed into Sentinel robes, and Abby had cleaned up at her new house and put on a fresh uniform, as it would be a few days before they'd be able to make anything in her size.

"You've killed people before," Abby guessed.

"Not like that," said Logan. "That was bad."

Luke was settling into his own place nearby. Bob had been invited to some kind of victory party with the Sentinels he'd fought beside, who were apparently an elite troupe and had welcomed him as one of their own.

"Look, he had it coming," said Abby. The wine was some hillbilly homebrew with the kick of spiked punch, almost sangria. It tasted like college.

"Oh, I'm not denying that," said Logan.

"Hey, did you mean that, about Valhalla? What you said to Stannard?"

He poured more wine. "Yes and no. This isn't the Valhalla he thinks of, of course. This is not the afterlife where we drink and fight and fuck and never die."

"Shame, really."

"I don't disagree. That said, it would explain a lot if one of these Arches had opened up to Scandinavia in the Dark Ages. Explorations of this world are likely where a lot of our Norse lore comes from."

"Do you really think that?"

"One hundred percent."

"Huh."

"Mostly, though, I wanted that racist fuck to die feeling stupid. That, I've got to admit, felt pretty good."

They watched the fire.

"Do you know how lucky you are?" he finally said. "Initially, they were going to kill you three. If Stannard hadn't come along right then—brilliant misdirection by Bob, by the way, the whole rifle thing—God, that would've been it. I'd have had to kill you, not Stannard."

"Fat chance. I'd beat the shit out of you."

"I don't doubt that. I've seen you with your shirt off."

She smiled over the rim of her cup. Her gaze lingered.

"Well, we're in it, now, aren't we, Professor?" she asked. "I didn't expect to go full Native, but here we are. Oh, God," she said, covering her mouth. "No offense."

"No, I get the reference," he said. "It's cool. I don't really take offense at Indian . . . well, sometimes."

"I mean, we live here, now," she said. "So, how does this work? What do we do for money? What do we do for jobs? I don't know anything about this place. How do we live?"

"This is a collective, as best I can gather it," said Logan. "They don't have an industry, as I understand it, but the Valla has some source of vast wealth that keeps this place running. Somebody makes these houses. Somebody makes wine. Somebody delivers the firewood. Hell if I know. You, me, Bob, Luke, we're advisors to the Valla now. Think of us as court-appointed royalty. I mean, as houses go around here, ours are very nice."

"This is very nice," she agreed. "So is mine."

"We appear to have a significant social standing. We're above the day-to-day necessities, we have bigger fish to fry. I don't have to know where the firewood comes from, because someone brings it to me every day. I think we'll be okay."

"So, you're one of them now, I guess. I guess we all are."

He shrugged. "I wouldn't go that far."

She sputtered for a moment, clenching and unclenching a fist beside her face. "That's the thing about you that makes me crazy. You know that? You've been doing it since I met you. Since the first meeting, with Decker and Paulsen. The moment someone tries to put you in a box, you fight it. Like no one I've ever seen. You don't identify as American, but you say you don't consider yourself French. You identify as American Indian, and I get that, but do you, really? Or only when you want justification for pissing people off?"

Logan ground his teeth.

"Call you a soldier, you'll go to the ends of the Earth to prove you're an intellectual. Call you an intellectual, you'll go do some kind of hooah, Operator, tough-bubba shit. Every time someone tries to pigeonhole you, you bounce off it. You're a human pinball. It must be exhausting."

"Identity issues are tearing our country apart," Logan assessed.

"Identity issues are the only thing holding some of us together."

"And look what it gets you," Logan said. "Every member of your team who's in some shit right now is in it because of who, or what, they identify as."

"That's part of it, though, isn't it? You choose your path. You choose your people. And you stick with them. 'The strength of the wolf is the pack. The strength of the pack is the wolf.'"

A moment passed.

"You know what's funny," Logan said. "My mother wasn't Blackfeet. Not legally. She was half Blackfeet, illegitimate, denied enrollment. Her father's family fought it all the way till the day she died."

"How the hell—"

"Long story, but a Blackfeet guy had a thing with my grandmother, who was white, and he died in a car accident right after she learned she was pregnant. She shacked up with some other guy, another white guy, to have her kid. That kid, half-Blackfeet, was my mom. My biological grandfather's family—my mother's biological dad's family—is basically royalty among the Blackfeet, powerful medicine going back a thousand years. They wouldn't stand for it. Wouldn't let the tribe enroll her, or us."

"But you grew up Indian?"

"Did I ever. I'm fluent in Blackfeet, for God's sake. I got all the trappings: powwows, rodeos, sweat lodges, government cheese. As a bonus, I got the shit kicked out of me every day for being part white.

"The fun part of this is, *I'm* illegitimate, like my mother. My biological father was some guy my mother knew in college. Never met him. My stepdad, who raised me, was Blackfeet. *His* name was Shines-at-Night. My last name growing up was Taylor."

"What?"

"Taylor," he repeated. "My mother's legal name. I changed it in the Legion."

She blinked at him a couple of times. "How do you keep this straight?"

"Hey, you wanted to talk about identity issues. Anyway, it all came together with my school records. When I returned to the States after changing my name in the Legion, I had to change my name legally to the new name on my French passport, and then show that paperwork, in order for any university here in America to accept my work at the Sorbonne."

"You are officially the most interesting person I've ever met. And in this line of work, that's saying something."

"Thanks, I think. But yeah, you're right. I don't identify. The one thing I've ever wanted to identify with in my life—being Blackfeet—fucked me over, and good. *That's* what you get for identifying."

It was her turn to be silent.

"But this?" He motioned around them, to the lights and the walkways. "The first time I truly felt part of anything was when Valla Kamè took my hand." *And,* he thought, *when Čer Aya railed my brains out,* but he didn't mention it. "I am part of these people. Or I can be. I should be. I guess I am now."

"I guess I am, too. So, do we take new names?"

"I think Abè Shad-hai is a wonderful name."

"Logan Kai," she returned, raising her glass.

Their eyes locked.

In the silence that followed she broke her gaze, and he watched as she scanned the canopy, the lights vanishing in the mist, the ring of distant laughter around communal fires, the cool air full of moss and wet earth. Ten stories in the air, surrounded by life.

Celebrating death.

"You know, we came here knowing we might have to kill you," she said.

"And I might have had to kill you. Funny old thing, life."

"Would you have done it?" they asked, nearly at the same time.

The fire crackled for a bit. Finally, Abby stood.

"So, what—o-o-okay, then," Logan said as she pulled her Frogskin and bra over her head in one motion.

"You, me," she said, unbuckling her pistol belt and tossing it aside with a clatter. She kicked out of her boots and loosened her web belt. "Right here, right now. Come on."

"You're serious ab—"

She grabbed his head with both hands and pulled him to his feet. Their lips met, and her hands searched his face as she nearly sucked his tongue out by the root.

"I'm serious," she breathed into him, and her hands were in his robes, fumbling with his belt. "How the hell does this . . . I don't—"

"—hang on, it's got a—"

"—what the—?"

"—it's a pin, it slides around the—"

"Okay, fuck it. What are you wearing under this?" she asked, pulling the robe up.

"Nothing,"

"Good." She yanked her trousers and shorts down, pulled them off and threw them aside with urgency. She rolled onto her stomach, raising herself to her knees with her face on the moss. Her breath quickened, hips turning figure-eights in the firelight.

"You can do whatever you want to me," she groaned, her hand between her legs, her voice a rasp. "Just make it hurt a little. Okay, more than a little. Make it hurt."

He knelt behind her. Shadows and flickers played across topographies of muscle and sensual power. An absolutely physically perfect woman. "You want me to—"

She grabbed his hand and clapped it to her with an audible smack, her curves stonelike. "Hurt me, goddammit."

"You want me to—"

She grasped him by the hilt, rummaged herself, and squirmed up against him, forcing him into her. She screamed so loud that birds flew from the canopy overhead.

"Jesus, Abby! Are you all right?"

"If you ask me that again," she gasped into the moss, "I'm changing my mind about shooting you."

What followed was two drops lovemaking, one gallon grudge

match. The ferocity of it was startling. It wasn't sex so much as friendly rivalry run amok—*watch what* I *can do.* He marveled at her athletic prowess, her sheer physical toughness and utter fearlessness as she asked for more and gave back, matching stride for stride.

He rolled them onto his back before he exploded, and he expected to take her head clean off when he did. She threw her face to the skies and convulsed, screaming in rhythm.

She gripped his chest, panting astride him, grinning, sheathed in sweat. "Older men," she rasped as she slipped free. "Legit skills." She collapsed and kissed him on the nose, and they were quiet until they got their wind back..

"So, was it better than your doctor-stripper fiancée?" she asked.

He kissed her nose in return. "Better than . . . anything. Ever." And it had been. It had even blown away his previous experiences with Čer Aya.

She rolled off him, snuggled up, and let out a long sigh. "Of course," she said, looking up into the tree wistfully, "now comes the Now What."

"Ah, yes. The uncomfortable conversation."

"I mean, come on, I just banged my boss."

"Not to mention an enemy of the state," he added, raising a finger to the point.

"I know," she said, and took his finger in her mouth and rolled her tongue around it. "God, that makes it so hot, though. We're on the lam, now."

"Maybe you go back, we remain mortal enemies, but you keep coming back here for closed-door negotiations?"

She squirmed and shuddered. "Ooh. Let's put that on the table."

Birds alighted in the branches above them now that things had calmed down. They fluttered and sang and the evening was perfect. "I think it's better if you don't go back," he offered.

"I agree. You're nowhere close to done, hotshot."

"Wow," he said, turning his head to look at her fully. "You know what'd be fun?"

"I do," she promised.

"Well, yes," he agreed. "But, I was thinking when Paulsen gets here, we can shave our heads and eyebrows, smear ourselves in body paint, and convince him the Sentinels have accepted us as their gods. Throw the entire project into irrevocable chaos."

The fire crackled. Lights flickered as far as they could see. Ethereal music played from somewhere, something strummed, something sung.

"I can see why the Vikings would have thought this was heaven," she said.

"I think we're going to be very happy here."

XVI

HERE BE DRAGONS

Seek peace with your words when it is possible.
— Heithavega, c. 35

ARCHSTONE

SFC Christopher "Chip" Martin sat on his main canopy pack, leaning against his ruck, which rested against the rocks not far from the stone Arch. It was night. A cooling wind carried the swampy aftertaste of low desert.

"A lot of stars," he commented. Five large, hazy blue stars formed a drunken, lopsided cross with several others, smaller but intense, dotting the area around them. "Way more than we have back home. Some big ones, too. Either that, or real close. Maybe a star cluster, or something."

Medved and two others scouted with drones from the mesa. The ops brief had been quick, the endstate simple: find and bring back survivors, if there were any.

It had been four days on Earth since Paulsen had launched a detachment and an augmented team, nineteen troops in total, none of whom had come back.

Chip been here for three hours, by his watch.

The pilots worked their video game consoles, relentless.

"They want the five of us to bring all twenty-plus of them motherfuckers back?" Braxton asked. He lay on the ground, his head on his canopy bag, watching the stars. He could fly a drone, but they'd sent the ACE guys as extra manpower, which was nice. Paulsen wanted the team rested when it was time to move. "We need a goddamn brigade for this op. We need the fuckin' Hundred and First out here."

"Eighty-Second," Martin corrected. "Hundred and First doesn't jump. What're they gonna do, fast-rope twelve hundred feet?"

"Shit, that's cold," said Braxton.

In the next indentation in the rocks, Fields, the intelligence sergeant for the team, shook his head and sighed, his red-blond shock of fuzzy hair like a signal flare in the light of the moon. He had a deep, soft, country-and-western-singer Appalachian drawl which seemed oddly incongruous in a lanky, red-haired, bespectacled Black man. "You know," he intoned, "we are the only assholes in twenty years to even do a combat jump, and this will be, what, our second in a week? What is wrong with this picture?"

"This is idiotic," said Martin, sucking at his bite valve. "They could have left us back at the FOB."

"Anyone we spot will be long dead by the time we get back and tell you, you make a plan, file it, requisition your gear, draw same, get briefed, and come back through the Arch," warned Medved, outfitted in camo and not looking up from his controller. "It could be six weeks here before you get back."

"We're here, now, and we have no idea what we might need," Martin argued. "We don't know what their situation is, and there's no way in hell for us to go back and resupply."

"That's not my problem."

"It will be. When the Dunning hits the Kruger out there—"

"Okay, that's funny," Medved admitted.

"—you're gonna wish we had more stuff. Or different stuff."

Martin went through the OPORD—the operations order—in his head. A five-man rescue mission with UAV support. Three attached drone operators, including Medved, posted up outside the Arch, making eight in total, using the birds to scout before anyone from the team went anywhere. Keep one UAV higher than the others to watch for gryphons and send two more down the canyon as low as they could get without the optics scrambling.

Hodges, Edwards, and Fields, like Martin and Braxton, were Special Forces sergeants. They'd lived, trained, and now deployed together as a detachment for over a year.

There were no SEALs on this mission. There were no SEALs left. The three who hadn't gone missing on an alien planet were laid up in the hospital at Fort Lewis. Martin tried to find some humor in the situation, some kind of Us Versus Them team pride, but he couldn't muster it. This was far, far too grim. Team Four, the team in reserve back at the FOB, was entirely Army. The SEALs were history.

"You know what I wish we had?" Martin asked Braxton.

"A bag of weed and no light discipline?" Braxton ventured.

"Fuckin' A," Martin admitted. "But also, PJ's. Parajumpers. That's who we need, here. High-speed rescue guys."

"No sweat, big fella. Let the nerds do their thing. No offense, Medved."

"None taken."

They lapsed back into silence.

Abby, Luke, Logan, and that crazy knife-throwing guy, all went over to the enemy? Paulsen's theory, that they'd fallen under some kind of PSYOP put out by Logan, made no sense. Those four somehow managed to wipe out a half a platoon of SEALs sent to stop them, while all of Detachment One got . . . lost. Over here.

Shit, he thought. Det One, plus Guff. Good old Guff. Just gone.

It didn't make sense, and it didn't bode well.

It felt like a suicide mission, and that wasn't what Special Forces did. The teams were supposed to observe, to learn about these people. Instead, ARCHSTONE was burning through multi-million-dollar-trained operators, well over half their roster, in combat with goddamned aliens.

And frankly, Chip didn't have enough regard for Stannard to risk his own ass pulling him out of a jam unless he was specifically ordered to, which he had been. Similarly, Decker, nor any of those SEAL clowns. Not after all the bad blood, the insults, the attack on Luke, the whole last six months of their idiotic macho bullshit.

"Does this seem sketchy to you?" Braxton asked.

"I was just thinking that," Chip admitted. "There's something going on over here, man. Something they're not telling us."

"I concur," said Braxton. "There's a lot of shit that men like the Professor and that knife dude are gonna know, that we don't know. Shit we won't think of. Maybe they thought of something, something they couldn't tell us, and they had to go check it out."

A quiet, reserved loner-type, Fields didn't speak often, and when he did, it was important. "Y'all are forgetting, too," he drawled, "there are other compartmented operations going on, here. Probably all around us."

"Yeah, you could tell us, but . . ." said Hodges, the medic. He was another quiet one: studious, tough, serious.

"But then they'd have to kill *me*," Fields joked softly, "And I can't have that. No, y'all have ARCHSTONE and ASCENDANT WARDEN, but there's a whole other project going on here, that I ain't even read into. It's Nuclear Sensitive, and I ain't got the clearance."

"What the fuck are you talking about?" asked Braxton. "Nukes?"

"A base material for miniaturized nukes, as I understand it," said Fields. "This place is loaded with it."

"If you're not read-in, how the hell do you know that?" asked Martin.

Fields shrugged. "Gap analysis. I see the traffic. Paulsen's been in daily contact with a place called Hayward Labs in California. It's a nuclear research facility. That's who's funding this whole joint. I don't know how we got roped into this one," he added.

"Anyway, those dumbasses at the labs have me on their distro as part of the Two Shop," Field said, referring to the Intelligence section of the Headquarters Command. "I ain't got the read-ins, so I can't open the attachments, but I see the messages and I sure as shit see the distro lists. Punched up a couple of the names from the distro in the academic portals, read their papers."

Martin's jaw dropped. "You are shitting me right now."

"Are you allowed to do that?" asked Braxton.

"I ain't allowed to not do it. There's some next-level shit going on here, boys. Like, way beyond this." He gestured to the ringed moon. "Paulsen's playing a whole other game, and we ain't invited."

"What kind of research do they do?" asked Hodges. "The people he's talking to."

"Yeah. I had to look that up. Most of the distro are doin' theoretical work in ballotechnic nanophase materials."

"You lost me," said Braxton.

"Fairy dust for skunkworks. All kinds'a applications. Nukes, stealth paint, even a new kind of laser that focuses gamma rays. The shit they study, we have to make it in a nuclear reactor. Given the traffic I seen, I assess with high confidence this valley is loaded with it, or something we need to make it, or somethin' we can substitute for it. Anyway, whatever it is they're after, it's almost certainly why the drones get zorched down there. It's why our comms went to hell."

"What the hell are you talking about?" asked Medved. A huge shooting star passed behind him, leaving a green trail against the sky.

"Just a workin' theory," said Fields. "Like I said, gap analysis. I see what they're sayin', and I see what they *ain't* sayin'. What they ain't sayin's gotta be what's goin' on."

"You think they're out there gathering fairy dust," said Braxton.

"I think at least one of the teams is. I think the professors and Major Easton? They're brokerin' a land deal. Look at it. The materials science guy, the incoming DIROPS CMO, and our senior Cultural officer and her sidekick? Do the math. I think one of the other teams, and probably us, are here to make sure they get back okay, that's all."

"And Decker and those guys?" asked Hodges.

"They had a different mission," said Medved, who seemed to talk a thousand times faster than Fields. "I can speak to that. They were exploring some kind of tunnels. I don't know any more than that, though. They asked for all the imagery I had of these tunnels along the right-hand wall. A few klicks down that way."

"Dude, the monster tunnels," said Braxton.

"Oh, wow," Martin agreed.

Medved put the drone into hover and looked up from the controller. "What do you mean, 'monster tunnels?'"

Buck Decker had been running for two nights and crawling for three. Down to his last dregs of water, his fighting knife, and sheer force of will, he measured his progress in yards. The moon taunted him, lighting him up, showing his exact location to . . . *them.*

He didn't have a name for the things, goddamn their souls if they had souls.

His leg itched, that was the worst of it. He wasn't sure how long you could keep a tourniquet on—two hours to keep the limb, but that ship had sailed—and at this point, he wasn't about to remove it. What was left below the knee, and he didn't want to think about it, festered, clotted with sand and who the hell knew what else. The itching was intolerable.

The leg was lost.

He needed to get to the Arch before another night with *them.* The lampreys, the snakes.

The monsters.

They'd caught him three times, now, and the last one had caught his bad leg and vacuumed most of the remaining meat right off the bone. They went for bloodied flesh first; he had no idea why. He'd burned through all his ammo keeping them away, thrown out his rifle, and he'd had to kill it with his knife while it tore at him.

He had one round left in his pistol, a hollowpoint at the bottom of his last mag; that one was his own.

Like hell he'd let them strip the meat off him by inches.

But there was no sign of them, yet, tonight. There had been fewer and fewer of them, the further he'd gotten from the caves.

Fuckin' caves.

Slow and steady, that was the key to the game. Minimal expenditure.

Don't sweat, he reminded himself. *Sweat is the enemy. Sweat will kill you.*

He lay in the shadows during the day, drinking his own piss, wracked with pain and roiling with nightmares of rasp-toothed monsters. He woke screaming.

He dug his fingers into the soft sand at the base of the ARCHSTONE mesa.

Soft sand meant no more lampreys. They wouldn't, or couldn't, cross a long stretch of sand. No idea why. They were only interested in the rocks. Rocks were death. Wriggling, slavering death.

Stay away from the rocks.

Keep moving.

One more night.

He rolled onto his back to cool off before he started the climb.

He looked up into the stars, intense even through the blare of disloyal, hateful moonlight. One, directly above, brighter than all the others, blinked red.

He heard voices.

Bob Valentine was drunk. Blissfully, amazingly, wonderfully drunk.

Beautiful Sentinel women hung on him, sometimes literally hanging, dangling from his neck, from his arm while he'd curl them like dumbbells, one squealing as she'd climbed him like a cliff while wearing practically nothing.

They wore little enough at it was. At a rager like this, the fire crackling, the music playing, clothing was apparently optional. Perspiration gleamed from silver- and gold-traced tattoos on the taut dark bodies of slender, angelic Sentinel women and the terrifying, fanged Sentinel men with tribal insignias and white scarifications across their angry seas of muscle, built like gymnasts at five and a half feet tall and ridiculously beautiful, all of them.

Luke danced with them, shirtless, tattooed, firelight playing across the furrows and creases of muscle that made up his body. He fit right in.

Bob had also lost his shirt earlier in the night—he had no idea where it had gone and he was sure as hell never getting it back—and the sweat of dance, of wrestling, of wine and honest labor, dripped from him, glistening in the hair on his shoulders. He was no Luke, physically, and they didn't care. He was a hero, tonight, a god, and these magnificent beings sang his praises and took turns feeding him and admiring his mighty form.

He lay back against a mossy stone before the fire, drums pounding, the world spinning slowly. A Sentinel woman, a soldier— half their soldiers were women, it seemed—massaged his upper arm. He reveled in her telepathy, and hers was simple, limited to images and emotions. Raw. Unfiltered. Powerful. He felt the marvel she beheld when her hands didn't touch as they encircled his biceps. He was terrifyingly huge to her.

Bob was a big guy. He was obese by American standards, fifty pounds above his college wrestling weight with a BMI that frightened the hell out of his doctors, but he rode a recumbent bike to work, and worked out with medieval weapons. He'd been meaning to get in the gym and spend six months shaping up, but he'd been telling himself he'd do it for years, and it hadn't happened. Let's be real, he told himself now, it wouldn't.

The Sentinel held her hands up to another woman, showing off the girth of his biceps and triceps, and they giggled. The other held up her hands in a slightly smaller circle, and they laughed for a long moment. He felt hands at the buttons of his trousers and working at his belt. As he leaned forward, someone pulled his head back and rubbed shiatsu points on his skull with fingers like iron and someone else fed him wine.

"Fine," he said. "Take me now."

He heard a squeal of discovery, and he wanted to lean his head forward for a moment because, come on, it sounded important. The woman on his arm slid down his body to join the other in his lap, the two of them pushing his legs apart with exclamations of awe intelligible in any language. He couldn't see to discern specifics, but what could only be two mouths and four hands started working on him while another woman—nope, a man, and fuck it—massaged his scalp, and in that moment, in the full view of the party and whatever gods oversaw this place, Bobby Fett Maverick Valentine was a hero, a conqueror, a legend among his found people.

Back at what he was now calling Chez Logan, Logan and Abby had moved to the bed, wrapped around each other, luxuriating. A fire crackled and snapped. The sting of woodsmoke and the tang of wet earth permeated the room along with the sweet musk of sex and healthy sweat. They had no idea what time it was; time had no meaning; distance had no meaning. There was only this moment: drunken relaxation, the heat of exercised bodies, the sensation of being safe for the first time in several days.

Release.

On so many levels.

Čer Aya let herself into the room, with another Sentinel woman behind her, both dressed flimsily, and Logan briefly panicked. "Čer Aya," he said, rising, and reaching for his leg.

"What are they doing here? What is this?" Abby asked.

"She's a Čer," Logan said. "An advisor to the Valla. She's my mentor." Pain shot through his chest from the pistol-bruise, now days old and getting no better, as he bent to pull the prosthesis on.

"You okay?" Abby asked, putting a hand on his back.

"Fine. Chest hurts," he wheezed. "Today took it out of me. I think I overdid it. Or you did," he joked.

"Please don't rise," Čer Aya told Logan, but he was already up. He waved it off.

"Did you enjoy her?" Čer Aya asked, matter-of-factly.

"Very much," he replied in Sentinel.

"You had said you two had not mated."

"We hadn't, at that time."

"You two make excellent mates. This pleases me. Allow me to introduce Čer Anh. She will guide Abè Shad-Hai in the way I have guided you. She will teach our language, explain our ways, and serve as liaison to the Valla."

Logan translated. Abby nodded. "Okay," she said. "Logan, what the hell are they doing in your house?"

"This is kind of how they roll," Logan said. "They have different ideas about, well, everything. Čer Anh," he said, motioning to her, "is your new guide, I'm sure she'll explain it all."

"She can explain it in the morning," said Abby. "Let her know I'm staying here, tonight."

Logan said exactly that, and the response he received wasn't one he was sure he should share with Abby.

"What did she say?"

"They wanted to know if we, uh, wanted them to stay with us. In bed," he clarified. "Basically, they want to join us."

"Well, now," said Abby. "That's a little forward, isn't it?"

"They look at these things differently," Logan said. "They're pansexual, as best as I can grasp it. Polyamorous. It's like a hobby to them. They take some getting used to."

"I've heard worse ideas," she admitted. "But I'm gonna pass."

Logan translated. There seemed to be no offense taken, no embarrassment at overstepping any social bounds. They simply nodded.

Abby pulled the covers tighter over herself.

"Our riders completed a pass over the old door," said Čer Aya. "They saw more from your world. Soldiers."

"There's another team at the Arch," Logan told Abby, then addressed Čer Aya. "Do you have a plan to deal with them?"

"Three escaped to your world. Our riders will surround and return the rest."

"Return," he repeated. "Return here?"

"The Valla wishes you to speak to them in the morning. We will bring them here. You will explain that the Valla forbids further incursion."

"Son of a bitch," Logan swore, in English. "They're going to capture them and bring them back here," he told Abby. "They want us to talk with them in the morning.

"Čer Aya, I would speak with them, now. Bring their leader here, to speak with me, now. Bringing them all here could place your people in jeopardy. I do not advise you to bring them all here.

"Abby," he said, switching back to English, his brain aching,

"We gotta move, Major. We gotta go, now."

"I was just getting comfortable," she griped, throwing the covers aside and swinging those magnificent legs out of the bed. Logan offered her one of his robes, and Čer Anh helped her with the belt.

"This is just like the Army," Abby griped. "Middle of the night, shit to do, when all anyone really wants is to get laid."

"Welcome to the war," said Logan.

Martin watched Hodges and Edwards disappear through the portal with Decker.

He hoped to fuck they returned with alcohol because the Commander's story was beyond grim. The entire unit wiped out? Giant lamprey-snakes coming out at night? A dragon in the caves? A for-real, no-shit dragon?

Decker had been out of his skull with pain and dehydration, and Martin had to wonder how much of it was hallucinated or shock-induced, but man, that leg wound had been nasty. Smart thinking with the tourniquet.

Tough motherfucker. Crawled for days. Killed one of those things with a knife. The mind reeled.

"Well, fuck," said Braxton. "Now what?"

"Now, we send the drone further down, see if anyone else is out there," said Medved.

"Never mind," said Braxton, and Martin heard a round being chambered.

At first, he thought they were winged horses, but they had eagle's heads and feathered, though otherwise weirdly mammalian, bodies, and they were massive. Three of them landed on the mesa. The beaks and the scaled, birdlike front claws were immense, moving in lizard-like jerks. Each had a rider in mail and a helmet sitting on its neck, forward of the wings.

"Hold your fire," said Martin, to Braxton. "Let's see what they want."

"Jesus Christ, you guys," yelled Medved at the two intelligence analysts who dropped their controllers and dove through the Arch. He put his hands up. "We're fucked."

"No," said Fields, calmly. "We're good. They could have killed us, but they didn't. We're okay. Everybody stay cool."

Two more gryphons—Martin remembered the name, now, a gryphon; he'd wanted to call them *sphinxes*, initially, but he knew that wasn't right—landed on the other side of them. They were unbelievably huge and terrifyingly alien, rippling with black-gray feathers.

"Okay, *now* we're fucked," Braxton admitted.

One of the riders, from the first three that had landed, pointed at them. "*Mar Tin*," he said.

"Okay, *you're* fucked," Braxton corrected.

Martin stepped forward. "I'm Martin."

"*Mar Tin*," the knight said again.

Martin slapped himself in the chest. "Martin."

The knight, and it was clearly a knight, motioned to the saddle behind him. "*Mar Tin*," he said again, emphatically. The gryphon settled and knelt on the ground. Martin looked to the others.

"I'm going," he said. He slung his pack and threw the Mark 48 behind his back by its strap.

"You want that parachute?" Braxton asked.

"What am I gonna do, hook the static line to him?" said Martin. "Besides, if he wants to kill me, I'm sure he'll find another way." He stepped up next to the gryphon, and the knight helped him get seated behind its neck. His legs had to fold under themselves, his feet over its wings; he was riding on his shins and sitting on his ankles. The knight locked both Martin's hands around his midsection.

The guy was *tiny*.

He moved his grip up the knight's body, reveling in the cool, almost liquid sensation of the chainmail, trying to get comfortable, and jerked his hands away when he felt what were undeniably boobs.

She put Martin's hands firmly around her chest. Right on her boobs. Her grip was powerful, urging him to hold the fuck on.

The gryphon rose to all fours, and he felt it hunch up and prepare to pounce into the sky.

He held the fuck on.

It had been five uneasy minutes since the gryphon had left with Martin on it. Soldiers stared at knights. Knights stared at soldiers. Gryphons preened and fluffed their wings.

Braxton checked his watch.

"So, what are you guys about?" he asked, looking at the four knights on their gryphons.

"They don't exactly speak English," said Medved.

"Naw, seriously. Come on down, man." Braxton motioned. He did it again, more emphatically, smiling. "Come here. Come on."

One of the knights, after consultation with the others, swung down from the gryphon and walked up to Braxton.

"Don't do nothin' stupid, Brax," Fields warned.

"I'm just bein' nice. Shit, they have us on all sides. What am I gonna do?" He slapped his chest the way Martin had done. "Brax," he said, and repeated it.

The knight slapped his chest. "Eera."

"Eera," Braxton said, and saluted.

"What the hell you do that for?" asked Fields.

"He's a pilot, he's probably an officer," said Braxton.

Eera put a fist on his chest and nodded, apparently their salute.

"See?" said Braxton. "The shit works."

Braxton held out his hand. Eera looked at the other knights, then stepped forward and put a hand out in return. Braxton was not a large man, but the knight was far smaller, even in armor and a helmet.

Braxton slowly reached for the knight's hand, clasped it in his own, and shook it, and the world around him shattered.

He could see all three of them from four angles, and saw himself from what had to be the inside of Eera's helmet. "What the fuck?" he asked. The knight kept holding his hand, and in a moment the images cleared, settled. A voice, bell-clear, appeared in his head.

We mean you no harm. Our leader seeks to speak with Mar Tin. You serve your leader as a soldier. We serve our leader as soldiers. We resemble each other in this way. We have no reason to harm you. We see our resemblance in you.

"Guys, this is fuckin' nuts, but this dude can . . . he's tele-whatever. Reading my mind. He's, like, talking to my brain."

"You're shitting me," said Fields, stepping forward.

"Oh, goddamn," said Medved. "You need to break contact, right now! There's like, secrets in there! What if they learn about us?"

"I'm learning about them, too," Braxton said, as calmly as he could. "They're just, I dunno, mooks, man. Like us. They're just doing their thing. They don't want to hurt anybody. They came here to get Martin. Their leader wants to talk to him."

"How the fuck do they know who Martin is?" asked Medved.

"Man, that's a good question. How *do* you know who Martin is?" Braxton asked Eera. When Braxton spoke, Eera seemed to understand clearly.

The vision that Eera put in his head as an answer would have likely been familiar to every soldier who has ever lived.

"They were asked to find Martin," Braxton relayed. "That's all they know. Shit, they're just like us, man. They don't know a damned thing. They're out here at Fuck Me In The Ass Hundred looking for some dude they've never heard of for no adequately explained reason."

"Tell me. I did a whole tour in Afghanistan like that," grumbled Fields.

"For all we know, Martin's the Chosen One," said Medved. "Foretold in the prophecies to lead their people to victory over the demonic hordes of the Lich-King of Anizosior." He found everyone staring at him. "Or some shit," he added quickly.

"Wow," said Fields. "Hey, Brax, ask him if they can all do this. The telepathy thing. Is that like a party trick? Or what?"

Braxton asked, and received an affirmative. A conditional affirmative, hesitant, then a little embarrassed.

"They can, some more than others. I think there's one of them who sucks at it, but they don't want to tell him," Braxton deduced, and when he said it out loud, Eera laughed in his helmet. "Eera, why don't your comrades come down? We'll set our weapons aside, we can all sit and talk until our people get back. This will be better than sitting here scaring the hell out of each other. We have food. Sit with us. Eat with us."

Eera spoke to the others from behind his helmet at length.

The gryphons knelt, and the knights stepped down. Braxton unslung his rifle and set it on his pack, digging out some beef jerky and a half-pound bag of Skittles. Eera unbuckled his swordbelt and went back to his mount, hung it on the saddle, and removed his helmet. In moments, the other knights, and Medved and Fields, had followed suit, and they met again before the Arch.

"Dude, she's a chick," said Fields. Eera was, indeed, female, or at least appeared feminine, with much finer features than the others, astonishingly beautiful. The other two were masculine, slightly larger than Eera, all of them dark-skinned, long-haired, and elfin, with pointed ears and white and silver facial tattoos in the moonlight.

"They're Drow," marveled Medved. "Wow. Like, real Drow."

"Vulcans, maybe," said Fields.

"Let's do this thing," said Braxton.

Hands extended, and introductions began.

Martin crashed against the knight as the gryphon touched down. His arms were rubber, his legs shaking. The creature knelt, and he tried to get off, tripped, landed on wobbly legs, and collapsed.

"Easy, Sergeant," said Abby.

Logan was there to give him a hand up. "How was your flight?"

"Weird," he admitted. "You want to tell me what the hell is going on, now, sir?"

"I was hoping you could tell me."

Martin crouched, his elbows on his knees. He breathed for a bit in the moonshadow of the Citadel.

"Well, we found Commander Decker," Martin said at last, standing. "He claims he's the only survivor. He lost his whole team in those goddamn tunnels."

"I told 'em," Logan said to Abby. "You told 'em."

"He lost his leg to some kind of snake, lamprey thing, he says."

"We've seen them," said Abby. "They're pretty gnarly."

"Apparently," Martin said. He unslung his weapon, and then his pack, and set them on the ground. When he stretched his back, arching backwards, Logan got a sense of how big he was. It exhausted him merely thinking of the amount of work it would take to kick Martin's ass if he had to.

"So, what's going on, here, then?" Martin asked. "You guys are, ah, out of uniform."

"That's one way to look at it," Abby said.

"Is Luke here?"

"Valentine, too," said Logan. "They had a big day. They're resting. Probably."

"Dare I even ask, sir?"

"We killed Stannard's team," said Logan.

"Oh—oh, *fuck,* man!" Martin stomped his foot. "Goddammit!"

"They were sent to kill us," Abby said. "You'd have done the same."

"No, goddammit," Martin defended, stepping forward and pointing at them both. "No, I wouldn't have, because *they wouldn't have sent them to fuckin' kill me.*"

"He brought a rocket launcher," said Logan, more calmly than he expected he would. "He tried to knock down the Citadel." He motioned behind him.

"This is it, huh?" Martin asked, looking up at the tower rising against the moon.

"Yeah. When that didn't work, he was going to use a flechette round on civilians, try to get them to surrender. We took his team out before they could."

"Well, fuck," said Martin, calming down. "Yeah, war crimes are kind of his thing."

"*What?*" Logan snarled.

"He did shit in Afghanistan . . . Oh my God, sir. We hate him so much."

Logan continued to swear under his breath in English, French, Blackfeet, and Sentinel.

"Chip," Abby asked—it was the first time Logan had heard Martin's first name—"are you serious about this? About Stannard?"

"I figured you knew this, ma'am. That's why he's here. His guys mowed down entire villages. It was their thing. They killed an informant's family in Afghanistan, that was the big one. Cooked one of the kids and made the father eat part of him."

"I'm gonna be sick," said Abby, and walked away.

"Decker needed a place to hide him, and a couple of his guys, off the books," Martin told Logan. "There are people looking for him, right now."

"They'll have to look hard. Pretty sure he's gryphon shit."

The sound of Abby vomiting in the distance broke the desert silence.

"Abby? You okay?" asked Logan.

She cleared her throat. "Gimme a minute."

"They fed him to a gryphon?" Martin asked.

"I killed him," said Logan. "I don't know where the body is. It wouldn't surprise me, though. There's a lot of reduce-reuse-recycle around here."

Martin grunted and started pacing in the moonlight. "Well, that's Team One, sir. If they weren't involved in the shit Stannard was doing, they were sure high-fiving those fuckers over it. Those are Decker's boys. Great guys all around, as I'm sure you could figure. Sorry not sorry, as they say. Still, though. I wish you hadn't killed them. That puts me in a bad position right now."

"Well, you know," Logan joked, "we have to fight the Navy SEALs over here so we're not fighting them at home."

Martin stopped pacing. "What am I supposed to do, sir?"

"Take a message back to Paulsen for me," said Logan. "That's why you're here."

"You need to come back, sir. Tell him yourself."

"That's not happening," Logan said. "We're not going back."

"They're gonna ask why."

"And I'm telling you exactly why. Tell Paulsen to cease all manned exploration of this place. We're training up the Sentinels' military."

"Respectfully, sir, you're gonna get your asses kicked."

"The four of us and a platoon-sized element of their infantry— led by Doctor Valentine, believe it or not—"

"No, I believe that," said Martin.

"—destroyed Stannard's team. We know how to beat you in this environment. The next troops coming through here are going to die. And it won't be pretty."

"You know they'll send *me* back over here with those troops, right?"

"That's a 'you' problem, Sergeant."

Abby had returned. "Chip, when you get back, stand yourself down. Go see Jamila Fournier. She'll advise you of your options. This whole operation is off-books, you probably have a lot of options."

"What? What do you mean, it's off-books?"

"It's backed by a private research lab out of California," she said. "Hayward Labs. Ask her about it."

"Hayward." It was the second time Martin had heard the name in an hour.

"It's likely not even an authorized project," Abby continued. "I can't figure out why the military's involved in this in the first place. This is probably illegal as hell."

"Explains why Stannard was here," Martin muttered. "Explains a lot, actually."

"This is colonialism," Logan insisted. "Paulsen is strategizing the subjugation of a First Discovery people and the exploitation of their resources. I'm not having it. We discover an alien civilization right next door, and his first act is to steal from them? He sends a war criminal to destroy their home?" He gestured around him. "This is humanity's greatest discovery since the invention of fire, and this is what he does with it?"

"Well—"

"We've chosen our side. Tell him."

"You're taking their side," Martin assessed. "Against the entire U.S. military."

"No, only against as many guys as Hayward Labs can afford to hire. I like our odds."

"Technically, I'm supposed to shoot you right now," Martin said.

Abby said, "You think you can pick that weapon up, load it, and open the bolt before someone here kills you?"

Martin flicked his eyes left and right. "No," he said with finality.

"Then it doesn't matter, does it?"

Martin clicked his tongue and sighed, crumpling slightly. "Not really, no."

"How long has it been, back home, since we first set foot here?" Logan asked Martin. "Since my first mission, here."

"Three days?" Martin guessed. "I think three days. It'll be more when we go back."

Logan sighed. "I feared as much."

"Why? What's up?"

"I put half an egg salad sandwich in my briefcase before we left," said Logan. "Can you please, for the love of God, find it and throw it out?"

Martin laughed and clapped him on the back, and the pain that shot through Logan nearly collapsed him.

"You okay, sir?"

"Bruised rib," he wheezed, then realized he was wheezing. He was definitely getting worse.

"You should probably have somebody look at that," said Martin. "They've got doctors, here?"

Logan was hunched over with his hands on his thighs. "They must."

"Take care of this guy, will you, ma'am?" asked Martin.

"I'm doing my best," she assured him.

The Sentinels, as they called themselves, had piled glowing stones together into something like a bonfire, slightly warm— Medved had noted that the Sentinels were sitting close to it, so it probably wasn't *too* radioactive—and, all in all, the night was going great.

Eera took the last piece of jerky from the bag. They'd had a wonderful conversation, starting with the shared experiences of eating dried food on maneuvers, and delving into rants and tales about vacuous officers, idiot underlings, requisition fuckups, broken gear, training injuries . . . Their army had many of the same problems, it turned out, as any army on Earth.

The teams laughed and talked in two languages, trading No Shit There I Was stories late into the night.

Braxton pulled out a flask of whisky, took a slug, and passed it to Eera. She sipped at it, coughed, choked, and handed it back, and the other Sentinels immediately wanted to try it.

They had the same reaction.

Poison, Eera joked. *Very bad wine.*

"Whisky," said Braxton, and passed it to the rest of the team. "Water of life."

He wasn't about to show them cigars.

The gryphon with Martin on the rider's back touched down, and he and the knight got off. They walked over to the circle. "What the hell, guys?"

"Drink?" Braxton asked, offering the flask.

"You're getting drunk with them?"

"Nah, just having dinner. What else we gonna do?"

Martin glanced across the circle. "I hate to break this up, but we have to go back. Right now. We have a message for Paulsen from the Professor and Major Easton."

"They're alive?"

"Oh, yeah. But we got problems. Come on, guys. Pack it in."

When Braxton reached for Eera's hand to say goodbye, she was admiring the plastic beef jerky bag, and when he touched her, he saw the thing through her eyes: jeweled, ephemeral, powerfully colored and gilded with alien writing. He marveled as she did at the exquisite mechanics of the plastic slide closure. Her desire for the bag was almost sexually intense.

"Please, take it," he said. "As a reminder of this evening. A reminder of the time when you and I stood as friends." He wished he had something more beautiful to give her, but it wouldn't have mattered; she was enraptured with the thing.

I will keep it forever, as a reminder of our friendship, she said. "Brax," she added, rolling the *r*. She put a hand behind his neck, pulled him down, and kissed him deeply, as if trying to suck his tongue out by the root.

Martin watched the whole thing in disbelief.

The riders handed each soldier a glowing stone, and one to Martin.

The gryphons lifted off in a thunder of hooves and wingbeats. Medved held his stone up and quoted, "'The light of *Eärendil*, our most beloved star.'"

"I knew you was gonna say somethin' like that," Fields said, watching the riders go.

They shrugged into their packs and carried their chutes in one hand, rallying before the Arch.

"That was outstanding initiative," said Martin. "Hearts and minds. You may have just done us all—I'm talking humankind, no joke—more good than you could possibly know."

"Turns out they're just soldiers, Top," drawled Fields. "Beef jerky and Skittles are a universal language, apparently."

"Sorry I missed it. Brax, I can't believe an alien kissed you just now."

"Yeah, I can't . . . really . . . either," Braxton stammered, his voice trailing off.

Martin stood before the team. "Look, before we go back, I need you all to know where the bodies are buried, so listen up."

XVII

FARAWAY SONGS

Saudade: Port.; a state of intense longing to be near again to something or someone distant.

Forward Operating Base WINTERSTONE, Mt. Jupiter, Washington State

Chip Martin sat in a comfortable chair across from Jamila Fournier's desk. Her office smelled faintly of essential oils; slightly hippie, very calming. It was a quiet corner office, away from the rest of the madness that was the Ops Center. Both windows faced the trees. It was definitely the nicest office on the base, he had no doubt. Everything was comfortable, the chairs were a notch above all the others, and hers looked like actual leather, a real executive chair, not a modern job like the officers. A polished steel electric teakettle sat steaming on a bookshelf behind her. There were pictures on the walls.

No one else's office had pictures.

Jamila was also unlike anyone else on the base. Statuesque and refined in a dark blue suit jacket and skirt, with a grace and delicacy to her movements and her speech, she seemed as alien to Martin as the Sentinels.

"There's a lot more to this," she was saying. "There is a lot you haven't been told. In fact, there's a background to this that I haven't even told this team."

"I trust you're not going to tell me."

She shook her head slowly. "No chance."

"Am I right about this Hayward thing?"

"You know I can't tell you that."

"Well, great, ma'am. Can you tell me what my options are? Legally."

She took a deep breath and let it out slowly, visibly buying time as she thought. "This is a military project. You have your orders. I'm not an expert on the Uniform Code of Military Justice, but I know you have the right to refuse an illegal order. However, going back into ARCHSTONE is a perfectly legal order.

"What you're alleging Stannard attempted, however, is definitely an illegal order. If someone asks you to do something illegal when you get over there, you can always say no."

Martin grunted. "No, we can't. Respectfully, that's a common misconception, ma'am. You refuse an order over there, they'll just shoot you and then lie about it. Especially those fuckin' SEALs."

"What do you mean?"

"You know exactly what I mean."

"I really don't," she said.

"Come on," he pleaded. "Let's just—Do I really have to say this out loud?"

"You can close the door, Sergeant."

"Count on it." He stood, and closed it. It was solid wood, heavy, likely soundproof, or as close as you could get in a modular like this.

"Ma'am," he said, once he'd sat again, "Stannard is a war criminal. A handful of his guys on Team One, with him. Maybe all of 'em. They did some pretty awful shit, for years. Under Decker. Everybody knows it. Decker brought them here, under this op, to hide them. If Stannard and those guys ever came off these orders, they'd be screwed. They'd be breaking rocks at Leavenworth. Or shot."

"You know this for a fact?"

"Everybody knows this for a fact. That's why our team hates those guys. I was on a firebase in Helmand when Stannard and his crew wiped out an entire village a few klicks from us. Murdered entire families, even forced a family into cannibalism at one point."

She fidgeted, and he knew he'd hit on something she didn't know. Couldn't know. "I—I need to look into this."

"You won't find it," he assured her. "It's going to be compartmented, just like this. You won't have access to view any reports on it, if there are any. I mean, if Decker didn't shred them. Even their orders would be redacted. You'll never find any proof they were there. That's how this works. It's how they get away with it. Decker stashed those guys here until the heat is off, until someone else commits a worse atrocity and becomes the cause *du jour.*"

She sipped her tea and he saw her hands shaking, the long, manicured fingers so delicate on the cobalt blue of her mug. A plain blue mug, no emblems. No affiliation.

No loyalty to anything; the adjudicator.

Or so he hoped.

"So," he began again, "isn't exploitation of a new civilization, like, all kinds of illegal?"

"Well, yes, but it's not that simple."

"I can't imagine that anyone here has the authority to make a treaty with another country. I'm obviously no lawyer, but I do have a poli-sci degree, with honors, so I know a little bit about this, I think. Correct me on this, but treaties must go through Congress. If the President of Iran wanted to make a peace deal with me, I couldn't do it. Neither could Paulsen."

"There's the Case Act," Jamila said, setting her mug down again. "Yes. The texts of all international treaties must go to Congress, you're right. International agreements require a delegation of authority from the Secretary of State. Colonel Paulsen has Mission Delegation Authority, but I'm unclear on where it comes from."

"Hayward Labs," Martin guessed.

"I don't have that information. I'd have to see it, to know if his authority includes international agreement authority. I doubt it does. However, this project is Congressionally waived. These kinds of laws may not apply to situations like this."

"I'd think these kinds of laws would apply exactly to situations like this. Otherwise, ma'am, what the hell are they for?"

"Well," she said, leaning her head back and staring at the ceiling in contemplation, "these laws aren't really used today."

She looked out the window for a long moment. He could see her chaining concepts together as he watched her eyes flash back and forth, which he found fascinating. He was used to working around very bright people with an affinity for arcane knowledge, but she was clearly brilliant on a level that made it engrossing just to watch her think.

"Historically," she said, slowly and after what seemed an eternity, "a nation had to occupy and possess a newly found area to claim it. The military usually did that by building settlements and forts. Today, though, it would more likely be done through, I don't know, a decades-long occupation under the guise of 'peace and capacity building,' usually with some kind of trade agreement and . . ."

Here eyes widened as she stammered. "—and . . ."

"Here it comes," Martin told her.

"Oh," she said as it settled in. "Oh-hh. Oh, no."

"You see where I'm going with this."

Jamila put her head in her hands. "Oh, fuck. Oh, *fuuuuuuuuck*," she groaned.

Martin slapped his thighs, stood, and picked up his coffee. "Well, I'll leave you to it, ma'am."

"No, Sergeant Martin, you keep your ass in that chair." She straightened up, energized, clicked a pen, and turned over a fresh sheet of paper on a notepad beside her. "I need you to tell me everything—everything—that's happened so far. Start at the very beginning, the moment you first went over there."

"Ma'am, it's seventeen hundred."

"We'll order-in food. Keep that door closed."

Braxton lay on his bed, listening to the rain, his brain reeling in devastated astonishment. He was exhausted; he'd slept out of necessity, but it wasn't even twenty-one hundred and now he was wide awake with Eera on his mind. The humor, the gentle smiles, the shared experiences although they'd been separated by . . . light-years? Eons? Galaxies? The immeasurable tenderness of that kiss spanned the cosmos. Literally.

Fuck me. I'm in love with an alien.

How in the hell could they make war on these people? Steal from them?

Subjugate them?

Blow them up?

Stannard and that flechette round . . . good on the Professor for killing his ass. He wished he could've seen it.

This wasn't what Special Forces was for. None of it. Not the stealing, not the land grab, not the blowing stuff up. Not this. This was grunt work, bullshit work. Door-kicker work.

Special Forces had been co-opted into lesser roles, before, certainly; they had a long history in the current wars of being muscled into glorified commandos by short-sighted commanders who, learning of an A-team on their base, immediately demoted them to a quick-reaction force, superfluously attaching the team to a perfectly capable infantry or cavalry platoon for no other reason than it would allow senior officers to crow about "commanding Special Forces,"—a lucrative resume bullet when they eventually retired or separated.

From their formation in 1963 to this day, Special Forces— SF—existed outside of direct-action lanes except through necessity. It was why Braxton had signed up: SF was responsible for training indigenous troops to overthrow countries from within, which is some of the most fun anyone can have in the U.S. Army standing up. American SF were, and remain, the only Special Operations component in the world with rabblerousing as a core competency.

Navy SEALs and Army Rangers, with whom SF were commonly conflated, were not Special Forces, but direct-action, commando-type Special Operations units. Commandos were go-fast guys who break shit and kill people, and SEALs and Rangers excelled at it. They were the door-kickers.

While American Special Forces could certainly deliver a beatdown as well as—if not arguably better than—SEALs, Rangers, or Marine Corps Raiders, their expertise at professional death was merely a byproduct of their mission scope. They could do it because their job was to teach it, which was the part that escaped nearly everybody, including about ninety-five percent of troops in the U.S. Army. Maybe ninety-nine percent.

Various and sundry Special Operations units in the U.S. military existed for specific functions outside of traditional warfighting, and this is what SOCOM, the U.S. Special Operations Command, was about: SOCOM housed a wide array of units including, but not limited to, specialized intelligence gathering, psychological warfare, humanitarian work, hostage rescue, counterespionage, conflict mediation, lasing targets behind enemy lines, and so on. There were Special Operations air units, Special Operations drone units, Special Operations cyber units, Special Operations boat units. Special Operations intelligence analyst cells furiously calculated second- and third-order effects of compartmented missions 24/7.

Every discipline under SOCOM attracted its own breed of soldier, which made balancing the personalities on a task-organized team like the ASCENDANT WARDEN detachments as important as balancing the skill sets, and this was where, Braxton had to admit, Paulsen shone. It was the piece that Decker and Stannard could never get their heads around.

Decker and Stannard wanted SEALs for everything, period. Nothing else would do; it was why nearly half the detachment roster were SEALs. Or, had been.

Every SEAL had been through identical training, so they knew each other's capabilities, and that, to SEALs, equated to trust, albeit on a level Braxton could never grasp. They were plug and play, and marvelously effective at simple tasks. This was fine; Det One had been the direct-action arm of ASCENDANT WARDEN.

However, exploring an alien world did not involve many, if any, simple tasks, which was why the other ASCENDANT WARDEN detachments were a mishmash drawn from the various components and mission areas: an SF commo guy, a Ranger linguist, a sniper from the Army, but who'd trained with the Air Force—and an officer at that. That crazy old bastard—Jack? Jake?—from the Army Reserves, who'd once fast-roped out of a chopper to sit at a negotiating table with no-shit witchdoctors from warring Amazon tribes.

A good SF team could do all of the above—okay, maybe not the witchdoctor part—but their job was to know every aspect of professional soldiering well enough to teach it to guerrilla armies fast enough that no one would notice, and train them up well enough that they could eventually use them to curb-stomp the forces of evil.

SEALs didn't do it. Rangers didn't do it. No other army in the world did it.

Only SF did it, and it's what Braxton had signed up to do. As a Special Forces Sergeant First Class, his job description was quite literally to raise and train a company-sized element of up to two hundred troops from next to nothing and lead them in battle.

The stuff Logan was doing.

With Eera's army.

Right now.

Against him.

He punched his pillow, fluffing it up, then decided he wouldn't sleep, tonight.

It started with a crackle in Logan's lung, which even Abby could hear as they walked back to their village tree.

"Logan, are you all right?"

"A little winded," he said. "I sucked in some sand, or something." He stopped for a moment, the Čers on either side of them, and bent over to get his breath.

When he stood up again, he collapsed.

"Son of a bitch," Abby said. Both Čers were babbling and singing to each other, and she didn't listen; it wouldn't have mattered. She knelt over him and checked his airway; he was breathing, but his lips were turning blue. She opened his robes and the clear indent of the pistol on his sternum, purple on blue, told her everything she needed to know.

She ripped open the medical kit on her pistol belt. It wasn't a comprehensive kit, but it had a thoracic needle and a chest seal, and with a pop and a hiss a moment later—and some grunting and bitching from Logan—she had the lung re-inflating.

"You dumb motherfucker," she berated him, equal parts concerned mom and irritated Infantry officer. "You didn't think you might have a collapsed lung? What, it didn't occur to you?"

"Never crossed my mind," he gasped. "Oh, wow, that hurts."

"Good," she said. "Maybe you'll learn something. Fuckin' commandos," she swore. "Okay, we need to get you to a doctor. Hopefully you've just got a contusion that's pushing on that lung. If you've got a sprung rib, and we'll know if this doesn't go away completely in a few days, somebody's going to have to cut you open, goddammit."

"I've gotta wonder if they have somebody for that."

"Our guys could do it," she said. "I'd give anything for Tommy right now."

Logan explained the situation to the Čers, and after some time—he still didn't understand how, but they had some kind of psychic 911 system down here—several Sentinels appeared with a litter made of ancient tooled poles and woven flax, far too small for him, and they rolled him aboard, his shoulders and arms hanging over the sides, his feet dangling. He fell asleep with fires twinkling overhead like stars in the canopy as they carried him home.

Braxton pushed open the door to Cooper's Grill at five to ten in the evening, went straight to the bar, and spied Medved and Fields at the far end of it. The place was nearly empty. It was—Tuesday? He didn't even know.

Whatever they had been talking about, they went back to their drinks upon seeing him, being the insular, weird intel geeks they were.

"Gunpowder gimlet?" the bartender asked. Her name was Lonni, and she was raw-food-vegan skinny with dyed-black hair, nose rings, and a sleeve tattoo on her left arm. "Double?"

Braxton sat down. "Have I been here that long?"

"Nobody—sure as hell no Army guy—orders a gimlet in a place like this. Much less orders top-shelf gin. And you tip well," she added with a smile. "Of course I remember."

She put it in front of him. "I'm flattered," Braxton said. "Lonni, right?"

"I'm flattered," she replied with another smile. "So, what are you guys doing up there? Come on. You can tell me. I'm not a spy."

"I dunno, I'd need to test your interrogation resistance," he joked.

"I get off at one-thirty," she said. "You any good with knots?"

"I was a Boy Scout."

They laughed for a moment, and she looked straight into him. "Seriously. What the hell are you guys doing up there?"

"If you must know," he lay down the official lie, which he had to admit was brilliant, "someone found a bunch of unexploded ordnance left over from World War Two. A plane that went down out here dropped all its bombs before it crashed. They landed on an Indian burial ground."

"I bet people are pissed."

"I can imagine."

"So, you're one of these guys who can disarm a bomb with a paper clip, I'm guessing?"

"As a matter of fact, I can."

She rubbed the bartop with a towel. "Figured. You're one of the smart ones. You, and those two over there," she said, motioning toward Fields and Medved. "You're way smarter than the usual

Army guys, and especially those dumbass Navy guys, who have been coming in here the past couple of months."

"I do my share," he admitted. He nodded down the bar. "What makes you think those two guys are smart?"

"Dungeons and Dragons. Only, like, really smart people still play it at our age, right?"

His tone was confused. "Dungeons and Dragons?"

"Yeah. They've been over there all night talking about elves, and dragons, and something about a castle in the desert. I don't know. They're really into it, though."

Braxton stood, and picked up his drink. "Get them another round," he told her.

"You play?"

"I know a thing or two," he said over his shoulder, moving to them.

Fields set his empty mug down on the bartop and picked up a full one. It was nearly midnight.

Brax watched Lonni walk away, a fresh round of drinks before them all. She was cute and funny, but he had more important things on his mind. Like, the future of the world. Maybe two worlds.

And that kiss.

"Lemme understand this right," Fields told Braxton. "You're in love with a woman from another freakin' planet. A woman you've known for, what? An hour?"

"She's telepathic," Braxton said. "I've seen inside her mind, and she's seen inside mine."

"And she still likes you?" Medved needled. Braxton shoved him.

"Asshole. I know her better than anyone I've ever met. And she feels the same for me. I saw it. I felt it. I felt what she feels for me. When have you done that, with any woman?"

Fields drawled, "How do you even know she's a woman? What if it's one of them 'Arcturian poontang' scenarios?"

"Good point," said Medved. "Are our species even sexually compatible?"

Braxton swirled his drink. "Define 'compatible.' We both have hands; we both have mouths. We'll figure the rest out."

Medved cocked his head in consideration.

"So, what, then," Fields drawled. "You're gonna turn your back on the entire U.S. military. On your country. On your friends, your family."

"My family?" Braxton downed his drink. "Fuck, man, my *family* was the G Street Mob in Walnut Hill. I ducked into a recruiter's office with the T Block Bloods looking for my skinny ass in the dumpsters one street over. Sarn't took me to MEPS in the trunk of his car. What, you think I write home?"

"Jesus, Brax," Medved said. "I had no idea. I'm sorry."

"Nah, it's cool, now. It all worked out. Fuck. I mean, almost everybody in SF comes from a broken home, at best. I know I ain't the only one comes from *no* home. But nobody in our line of work has family. Look around. Ain't nobody on the whole team has family to speak of. Think about it. Is *anybody* married? Anybody on our team have so much as a damned goldfish at home?"

"I—" Medved started, then paused.

"What's up?"

"Nothing," he said. "I was going to say something about my family being irretrievably fucked, but I'm not SF."

"You're one of us," said Brax, clapping him on the back.

"I'm not an operator," said Medved. "You guys are . . . different. I understand. I'm not in a position to even remotely judge you for the decision you're talking about, because you've seen shit I haven't. You understand things on a level I don't."

"Hah. Listen to the intel genius over here, tellin' me I understand stuff he don't."

"No, Brax," Medved insisted, "you do."

"Well, I understand shit *you* don't," Fields assured Braxton, "and that's why you ain't goin' back there without me."

"You're serious, now?" Braxton asked. "'Cause I'm drunk. Don't be fuckin' with me, Fields."

"I've been thinkin' about it all day," said Fields. "I've got far many more reasons to go than to not go. Not the least of which is that those guys are trying to do exactly the thing that we're trained to do, you and me: raise an army. If they're gonna have a chance in hell, they're gonna need actual Group guys. If you're goin', I'm goin'."

"I had that same thought," said Braxton. "That's what led me down here, to start drinkin'. Goddamn. We should be over there doin' that."

"Drinkin'?"

"That, too."

"You guys have all the fun," said Medved. "I'd go in a minute."

"Seriously?" Braxton asked. "You? I figured at least you were smarter than this."

Medved blew out a disbelieving breath. "I'd give anything to go. Are you shitting me? Live with the elves in their magical underground realm, on an *alien fantasy world?* Maybe it's someplace I can, I don't know, find my purpose. Make something out of myself besides being Decker's office bitch."

"Oh, you know that man is gonna be insufferable when he heals up," Fields assessed. "He's gonna roll heavy on those guys, too. Balls to the wall. It's gonna be ugly. Motherfucker's gonna be ramping tanks through the Arch."

"They'll need somebody who knows U.S. military capabilities," Medved said into his drink. "Like, really knows 'em."

"Yup," Braxton agreed.

"Sure will," said Fields.

"It's one thing to train those guys up, and good on you," Medved continued, "It has to be done, but without a thorough understanding of ops and intel? You're gonna get rolled."

"Yup," said Fields.

"Yup," said Braxton.

"They need someone really smart," Medved went on, completely missing the looks he was getting. "Like, one of our guys from the ACE, probably. You'd need to know Special Operations capabilities, you'd have to know how to set up an intelligence network, teach the sensors what to look for. No offense, Fields, but even you don't have the kind of strategic-level analytical chops you'd need to—"

"Oh, I know," said Fields.

Medved finally glanced up from his drink to find Braxton staring at him from one side and Fields staring at him from the other.

"What?" he asked.

Braxton clapped him on the shoulder. "How long since you've rucked, Ranger?"

In the end, had they ever compared notes with Major Easton about it, the four of them would have been amazed how many actions of consequence had occurred in the middle of the night, on a porch, in the rain.

"You really think we should wake him up?" asked Medved.

"You wanna leave him behind? He'll totally hunt us down."

"If he doesn't want to come, he's gonna hunt us down, anyway."

The wind intensified.

"What if he's as drunk as we are?"

"I'm not drunk," Braxton insisted. "I'm in touch with the first intellect. Sensory perceptions are memories from before the soul entered the body. You stay sober, you're short-circuiting any kind of intuitive connection, man. How else we gonna navigate the intricacies presented by these conceptions of clairvoyance and telekinesis with our new brethren?"

"You are definitely drunk," Fields assessed, and knocked on Martin's door.

"You know if we do this, we're enemies of the United States, forever, right? We can't ever come back," said Braxton, which felt naïve, even given as many drinks as he'd had.

"Hell, I've already got twenty-two countries I can't set foot in anymore," said Fields. "Add it to my tab."

Martin opened the door, dressed to roll out, filling most of the doorframe with multicam. "I'm packed." He pulled on a boonie hat and picked up a camouflage duffel from beside the doorway. "Let's go."

XVIII

BONES

Judge a man by his questions rather than his answers.
— Voltaire

Steve Paulsen's jaw hurt from grinding his teeth.

A manning roster filled one of the screens in front of him, and what he read was worrisome.

He was running out of troops.

Det One—Decker's SEAL platoon, the strike force—was gone completely. Half of Det Four, as well; those SEALs who hadn't been cross-leveled into Det One had shipped out with Stannard, and, who the fuck knew how but, apparently Logan and the Sentinels had wiped them out, too.

All but four members of Detachment Two, Major Easton's team, had either been killed, injured previously and taken off the FOB, or gone over to the enemy.

And that was a problem on its own; he had two troops, along with two academics who were, he had to admit, smarter than he was, who had decided to go and help whoever the hell these

Sentinel people were, and he still didn't even know what they were about or why they were killing everyone else he sent over there.

It didn't make any sense, no matter how much he beat his head on his desk about it. What had these Sentinel people offered Logan? What would make Abby, Gunny Foster, and now Dr. Valentine all decide to climb on board?

Money?

Sex?

Power?

Sergeant Martin's report was a confusing mess. Logan had killed Stannard, and the four of them were staying over there and training the Sentinels, raising an army. Which was equally insane, because that was Special Forces work, and not one of them was SF.

He doubted they could pull it off.

That said, they'd managed to annihilate Stannard's team.

Surprising.

He could put together a plussed-up Detachment with the dregs of Det Four and the remainder of Det Three, who had only lost one heavy machine gunner, the SEAL Senior Chief who'd thrown his hat in with Stannard.

But then, what?

Jamila had come to him first thing that morning with a sheaf of redacted documents from Hayward Labs, and something about not having Congressional authority to make a treaty, and fuck, who'd seen that coming? And who was talking treaties, anyway?

It wasn't that he had bigger problems than losing seventy percent of his roster in four days, just additional problems.

The American Special Operations solution was money. This was a black operation, completely off the books. However, Hayward's development programs were a matter of national security, and though Paulsen wasn't sure exactly how it had propagated, it had to have been a handshake deal in the basement of the Pentagon—or over dinner at The Palm—that got Task Force here in the first place. They had literally all the money they would ever need.

Money wouldn't solve this, though. He needed troops; hardened desert troops, men who'd do the hard thing, the right thing. Anybody he sent in there now was going to run up against the locals, who were being coached by one bad motherfucker.

Task Force didn't have the bodies. He'd have to pull them from another command, somewhere in SOCOM, probably. Ranger Regiment? He needed direct action troops at this point, not world-builders.

Whomever he got, he'd have to read them in on to the project, which meant reading the missing and dead off from the compartmented information, which was going to be awful. There were casualty reports to write, probably a full investigation. Holy shit, what would that even look like?

In the meantime, he needed bodies in slots. Quickly. Before Logan could inculcate the locals in commando tactics. Before Logan could train up an army to do whatever they'd done to Stannard's team and do it on a large scale.

He thumbed through the pile of reports from Jamila. She had it all. He wasn't exactly in trouble, because he hadn't done anything technically wrong, but there were questions, and there were about to be more questions. And questions were not the sort of thing you wanted with any kind of classified operation, and certainly not one this classified.

Dear Christ, she'd attached sticky notes to everything.

His email chimed with an update on Decker. He skimmed it: stable, critical. The leg was gone below the knee.

The coincidence was staggering. It was almost an identical injury as Logan. Decker's days as a SEAL were over. It was like watching the passing of a great statesman.

Where did a guy like Decker end up? What was next for someone like him, someone with a trail of bodies behind him stretching across three continents and now, two worlds? What would he do? Hang it all up and go fishing? Write a book? Give motivational speeches at graduations?

And then it came to him. He knew exactly the kind of people who'd take Decker in, who'd make him a leader, who'd put him right back into the thick of it, doing the thing he did best. There were merchants for the kind of work at which Decker excelled.

The kind of people who could beat Logan at whatever game he was going to play.

He pulled a small, slim phone from his desk drawer, powered it on, and unlocked it with a fingerprint after three tries.

He punched two numbers.

There was no ringing; it picked up immediately.

"Talk." The voice on the other end was Dr. Xander Lynch, VP of Special Projects at Hayward Labs, who graced the boards of directors of several weapons research companies.

"You should see this," said Paulsen.

"I've seen it."

"See it again."

A momentary pause. "What's wrong?"

"Complications. Casualties. And some defections. We may have a problem."

"Defections?" Disbelief; the word enunciated as if he didn't understand the meaning.

"Yes."

Another pause. "Is tomorrow too late?"

"Tomorrow's fine."

Goodbye was not part of a Xander Lynch conversation. The light blinked off as the call dropped.

He reached for his next pile of paperwork: a sheaf of 96-hour passes for nearly all the surviving members of Team Two, and why the hell not? Four Seasons, Seattle. Martin, Braxton, Fields, and Medved with them, which he thought was interesting—Todd hadn't been with them on the ill-fated op, but hell, if they were getting along, chalk one up for cross-functional outreach.

A few days in the city to blow off steam would be good for them. Though, to his knowledge, Todd had never taken a vacation in his life.

He signed each and laid them in his outbox. An NCO would get them in the morning and send them up to HQ. According to the forms, the boys were already gone, and that was fine. Paperwork sometimes arrives late. It was the nature of things.

XIX

EDEN

Danser après le mariage pas avant:
tr. "Dance after the wedding, not before."
                    —French proverb

Her name was Ullè Soa. She was a Sentinel warrior, a commander of an *Ul*—thirty troops. A platoon officer, as Bob understood it.

She'd been immediately on Bob's right, charging Stannard. It had been her troops he'd led, although he didn't know he'd been leading at the time. He knew, from speaking with her—well, what they considered speaking, but that was coming in time—six of her soldiers had gone down, extinguished forever, and she herself had hesitated at the sheer power of the machine guns.

He'd spoken with her after the fight and again around the fire that evening, seeing himself lensed through her experiences: an aggressive, lethal, oversized human who'd run ahead into the jaws of death and captured the enemy leader when the bravest Sentinels she'd known in hundreds of years had balked, breaking their lines.

Which was kind of cool, because that wasn't the way he had ever seen himself, or at least the way he'd imagine a professional soldier would have seen him.

She stood a distance from him, staying out of arm's reach the way you'd stand off from a Mastiff or Great Dane you'd once seen run down an intruder. Not fear so much as respect.

He couldn't fit the beauty of these people into his mind. There wasn't room. He had nothing to compare it to. A sunset. The stars at night. Shall I compare thee to a summer's day and all that. He bookmarked some Shakespeare in case they got to that point.

Ullè Soa was tall among Sentinels, with a chiseled physique and spectacular curves under a gauzy green and silver number barely reaching her knees that looked like it was made of moss and spiderwebs. These were not a modest people.

She wore a sword and knife on a belt; an Ullè was never weaponless. The soldiers here wanted you to know they were soldiers. And that was something he hoped he could eventually work with, because there were some major problems with their soldiering.

At the party the prior night, she'd asked him to teach her how he'd done it, and it was all he could do to not let her know that he, himself, had no idea what had compelled him to run into danger. It was war; it was what you did.

At least, he'd figured it was what you did. War wasn't his thing. He didn't know a damned thing about it outside of pure academia. Blowing the dust off ancient tomes to find ways to beat a guy like Stannard was so ridiculous a concept that it honestly hadn't occurred to him.

What he did know was, he'd never won a match in any sport by letting someone who outgunned him in a key capacity dictate the terms of the fight. That was all he'd had going for him, and he'd doubled down. He hadn't been about to wait for Stannard to engage him with a rifle, for fuck's sake. He'd had a half a second of surprise and a shitload of momentum, and it had turned out to be all he'd needed.

Truth told, Bob hadn't even known it was in him; courage was simply what everyone else around him had, and he wouldn't have been able to live with himself—more to the point, he wouldn't have been able to keep living with *them*—had he not done it. In the back of his mind had been a running worst-case/best-case equation, and the absolute worst outcome he could think of when the smoke went up was getting gunned down by Navy SEALs on an alien planet and living on in song among his chosen people. He could imagine far more inglorious denouements.

However, charging machine guns wasn't what the Sentinels did, which is why it had blown their minds, and this was something he'd have to confer with Luke and Abby about if they were to have a chance in hell of teaching these people the sacraments of swift and violent action. The Sentinels weren't wired for it. They were wily and cautious, not about to throw away thousand-year lifespans full of sex and wine and music.

And sex.

My God, the sex.

He set lightstones on the corners of a map on the table and beckoned her closer. It was a large map of the valley and the flat areas around the Citadel, immensely detailed.

She put a hand on his arm. The warmth of her touch was astounding. *Talk with me. Ask me your questions.*

He decided to swing for the fences right off the bat. "The dangerous thing . . . the thing you curate. When we know where you keep it, we will know where the New Humans will send their next patrols. They will have ways to find it, next time. They will go directly to it. If we know this, we know where they will go, and we will know how to beat them."

The dangerous thing—she had an impossibly long word for it— but the image in his head was clear: volatile, world-wrecking, civilization-threatening.

Liquid. Red. Heavy.

The Blood of the World.

"Yes," he said. "This."

We do not curate the Blood of the World. The Sheth curate it. We direct the curation. The Sheth do not make wise decisions.

"But the Sheth protect the dangerous thing."

They do. As do we. We cooperate with the Sheth to protect and curate.

Cooperate wasn't exactly the word she used; there were shades of meaning behind it, a master-servant relationship. The Sentinels, it seemed, oversaw the Sheth. Which made sense.

"Can I see the dangerous thing?"

Absolutely not. The Blood of the World will kill you.

"My people handle the dangerous thing in small amounts."

It only occurs in small amounts. The Sheth keep it divided in small amounts. The many small amounts comprise one large amount, and the large amount will kill a human. The large amounts will slowly kill a Sentinel. They most slowly kill a Sheth.

Bob thought about this for a long moment. He had an image of a card catalog, of all things; drawers, files, lockboxes of some type. It wasn't literally that, but it was the picture that formed in his head when she thought of the—she didn't have a word for it, and he realized that she herself had never actually seen the red mercury, nor how it was curated, and was only working off hearsay. He had no sense that she was lying to him. The Sheth did the heavy lifting because they had a tolerance for it; the stuff was lethal to Sentinels over long periods and likely immediately lethal to humans in large amounts.

And then he had another thought.

"How do you know it will kill a human?"

Logan's house was quiet. It was late afternoon, and he was propped up on pillows against the wall at the head of the bed. He couldn't sleep. Čer Aya sat next to him, running her fingers through his hair, comforting him in the way a master might gently reassure a gravely ill dog.

Every time he got up, the damned lung collapsed again, like a Charlie horse in his chest. It was bad, and he knew it; he was going to die here, a million light years from home, in a strange bed beneath alien stars. There were worse things. He'd killed Stannard, and whatever nightmares those snake-lamprey things in the tunnels were, they'd done a number on Decker's team, and they might have saved this world, all of them combined, assuming it had scared Paulsen off, but who the hell really knew. Paulsen was just smart enough to think of another plan and just dumb enough to try one.

He expected anything from Paulsen, but he didn't expect it soon, and he didn't expect it to work. Perhaps that was enough.

Abby eased the door open. "Logan?"

She saw Čer Aya in the bed, her fingers in Logan's hair, and before Logan could say anything, Abby turned white and started shaking.

"Čer Aya, please leave us," said Logan, in Sentinel. "We have much to discuss."

"As you wish," she said and kissed his head and excused herself. Abby watched her go.

"So, this whole time you've been balls-deep in that elf . . . whore?" she asked.

Logan moved around on the pillows. "Okay, first off, they don't have whores. The concept is—you know what? Never mind. It's not germane. Secondly, it was before you and I were—well, this—"

"*This?*"

"You tell me. What are we?"

"Oh, My God."

"Anyway, Čer Aya and I are . . . bonded, I think."

"Bonded?"

"It's hard to explain."

"Try me."

"Okay, yeah. It started with a sexual thing. Back before you were here. But it wasn't intentional."

"Oh, this ought to be good."

"She was showing me how the shower works—"

"The shower."

"Yes. The way the, the whatever-the-fuck, the bathing waterfall, I guess you'd call it, that thing," he said, gesturing, "comes out of the wall. The stones, you step on them to set the temperature. Anyway, I got in the shower, and then she got in the shower, and—"

"*And?*"

"Well, did you ever see that old commercial where the chocolate meets the peanut butter?"

"You're lucky you're injured right now."

"Nothing has happened between her and I since you and I—"

"—fucked?"

"I was looking for another word, but sure."

A beat; a crack of the fire. A breath of the world.

"Look," he said. "Sex to them doesn't mean what it means to us. You need to understand this if you're going to live here. Mated Sentinels have a whole other thing they do among themselves that transcends physical sex. They have some kind of psychic, telepathic sex thing that we can't even—"

"Oh, really."

"Yes, really. The physical side of sex means as much to them as a backrub does to us. Everybody fucks everybody. It's like getting together to work out. It doesn't mean anything more than that. You haven't had this discussion with Čer Anh?"

"Why would I?"

"Well, you should, because sexual mores are a critical component of a society."

She blew out a spiteful laugh. "Wow, this is an anthropologist's dream, I guess."

He leaned back, shifting to get comfortable. "Actually, it is. Their history, their literature, their songs—much of it is about sexual exploits. You rarely see sexuality out in the open like this."

"You'll never see it in here again, that's for goddamn sure."

"Seriously, Abby. There's nothing going on between her and me. I don't think there ever was. At least, I don't think she thinks so."

"Wow. That . . . that makes it so much worse. Somehow."

"What? It doesn't mean anything to her."

"I don't care what is means to her! I care what it means to you."

"It doesn't mean anything to me," he said, "because there's nothing there for her. My God, how I had once wished there was. But there's this whole other thing that she needs, that I can't provide. Anyway, you were trying to kill me. Things have changed."

"Don't count on it."

She turned, and faced out the door.

"Is she what you want?" she asked, after a time.

"No," he said, and it came out surprisingly firm.

She was crying, but she wouldn't turn to him. "I gave up everything," she sniffed. "My life. My friends. The Army. Everything I've ever done! I'm so fucking scared right now. I need you, Logan. I need you in my life."

"I'm here for you."

"Are you?" she asked, and the dam broke. "Are you really?" she sobbed. "Because I just saw you with her. You incredible, selfish asshole."

"*When I was fucking her, you were trying to kill me.*"

"I wasn't."

"You shot at me."

"I missed," she sniffed.

"Well, we're both here, now. We have to leave some things behind, Abby. Among them are some of our values and beliefs. There are aspects of their society we need to embrace if we're going to assimilate."

She wiped her eyes. "Why should we have to change who we are to live here?"

"Holy shit, that is the most American thing I've ever heard. You're an immigrant, now. Your success is predicated on your ability to mold yourself to the culture you've emigrated into."

She wiped her eyes again and grunted. "Well, I'm not fucking anybody else."

"I'm not saying you need to. What I am saying is, we both need to let go of the idea of sex partners as personal property. It doesn't work like that here. Nobody stakes claims. For all I know, Čer Aya is on her way home to get railed by some Sentinel dude. And it's none of my business, unless they invite me to join."

"Oh, you'd love that, I bet."

He didn't take the bait. "I have no right, here, anyway—and shit, maybe, looking at it, I think more and more, I never did on Earth— to feel jealous, or left out, or backstabbed by whatever she decides to do. Because *they* don't feel that way. I can only control how their actions make me feel, and to do that, I have to think like them."

"You don't have to act like them, though. You're not one of them."

"We've had this discussion. I'm not one of anybody, but I'm giving this a shot."

" *We're* giving this a shot."

The world stopped turning with such force it nearly threw him out of the bed.

"We what, now?" he asked.

"I'm with you," she said, facing him. "All the way. All of this— this world, the war, the Army, the red mercury—I don't care. I mean, I do care, but . . . well . . . I wouldn't be here if you weren't here. This matters to me because you matter to me."

The talking was making his chest ache, and he wasn't sure if it was the subject or the physical exertion involved. He breathed carefully because he wanted to finish this without passing out. "Abby, you shouldn't be here for me."

"Why not? The sheer audacity of you, doing this, is . . . Oh my God, Logan! There is no one else in the world like you! Not in this world, that's for sure, and sure as hell not in ours. I fell in love with you the minute you spoke to the team."

"Wait—you what, now?"

"I love you, Logan," she said. "It took me until I was shooting at you to realize it. Now you show me a world where a man like you wants to live his life and make his mark? A world a man like you wants to side with? We *all* followed you here."

"Great. That's in no way stressful or concerning."

"You're seriously not fucking her?"

"I'm not. Not since you and I—no. She even told me she thinks you and I make good mates. She cares for me, though, on a level that I will probably never understand. Čer Anh probably feels the same for you."

"Čer Anh is a chick," Abby said. "It's not the same."

"They're pansexual. They don't care. She'd totally do you. In fact," he said with an evil grin, "I'm surprised she hasn't."

"I'm not gay, you know," Abby stated, and he had to wonder how many times she'd had to say it aloud in her life. Too many, he could tell.

"Neither are they," he replied. "They don't even understand the concept."

There was a long pause. She nodded. "I'm going to get on the bed with you, now. Don't get any big ideas. I just . . . need someone to hold me."

"Yeah, so do I."

It was late, past dinner, when Abby let herself into Bob's house. No one knocked, here, so neither did she. Fires were going throughout the trees, and music, laughter, and sex had begun, judging from the noises she'd heard emanating from houses on her way over.

"Hey," she said.

"Major." Bob was seated at his table, in a Sentinel robe much like hers, dark brown with silver edging, studying a map that covered his table and making notes in a massive book. "How's Logan?"

His treehouse looked almost exactly like hers, which looked almost exactly like Logan's: woven floors planed smooth and hand-rubbed to a polished finish, a bed, a table, a firepit, comfortable places to sit or lie.

Bob's home had more art in it than either of theirs. On closer inspection, Abby saw it wasn't art so much as knickknacks. He also had several weapons in his possession, which stood against chairs and walls. A shirt of chainmail hung over the back of a chair.

Abby and Logan had homes; Bob had a live-in office. It was likely how he lived back on Earth. There was an ease to it, far removed from the military regularity of her place and Logan's. The dishes were clean, the floor was swept. There was a lot going on, a project everywhere she looked.

"Logan's resting," she said. "It's not good, and it's not getting better. He's not coughing up blood, but we took the catheter out and the lung collapsed overnight, so we had to do it again this morning. It's likely a hemothorax either from a bad bruise or a broken rib. If it's a rib, and it's tearing something up in there, leaking into his chest cavity . . ." she trailed off. "I don't know. I don't know what we're going to do. They have healers, but this is a pre-industrial society. I don't like the idea of anyone here doing thoracic surgery on him."

"I understand that."

She picked up one of the swords. It wasn't as heavy as she'd imagined. She set it down again. "What are you looking at?"

"This map. Have you seen a map of the surrounding areas?"

"Not really, no. The ridges along this canyon, sure."

"Come look."

He'd secured the map with wine goblets on each corner, and specific sections were illuminated with lightstones. She ran her hands over it, and found it was some kind of white hide, scraped clean and creamy soft. The mountains and canyons were penned so clearly, she felt she could pierce her hand on the crags. "Amazing," she said.

"It really is. We're here," he said, tapping the map with a finger. "This canyon is a backwater strip of desert no one comes to. It looks like this canyon is in the middle of a nation run by humans."

"Humans?"

"Humans," he repeated. "The nation, pretty sure it's a nation from the way Ullè Soa has been explaining it, is called the Free Hold."

"You're kidding me."

"The Sentinels are not the dominant species on the planet."

"What the hell are you talking about?"

"Stretching out in every direction from the Free Hold, there are massive, interconnected human societies. Kingdoms. Fiefdoms. What sounds to me like an early feudal system based on something roughly analogous to Germanic tribal law. Hell, there's a human village probably ten miles northwest of here, the first in a string that leads through the mountains to a human kingdom called Falconsrealm. Which sounds cool as hell."

"Can we meet these humans?"

"I don't know. Probably?"

"I mean, ten miles—that's, that's not even the distance back to the Arch. We just went the wrong direction."

"I've been thinking about that. Had the drones had line of sight to that human village, or if they'd sent the drones over the western plain, we'd likely be treating with humans right now."

"You couldn't engineer these circumstances if you wanted to," Abby recited, quoting Paulsen from what felt like a hundred years ago.

"No, you couldn't. Sheer luck."

"There's a lot of that."

"Also, we have a much larger problem, now. We have human nations, and God only knows what their political structures look like, that we're going to have to consider when we anticipate what Hayward Labs does next. If memory serves, you're the intelligence officer. This is your thing."

"I guess it is," she agreed.

"What we do not want, if I read the situation correctly, is for Hayward to learn about the humans. They could just as easily launch a recon mission toward the human settlement, skip this valley entirely, and . . ."

"Oh, God," said Abby.

"Oh, God," Bob agreed. "To our advantage, this canyon is isolated. Ullè Soa tells me it's why the Sentinels and the Sheth live here."

"You've been talking to her a lot, huh?"

"Quite a bit," Bob admitted.

"Getting any?" she asked with a grin.

"Quite a bit," Bob repeated. "They have a—um, different view of sex than we have. It's ridiculously sex-positive. They come over here, and it's like they're asking me to, I don't know, go out for lunch or something. It seems to mean about as much. They're pretty free about it."

Abby said nothing.

Bob continued, "Anyway, humans don't venture into this valley, she says. Come on; there's no reason to, you'll die getting here, plus the Sheth have figured out camouflage, so God help an intruder. On top of that, every now and again entire sections of these mountains explode."

"How long until that happens again?"

"No way to know. As long as nothing interrupts the processes around here, it doesn't seem to be a problem. They've gone hundreds of years without an incident."

"Here's hoping," Abby muttered. "So, if there are humans over there—the Sentinels aren't from here, then? This is a human, um, world? Where are the Sentinels from?"

"I wouldn't call it a human world, but the Sentinels are descendants of a race that lives in the forests a few hundred miles north of here. You have to travel under the mountains, and under this river." He traced it with his finger as it snaked through two lines of mountains north of their position. "They don't even call themselves *Sentinels* up there; they call themselves *Vé*. They call their homeland The Stronghold."

"So, they're related? The Vé?"

"Sentinels are the Vé. They're members of the Vé who long ago accepted shorter lifespans to curate the red mercury and keep it from destroying the world. At least, that's how it was explained to me."

"Holy shit."

"My sentiments precisely. Not only that, they initially thought *we* came from *here*. From some land here they'd never heard of. This is why they were so blown away by us. They couldn't figure out how we were getting back and forth so fast."

Abby frowned. "Don't they know about the Arch?"

"They do, but they don't use it. It's forbidden."

"They didn't think someone else would use it?"

"They're not wired that way. They're extremely insular. They don't do it; therefore, they can't conceive of anyone else doing it. They know there are other people on this planet, but those people never come here. Sentinels live under Sentinel law."

"So, who came through and tore those hikers up? I mean, that's what kicked this whole thing off. The hikers the sheriff's office found, what, six months ago?" It seemed like a lifetime. So much had happened.

"That's the big question, isn't it?"

"Sheth, maybe?"

"Or some really pissed-off humans. We have no idea what the humans here are like.

"All this aside, here's the important part. In my conversations with Ullè Soa, it's become clear that the Sentinels have a unique outlook on the value of their lives, and that's something that you, as our Cultural Officer, are going to have to work around."

"Talk to me."

"These are not people who will charge a machine gun nest, Major. These are not people who will readily perform a frontal assault into withering fire. They don't view combat the way we do; they rarely even fight to the death. The Sentinels live for hundreds of years. The Vé, from whom they're descended," he repeated, "can live for thousands of years. For all anyone knows, short of an accident, they may never die. They're not about to throw their lives away over what they see as a momentary concern. It would be like us volunteering to get shot, over, I don't know, a parking space or something. There's a value equation at work."

"That will make training them a laugh a minute."

"It certainly will. However, this is the thing you might be able to take to them, though I don't know how you'd do it: the Sentinels have all accepted shorter lifespans to curate the red mercury. They've already given their lives up. You need to find a way to conflate that sacrifice with this one."

Abby let out a long breath. "That's going to be a hard sell."

"I don't think it necessarily will be. The trick will be convincing them that whatever Decker and Paulsen send through that Arch next is an existential threat, not only to the Sentinels, but to this world. Convince them of that, you'll likely convince them to lay down their lives for it."

Čer Anh appeared in the doorway with Ullè Soa almost as the words left Bob's mouth.

"Let me guess," said Abby.

She joined hands with Čer Anh, and the immediate image she received was of the pressing need for her to learn the Sentinels' language. She agreed.

A second set of pictures and emotions encompassed a group of American soldiers at the Arch, and something about equipment. Possibly staging for an assault. Scouts on gryphons had spied them, and a larger aerial unit of Sentinels was spinning up.

"Can you get me on one of those gryphons?" Abby asked. "I'll talk to them."

XX

VANGUARD

"Onward we stagger, and if the tanks come, may God help the tanks."
— COL William O. Darby, US Army Rangers

ARCHSTONE

Abby wasn't afraid of heights. She had almost no fear of high places, no vertigo.

Her fear was a lack of redundancy.

Rappelling, rock-climbing, hanging out the side of a chopper, as long as she was belted in? No problem. Skydiving and airborne drops? There was a reserve chute; the odds of two failures in a row were miniscule. Again, no problem.

Conversely, fast-roping—sliding to the ground from a chopper using only hands and feet on a line—made her heart pound. No margin for error. No backups.

No redundancy.

And this . . .

She gripped the rider for all she had, wildly unstable atop the saddle, kneeling, her center of gravity perilously high. There was nothing, literally nothing, keeping her from falling a thousand feet other than her sheer will and grip strength.

She had a hell of a lot of grip strength. And even more will.

Wind was static around her ears, the air cool. Well, cooler, anyway. It was morning, and not hot yet. Feathers ruffed and sighed through the heavy air; the thermals coming off the desert floor were enough that the birds barely had to flap to stay aloft.

They edged up to the Arch with five other gryphons around them.

From a hundred yards out, she could tell it was Martin, Braxton, and two others—Fields, it looked like; and someone else with them, in camo, thin, his face painted.

And pallets.

Dear God, she thought as they touched down with immense grace and almost magical ease, the pallets.

Five pallets, stacked high, wrapped in taut plastic that gleamed in the sun.

"Good morning!" Martin called.

Abby slid off the saddle and landed in a three-point superhero crouch, then stood. "They thought you guys were prepping for an assault," she called back.

"Prepping to repel one," said Braxton.

"Ride's a little sketchy, huh?" Martin asked, coming over to meet her. There was no saluting in the field; he brought her close in a quick Bro Hug.

"Yeah," she admitted. "Good to see you."

"You too, ma'am. We brought you some goodies."

"Wow," she said, feigning thanks, a hand on her chest. "This is all for me?"

"Well," said Martin, as the three others fell in behind him, "we figured we might stick around and show you how to use it. Because we were thinking about this, ma'am, and it's like, you were trained by the Air Force, and the professor is French, so how much could you two possibly know?"

"Oh, fuck you." She laughed and reached up to shove his

shoulder. She looked over the pallets, shrink-wrapped, hundreds of ammo cans and wooden crates under a sheen of heavy plastic with more boxes banded and belted down on top. One pallet had a pile of rifles, either M4s or HK 416s, snugged in between ammunition and God knew what else. "How the hell did you pull this off?" she asked.

"Medved's idea, ma'am," said Martin.

"Medved," Abby said. "I didn't recognize you. Never seen you in uniform."

"It's been a minute, Major."

"Ranger tab," she noted. "Doesn't surprise me."

"Deployed with the Second," Medved said. "Two tours, in the Two Shop. I'm not an operator. But I thought I could help."

"So, Medved, here," Martin continued, "boosted an all-terrain skid loader from the motor pool. We spent the evening making runs back and forth from Logistics."

Abby closed her eyes and raised her eyebrows in disbelief and prayer, in the way only an experienced operations officer can. "Nobody saw you?"

"Oh, everybody saw us. They just didn't say anything."

"There are cameras, there are lights. We had to sneak down to the Arch," Abby insisted. "How did you—"

"Medved wrote up a phony OPORD for a training exercise and distributed it up the chain. Everybody thought it was legit."

"We all put in for two weeks' leave, too," Braxton added. "I went up to Seattle and rented a room at the Four Seasons for the duration, checked us all in. We left the hotel as our contact info. As far as they know, we're up there right now. Texted Colonel Paulsen the room number and everything."

"Two weeks at the Four Seasons? That's going to cost you a fortune."

"Do they have bill collectors over here, ma'am?" Medved asked, smirking.

Abby sighed. "You fuckin' guys. Wouldn't your badges give you away?" She knew as she said it that they'd already figured it out.

"I control the visitor badges," said Medved.

"Yes, you do," she breathed, her hands on her face. "Oh, God. So, you issued yourself—"

"Like hell. I issued it to Staff Sergeant Rod Bonesteel," said Medved. "My alter ego."

Čer Anh, who had ridden behind another soldier, touched Abby's arm and inquired what was going on. Abby explained that they had come to train the Sentinels, and had brought weapons and tools, and had secured their escape.

Sheth will arrive soon. We alerted them. We must remain until they arrive. They will greet these humans with hostility should we not remain.

"The bitch was," Martin continued when she was done, "we weren't sure how the pallets were going to stack up this side. Once we touched the Arch with the edge of the pallet, it just zapped it right through. They seemed to land okay. Now, though, well . . . yeah. They're heavy."

"We need to move these weapons back to your home," said Abby to Čer Anh. "Back to where we can train your people."

Sheth will carry weapons.

"The Sheth are coming," said Abby. "They'll carry it for us. Just sit tight and guard the Arch. How much is here?"

"Two hundred thousand rounds of five-five-six, about half of it belt-fed," said Martin. "We figured you'd have the Mark 46s from Stannard's team, so we wanted to fit those out. About fifty thousand rounds for the 48s. We've got fifty carbines—not a lot, but it's what we could get. Enough to train them up on, anyway. A couple of Mark 19 grenade launchers, really just area security—figure we post those up by the Citadel—and a thousand rounds. There's a few thousand rounds of nine ammo, and then some odds and ends. Grenades— M67, thermite, some of the new modular grenades, too, these are pretty cool, you can stack 'em—NVGs, scopes, spare mags, bayonets.

Couple of drones, radios, solar chargers for everything. I dunno. We were in a hurry, but on the other hand, they let us pretty much clean them out. MREs, uniforms, camo paint, whatever."

"A couple of whiteboards, some markers," Medved added. "Plus, wall-size plots of all the maps we've made, and acetate."

Her jaw worked but no sound came out.

"They may never even realize this stuff is gone. They certainly won't know until someone reconciles the logs when a new commander comes in. That could be years. It's not like we were ever going to use it. There's only one detachment left, and you know Paulsen's going to keep them in reserve. He has to. He can't send another team through here until he replaces everybody. That's going to take weeks, maybe months, which could be a year or more here."

"Glad you're on our side."

"Right back at you, ma'am," said Medved.

The air behind Abby and the Sentinels shimmered like heat waves, and a platoon-sized element of eight- and nine-foot monsters in leather and mail armor with gray skin, tusks, claws, and cabled arms the diameter of Martin's thigh thundered into existence.

Ogres. Trolls.

Braxton stepped back. "Holy shit."

"How do they do that?" Medved asked.

"I don't know," said Abby.

"These are Sheth?" Medved asked.

"Yes."

One of the Sentinels spoke to the Sheth in a low, growling, snarling language, and the others nodded and grunted. There were eleven of them; two each picked up a pallet between them and the last fell in behind them, pulling security, as they carried the gear down the hill with roughly the same effort as two human beings moving a sofa.

"Jesus, we were gonna fight those things?" said Braxton.

"Once, but not now," said Abby. "They answer to the Sentinels.

Mostly. Get your gear on, there are gryphons coming."

Martin threw Sally, his massive machine gun, on one shoulder. All he could think about, watching tree-trunks of legs and gorilla-sized arms carrying a thousand pounds with the same effort that he, himself, carried a little over a hundred on his back, was how they could maximize the impact of the Sheth, not the Sentinels.

He decided not to mention it, yet. There was likely a good reason that the Sentinels did things the way they did, and before he started fucking around with their process, he needed to see what worked and what didn't.

Christ, they were impressive.

Another flight of gryphons landed, feathers, wings, talons, beaks, yet oddly dinosaur-like, moving with the lizard-like quick jerks and bobs. The riders, pilots, whatever they wanted to call themselves, hailed the team with fists on hearts. The American soldiers returned it with formal salutes.

"Brax!" one called, and Braxton knew the voice.

"Eera!" he replied.

Martin slapped him on the back and shoved him toward the second flight of bird-monsters. "Go, man. You came all this way."

"I'll see you over there," said Braxton, shouldering his pack with a grin.

Abby motioned at them. "Everybody, climb on behind a soldier. The Sheth will outpace you down there, you'll never keep up. Don't worry about them. Just hold on when you get up there."

They slung their gear and mounted up.

Logan awoke with a chill. His back ached. He lay on what felt like a block of ice. The room was bright white, sterile, and extremely well-lit.

Looking to each side, he saw he was sprawled out on a quartz slab, surrounded by Sentinels in gauze-colored robes as white as wedding dresses. An array of surgical instruments was spread out behind them.

"Aw, fuck," he grumbled.

Čer Aya was there, also in white. She put her hand on his.

"They must repair you," she said. "You will feel much pain. We fear if we make you unconscious for this, you will not survive it. They apologize for what you will feel, but you will survive this and emerge stronger. They mean you no pain. They apologize for this."

"I won't enjoy this, will I?" he joked.

"You will not," she said. "I will remain with you. You may give me some of your pain."

"I wouldn't do that to you."

"This healer has čyeen," she told him. "However, you still lack the necessary čyeen to endure this without pain. He apologizes for this. He means you no pain. However, he must do this, or you will die."

As she spoke, Logan felt pressure on his legs, then his arms. They were strapping him down. Hot, red, animal panic surged. His heart slammed against his chest. Sweat poured.

"He must do this, or you will die," Čer Aya repeated. "We do this, so you do not die."

The healer's skin was almost obsidian black, his face ancient with crags, terrifying in its sternness. The fangs didn't help. He held a knife before Logan, a small blade, steel, matte, nearly a hobbyist's knife.

"He will repair you with this knife. He will reach the offending piece of bone, then remove it."

"Fuck me," Logan groaned in English.

"He must do this, or you will die. He apologizes. I love you, Logan Kai. Know that we love you and we do this because we value you and need you. This pains us deeply. We abhor that we must do this, but we have no other way."

"Oh, fuck," Logan breathed again. He felt Čer Aya's hand on his arm. The surgeon nodded to another Sentinel, who closed the door.

The knife dug.

Logan wept, and waited for it to be over.

The team stayed behind to load and sort gear into a chamber off the anteroom. They waited for the Sheth, who would be along in an hour or two.

They sat on their backpacks in the shade and drank water.

"So, this is it, huh?" Medved asked. "Kind of a dump."

"Not exactly," Abby said. "This is just the guard shack."

"Patience, young Jedi," said Martin.

Two Sentinels in formal robes fairly ran to Čer Anh, and they spoke for a moment before Čer Anh motioned to Abby.

"I need to go," Abby said. "Excuse me."

Čer Anh led her through the doorway, and down the stairs to the hallway leading out to Red Sky Green.

"Logan?" Abby guessed. "Logan Kai."

"Logan Kai," said Čer Anh.

It was a two-mile run, and Abby ran it. Čer Anh had no chance of keeping up.

When Abby reached Logan's house, up a couple of hundred stairs, she was winded, sweating, red-faced. Logan, who was in his bed, unconscious, folded bandages on his chest sponging through with spots of blood. Čer Aya sat beside the bed on a padded stool.

"Fuck." Abby rushed over to him. "I'm here." His hand tightened on hers when she grasped it, but he remained asleep. "Oh, baby. What did they do to you?"

"They saved him," said Čer Aya. She recoiled as Abby stood

and shot a look at her that may not have killed on its own, but clearly demonstrated the intent.

Čer Aya put a hand on Abby to communicate. Abby threw it off, then took a few deep breaths, and put her hand out, realizing it was the only way to know what was going on.

Logan will not remember this, Čer Aya told her. *The healers had to do this without him losing consciousness. He endured tremendous pain, and we apologize for this. We meant him no pain, but no other option would keep him alive.*

"You operated on him while he was *awake? Conscious?* What the *fuck?!* What kind of barbarians—"

We have removed his memory of the pain. He will not experience it again. He will not know about the pain when he awakens. He will awaken, in time. Many days. He will want to see you. If you wish to stay with him, you may. We will bring you anything you need.

"Wine," said Abby. "Bring me wine. Then bring me more bandages. And find the goddamn surgeon and get his ass up here. I want to talk to him."

Back at the entrance to the Citadel, the team had watched Abby speaking with her—none of them knew what to call her. A guide? Translator?—and run out of the room through a wide door in the back.

"Gotta wonder what that was about," said Martin.

"That was a 'report to the commander' if I've ever seen one," said Braxton.

"Had a few of those in your time?" Martin needled.

"Now and again."

"So, guard shack, huh?" asked Medved, looking out an

arrowslit. "I'm guessing there's more?"

"There's more," said Martin, gesturing to the back of the room, where Abby and her guide had left the door open.

They slipped through, quietly, with the crushing sense of being somewhere they didn't belong. The invitation was missing, and it's what Martin realized he was waiting for; they'd merely arrived here, and offered to lend a hand, but hadn't actually been asked.

Scores of Sentinels in multicolored robes walked the stairs all throughout the massive chamber, disappearing into hallway after hallway. Abby was nowhere to be seen.

The dizzying sets of stairs reminded him of an Escher painting, only they all led down.

And down.

And down.

"That underground world you were talking about," said Martin.

"Those robes look cozy," Medved noted.

They let themselves back into the anteroom, where Brax and Eera, who was still in her armor but had shed her helmet, were talking to Luke and a tall Sentinel man, each wearing black and red gowns markedly different from the slender garb of the Sentinels; nearly kaftans but knee-length, inscribed with silver thread, and expensive-looking. Brax and Eera held hands. Luke and the Sentinel held hands.

"I forgot to mention," said Martin quietly, "Luke's gay."

"I forgot to mention," said Medved, just as quietly, "I don't care."

"I'm just saying," said Martin. "They might be holding hands, or holding hands, holding hands. You dig?"

"I think that's just how they communicate," said Medved.

"I'm just saying," Martin repeated.

"Relax. I'm cool."

"Luke!" Martin called.

They embraced.

"Glad you're here," Luke said.

"Nice threads. Lookin' good."

"It's a, uh, thing. We'll talk," said Luke. "Martin, Medved, please meet Via'k Ul."

The *'k* was a click, the sound used to urge on a horse. "That's gonna be hard to say," Martin admitted.

"You'll get it," Luke promised. " *Via'k* is a title. You can certainly refer to him as *Ul*, or *Master Ul*, until you learn their language. A *via'k* is a, well, you could think of him as a sorcerer, but more like a very learned shaman. A teacher, a spiritual instructor. He's a powerful man, here. He's a very, very powerful, well, wizard. No shit."

"Are you and Ul, um . . ." Martin wasn't sure how to say it. "You two, uh . . ."

"Not exactly," Luke said, speaking carefully. "They have a thing they do that's past physical sex, and, well, I'm learning that. Now."

"What's this?" asked Braxton. "What do you mean, 'past physical sex?'"

"Stick around. You'll see," Luke promised.

"God, I hope so," Braxton breathed.

"Anyway, we've moved on to . . . this other thing. The gown," he said, looking down and straightening them, "I'm an adept of the Via'k. I'm studying."

"Are you shitting me?" Medved asked. "You're telling me you're studying magic? You're going to be a wizard?"

"Yes and no," said Luke. "More like he's helping me discover, and eventually strengthen, psychic abilities. Which, it turns out, are much easier to tap into here."

"Sweet Jesus," said Martin. "A psychic sniper."

"Psychic warrior monk sex wizard," Luke corrected. "And math genius Scout Sniper."

"Be all you can be, baby," said Medved. He put his fist out, and Luke punched it.

"Do I understand you guys are bringing ammo?" Luke asked.

"And weapons. HKs, grenades, some goodies."

"That's great," Luke said. "We need extra ammo. We need to rework the ballistics tables for everything."

"What do you mean, 'rework the ballistics tables?'" asked Medved.

Luke explained in detail about air density, gravity, and curvature of the planet.

"So, you're telling me—" Medved started, and stopped again. "—okay, I don't know what you're telling me."

"I can't hit the floor past two hundred yards," said Luke. "Five-five-six is all over the place, and we need probably a thousand rounds to dial it in. The failure rates are insane, too, which I'm going to guess has something to do with the gravity, or maybe some kind of magnetic weirdness in this valley. Belt-feds jam, nines stovepipe. Not regularly, but far more than nominal."

"Have you told anybody back at the FOB about this?"

"Of course not. I haven't talked to anyone back at the FOB since we learned about it."

"This is interesting," said Medved. "We have MASINT suites on the drones, so we can look into some of this. We didn't think to check, like, gravity, for fuck's sake. Curvature of the planet? Who thinks about this?"

"Can you measure the curvature of the planet?"

"Absolutely," said Medved, as if it was the easiest thing in the world.

"Well, hell, let's get an HK on a bag and start shooting groups," said Braxton. "We've got more than enough sand around here."

"Who's the best shooter we've got?" Fields asked.

It was a tough question, and a serious one among a Special Forces team, all of whom were expert marksmen with literally every weapon in the U.S. arsenal. And many foreign arsenals.

"Outside of Abby? Sorry, guys, that's gonna be me," said Luke.

"He's not wrong." Braxton shrugged. "Fuckin' Marines, take the fun out of everything."

"It's what we do," Luke said with a grin.

"You've got your work cut out for you, kid," said Martin.

Luke put his hand in Via'k Ul's and explained the situation. The master nodded, let go of his hand, and kissed him on the forehead before nodding to the others and leaving the anteroom.

"Does he ever talk?" Martin asked.

"He's telepathic," said Luke. "If he wants to talk to you, he will."

"So, he's cool with you doing this?"

"This is why I'm here. This other thing is sort of, well, extra credit."

Braxton's shoulder and head hurt. He'd turned the shower on as hot as he could get it, stayed under until he was pruny, and he was still jacked up. Changed into clean trousers and a fresh T-shirt, barefoot on the wooden floor, he rubbed his neck and cursed. It had been a long day of shooting, staring into a spotting scope, and making notes.

Again and again; a thousand rounds.

It had been a long day of swearing, as well. Spotting was crap work. And it was frustrating. Today didn't make any damned *sense*.

It wasn't that the rounds had been high or low, but that the spread had been inexplicably wide. Luke had gone into detail about external ballistics—ambient pressure, gravity, altitude—but nothing had been able to account for the spread. At a hundred yards—on Earth, anyway—Luke could regularly cloverleaf three rounds, putting them into a piece of paper with the impact holes, each smaller than a quarter of an inch in diameter, touching. They'd all seen him do it. It was some freakish gene for muscle control and somatic memorization that every sniper had; the ability to time the trigger pull with breath and pulse, to make the weapon an extension of the imagination.

Here, for reasons that no one could explain, those three rounds opened to an unreasonable two, even three inches of gap at a hundred yards. Recruits right out of Army Basic Training shot tighter groups.

Most frustratingly, it wasn't consistent. The Army standard at twenty-five yards was six successive rounds in a four-centimeter circle. At twenty-five yards, Luke was putting rounds in the same hole. At fifty, the rounds started to open so the holes wouldn't touch. At a hundred, they were the spread of a handspan. And that was unacceptable.

They'd worked the math. The spread could be reproduced, but the variations couldn't. They'd gone through every single variable and permutation anyone knew of; stripped the rifle down to its bones and double-checked tolerances; tried other rifles.

The oxygen in the atmosphere was a variable they didn't have and wouldn't have until one of the drones and one of the laptops had charged, which would likely be the next day, but Luke had promised them it wouldn't matter, because the powder in the cartridges had its own oxidizer. The rounds would theoretically fire underwater, or even in space.

Whatever was happening with the guns, a shooter would have to be within a hundred and fifty meters to drop a man-sized target with a carbine on this planet. Leave it to greater minds than their own to determine the whys and hows. In the meantime, they'd work around it.

If they couldn't remedy it, they could at least be aware of it, and that was something.

If they were aware of it, and whoever Paulsen threw at them wasn't, it would be a considerable advantage.

Initially. It would buy them one encounter, which was not remotely enough to win a war.

Braxton's house was on a different tree from Abby, Bob, and Logan. Martin was a few houses above him on the walkway that circled the girth of the trunk; Fields the next house on the downhill side. Luke was living with his mentor with the impossible-to-pronounce name.

There would be language lessons.

He went over his notes again, in a handmade book on the table. They still made no sense.

The pen, the book, the table, the house—handmade, artisanal, breathtaking.

He hooked his phone into a small solar charger on the windowsill. He'd have no service, of course, but he'd have a bank of photographs, messages, and saved images. All that remained of home.

That was the difference. It was radically different from a deployment because there was no four-month rotation back to the world. No reassurance that, yes, one day there would again be an evening watching Jeopardy while scarfing down a Whopper with cheese and chasing it with Jim Beam in Cherry Coke.

No more internet. No more social media.

No more Earth.

He'd have to learn entirely new processes, new patterns, new skills. On the one hand, it was thrilling; on the other, it was terrifying. And what a subtle difference that was, the shades between anticipation and abject terror.

He'd bought a one-way ticket. And this was his first evening here—a bed made of moss, which was pretty dope; a shower that was a *waterfall* right out of a millionaire hipster's wettest dream, organic and bougie as fuck. He'd come how far from a graffiti-riddled St. Louis shithole?

He looked out the window. No glass. The wind fluttered softly through the room.

Someone had built him a fire. He had no idea who.

Someone had filled a decanter with wine. He had no idea who.

He poured a cup of wine that tasted like spiked punch.

A plate of raw strips of meat, berries, and what looked like bread made from nuts and seeds sat on his table. Again: no idea where it had come from. There was a low metal frame over the central fire, and a series of skewers next to the plate. It didn't take much time to figure out the meat was to be skewered and placed in the frame to cook.

Done, he thought, and done.

No idea what the meat was. Little if any care.

No word from Logan. No word from Abby. No word from that knife guy, the medieval weapons guy. He'd be handy to have around.

Same old shit: officers in one world, sergeants in another.

He looked up from the table to find Eera walking in, wearing a white gauzy robe with a green overdress, tunic, he had no idea what to call it. She looked amazing out of armor. Hell, she looked amazing in armor.

She touched his hand, then took his other hand, then kissed him.

I enjoyed seeing you today. You flew with me!

"I did," he admitted. "I am making food. Do you want some?"

I will eat with you, yes. Tomorrow the Valla will assign you a mentor, to learn our language. It thrills me to know you will soon speak our language. We have so much to say to each other!

He led her over to the fire and turned the skewers.

"Food," he said.

"*Nah- yer,*" she replied.

"Nah-yer," he repeated, motioning to the strips of meat, and she smiled.

She put her hands back on his. *Why have you come?* A simple thought that was painfully clear.

"I'm here for you," he said. "And for my friends. And for your people. To help you make good war. My job in our army is to teach soldiers. I'm here to help you with your war."

You make war.

"I do."

It had been all he'd done for the past nine years. He was here because he wasn't good for much else at this point.

With a heaviness in his chest, he realized he was tired of war. Tired of bad war, anyway. Tired of pointless war, endless war. Tired of war for fuck-headed reasons. The entire thinking behind a career in SF was—well, okay, it was fun as shit shooting stuff and blowing stuff up—but more than that, it was the concept behind American Special Forces: *De Oppresso Liber,* to liberate the oppressed. Overthrowing despotic regimes. Raising and training freedom fighters. Changing the world for the better, one downtrodden backwater at a time.

Seeing justice served to assholes.

"I believe we're here to leave a mark on the world," he said. "All of us. For me, that mark is war. War, for good ends. War, to save the oppressed. War, to set things right. My people have not made that kind of war in a long time. They trained me to make that kind of war, and they haven't let me do it. Here, helping your people, I can. This is a thing that my people are doing wrong, but I believe in you and your people. I believe, together, we can change this. Together, we can save your people, drive the bad people from my world away. This is why I'm here."

That was all Braxton had time for before she was in his arms, her hands on his face, her lips tender and hot on his. The fire dimmed by comparison.

He had no idea where these beings had come from, otherworldly in their perfectness, some pure improvisation on the part of all that's beautiful in creation and hid away from the rest of humanity for safekeeping. His hands roamed her, and she returned it, frenetic. He felt her intake of breath with her reading of him, as if it had only now occurred to her how much larger he was by comparison.

He worked his way down her neck, holding her head like a baby bird in his hands, and her robes fell away with a deft touch of her fingers at the belts. He bent her back onto the bed as he kissed down her chest, taking each dark areola in a mouthful, tracing the curves of her breasts and reveling in the noises she made, until he left them, too, moving downwards like a leaf falling, spinning, rejoining the Earth.

He thrilled at new textural discoveries, flavors, subtleties of topography as he snaked his tongue down the silvered trail, heady with the candied scent of her sweat, opening her legs to reveal wisps of hair along black-rimmed folds of shocking pink, perfectly formed and human-looking.

The fire raged late into the night.

XXI

OBLIVION'S EDGE

"There go the people. I must follow them, for I am their leader."
— Alexandre Auguste Ledru-Rollin (1807-1874)

ARCHSTONE

Xander Lynch, the Vice President of Special Projects at Hayward Labs, was tall, pale, and heavy browed, his head shaved clean. He wore khaki fatigues and Cartier aviators, a bottle of water in his hand. He carried no weapons. He was markedly unmilitary in bearing, slender to the point of frailty compared to the operators around him.

Half of Team Four, six troops, fanned out behind him as he stood before the Arch in the heat, one hand on his hip. The sky gleamed sapphire over white-gold mesas and red-black shards of volcanic peaks, the world primeval. The spiked mountain, godlike, tore at hazy clouds tinged with heliotrope from the ringed moon.

"That is a hell of a view."

"Yes," said Paulsen, on his right in full kit. The scope of it still took his breath away. "Yes, it is."

"So, what's this problem you could only tell me about with me standing here?"

"Walk with me," said Paulsen. He winced inwardly at giving Lynch instructions, but in this particular situation, he was definitely in charge. They stepped away from the team and approached the edge of the cliff. The dust kicked up and shimmered in puffs of wind.

Paulsen's eye went to the static lines hanging from the rock, wildly out of place against the valley, bright yellow in the sun and tentacular, sharply defined in the alien purple-pink highlight of the moon.

"The problem is," he told Xander, "we're down to fourteen operators. We've lost almost three-quarters of our people out there."

"That's not good."

"My sentiments, exactly."

"What's happening down there?"

"We have reason to believe the natives are hostile to our intentions. It's going to require overwhelming force to rectify, and we don't have it. Can't get it. I don't have the reach within DoD to bring in a company-sized element on this op. That's what we need. We need two hundred guys. Good ones."

"So, why am I here? Son of a bitch, it's hot."

"You're here because I needed you to see this. There is no other way to grasp the importance of what we're doing. This is no longer merely a question of securing the material you need. We're looking far beyond that. We're talking about administrative and military control of"—he motioned across the valley—"this."

"Control," Lynch repeated. "You're talking about control."

"I am. I need bodies, and not the kind that come cheap. We can't go to DoD on this, like I said. We don't have the time, and we can't risk spillage."

"What's the play?"

"I need you to make some calls. Call TriCorps, call Omega, call whoever you need to call. We start a new op. New read-ons. I need a logistics company in here in thirty days to set up a combat outpost—a COP—at the base of this mountain and a series of posts along that ridge, but I also need two hundred good men equipped for an assault on a fixed position, cocked and locked, once they have it built. And in one year, I need the COP turned into a FOB. Air, logistics, hospital, firebase. The FOB will need to be bigger than WINTERSTONE. A thousand good men."

Xander Lynch stared out at the ridge and the ringed moon for what felt like forever. "Colonel, that's a big ask."

"You get me this, and I'll get you everything else you'll ever need."

"You're talking about colonization."

"Yes," said Paulsen. The word bugged him. It was exactly what Logan had warned him not to do, but looking back on Logan now, it was clearly a warning born of indignation. Giant flesh-sucking snake-lampreys, air assets, infantry with hand weapons; fine. There was nothing here that could stand up to a company-sized element with artillery backing them up. Going in there with twelve guys was one thing. Going in with two hundred was another league altogether.

"Once we have a FOB set up," Paulsen said, "this is yours. All of it. We'll make you viceroy. You can come in here and rule this place like a king, for all I care. We'll name it after you. Planet Hayward."

Another long pause as Lynch unsnapped a pair of binoculars from his belt and scanned the desert for a full minute. Paulsen knew it was a minute, because a blue Patek Phillippe Nautilus on the wrist of the hand working the focus ring swept its seconds marker fluidly in a full revolution. It was a quarter-million-dollar watch. What do you give the man who has everything?

"Hayward Valley," Xander said at long last, putting the glasses down. "Planet Lynch."

AUTHOR'S NOTE

After extensive evaluation by U.S. Intelligence and Special Operations personnel, several draft chapters detailing the Special Forces tradecraft of raising and training an indigenous army, including, but not limited to, descriptions of tactics, techniques, and procedures instrumental in training up a small and comparatively low-tech guerrilla force to defeat a modern company-sized direct-action element, have been omitted entirely, as has a chapter dealing with USSOCOM and USGOV policies on the training and evaluation of indigenous troops and the doctrinal role of Special Forces in foreign internal defense.

After consultation, said personnel determined that including even purely theoretical unconventional warfare tradecraft flirted with aggregate classification issues, and more than that—given the political atmosphere in the United States as this was going through initial Security Review during the 2020 election—all agreed it was a terrible idea. I respectfully ask you to honor their input. This is perhaps even more relevant as Stonelands *goes to press in 2025.*

If you really want to know how to train up and lead an army of your own, head down to your local recruiting office and ask about an 18X contract with an Airborne guarantee. Have fun, and tell them I sent you.

Envision, if you will, a spectacular training montage involving elves, gryphons, and machine guns as we time-jump forward 45 days in the Stonelands and approximately eight months on Earth.

XXII

THE SCAR IN THE SKY

In WWII, "Mad Jack" Churchill became the only soldier in the Twentieth Century to be credited with a longbow kill.

Red Sky Green

Logan awoke from panicked dreams of swimming until he could no longer see the shore. A haze of half-memory dragged along behind him—years of nightmares, of drowning, of being pulled to the surface time and again.

Ghosts of meaning fled back into darkness, and he was left in the chill and the light. His eyes traveled the room, familiar yet oddly distant. It took long moments before he remembered this place.

His new home. His Sentinel home.

His Valhalla home.

Čer Aya was next to him, dressed in a filmy little thing, holding his hand. Abby, dressed in black and gold robes, held the other.

"Hey," Abby said.

He smiled. "Made it to Valhalla."

"That, you have," she said, in perfectly accented Vé.

He couldn't ask her how long it had *been*; they had no word for *be.* It took him a minute to formulate the question. "How many days did I miss?" he asked her, also in Vé.

"Forty-five days."

He swore in French.

"The healers used *čyeen*," Abby said. "The magic—" he now understood *čyeen* as meaning something closer to *gift* "—but they appear to have overdone it. The healing magic contains a restive component, and it landed on you very hard."

"You speak better than I do," he observed.

"You'll catch up," said Abby, only it wasn't entirely *catch up*, but rather *catch the bird,* though he understood its meaning. Čer Aya squeezed his hand.

"Hello, Čer Aya," he told her. "Thank you."

"You rested," she said. "You healed. We tended you as we would a hero of our people. How do you feel?"

"I feel—" He stretched out his shoulder; it was tight. There was a scar across his chest, still pink-white and tender, which he absolutely didn't want to fuck with. "I feel terrible. Tired. Pain. Manageable pain. I would like to get up, please. Find me my leg."

"You may find walking difficult for a time," said Čer Aya. "We will help."

"Fuck," he grumbled in English.

"We've had someone on you every minute," Abby assured him. "Working with you, massaging you, moving you around, making sure you can walk when you wake up. Much has happened that you need to know." Her Vé was flawless, down to the inflection. "You will enjoy seeing how the training has progressed."

"Training?" he asked her in English. "What training?"

She dropped into English to meet him. "Martin, Braxton, Fields, and Medved all joined us. They brought a shitload of guns and ammo, pallets of it, and they've been training up the Sentinels."

"You're kidding me."

"Nope. They brought, like, a quarter-million rounds."

"Holy shit."

"We've trained up a couple of rifle platoons. They also brought a handful of belt-feds, and a few grenade launchers."

Logan was pulling the liner over his stump. He stopped, getting her full attention. "Rifle platoons?"

"These guys are Special Forces. It's what they do. They make soldiers."

"Apparently. And Bob?"

"If you mean 'Siege Lord Valenteen'—"

"I didn't think I did."

"Bob's now in charge of the defense of the Citadel. He teaches classes on Earth military history and strategy to their officers and senior leadership."

"Okay," he admitted. "That, I get. How's Luke?"

"Luke is . . . well, he's Luke," she said. "There's a lot going on, there. He's been helping with the training, but he, um . . . better if he tells you, I think."

"That doesn't sound great."

"No, it's wonderful," she insisted. "It's just unexpected."

"What, is he pregnant?" Logan asked, settling his blade prosthesis and pumping the air out of it. He'd lost some weight.

"Not quite," said Abby.

"What's not quite pregnant?"

"You could say he accepted an apprenticeship. He's, he's gonna . . . okay, fuck it. He apparently has some kind of knack for their magic. So, he's been splitting his time between the project and his devotions."

"Devotions."

"It's kind of a monk thing," Abby said. "There's a lot of meditating and, you know what? I don't get it all. I'm not going to pretend to."

He tied his hair back. "I know how you feel."

"Anyway," she said, helping him to his feet, "we need you healthy as soon as you can manage, because Swackhammer and

Company are building something at the other end of the valley."

Čer Aya got under one arm and Abby got under the other. The room swayed.

"Building something?" Logan asked. "Building what?"

"We're not sure. That's why you need to get your shit together. One foot at a time. We gotta move."

Logan hadn't used a cane in years. This was a nice one, as carved and braided and polished as anything else in Red Sky Green, and, for all he knew, it could have been two thousand years old.

It had been a long hike to the stairs. And a lot of stairs. He'd had to take them one at a time, resting on each. Hours. It had been hours.

"I'm just going to live up here from now on," he told Abby once they'd reached their destination, a library under the Citadel with well-lit shelves stacked with leather-bound tomes and racks of parchment scrolls. Like everything in the forest and everything in the Citadel, the furniture was solid and ancient. The room glowed from a hundred angles with the sheen of burnished leather and hand-rubbed wood. "Forward my mail."

Chip Martin was already inside, flipping through a book. He rose from the table, looking impossibly large among the Sentinel-sized trappings. His robes, also gold and black, very formal, had an extra panel across each shoulder; the Sentinels' looms weren't large enough to make clothes to fit him. "It pleases me to see you, *khos* Logan *Kai*," Martin greeted in Vé as smooth and beautiful as Abby's.

"It pleases me to see you, Martin *Shad-Hai*," Logan returned.

"It pained me greatly to hear of your injury, Master Khos. I visited you many times. Your recovery and presence here today pleases me. How do you feel, sir?"

"You have an impressive command of Vé," said Logan. He felt

like he was speaking through molasses, comparatively; as if he were speaking measured, deliberate, British English and they were rattling off between each other in Basque at a third again the speed. "I need you to speak English to me until I catch up," Logan said in English. "There are going to be concepts here that I want to be sure I grasp in their entirety."

"No worries, boss," said Martin.

Logan stayed standing, stretching in micro-increments as Martin went into detail about the troops, the training, and the issues with the guns. Abby had explained most of it along the way, but it was good to hear it from the NCO side and to see that a lot of it lined up from both labor and management.

A cool wind rolled through the anteroom, gentle, smelling of bookdust and good oxygen. The lights in here were veins of crystal set in a polished stone ceiling of red and black, impossibly gorgeous, at odds with the deepening disquiet as Martin went on about the issues involved with training up squads of Sentinel riflemen.

"At first, we thought it was an ammo problem," Martin was saying. "You remember the first mission in the valley? I was having stoppages."

"Vaguely." It had scratches of significance, but it was so incredibly long ago. Everything before the surgery now felt like a dream, mere shreds of memory. Ten years prior, the same thing had happened to his life before the IED. Trauma had a way of blasting away the Before Times like a flamethrower, ephemeral husks of relevance vanishing in a torrent of cinders. He could see something had been there once, but that was it.

"Well, the ammo's fine. All the weapons shoot the same— shittily," Martin added. "We've stripped them down to the bones. It could be the tolerances, the air pressure, some chemical composition in the air."

"Well, that can't be right," said Logan. "The bullets have their own—"

"—their own oxidizer in the powder," Martin finished. "Yeah, we thought of that. But it's more or less like trying to fire a belt-fed underwater. I mean, yes, it'll kick the bullets out. It'll go bang. But underwater, it won't continue to cycle; there's not enough force in the combustion to push the bolt back against the hydrostatic pressure each round, and eventually it fails. Two or three rounds, and it shuts down. You with me so far?"

"Sure."

"This isn't as bad as shooting underwater—obviously, because if there was something fucking up the guns to that degree, whether it's air pressure or some trick of the atmospheric chemistry, we'd all be dead. Chemistry's chemistry; you run off chemistry, I run off chemistry, the guns run off chemistry. But whatever it is, I can get off ten, twelve rounds with a belt-fed, but the failures amplify over time and after that, it jams. So, we've been training the machine gunners on three-round bursts."

"Better than nothing," said Logan.

"Definitely. Also, we're finite on ammo," said Martin. "So, there's also that."

"They're also not very accurate, anymore," said Braxton, walking in behind them. "How you doin', Professor?"

"Hello, my friend," said Logan. They embraced.

"You look like shit, man," Braxton offered. "I mean, a cane? Really? How old *are* you?"

"Call it an affectation," Logan said. "I may keep it."

"It suits you. Anyway, the accuracy. After about a hundred and fifty meters, you're at almost five MOA,"—minutes of angle; an inch of variance per hundred yards that would manifest even with the gun held in a vise—"we're tracking a seven-inch spread at one-fifty. At two hundred, that cracks open to well over a foot. There's nothing you can do. Bullets don't fly straight, at least not at this end of the valley. They seem to work better the further north you go. Magnetism, magic, we got nothin'."

"This is interesting, though," said Abby, "because nothing Paulsen's guys bring over here is going to work quite right unless they laser-guide it. They won't know anything's wrong until they start shooting and can't hit anything at any consequential distance."

"Roger that," said Martin. "Also, their belt-feds will be as limited as ours, so once they start really hosing through ammo—say, they bring a CROWS or a minigun or something, and come on, you know they will—they'll hit a learning curve. At least, if we can get 'em into this end of the valley."

"We can capitalize on that," said Logan.

"Roger that, sir. Let's sure as hell not tell 'em," Martin suggested.

"Medved's here," said Braxton. The skinny intel analyst with the mop-top, now in black and silver formal Sentinel robes and Birkenstocks he'd obviously brought from Earth, waved and approached carrying a book under one arm and a rolled paper in his hand.

"Got the latest," he said. "Good to see you, Professor."

"You're the, ah, intel guy," Logan remembered. "I missed your name, I'm sorry."

"Todd."

"Todd," said Logan. "Okay. Well, we have a real party, here, don't we, guys?"

"We're about to," said Braxton. "We lost a gryphon to a drone about halfway down the valley two days ago. They are here, and they are definitely probing this way."

"Armed drone?" Logan asked. "Took down a gryphon?"

"Negative. The gryphons eat them. The parts—well, sir, it's ugly. Every time they send up a drone, we lose a gryphon a few days later. The gryphons can't digest the pieces. Fuckers."

"Roger that," said Medved. "So, sir, we've been building an intelligence network, setting up camouflaged observation and listening posts—OP/LP's—throughout the valley. The Sheth are now sensitized and actively reporting to Sentinel overseers every day.

Those reports come back to me, and they're logged in the book."

"Todd gives a summarized daily report. In Vé," Abby added. "He's effectively been writing the history of the valley one day at a time."

"All this in six weeks?" Logan marveled.

"Do we have the time to spare, you think?" asked Martin.

"You tell me."

"I'm gonna say no," said Medved, and unrolled the paper. "Ma'am, you've seen some of this, but I need to brief the Professor, so excuse me for going back over old data."

It was lines, crude, expressionist charcoal on paper reduced to the abstract in alternating fat and thin marks, covered in scribbles. Dark strokes outlined huge squares, two-dimensional, a child's rendering of a dragon-creature puking into a huge wastebasket, maybe.

Medved helped him along by saying, "This is a sketch one of the Sheth drew of what he saw at the end of the valley."

"Was he having a stroke?" Logan guessed.

"No, sir. I had the same reaction, initially. You have to see what they see. It's like speaking Vé. You have to think like them. The Sheth take what's important and draw it more emphatically. So, look at the dark lines and ignore the scribbles. Look at the squares. The dragon."

It fell into place, shimmering and morphing like a Magic Eye puzzle when Logan unfocused his mind and stopped expecting to see anything.

Construction. Flat rocks piled up—sandbags. Walls. Behind the dragon, a three-story tower with a roof, against the base of a cliff.

"Those are Hesco barriers," said Abby. "Expedient blast walls. And that thing filling them, that he thought was a dragon, is a front-end loader. A big one, by the looks of it."

"The standard Cat front-end loader, the Nine-Six-Six, is eleven feet wide," said Medved. "If they can get that through the Arch, they can get armor through."

"They haven't yet, have they?" Logan asked.

"Not that we know of," said Abby. "But they're definitely putting up a COP. They're here to stay."

XXIII

ECLIPSE

Ultima ratio regum. ("The final argument of kings.")
— Inscription on French cannons, on order of Louis XIV

Sentinel Observation Post, above Phase Line FREHLEY
Hayward Valley, Planet Lynch

The drone soared above the valley, sending back gorgeous video from half a mile in the air.

Logan's team back on Newfoundland used something similar, a French drone that Kenny, his research assistant, flew with a game controller. This one was smaller, yet denser, built from black carbon fiber with sleek curves, industrial, clearly military. The feed linked directly into Todd Medved's phone, which charged with a flip-out solar panel on his pack and was now clipped into the controller.

They'd draped the observation post in camouflage netting over enormous boulders shoved together. Flat rocks served as chairs, benches, and work surfaces. There was jerky, dried berries, and plenty of water in skin containers. Todd's feet were kicked up on a flat bit of stone, and Logan leaned up against a slab behind him.

Three Sentinel soldiers took turns watching the valley, unblinking, with a sobriety and focus that would have made a Buckingham Palace Guard blanch. Every half hour or so, one would sit and another would take their place.

"How does it do that without cell towers?" Logan asked. His legs were feeling better; he'd been coltish for a few days, but it had come back soon enough. The walk out here had actually, and he hated to use the words but he would, if pressed, been good for him.

"You can transmit video up to ten miles," Todd said. "You just have to know what to look for."

"What do you look for?"

"If I tell you, you'll tell someone else, and pretty soon everyone has one of these and I lose my competitive advantage. I'd be out in the civilian world, and then I'd have to work for a living."

"You see any other civilians around here?"

"We're about to find out, sir."

Logan looked over Todd's shoulder as the camera zoomed in on a combat outpost built to the Army standard: a maze of Hesco barriers, hard-roofed dug-in buildings, and a rear exit up the soft sand of the mesa toward the Arch. The tower was clearly defined, along with what would be belt-fed emplacements on the exterior corners, sandbagged, open to the sun. Manning the position would prove brutal, but Logan imagined no one expected to be up there long.

No one ever did. It was the allure of superior firepower: belt-fed weapons with their come-hither eyes promising quick and easy conquest of those dirty indigs . . . and the inexorable betrayal of weapons technology. Ammo ran out. Barrels overheated. Enemies found the lone sector the guns wouldn't traverse and tightroped that shit.

Or, he remembered, sometimes they brought bigger guns of their own.

The jihadis in the southern end of the Sahara had outfitted

pickup trucks with Oerlikon 20mm anti-aircraft guns and Russian-built ZU-23's on modified mounts that fired horizontally, raining slugs the size of a man's thumb. Shadetree engineering at its finest.

Worse than that, though, were the 40's.

40-millimeter anti-aircraft cannons firing explosive-tipped rounds were the jihadi's must-have toy, year in and year out. Humanitarian groups had reported houses and entire families literally vaporizing under them.

You could never underestimate what the local boys will bring to the party. He shuddered.

"See those?" Todd said, pointing to the screen. He pinched it and pulled it larger. "Right there."

"Solar panels." He'd had a similar array at his last dig site. Thin, sleek, modern. Ridiculously expensive and sublimely powerful, absolutely state of the art. "That's an Archimedes system. Or a knock-off."

"That's their Achilles heel," said Todd. "We wreck that? They're done." He scrolled to the right. "I thought I saw . . . hang on . . ." He zoomed in a little more. "See it?"

Logan saw it. "Tracks," he said.

"Tracked vehicle tracks. That's not a loader. That's either a tank, or a self-propelled howitzer. It's probably under something, could be as simple as plywood and sand. Build a bunker, dump sand on it until it blends in. We won't see it from the air."

"Holy Christ," said Logan, "they brought armor."

"It sucks being right all the time."

"Can you tell where it is?"

"Not from here, and we're short on juice." Todd clicked the phone several times, taking still photos, and called the drone back in.

This was the dangerous part: you had to make the decision between getting the bird back to you as fast as possible and risking detection with every passing second.

It wouldn't take much—a glint of the drone in the sky; an EM burst picked up by whatever they had hiding underground whether it was a tank or a howitzer; another drone they couldn't see locking onto its signal as it beelined for them; any of it would spell disaster.

Todd always opted for the beeline approach, given the opportunity.

Logan heard the quadcopter humming as it closed. "Don't bring it here. Run it in a straight line and land it in those rocks." He pointed south along the ridgeline about five hundred meters off.

"You want to walk that far?"

"We're going that way, anyway. We'll pick it up as we go. Run it straight for those rocks. Trust me."

The drone changed direction, picked up speed, and raced for a rocky protrusion on a spur overlooking the valley. Todd was dialing it in and slowing it down when an earthquake shook the canyon, impossibly loud, rattling the very foundations of the planet and kicking up dust around them. The Sentinels all took cover. Logan threw Todd down and lay over the top of him.

"The fuck?" Todd asked.

"That's what I thought," Logan said.

"Stay very, very still," Logan told the Sentinels in Vé. "A steel dragon awakens, and he looks for us. He will see you if you move. Do not move."

"Shit, that thing's live," Todd said in a quivering voice.

"Tank?" Logan asked.

"Howitzer, maybe. Either way, those things have millimeter-wave radar. Out here, with no foliage? Totally unattenuated. It could see a hummingbird in flight."

"Jesus. Technology."

"Fuckin' A. We're boned."

Logan slid off him and low-crawled for the post's rear opening. He peeked out. The rocks on the spur half a kilometer away had been leveled. Smoke and dust rose into the sky. Whatever it was, it had blown the top of the ridge completely off.

"The good news is, they probably think that was our OP."

"The bad news is, they're definitely scanning this ridgeline," said Todd. "We're stuck." The crushing weight of not knowing, of being hunted and powerless, was new to him. The crosshairs of the howitzer were an anvil on his chest.

"Stay down," Logan told the Sentinels. "If you move, we all die. We will show you a manner in which to move but we can't do so safely, yet."

Logan dragged each of their packs and rifles across the sandy floor, painfully slowly.

"Sentinels," he said, "We leave now. Stay low. Keep the rocks between yourselves and the dragon. Do not, do not," he repeated, "stand, run, nor breach the ridgeline once we crest this hill. We move from rock to rock. Keep the rocks between you and the dragon. The dragon cannot see through rock. If he sees you, we will all die. Do you understand?"

"We understand," one of the Sentinels said.

"Follow us, one at a time," said Logan. He pushed out through the camo netting and slithered up the soft sand to the crest of the ridge, keeping the rocks behind him, waiting to be wrong; waiting for the blast that would take the top of his hill off and end all five of them.

It never came. He dropped over onto the other side.

The glare from the sand was punishing, even through his sunglasses. Christ, it was miserable out here. Why was he fighting a war in this shit yet again? He distinctly remembered a pact he'd made with himself in the distant past to stay the hell out of the desert.

Todd was right behind him. Logan could see he was still thinking about the tank, or whatever it was. He knew there was a delineation between a tank and a whatever, but if it had tracks and a gun, to him it was a tank.

Todd spit out a curse. "They could use it for counterbattery if we hit them with the Mark 19's. I didn't even think of that. We are fucked, man."

"What's the range on that radar?"

Todd shrugged. "Ten klicks?"

"You don't sound very sure."

The first Sentinel slid down the sand and dropped to the rocky floor behind them, armor jingling and clattering. Logan clapped him on the back.

"That's the book answer," Todd admitted. "I'd have to look it up on a classified system to know for sure. Call it ten klicks. I mean, physics."

"There's no line of sight to the Citadel from that outpost," said Logan. "The canyon makes that jog to the left, and there's that big-ass piece of rock in the way, the Knife. They'd have to lob one, like, miles up and then bring it down, right? Can they do that?"

"Hell if I know. There's nothing stopping them from trying. This whole place is basically their firing range, now. Plus, all they've got to do is roll that bitch down the center of the canyon, or back it up the hill, until they've got a clear shot. It isn't hard. They could do it in an hour. Maybe minutes."

Todd slugged water from a Nalgene bottle as if he suddenly couldn't get enough of it. Logan watched his hands shake and remembered the first time he'd been shot at in anger. He hoped, for Todd's sake, the young analyst wouldn't ever have to get used to it.

The third Sentinel joined them, the team of Svartálfar implausibly disconsonant in leather breastplates over mail hauberks with Coppergate helmets and HKs slung on their shoulders.

They stuck to the rocky hillside and traversed as quickly as they could manage.

"You're telling me they brought a goddamned self-propelled howitzer?" Martin asked. He clutched his head.

They sat at tables in the library-turned-intelligence center, sipping wine. Logan and Todd had changed into Sentinel garb, which was insanely more comfortable than pants. *This is it,* thought Logan, *when we solve this for good, I'm never wearing pants again.*

"Probably," said Todd. "Might be an Abrams, but there'd be no reason to bring a tank. There's nothing to shoot at. You don't need a tank here. You need stand-off. And they need negotiating power. Stick a one-fifty-five at the other end of the canyon? You'll get our attention."

"They've got it," Logan agreed.

"So, how do we get rid of it?" Bob asked.

"Blow off a track and turn it into a pillbox exercise," recommended Fields, from a separate table. "That's . . ." his voice trailed off. "That's all's we can do. That's all's you *can* do."

"That brings up a whole other set of issues, though," said Bob. "These people, they're not wired for that. You'll never get a team of Sentinels to run up the middle into a tank to draw fire. I've been going over their military history, if you can even call it that. There's nothing to suggest that the thought has ever crossed their minds. To my knowledge, there's never been a Sentinel in their entire history who's done anything of the sort."

"Well, then we'll do it," Martin said.

The room stared at him.

Logan broke the silence. "The hell we will."

"We can't ask them to do something we're not willing to do, ourselves," said Martin.

"Oh, yes, we can," said Logan.

"That's not how this works," Martin insisted.

"Understand the relative worth," said Logan, and before Martin could get upset, he clarified. "Look, it's a shitty concept, and it's foreign to you as an American soldier, but if the six of us get mowed down rushing that thing, who do these people turn to when Paulsen sends the next wave in a few months? How do they know what to expect from the next assholes? More than that, who trains the next fighters up? Who explains to them what the fuck a millimeter-wave radar system is? Who figures out what Paulsen or whoever are doing, next?"

"The trick is, getting close enough to damage the thing in the first place," said Abby. "I mean, if they've got that kind of hardware, they've certainly got thermal. How do we get in there? Even the Sheth can't get that close, as good as they are."

"That howitzer is their Fuck You," Todd insisted. "We neutralize it, they won't have anything to negotiate with. That's got to be our end game."

"We neutralize it," said Logan. "And we overrun the compound and burn it to the ground."

"We should be looking for a way to destroy the Arch," offered Fields.

"We thought about that," said Abby. "Bob?"

"There's far too much power flowing through that thing—however it works—to risk damaging it," Bob said. "I mean, we could be basically setting off a nuke in that end of the valley if we do. This valley is full of radioactive material on the verge of going supercritical, anyway. If they had any brains, they wouldn't even be considering shooting artillery off around here."

"Wait," said Logan. "The red mercury. It's used in radar-absorbing paint, yes? Paulsen was talking about it."

Bob perked up. "So, we're told. Interesting. Yeah. Huh. Okay."

"Is there any way we can . . . I don't know . . . use it?" Logan asked.

"It's so goddamned dangerous," drawled Fields. "Direct contact with more than a few tablespoons of it can kill you, from what I've read. If you're thinking of smearing yourself in it to sneak up on a tank, you'll be dead before you hit the ground, I'd bet. Besides, there'd be no way to test whether or not it works. You wanna go stand in front of a tank and wave your arms around? Be my guest, Professor."

"I've got depleted uranium rounds," said Abby. "One mag. Ten rounds. If it's a Paladin, or some other self-propelled gun, I might be able to kill it. If it's a tank, though?" She shrugged. "I might as well be throwing rocks."

"There's that big of a difference between a—what did you call it? A self-propelled gun? And a tank?" Bob asked.

There were nods around the table.

"Tanks are meant to get into fights," said Fields. "Way more armor, faster. The guns have a higher rate of fire, but less range. Tanks are for front-line support. They shoot depleted uranium rods, not arty rounds. Totally different."

"It's probably a self-propelled howitzer," said Medved. "It wouldn't make any sense to bring a tank, here."

Martin changed tacks. "Hell, we've got thermite grenades. Take a drone, rig a thermite grenade on it, set it down on top of the bunker where the piece is."

Medved shot that one down. "Someone has to pull the pin."

Martin sighed in exasperation. "Man, that sucks. We've got these modular grenades, too, you know? Stack 'em two, three, hell, ten at a time."

"Ten? I thought you could only stack three of those," said Abby. "I remember reading a thing."

"Well, yeah, technically," said Martin. "When we were first working with these, back in concept, we stacked five of them, once. God, that was awesome." He grinned at the memory. "Anyway, I think there's a regulator or something in them now so you can only stack three of them, but these we brought? These are the old prototypes. Pretty sure they're the same as we used to fuck around with. If we can daisy-chain ten of them, we could wreck that thing. The spalling effect alone would trash everything inside. You're talking about over a kilo of Composition B.

"But I'm dreaming," he decided, crestfallen. "Dammit. Somebody has to pull the pin and hold the damn handle down. Three-second fuse." He bit his lip in thought, then shook his head. "There's no way. There's got to be a way."

Braxton laughed. A quiet, simple laugh.

"What's so funny?" Abby asked.

Braxton set his wine glass down on the table as the team quieted. He met everyone's eyes in the room before he spoke.

"You guys," he said plainly. "I'm dating a pilot."

It was a multi-pronged, phased operation: simple, solid, Special Forces 101.

The Sheth, hopefully under the cover of camouflage, would attack the walls and look for a weak spot, draw fire, and melt into the landscape in the hopes that the tower gunners would waste ammo. They had missile weapons, particularly slings that could throw rocks up to a few pounds, and it didn't matter what kind of body armor you were wearing, catching a three-pound rock at a hundred-plus miles per hour was a bad day.

Two platoons of Sentinel riflemen would position around the COP, using the rocks for cover and spreading out as best they could; no sense in letting The Dragon, as they were calling it, get more than one of them at a time. They'd shoot once, move, shoot again once they were set. This would distract any other gunners. The team expected workers to return fire with small arms, and it was entirely possible that there was already a military or mercenary quick-reaction force on site.

While the gunners were engaged, the gryphons would attack from above, several flights, two riders to a bird, the rear rider dropping grenades. There would be two flights of grenadiers with standard M67 frags with a five-second fuse, and three dive-bombers—Braxton, Martin, and Fields—aiming for the solar farm and the Dragon with daisy-chained modular grenades.

Bob would remain at the Citadel, as Siege Lord, and direct defenses in case the attack failed or a counterattack broke the lines.

Abby and Luke would provide overwatch from a rocky outcropping two thousand meters to the east, delivered by gryphon, as whatever weird-ass effect the Citadel was having on accuracy would be minimized at the north end of the valley. They'd also have eyes on the Arch and a clear shot at the ridgeline in case reinforcements appeared.

Logan would lead the attack from the ground.

It had taken over three hours to explain it to the Valla and the Čers, backed up by Ullès attesting to the power of the grenades and the three soldiers who had seen the power of The Dragon.

Valla Kamè was quiet for a long time, during which the team stared at each other.

"We appreciate all you have done," she said at last.

"But," Braxton anticipated under his breath, in English.

"However," said Valla Kamè.

"Son of a bitch," Martin breathed.

"Your value to our people lies in your strengths as teachers, as *khos*," Valla Kamè said. "We cannot risk losing you. We can create more soldiers and more *uls*, even more Ullès. We need you alive, training them."

"Well, we appreciate that," said Logan, "but—"

"Our ancestral homeland, the Stronghold, lies to the north, beyond the mountains. You will reach it through our lands, a safe underground passage beneath the northern mountains and beneath the great northern river. Our people will take you. When you reach the Stronghold, we will inform The Old Ones of your value. You will train new Sentinels in your ways of war and they will travel here to help us make war. This way, we will sustain the war without jeopardizing you."

The team discussed it among themselves.

"We have no interest in that," said Logan, speaking for the team after they'd talked for a bit. "We came here to fight. We came here as soldiers."

"You came here as soldiers, but you serve as khos," said Valla Kamè. "We will not discuss it further."

"We must," said Bob.

Oh, shit, thought Logan.

"We can't train your soldiers in the intricacies of our people's ways of battle in the time remaining," said Bob. "We need to accompany them on the field and direct them. Our people must work the explosives, which require specific application. I need to remain here, as Siege Lord, and direct the defenses in case this fails. We cannot, and will not—"

His argument was lost in arguing and commotion among the Čers and the Valla, which went on for some time before Valla Kamè made her pronouncement. It was as simple as their plan:

"Any of you who survive this military action will travel to the Stronghold. There, you will serve the Vé as khos, and they shall know you do this as warrior heroes blooded against our foes. You will live full and prosperous lives among the finest of our people, and one day go to your graves having made good war."

"Shit, I can work with that," said Braxton.

Logan looked at each team member in turn. Everyone nodded.

"We accept your most fair and noble decree, Valla Kamè," said Logan.

"Go forth," said Valla Kamè. "Do well."

XXIV

GERONIMO

Going Geronimo: American Indian slang for losing one's temper; compare with the wider American use of "going postal."

An hour past dawn, Logan peeked out from behind the rocks at the edge of the combat outpost—the COP—still not entirely believing they were going to try this.

He'd done his face up in brown, sand, and white, forgoing the military-standard stripes and splotches of desert camo for Blackfeet war paint: a white triangle from his nose to either side of his chin; dark brown masking from his forehead to his cheeks; and, as a nod to his Sentinel brothers and sisters, a series of white dots down each side of the mask. His hair was braided tight, held in place with a Sentinel man's silver barrels, swinging free behind his low-profile helmet.

Danger filled the air, compounded by raw fatigue and an officer's ever-present misgivings, the unspoken, soul-killing distrust of self that accompanies command. And while in many ways he was right back where it had started—hiding behind one of these massive boulders, slowly roasting in the heat, hoping to fuck he didn't get seen—there was an inescapable inequality.

This time, he knew exactly why he was here.

He shouldered the HK and scanned the Hesco wall through the scope. He made it out to be two hundred yards, a little under. They were close. Almost too close, depending on what weapons the COP had on the towers.

He could hit at this range, easily; the Sentinels with him? Maybe? He'd seen them shoot, and they weren't bad, if mechanical. They'd been practicing at a hundred and fifty. They'd taken to guns remarkably quickly, employing a knack for technical knowledge that surprised them all. Abby and Bob assessed that it traced back to their social organization as artisans. They loved intricate, complicated things; the practically jeweled movements of the HKs fascinated them, and they treated the weapons like precious relics.

As long as they kept their heads down and didn't let anyone kill them, they'd be fine.

Getting it through their heads that they weren't there so much to destroy the enemy as much as to keep them scared and behind cover had seemed to work well. Overwhelming firepower was an easy sell.

Whether he could do it with fifty guys? Well, he'd see.

They didn't have exact numbers on the personnel at the base, but it didn't seem like many. He wondered how Paulsen had gotten so many personnel read-on to ARCHSTONE so quickly. These guys didn't look like commandos. They looked like regular Joes, and as he watched them in the morning light, they really were Joes, working stiffs in khaki coveralls. Shovels, cigarettes, coffee. Baseball caps. Foremen leaning on walls and shooting the shit. All that was missing were lunchboxes.

And then it hit him.

This had nothing to do with DoD at all.

This was a Hayward operation; off-books, privately funded.

Colonization. Privatized rule.

He snicked off his safety and bracketed the loader operator, oblivious inside his transparent-armor cage, the view panels rated against smaller weapons, likely, but sure as shit not a 5.56 at this range.

The cab spun.

The moment came, as it always did when looking through a gunsight: what had this guy done to him? Just a guy, doing his thing—in this case, working heavy equipment—making a hard buck.

This was the way of warfare; rarely did the ones doing the wrong thing ever know they were doing the wrong thing. You had to show them.

And this was where, for literally eons, the Blackfeet people had excelled.

He had a flashing memory of childhood afternoons listening to the stories of his people, of Star Boy and Badger and Coyote, and of how the great leaders had been fucked over mercilessly and relentlessly. Memories of his father, drunk as shit and raging at the world for another of a hundred transgressions gone unanswered: another land grab, another water-rights dispute, another ancient hunting ground turned into million-dollar mansions. Any given Tuesday evening at Chez Shines-at-Night.

Ancestral spirits kicked up behind him in the dust. Drums pounded with voices raised in cadence, echoing through the valley as real as anything, songs from a thousand years before, haunting him now, here, feathered spears shaking.

He snugged his elbow in tighter, welding himself to the rifle with the sling. After all this, after all the running and all the reading and all the protestations and the swearing at his guardian spirits, the Creator had dragged him across the universe to go to war. Again.

A single tear rolled down the warpaint on his cheek.

He breathed in, and out, held at nothingness, and felt the trigger break.

Abby heard the shot. 5.56, unsuppressed, sooner than she'd expected. It was time to go to work.

Luke was an arm's length away, a lump of burlap jute among the rocks, invisible to the eye at nineteen hundred meters from the tower. There was no vegetation in this valley, but at this distance, they'd be nothing but smears among the stone.

"Loader operator's down," said Luke. "Lots of movement, QRF,"—a quick-reaction force—"tower, stairs."

"I got 'em," she said.

"Ma Deuce." In the dots of the scope, a fast-mover in the QRF was climbing behind a Browning M2, a 50-caliber machine gun on a tripod; this one had been outfitted with armor plates across its front and surrounded by a few feet of sandbags to turn it into a makeshift turret on the second floor of the tower.

"I see it."

A low sandbag wall such as had been erected around the Browning was ideal against someone shooting from the valley floor. However, Abby and Luke were two hundred feet above him, shooting down, rendering it useless.

"Send it," said Luke, "now . . . now . . ."

The .338 boomed through the canyon.

Whatever the hell had been going on with the rifles by the Citadel jacking up the points of impact, it wasn't happening here. The round rag-dolled the gunner on the Browning two seconds later, sneaking over the makeshift turret's front armor plate and tearing his chest open.

Two more men, working ammo, turned to face him—it would be another three and a half seconds before they heard the shot—but she'd already fired twice more, throwing the bolt without breaking eye relief while they knelt, frozen, staring at their buddy who'd inexplicably exploded. A stunningly stupid way to die.

As the .338 reports reached the base, the remaining QRF bailed out of the tower. No one dared go near the big gun knowing a sniper had it indexed. Grunts had a word for such a thing: *bullet magnet.*

Abby and Luke slithered back behind the rocks and started the climb for the next hide.

Weaponeers had modified the gryphon saddles, adding extra straps for the lower legs of the second riders. Martin was far more at ease this time with his ankles and the tops of his calves snugged down, freeing up his arms. He could sit back on his ankles, and it was fairly comfortable. He wished he'd done more yoga.

He carried two pouches of hand grenades—a bag of old-school baseball frags, and over his shoulder, two stacks of ten goddamned modular grenades. His HK was clipped to his shoulder through its strap, and this was the craziest fucking thing he'd ever done.

The first flight of gryphons started its run.

A five-second fall for the grenades was right at four hundred feet, which put the birds at risk from ground fire. They overcame this by diving at what had to be falcon speeds, a hundred miles an hour, perhaps more, flashing by overhead and dropping grenades into the perimeter. It didn't matter if they hit anything; the barrage itself was enough to keep everyone hunkered down. Two flights of ten gryphons, a ridiculous amount of explosions, and they circled back around the mountain, out of line of sight of both the gunners and the tracked weapons system's radar. Some of the grenades went off early, because the Army's quality control was shit, and that was fine, too. The damage to the facility—to equipment, to structures, to people—was terrific.

He could see the Sentinels peppering the walls with small-arms fire, and he shouldered the HK and took several shots at a machine gun crew on one tower as they readied their first pass. Above the crack of the grenades, the thunderous boom of Abby's rifle rolled out like the voice of an angry god.

He got a mental picture of where the armored piece was going to be—the only place it could be—on the western side of the COP, where there'd be room between the bunker and the compound wall to move it out and maneuver it if needed. There were no landmarks around it, so it would be a bitch to find.

The best thing to do would be to drop a big one in the vicinity and see if they could scare it out, or possibly even damage the bunker and give the others a visual.

"Go!" he yelled at the rider, in Vé, and they swung around to put the sun at their backs, getting ready for their first run.

Behind Eera, Braxton fired several rounds at a machine gun crew from a hundred and fifty meters up and two hundred meters off. Nobody was firing at the gryphons, yet; there weren't enough bodies on guns to return fire at the Sentinel riflemen, keep cover from grenades, and watch the skies.

Overwhelming numbers and superior firepower carried the first wave of the assault. They'd literally caught them having coffee.

The Sheth appeared at the front gate, shimmering out of nowhere, and tore the sandbagged position down. A couple of soldiers or guards, whatever they were, got rounds off and two of the Sheth collapsed, but the others smashed through the construction and got hands on the much smaller humans, and what followed was horrific.

Hesco barriers funneled the Sheth into the compound, and the

QRF dodging the tower moved to intercept, guns blazing as they rounded the corner. The timing was off, Braxton realized; what they really needed was another aerial strike and the other two wings were on the far side of the mountain. He peppered them with the rest of his magazine. The Sheth had slings, and their rocks were brutal, but they withered before the onslaught of small-arms fire. They shimmered and vanished, leaving the gun teams staring into nothingness.

"Welcome to Valhalla, motherfuckers," Braxton shouted.

Movement—big movement—caught his eye, and he saw an enormous tank barrel with a fat compensator on the end extend from nowhere, mustard yellow against the white-pink sand and impossibly out of place, followed a moment later by the block of a yellow armored chassis.

They were bringing her out.

There was no way they could use the main gun against anyone or anything attacking them, but whether it was a tank or self-propelled howitzer—and he might know which, here in a minute, if it rolled another ten feet—it would have a manned belt-fed weapon, or even rockets, on the turret, and that could be a game-changer.

The track crept forward, a bear reluctantly coming out of hibernation, until the gun systems were clear of the overhead cover, and Braxton had a good look, high and broadside.

It wasn't a tank.

It was too blocky, the turret too tall and mounted too far back. The main gun was ridiculously oversized.

An M109 155mm self-propelled artillery system: a Paladin.

It rolled until it cleared the hard cover entirely, the comparatively bright yellow body—not American Desert Tan but some despotic regime's closest approximation—fully exposed against the red-gold of the sand.

It pulled a sharp right and traveled two, three lengths, diesel soot spewing, before spinning left and reversing up the slope. The main gun elevated, painfully slowly, aiming toward the Citadel.

"Fuck!" Braxton told no one.

Ahead of him, Martin had started his approach.

"Paladin," Luke said. "Looks like an Alpha-Six. Not the new one. Low-rent motherfuckers."

"Tracking," said Abby. She dropped the magazine from the big gun, rummaged a pouch, and pulled out another, ridiculously heavy.

"He's coming our way."

"I see him." She fitted the new mag. "Switching to DU. I make that, what, seventeen and change?"

"Seventeen-twenty. Correction, ten. Correction, one-six-niner zero and closing. Hurry, goddammit."

The Paladin carried three centimeters of armor around its turret, but considerably less over the engine bay; the idea being, the engine would serve to stop an armor-piercing round or enemy shell from entering the crew compartment. Self-propelled guns were not built to trade fire. Once the engines were gone, they effectively became gun emplacements.

"I'm up," she confirmed, and locked the bolt home with the force of a vault door slamming shut. "Get ready to move."

The DU rounds were heavier, slower, and required some quick math at this range. "You're gonna want to go up three," Luke recommended.

"Reading my mind." She spun the elevation on the scope and waited for the Paladin to stop, because who the hell knew where it was going to be after two seconds of flight time.

There was a man on the top, in the open hatch, behind a DShK, the Russian answer to the fifty-caliber machine gun. The leviathan main gun was pointed due south and was elevating at what felt like an inch at a time, as if hand-cranked, while the tracks edged the beast up the hill.

They were going for elevation.

They were going to fire on the Citadel.

Abby fused bone to polymer, inhaled, and touched the trigger.

"Send it," Luke said, as the gun hit its mark and stopped moving. "Now . . . now . . ."

In the close-up world of the reticle, the Paladin kicked as the trigger broke, disappearing in wafting powder sand. At first, she thought something was wrong; there should be two seconds of flight time, and there was no way the impact could . . .

"Aw, fuck," said Luke, but it was lost as the roar of the Paladin's cannon washed over them.

Abby fired three more shots into the side of the Paladin, below and to the front of the turret.

As the last echoes of the .338 rumbled through the valley, a narrow blue-black plume, faint but definite, rose from the front cowling; engine damage. A moment later the Paladin belched smoke out the exhausts—first a cough, then a steady vomit of blue combustion byproducts as oil poured through smashed cylinders and around pistons pinned in place with depleted uranium projectiles far harder than steel, catastrophic and irrevocable mayhem from a twenty-thousand- dollar rifle to a twenty-million-dollar platform.

The main gun started its laborious traverse to their position; the radar had certainly picked up the DU rounds and identified a point of origin, and they had fifteen seconds until it could shoot again; maybe ten, which meant it was time to go.

They scooped up their gear and scrambled out of the hide to the back side of the rocks, leaping from the cliff into soft sand ten meters below.

"We gotta get out of here," Luke muttered, wading knee-deep in powder and cradling his scope.

"Down!" Abby yelled, and shoved him flat. The world exploded above their heads, and shards of stone rained around them for what felt like eternity.

"You good?!" she asked.

He shook himself off and pulled at the crotch of his trousers. "My nuts are stuck halfway up my ass," he griped. "Gimme a minute."

"We're okay," she assured him. "Now, they think we're dead. Let's get back to that first hide, but we don't shoot again unless we have to."

Logan watched the Paladin fire into the sky and wished to God he had binoculars to look down the valley.

There was no way to know where the round had gone, only south, and high. A moment later the .338 added its vote, three times, and the behemoth started to smoke.

The Sentinels continued to harass with carbine fire. The Sheth were inside the perimeter, and now came the moment: did they rush the compound? Kill everyone? Burn it to the ground?

Did they teach them a lesson? Or was wrecking the howitzer enough?

Had it been enough?

It was still operational. He watched it fire into Abby and Luke's hide, sickened at the amount of damage it caused to the mountain, but it had been forever in sniper time and he had no doubt they'd been nowhere near when the round impacted.

Coming out of the sun above him was a gryphon, diving like a falcon in an arrowhead shape, with what could only have been Martin on the back behind a Sentinel who looked tiny by comparison. Logan put the Paladin's DShK gunner in his crosshairs and emptied his magazine, but the man was brave as hell and let the armor plating take the rounds, indexing on the incoming threat.

"No, no, no!" Logan yelled, and wished to Christ he could wave Martin off. The DShK rattled off a long burst, and the gryphon let out the same frantic, panicked shrieking he'd heard from the bird who'd been caught in his parachute. Feathers flew, wings flailed, and the gryphon and both riders impacted fifty feet short of the gun, leaving a crater in the sand.

High above, in a glint of light, a stick of grenades arced gracefully, a Hail Mary Pass from a sacked QB; Chip Martin's last contribution to the world.

"Oh, you magnificent motherfucker," Logan said, watching the row of explosives spin in the sunlight and come down atop the barrel mount, almost in the gunner's lap.

There was a fraction of a second of dawning realization on the man's face, and it was spectacular.

The concussion was terrific. Even at two hundred yards, it was like being slapped on all exposed skin. It blasted the smoke away from the damaged hulk, and in perfect sunny daylight the guy in the turret vanished from the waist up as pieces flew off the Paladin in all directions.

A clear black dent with a white center was visible where the bomb had landed, above the barrel. The engine choked, sputtered, and died.

The smoke resumed, less insistent, now.

No one climbed out of the turret. The side hatches were still. The spalling effect inside the crew compartment would have not only trashed equipment and electronics; it would have liquified organs, which would be spilling out through every orifice. A total hose job for the recovery team.

Logan looked to the skies to thank his ancestors.

The gryphons were coming around.

Braxton and Eera circled the COP, looking down at Martin's wrecked gryphon. He was clearly dead, as was the rider, as was the mount. They had probably hit the ground at a hundred miles an hour. There was a hole in the sand.

There was no point in going down there, and a QRF was already moving for the Paladin. It would be pure suicide, and no one to recover.

"God bless you, brother," he said, and he dropped two grenades onto the QRF as they passed over, because fuck those guys.

The next flight of gryphons was bombing the base, and to the south, Logan was leading the Sentinel riflemen back through the rocks in a hasty retreat, a shitty peel, but it was getting the job done. They'd be out of range in another minute.

The Sheth were reappearing further back in the rocks, dragging their wounded, flashing in and out of the visible spectrum. The fight was over; everyone was leaving.

He had to wonder who else was dead. It looked bad down there.

"We need to go," he told Eera. "Tell your people, we must go."

The gryphons winged back around the mesa and climbed out of range of small arms, heading for the Citadel down the back side of the ridgeline.

Smoke rose from the south end of the valley.

XXV

CHILDREN OF THE WAR

"Obstacles don't block the path. They are the path."
— Zen proverb

Bob kept his people calm. Kept himself calm.

Todd Medved, however, was not calm. He had a team of Sentinels packing up the library as fast as they could, putting everything in trunks and carrying it into Red Sky Green, moving it as far into the underground realm as possible.

"How can you be so cool about this?" he asked in exasperation.

"There is literally nothing we can do," Bob replied in English. "It will go when it goes. They're saying we have a day, probably. Maybe two."

"How far away can we be in a day?"

"Not far enough," said Bob. He had knots in his stomach, but he strove to not show it. "That's why I'm saying, don't worry. Make the most of it. Me, I'm going to get drunk as soon as those guys get back."

The artillery round had bounced above the Citadel, telekinetically deflected by Via'k Ul. He had channeled so much energy into it that it had killed him.

And he'd fucked up, too; the round had hit the next hilltop over and collapsed several storage tunnels for the red mercury, which meant it was pooling at an unknown rate somewhere inside the mountain. Eventually, it would reach supercriticality and heat up until it melted through the rocks, at which point it would slowly sink until it hit the water table. There, it would trigger a massive steam explosion, blowing a good section of the valley apart and irradiating it for miles in a nuclear volcano.

Even sorcerers were fallible, it turned out.

Bob's disappointment was palpable in the room.

Meanwhile, the Sentinels were traveling as far into the underground realm as they could. Miles, they hoped. It might be enough. It might not. This happened every thousand years or so; they never knew when. It was part of who they were.

"We could get on gryphons," said Todd. "We could fly away."

"We could," said Bob. "And then what?"

"Are you kidding me right now? It's a medieval world, and we have guns."

"That's Paulsen talking. I won't do it. I won't use our superior knowledge and firepower to put these people . . . beneath . . ."

Todd waited for the thought to finish.

". . . beneath me," said Bob.

"Right?" Todd asked.

Bob groaned. "Oh, shit. I have, haven't I?"

"Yes, you have, Siege Lord Valenteen. You have, indeed. Now, I'm gonna grab a couple of guns, and a couple dozen mags, and a shitload of water, and take one of those goddamn gryphons and fly until I hit civilization. And with any luck, I'm taking Fields with me."

"Fuckin' A I'm goin' with ya," said Fields, walking in the room. "Where are we goin'?"

"Out of the blast radius."

"What are we waitin' for?" Fields asked.

"And then?" Bob asked.

"I don't know. Prevailing wind's from the north, so we head anywhere but south, I'm thinking. I've seen the maps. Probably east. Hopefully find a local lord, or king, or whatever the fuck they have in the next settlement over, and we'll build an intelligence network for him. The shit worked here."

"You're giving up on these people," Bob said.

Todd gestured wordlessly in three directions, exasperated. "Yes! Holy shit, dude. That's exactly what I'm doing. Our work, here? It's *done.* We can do more, if—only if—we stay alive."

Fields glanced between them and nodded to Todd. "Yeah. I'm with him," he told Bob. "Don't worry about us. We'll make a go of it. Tell 'em where to find us."

Bob stuck his hand out to them.

"What's that?" Fields asked.

"Good luck," said Bob. "I hope it works for you."

They all shook hands.

"You really don't want to come?" Todd asked. "You did good, here."

"I'm their Siege Lord," said Bob. "I'm going to stand my post until the fiery end, and they're going to remember me in song for eternity. There are worse fates. Especially for a historian. Besides, I'll be standing on top of a volcano when it goes. It's not like it's going to hurt."

"You've got some balls on you," said Fields, with appreciation. "You salty bastard. You should've been SF."

"In the next life, I promise," said Bob.

"We'll hold you to it," said Fields. "Good luck, Doctor."

Todd followed him out of the library and up the Great Stairs.

Bob gave them some time, watching as robed Sentinels continued cleaning out the room, organizing and stacking, filing his reports into chests and trunks and lugging them deep into caves below the surface. Once he was sure they were gone and the work would be safe, he left and headed for the Citadel.

Todd Medved's legacy with the Vé, and arguably the single greatest intelligence feat in the history of the world of Elalion, will forever reside in an ornate chest, in a corner of an underground vault, in a collapsed section of a mountain that no human or Vé will ever see.

Logan's gryphon and rider touched down behind Abby's, which was only minutes behind Luke's. Smoke rose from a hole in the side of the mountain beyond the Citadel to the south.

The Sentinels were in a state of what Logan could only construe as refined panic. They weren't exactly freaking out, but they were moving with a purpose.

Čer Aya explained the situation to Logan, and Čer Anh explained the situation to Abby. The Sentinels headed back into the mountain as far as they could go. Logan and Abby were to head immediately for the depths of the mountain, via gryphons; the Čers would accompany them, and they would fly to the Stronghold and report everything they had seen and done, then start a new life training up a new generation of soldiers.

"Okay," said Logan, without argument. "Abby, let's go."

"Wait," she said. "Shouldn't we wait, here? What if Paulsen sends more guys? That wasn't even a full company. You know there'll be more."

"So, he sends them," said Logan, "and this place goes up in a blast of nuclear hellfire. That's what we used to call a self-correcting problem.

"What about my men?" Logan asked Čer Aya, switching back to Sentinel. "What happens to my men?"

"If they wish, they may accompany you. If they wish, they may flee. Under the mountain, to the human lands overland, as they wish. They must decide quickly."

"I'm staying," said Luke, in English. He had come back to Abby and Logan, surrounded by four Via'k adepts, who were even more somber than usual.

"Why?" Abby almost screamed.

"Bob's staying," said Luke.

"Bob's an idiot," said Abby. "Come with us."

"Via'k Ul is dead," Luke said. "He died saving these people. That's what I should have done."

"Yeah, but you didn't, though," she argued. "You saved them, and you lived. That's completely different."

"Everyone I've ever loved is dead. I'm batting zero." He collapsed a few inches. "I'm so tired of fighting, Abby. I'm so sick of this shit."

"Luke, you don't have to fight anymore. No one's asking you to. You have a gift that these people wanted you to . . . I don't know, refine. Utilize. You can use it to help these people. You can become one of them, at a level we never could."

"Can't you be a Via'k adept in the Stronghold?" Logan asked. "Someplace where you won't get, you know, vaporized? Because, I mean, that seems like it would be better. Just throwing out options, here, Gunny."

Luke sighed. "I am so tired of people around me dying. I'm just . . . tired."

"So, come live in the Faerie's secret magical kingdom, where people don't die," Logan suggested. It made the most sense of anything he'd said out loud since discovering the Paladin. War fucked him up; lizard-brain was in full survival mode, and it would stay there for hours, if not weeks. Every now and again, though, something peeked through, and this was one of those moments. "I mean, look at it this way," he said. "Come with us, and everybody you meet from now on will outlive you."

Luke appeared to think about this.

"Brax!" Logan yelled, as he saw the smaller man running past. Braxton and Eera came over at a trot.

"Hey," Braxton said. "Martin. Did you see? He didn't . . . ah—fuck, man," he said, sighing and sagging. "Goddammit."

"I know," Logan said. "I'm sorry."

"Hey, who gets to go out like that? That was awesome."

"We're flying to the Stronghold," Logan said. "Traveling underground. It's safer, they say. You're welcome to come, both of you. We're leaving right now."

"We just talked to Dr. Valentine," said Braxton. "We're going to find the other guys. Or try to, anyway. Fields and Medved boosted a gryphon and some guns and headed east."

Abby rolled her eyes. "Of course they did."

"Exactly," Braxton said. "We're gonna load up real fast and try to catch 'em. Make a go of it in the human lands."

"Really?" said Logan, surprised.

"Yeah," said Braxton. "There's a whole world out there, man. Those guys have the right idea. Someone will pay handsomely for the shit we know. Anyway, my plan is to be as far away from here as we can be by nightfall, and nowhere downwind. We're gonna reload water and provisions, grab some more ammo and a map, and head out. In, like, *ten*. It's been fun, sir. And ma'am. Luke," he added.

"You know where we'll be," said Logan. "You're welcome with us any day."

"Same," said Braxton. He saluted, and they each returned it, Logan with the Foreign Legion salute, palm out.

"That was fun," Braxton assured him with a smile. "Thank you." With that, he and Eera headed for the Citadel at a run.

"Let's get the hell out of here," said Logan. "Čer Aya, lead the way."

"We have mounts waiting," she said. "You must come. I have secured your things. Your other leg, your other things from your world. We must go, now."

"Where would I find Bob?" Logan asked. "Siege Lord Valenteen?"

"You would find him climbing the tower, awaiting the end," said Čer Aya.

"Yeah, screw that," said Abby.

"Come, now," Čer Anh told her. "We must go. Now."

Logan took Abby's hand and followed the Čers. Luke took a moment to confer with the Via'k adepts, then followed at a run.

Logan offered his other hand, and Luke took it. They proceeded into the Citadel for the final time, leaving two worlds behind them, seeking yet another.

DECLASSIFICATION REVIEW
Change/Classify to: (U) per GENERAL RELEASE
With concurrence of: SAG/G2
After: 20210503
By Stevenson, R. SIA GS-15

MEMORANDUM FOR

SUBJECT: ~~(TS//SAR-ASW/SAR-DST//WAIVED)~~ Termination: ARCHSTONE; WARNO: DREAMSTONE

1. ~~(TS//SAR-ASW/SAR-AST//WAIVED)~~ All ASCENDANT WARDEN and ARCHSTONE operations are suspended effective immediately.

2. ~~(TS//SAR-ASW/SAR-AST//WAIVED)~~ Multiple USPERS have become naturalized ARCHSTONE Local Nationals (LN) and likely Key Leaders (high confidence).

3. ~~(TS//SAR-ASW/SAR-AST/SAR-DST//WAIVED)~~ Area of Operations ARCHSTONE (hereafter AO LYNCH) is hereby considered a hostile zone. ASCENDANT WARDEN operations going forward will be performed per ███████████████. All Teams will follow ███████ and doctrinal NRC protocols without exception.

4. ~~(TS//SAR-ASW/SAR-AST/SAR-DST//WAIVED)~~ Effective ███████ DREAMSTONE (DST) supersedes ARCHSTONE (AST) as compartment for operations in AO LYNCH.

5. ~~(TS//SAR-ASW/SAR-DST//WAIVED)~~ All DREAMSTONE and follow on ASCENDANT WARDEN operations will integrate a zero-interaction baseline with AO LYNCH LN personnel.

6. ~~(S//NF)~~ POC for this memorandum is the undersigned at ███████████ ██████ DSN ████████

COL, SF
Commanding

XXVI

HEREAFTER

"If you would be a real seeker after truth, it is necessary that at least once in your life you doubt, as far as possible, all things."
— René Descartes

The view from the final pass into the Stronghold, the Vé ancestral homeland, was staggering. The winter air burned Logan's face. Čer Aya rode behind him.

They'd been traveling twenty days. Underground, aboveground, through mountain passes carpeted with trees and over spearpoints of ridgelines crusted with snow.

Logan's beard had grown in, flecked with gray since the coma. Abby, on a gryphon behind him and to the right, had never looked better. The wilds of the world were good for her. Čer Anh rode behind, her arms locked around Abby.

The dual-seat saddles were a godsend.

Luke was off to their left, astride a gryphon of his own, grinning as he always did. He loved flying.

As they crossed the last ridgeline, the Vé realm spread out

before them, thick with emerald woodlands to the horizon. Silver rivers, bright with glacial chill, carved swaths through the forests. Mountainsides stabbed the sky, an eternity distant and framed against violent, rainbow-tinged clouds pregnant with rain. It was nearly evening, the sun going down to the southwest behind them.

Immediately beyond the first river, in a clearing, stood a group waving pennants in silver, red, and blue, beckoning them in. The gryphons banked, dropped, and pulled in for an easy landing.

Dismounting was easier than it had been.

Their riding was stronger than it ever was.

Their command of Vé was stronger.

They were ready.

The leader of the Vé delegation strode out to meet them. Wrapped in furs, jewels, and medieval-looking earth-toned tunics against the cold, he was half a head taller than any Sentinel, with golden skin like cedar bark, violet eyes, and tiger stripes of black in his wild brown hair.

The Vé robes were subpar for the chill of this place. Only Luke, in his Via'k vestments, seemed okay with it. Logan and Abby shivered.

"Logan Kai," Čer Aya introduced, "meet Akiel Corimann, prince of the Vé."

Čer Anh spoke. "Prince Akiel, Logan Kai and his people fought a great battle against an invading force who used the Old Door above the Stonelands."

"And how did they fare?" asked Akiel.

"They prevailed, at great cost. Our curation failed as a result of the battle, and we have lost the Citadel to the Great Fire. However, Logan Kai and his soldiers stopped the invaders. In repayment, Valla Kamè sends them to you as teachers of war. This she asks, so that you may send those they teach back to the Stonelands after we rebuild. And that they may teach your people in the interim."

Akiel nodded, looking them over. "And you accompany them,

Čers? You take responsibility for them?"

"We do."

He paced. It made Logan want to stand at attention for the first time in a long time.

"We have not welcomed humans into the Stronghold in centuries," Prince Akiel said. "We forbid outsiders. However, we will never again consider you outsiders. Understand the privilege we afford you.

"Understand, also, as a human, once you venture beyond this clearing, you may only return through it with my express permission. Even then, you may never tell another human anything of what you see, here.

"Tell me you understand this. Tell me you have prepared yourselves for this."

Logan looked to either side. "Everybody good?" he asked, quietly, in English.

Abby nodded.

Luke nodded.

"We understand," Logan acknowledged. The three of them saluted. This took the prince aback, and he returned it with the Vé salute, the same as the Sentinel salute: fist over heart, and then an open hand in offering.

"She sent us soldiers of an outworld, indeed," he agreed. "Please, soldiers. Teachers. Join us, as my honored friends. As my honored guests. As heroes of our people."

Logan took Abby's hand. Abby took Čer Anh's hand. Čer Aya took Logan's other hand, and Luke took hers.

They followed the prince and his cohort, flags still waving, through the treeline on a wide path leading down a hillside through deepening trees and encroaching dark. When the world reappeared, the path opened into a valley strung with lights and humming with music. Laughter rang from treetops. Sprites danced. Fires glowed.

Abby's hand tightened on Logan's.

A world without cares, Čer Aya said, in Vé. *Without war.
Without loss.*
A world of fair promise and uncompromising light.
"Welcome home," Logan told himself.

THE END

ACKNOWLEDGMENTS

I want to extend my thanks to a great many people for making this book possible.

My wife Katie continues to be my massif of support and stability. None of this would be possible without her.

My agent, Sarah Hershman, went above and beyond through all this, particularly during what turned into a labyrinthine security review at the Department of Defense.

I want to thank Kelly McHale, John Jacobsmeyer, and the rest of the team at the Defense Office of Prepublication and Security Review (DOPSR) for threading a difficult needle between preserving my artistic vision and preventing me from having to testify before Congress.

Author Sam Odiorne and Army MSG (Ret.) Edwin Kay served as my Sherpas over this mountain. It bears mentioning, here, that I didn't know MSG Kay when I named the asshole character in my debut novel *Dragon's Trail* "Edwin."

If you're current or former SOF, or have worked or deployed anywhere in their orbit, and you've been reading this and saying, "That's not how that works," or "That's not what that's called," understand that key aspects of tradecraft and capabilities in *Stonelands*, as well as some DoD agency names, functions, and operational compartments, may have been changed to comply with findings by USSOCOM, DIA, or DOPSR. If you haven't served in a Special Missions Unit and held a compartmented clearance, then very little of this story's setting will reflect your military experience. More of it is authentic than you'd believe.

If you wanted to stage a series of Special Operations missions to explore a fantasy world through a portal found on U.S. soil, *Stonelands* is pretty close to what it would look like. The chain of command, policies, procedures, logistics and support requirements, cover stories, legal complications, mission design, personnel selection, tradecraft, briefings, team dynamics, paperwork hassles— everything—is exactly the way it would look and function, at least within the limits of what I can say publicly without being blindfolded and shot.

At the time of Project ARCHSTONE, women were not allowed in Combat Arms MOS's, nor schools such as Ranger and Sniper. MAJ Easton's path into SOF is illustrative of the hurdles facing women in a Special Missions Unit at the time. The U.S. military being a dynamic environment, this changed while I was writing the manuscript.

I had a long thing ready here about how far these issues have come since the end of the Global War on Terror, but in the span between declassification and publication—lengthened considerably by a publisher with its thumb irretrievably up its ass—the new administration has rolled back nearly all progress regarding Intersectionality in the Federal Service and the U.S. military, so here we are, suddenly relevant again.

The interplay and tension between the operators from various disciplines, and the challenges of identity and intersectionality that they face throughout the missions, are all issues that I witnessed firsthand during my career. For that reason alone, I thought this would be a wonderful time to release this story; I love anything that causes trouble.

Logan's desert warfare tradecraft is straight out of my own experience training with the 13^e Demi-Brigade of the French Foreign Legion at their Desert Commando School / *Commando Entrainement* in Arta Plage, Djibouti.

All characters are products of the author's imagination and bear no resemblance to actual people, living or dead, save one: the prior-service Marine who trained me up as a wet-nosed Army Specialist, and who later served as Vader to my Palpatine in the intelligence section of a SMU, during which time I wrote *Stonelands*, helped come up with the Guff character. I will neither confirm nor deny how much of Jake Guffman is real, but what's in there is used with permission.

SGM (Ret.) Mike Jarnevic, U.S. Army Special Forces, remains my Ramakrishna of rabblerousing and killing stuff, awaiting me cross-legged on a mountaintop in all his immense patience with a beer, a red pen, and an occasional well-deserved smack in the head.

SFC (Ret.) Dan "Mongo" Damian, U.S. Army Civil Affairs and former Automatic Rifleman in 1-23 IN, was, and remains, my go-to on all things belt-fed and crew-served; it was his idea to use the Mark 48/46's "even though they're fuckin' French."

Thanks to my good friend and longtime sparring partner Michael "Tinker" Pearce for an evening on the phone helping me figure out the issues inherent in long-range shooting on an alien planet. (The quote on Page Two about "Cut the strings and the puppet can't dance" is a Tinker saying from edged-weapons training decades ago.)

The quotes from the *Prose Edda* are from Arthur Gilchrist Brodeur's 1916 translation of the *Gylfaginning* by Snorri Sturlson. Sturlson, a 13th-Century Icelandic Christian, cobbled together fragments of ancient texts in an apparent attempt to pen a rational explanation for Norse myths and legends. I discovered Brodeur's translation in a library in Reykjavik in late 2017 and copied several passages into my journal. Snorri Sturlson's search for explanation kicked off the initial outline for *Stonelands.*

My inspiration for the first-contact interactions with the Sentinels began with a conversation with Emily Dunham during MisCon in Missoula, MT, in May of 2018. Emily was modeling an alien costume by local makeup artist Nina Alviar, one so intensely believable that I went straight to the bar and knocked out several pages of concepts for the first-contact sequences of the novel I'd been plotting since finding Brodeur's work in Iceland. The lesson here being, always carry a pen.

As some of you have figured out by now, yes, the Project ARCHSTONE reconnaissance missions in *Stonelands* explore the world from my first two novels, *Dragon's Trail* and *The New Magic.* The missions in Hayward Valley are almost precisely contemporary with the forthcoming third book in the initial planned trilogy, *Coin of the Realm.* While *Stonelands* is a spinoff and stands alone, it was necessary to write it and outline its sequels before I could continue.

For practical purposes, you can certainly read *Stonelands* as a sequel to *The New Magic,* as it does follow in temporal space; or you can read it as its own adventure; or, for that matter, read it while considering it's all the same world, which will give you a glimpse of the greater series arc. If you're a fan of my earlier work, you'll find some Easter eggs, so have a good time with them. If this is your first exposure to my writing, welcome, and thank you.

Thank you to Badger, Keeper of Stories.

The world's best dog never saw this book finished but man, he would have thought it was cool.

TRANSLITERATION REMARKS: ON SPEAKING VÉ

Wherever feasible, I have used direct translations in this novel. However, *Vé* names, and some terms in *Vé*, have no English equivalent. In these instances, I have transliterated the language as faithfully as possible. That said, several unique and confusing phonemes exist in the *Vé* language and the Sentinel dialect, and I will discuss them here.

The notation *Č,* seen in Vé words like *Čer* and *Čyeen,* is pronounced much as the English "ch," ʧ in the International Phonetic Alphabet (IPA). I have used the standard American *Č* notation to limit confusion, as spelling a title like *Čer* phonetically as "chair" would make sections of the story hard to read.

All *r*'s in Vé are a voiced alveolar flap, IPA ɾ, with no English approximation. It may be helpful to think of the Sentinel *r* as a short trilled *r.*

The IPA transcription of *Čer* is therefore ʧɛr, or, most closely in English, "chair," but with a rolled *r.*

The Vé long *a* sound, "ay" in English (IPA: eɪ), is denoted by *é* when stressed, or *è* when unstressed.

The name of the **Vé** people and their language is therefore pronounced "Vay." (IPA: veɪ)

Valla Kamè is pronounced "VAL-lah KAH-may. (IPA: vɑl' ə kɑm' meɪ)

All *a*'s in Vé words are open-back, unrounded vowels

pronounced most closely as "ah" in English; IPA ɑ.

The Sentinel **Čer Aya** therefore pronounces her name "Chair ah-YAH" with a short flip on the *r* at the end of "chair." (IPA: ʧɛr ɑ ja')

The Vé *kh* is a voiceless velar fricative with no English equivalent; IPA: **x**.

The Sentinel *'k* is a voiceless lateral click, the sound Americans and British use to urge on a horse (IPA: **kǁ**). *'k* is also often tacked onto the beginnings of words, or thrown out on its own with a random vowel appended, as an expression of disapproval or irritation.

The Vé language, and with it the Sentinel dialect, lacks the verb *to be* in any form. In this respect, the fundamental syntax of Vé compares with the variation of English known as E Prime. Since the Vé live for thousands of years, their language has evolved to describe everything as transitory or somehow provisional, rather than making any definite pronouncements on nature and belonging. Nothing, to a Vé, ever *is*; things simply appear a certain way given the information available and the point of reference at the moment.

The final, and missing, piece of the Vé language, which proved confounding to capture in translation, is their predilection for speaking in a specific metrical pattern consisting of an unexpanded choriambic nucleus with a complex phonetic weighting scheme. The Vé will speak in circles around a concept, in a game of sorts, rambling on, choosing synonyms, and straying wildly from central points in their discourse in order to stick to the meter as long as possible. It can take a Vé all afternoon to describe a single experience if there's nothing else immediately pressing. I did not attempt to capture this affectation in my translations of Vé, as it makes an unreadable mess of the dialogue.